KIM KARR
CRUSH

HE'S TEETERING BETWEEN
REASON AND INSANITY.
ONE PUSH MIGHT JUST CRUSH HIM.

Crush
Copyright © 2015 by Kim Karr
All rights reserved.
ISBN: 9781518718311

Editor:
Mary-Theresa Hussey, Good Stories Told Well

Interior design and formatting:
Christine Borgford, Perfectly Publishable

Cover designer:
Hang Le, By Hang Le

Photographer:
Brice Hardelin, Brice Hardelin Photography

Cover model:
Cyril Mourali

chapter
ONE

LOGAN MCPHERSON

S AY YOU WANTED SOMEONE eliminated . . .
   Killed.

It doesn't matter who—your mother, your lover, your enemy.

There are guys out there who will do it for you.

It's a fact.

Not someone from the Mob.

Not someone connected to the Mob.

Not anyone you know.

A hit man.

I've heard of ways to contact one. Someone who knows someone who knows someone.

Someone from the old neighborhood. Someone with prison tats. Someone with long hair. Someone with no hair. Who the fuck cares—he could look like Mötley Crüe. Hell, on the other hand, he could be a businessman wearing a two-thousand-dollar suit.

I really don't give a shit.

What he looks like is irrelevant. It's what he does that matters.

Sure, there's a steep monetary price attached to the deed. That's not what worries me.

I'd give every cent I had if it meant she'd be safe.

It's what it would really cost me—how big of a piece of my soul it would take—that keeps me from making that call.

I re-read the note, "That E wasn't meant for Emily."

One thing was clear . . .

He knows about Elle and me.

Tommy Flannigan, my enemy, my foe, the Mob boss's son, the one I have been forbidden to make contact with, knows I have someone in my life that I care about. He might even know I love her. And she's not his sister. She's not Emily. Because I defied him, because I dared to move on, I know he'll taunt me, try to break me, try to drive me out of my mind.

For over a decade he's loomed over me.

Like a shadow.

A black spot in my life that I always knew was there.

In the past he'd threatened me, mutilated a girl I'd dated, scarred me, but that was a long time ago. I hadn't heard from in years, until just last week when he harmed someone he thought was Elle.

He was back in my life.

Everyone knew he was into drugs as a user, but not many knew he was a cutthroat player in the drug world; not even his old man knew to what extent he was involved. The thing was he was always crazy, but lately he'd been breaking all the rules. Homes. Women. Mothers. Children. Nothing and no one was safe from him anymore—it was like he had nothing left to lose.

With that, breaking the treaty forged years ago when it came to contacting me wasn't a surprise.

I think I'd been waiting for him to cross that line for a very long time.

The thing he doesn't get is I'm no longer fearful. That I'll do the very same thing. As of right this minute, as far as I'm concerned, the rules of the street no longer apply to me. There is too much at stake for me to care about what could happen if I went up against the Blue Hill Gang. I have to think about what has to happen in order to keep Elle safe. And that's one thing, and one thing only.

Tommy's threat has to be eliminated.

Somehow.

Some way.

But murder for hire would have to wait.

Paralyzed.

Frozen in place.

I looked over into Elle's green eyes.

Wide.

Scared.

Still beautiful.

I haven't even known her for two weeks but she's a part of me. I can't—no, I *won't*—let anything happen to her.

"Logan," she whispered quietly.

Escaping from my thoughts, I wanted to say something. Something profound. Something that would make sense. Something that would make everything okay. But there was nothing.

Without hesitation I searched her face. As soon as I did, I saw the once glimmering green in her eyes was now dull, her skin pale, and her lips quivering.

The sight made my chest tighten.

But it was when I saw the apprehension in her body language, the hairs on her arm rise, the unsteady rise and fall of her breathing—the fear she didn't want me to see, the fear she was trying to hide from me—that I knew what I had to do.

I had to find him.

Now.

I was going to settle the score with Tommy Flannigan once and for all.

Whatever the outcome.

The note crumpled in my fist and I let it drop to the floor. Tugging my shirt on, I once again looked over at her. "Stay here, lock the door, and don't let anyone in. I mean it, not anyone except me. I don't care who they say they are."

KARR

"Where are you going?" Fear laced her voice.

"To find Tommy."

"But the news, they said members of the Flannigan family had been arrested. Maybe he's already in custody."

I looked at the note on the floor. I had a gut feeling he wasn't. This wasn't something he'd send someone else to do. This was something he'd take too much pleasure in doing himself. "Maybe he is," I said to help calm her nerves, "but someone arranged to deliver that note to this room, and I'm going to find out who it was."

"Logan, no." She reached for me as I slid my feet into my shoes.

I had to shrug away from her.

I had to do this.

On my way to the door, I stopped for just a single moment to look at her. In that moment there was nothing more I wanted than to feel her arms around me, press my body to hers, look into her eyes and tell her we were going to be just fine.

But that would be a lie.

And I wasn't going to lie to her.

Not about this.

"Logan," she pleaded.

I heard the pain in her voice and my heart stopped. Still, I kept moving. I had to do this—for her. For me. For us. The door closed behind me and the sound of the latch told me she'd be safe—until I returned or . . .

My despair was immediately replaced with rage as my eyes fell on the white jacket of the guy who had delivered the note. He was standing in the hallway with his back to me. Unable to control myself, I rushed for him, but came to an abrupt stop when I got a little closer. He wasn't alone. He was kissing a girl, also in uniform. I waited. She giggled, smiled, and finally gave him a wave before she walked down the hall. As soon as he entered the waiting elevator, it started to close, and I darted for it.

My hands jammed between the panels and the doors

flew open.

There he stood.

Lipstick on his lips.

Smiling.

Like he didn't have a care in the fucking world.

He couldn't have been more wrong.

I lunged for him.

Had his lipstick-stained collar in my hands so fast, I could barely see the fear in his eyes. "Who put that note on the food cart?" I hissed.

He was shaking. "I don't know what you're talking about."

With a tug, my grip tightened. "I'm not going to ask you twice, who put the note on the food cart?"

There was a dripping sound on the elevator floor. I think he pissed his pants. "Some dude paid me fifty bucks to slip it onto your tray. He said it was a joke between you and him."

I slammed him against the wall. "What did he look like?"

Mumbling, words barely cohesive, he answered, "Short, brown hair, piercings, and he had a limp."

Tommy.

"Where is he now?"

"I don't know."

"Where is he?" I asked again through gritted teeth.

The guy was crying. "I don't know."

I loosened my grip. "Where did you leave him?"

He crumbled against the wall. "Outside the kitchen door."

I hit the service level. "Scan your card. Show me."

Shaking, he nodded. "Look, mister, I didn't mean to cause any trouble. He said it was a joke. I believed him."

My body went rigid.

A joke!

When I slipped my hand in my pocket, he raised his palms. "Don't hurt me. I didn't mean anything by it."

Ignoring him, I pulled out my wallet and handed him a fifty. "Just show me where you saw him last. I'm not going to hurt you."

Visibly relaxing, he scanned his card and the elevator glided down toward the service level.

Within minutes we were just outside the kitchen.

With a shaky finger he pointed. "He was standing right there when he approached me but once he gave me the note, he headed for the stairs."

"Where do they lead?"

"To the lobby."

I gave him a nod. "Thanks, man. I didn't mean to scare you."

His laugh was more like a cry. "Na, I wasn't really worried," he said.

Now that was a lie.

Taking the stairs two at a time, I pushed open the door and hit the service hallway. Once inside the Mandarin lobby, I scanned it and then swept the lounge. *Nothing.* No sign of him. I searched the bar. The restrooms. The offices. *Nothing.* I climbed the grand staircase and then combed the exterior of the building. *Nothing.* He was nowhere in sight.

That didn't mean shit.

chapter
TWO

Elle Sterling

E MOTION RUSHED THROUGH ME.
      I wasn't going to cry.
   My clothes were scattered and I busied myself dressing.
   Seconds passed.
   Minutes passed.
   Pacing, counting steps, back and forth from the door to the window, I wore a path onto the carpet.
   Finally, I couldn't take the monotony and flopped on the bed. Unsure of what to do, my thoughts started to wander.
   My defense mechanisms weakened with each additional tick of the clock and soon I found myself swallowing against the knot that was lodged in my throat, but I could do nothing about the sting of tears behind my closed eyes.
   Logan and I had come so far, so fast.
   Neither of us had expected to meet in my brother-in-law's law office just a week ago. Neither had expected to run into each other at Molly's Pub later that night. And certainly neither of us meant to have this intense connection.
   It was all so surreal.
   Somehow we'd become entangled in a drug war brewing amid the Boston Irish Mob, and we weren't the only ones.
   There was my missing sister. I had no idea how innocent or guilty she actually was. Then there was Logan's father,

who had been skirting the edges of the law with the Blue Hill Gang for years. There was also Michael, my brother-in-law, who was acting suspiciously. On top of all of that, Logan was working undercover with the DEA but also trying to protect me from everyone.

And me? I just wanted to keep my niece, Clementine, safe. And if things went well, have Logan be a part of my life.

The odds were against us.

Was this a sign? Was everything that was falling apart around us fate telling me I should have known better than to think we could belong to each other?

I refused to let my thoughts go down that road.

Logan was different.

This was going to work out.

Pushing my issues and insecurities aside, I had to believe that we were going to make it. That Logan would be strong enough to fight his demons. That Logan was going to get through this and that I would be by his side to help him.

After all, it was just a note.

Words on a paper meant to scare him.

Meaningless—or so I hoped.

I was certain that after the initial shock, Logan would see it that way too.

I had to believe that. I just did.

Anyway, by all accounts, if the news was correct, Tommy was in jail and no longer a threat to us. *To me.* To Logan.

I pressed my lips together, keenly aware of the passage of time.

My attention went to the TV where Channel 7 news was still on. They were replaying the arrest. I turned the volume up. This time names were flashing across the bottom of the screen.

"More breaking news," the TV correspondent announced. "Members of the powerful Flannigan crime family are among at least twenty-four people arrested tonight in a major drug raid. Details are sketchy, but a confirmed two million dollars in cocaine has been seized. Among those arrested tonight, the alleged head of the Irish Blue Hill Gang, Patrick Flannigan. Sources acknowledge some high-ranking members are still at large, but all efforts are being made to bring them in. If you have seen any of these men, call our hotline."

I crossed my arms, fighting off the chill that had seeped into my bones. There, before my eyes, was a picture of Tommy Flannigan. I hadn't known what he looked like before now, but I knew I'd never forget it. Those cold, brown eyes, the lifeless look on his face, the evil that was written all over him.

Knock. Knock.

I jumped, startled out of my own skin.

My heart started to race.

My pulse thundered.

Fear began to set in.

It wasn't like me to be afraid.

I was strong.

I was resilient.

I'd been through a lot in my life and I'd come out on the other side.

Hardened.

Determined.

Immune.

What had changed?

"Elle, it's me, open up." His voice was husky, commanding.

Relief washed through me. "Logan!" I rushed to the door and threw it open.

In a flash, he was inside. Tall, hard, and imposing, the more-than-competent man locked the door behind him. As soon as he did, his eyes moved over me like he wasn't certain I was really standing here before him, alive, unharmed, in one piece.

With a determined step, I wanted to reassure him, so I

pressed myself against him and stroked my fingers through his beautiful hair. It was rumpled and sticking up everywhere and still, he was breathtaking. "Did you find him?"

He let out a long sigh. "No, not yet."

The words *not yet* made me shiver. I pushed my fingers through his hair again. "His picture is on TV. They said he hasn't been picked up."

Logan's eyes closed as if in pain and then he leaned in and let his forehead rest against mine. "Get your things together. We have to go."

Pausing, I breathed him in—my friend, my lover, the man I loved. I didn't argue. I knew we had to leave. *I just wished we didn't have to.* "Give me a minute."

He nodded.

In the bathroom, my reflection confronted me. My hair was a mess. My eyes were red. My face blotchy. My clothes in disarray. Could Logan see that I was scared?

I hoped not.

With a deep breath, I shook off my own fear.

It was just a note.

It didn't mean anything.

What really frightened me wasn't what might happen to me, but what might happen to him.

I heard his voice. He was on the phone. "Fuck you. You said you'd get him, you reassured me that he, of all people, would be brought in."

Silence.

"Don't tell me what I can and can't do. I'm going to find him."

Silence again.

"I can't guarantee that."

There was a crash, a thud.

Then silence.

More silence.

I waited to open the door.

He was going to go after Tommy, and there was nothing I could do to stop him.

I was scared. I was scared for him. Sure, he was competent, strong, capable, and dauntless even, but Tommy was a part of the Mob, and the Mob wasn't just one person, not just one set of eyes, or hands, or legs, or barrels of guns ready to hunt him down—it was dozens, potentially hundreds.

When I finally opened the door, Logan was composed and dressed in the same clothes he'd arrived in only hours ago. But it seemed like a lifetime ago.

"Who were you talking to?" I asked.

He rolled the sleeves of his white shirt up to his elbows as he spoke. "Agent Blanchet of the DEA."

Ironically, knowing he was working with the DEA helped soothe my nerves. "What did she say?"

He shrugged. "Nothing. Absolutely nothing. They don't know where Tommy is. Come on, we have to go."

"Where are we going?"

He indicated I should walk toward him. "I'm going to take you to my father's house. Right now it's the safest place."

"Isn't he Patrick's counsel?"

"Yeah, but Patrick has a half-dozen attorneys. My father isn't one he'd use to get him out of jail. Besides, I can't imagine he'll even be given bail. He's too much of a flight risk."

My steps were slow. "And what about you?"

With an extended hand, he urged me to move faster. "I'm going to find Tommy."

Hearing him say it again didn't make the blow any easier. I stopped. "Logan, please don't do this. The police are looking for him. Let them find him."

His headshake was determined. "They'll never find him. He might not be very bright, but he's not stupid."

My fingertips reached for him. "I don't want you to get hurt."

There, I said it.

He took my hand and tugged me toward him. He didn't

say anything to me. Didn't give me false hope. Instead, he kissed me like I was his world. I could feel him, I could taste him, I was *him*. His hands clutched my face tightly as his lips moved against mine. My hands rested on his chest but then moved up to wrap around his neck. I needed to be closer. He did too. He pulled me even tighter to him and started grabbing fistfuls of my hair. In that moment, he held me as if it were the last time we'd be like this. I wanted to fight for control with him, tell him not to kiss me like this, but our lips and our bodies were moving in such perfect sync, I couldn't. It was as if our minds were branding this feeling into our souls and I didn't want the moment to end until the full image was captured.

When he pulled back, I looked at him. I wanted to beg him to stay with me. Not to go out into the night alone. Yet, I knew there was no arguing with him. He was determined to protect me no matter the cost. Besides, he had already made up his mind, and the way he was staring at me told me what I already feared—if he didn't succeed in finding and stopping Tommy, he was going to leave me in order to save me.

And crush my heart.

chapter
THREE

Day 9

LOGAN

R ELYING ON OTHERS FOR help felt strange.
I'd been on my own, forging my own way, and dealing with my own shit for so long, asking for assistance didn't seem right.

Yet, I didn't have a choice.

I couldn't be in two places at once, and Elle's safety was at stake.

The ride to my old man's was quiet, both of us lost in our thoughts. When we pulled into the driveway, I turned off the ignition and looked at her. I knew she was upset. "Talk to me."

"What do you want me to say?"

"Whatever you have to," I said. "Whatever you need to. Just get it out."

She closed her eyes. "I don't want you to go after Tommy."

Trying to comfort her, I reached for her hand. "I have to. Don't you see? If not I'll go insane constantly looking behind my back, wondering what's lurking around every corner, waiting for what's next."

She pulled her hand away. "Then there's nothing more to say."

"Elle," I sighed.

Her eyes met mine. "Logan, I'm tired. And I'm worried . . . for you. For Clementine. For Michael. And for me. I just want this to be over."

I nodded. "So do I."

She turned her head and her eyes were hidden from me, but I had already seen the tears that were glimmering in them, and it killed me.

"Let's get inside." There really wasn't anything more to say. She'd said it all. The truth was . . . I was worried too.

It was almost two in the morning and the house was lit up like a Christmas tree.

I'd called my father as soon as I left the hotel room and given him a very watered-down version of what had happened. Then I'd called Declan Mulligan, a guy from my past who I hadn't expected to be a friend, and Miles Murphy, who wasn't ex-military like I thought but ex-BPD, who'd worked in the gang crimes division for years until he was shot in the line of duty sometime last year and subsequently decided to retire. I filled them in and asked for their help. Miles had agreed to call some of his ex-cop friends to come over to my old man's tonight to look out for Elle. He was coming to keep guard as well, and then if it came to it, he'd help take her home in the morning and get her house and business wired securely. Declan was showing up as well, but not to keep watch; he had the best intel on Tommy.

"Wait for me to come around," I told her and then got out. As soon as I did, the kitchen door flung open. My old man stood there, gun at his side, eyes shifting in the night. I gave him a nod and rushed over to Elle's side. I tried not to show her the fear that was flowing through my veins.

With my hand on the small of her back, I guided her toward what used to be my gramps's house and was now my old man's. She fidgeted. Her fingers combed through her hair and she smoothed it. It was then that I realized she hadn't formally met my father yet. The run-in at O'Shea's law office, more than a week ago, wasn't the impression I wanted her to have of him.

My old man stood stoic as we hurried through the door. His eyes met mine when I passed him and I could see the disapproval in them over the deal I'd made with the DEA, but he said nothing. Instead he followed us in and secured the door behind him. Once he slid his gun inside his waistband, he surveyed us. The creases around his eyes and lines on his face told me he was worried too.

We were all standing in my gramps's kitchen and the ghosts couldn't have had any larger of a presence. With lingering visions of blood everywhere, I closed my eyes and had to forcibly suppress the memories of the night Tommy attacked me and my then somewhat-girlfriend Kayla in here.

"Logan," my father said quietly as if he knew what I was envisioning.

The sound of his voice made me blink out of the horrific flashback.

Focusing on Elle, I knew it was time to break the ice and do the formal introductions, as awkward as they seemed in a situation like this. "Pop, this is Elle Sterling. Elle, this is my father, Sean McPherson."

She held her hand out. "Nice to meet you, Mr. McPherson."

To my surprise, Sean McPherson, attorney-at-law, admitted alcoholic, my part-time boss and my old man, stepped forward and hugged her. "Call me Sean."

The embrace wasn't long, but it was enough that I could see the look of relief on her face. Had she been worried about meeting him?

"Coffee?" my old man asked, stepping back.

"No, thank you," Elle replied.

"Yeah, I wouldn't mind a cup, if you want to make a pot. I'm going to take Elle up to my room. She's tired."

My father nodded and then started for the sink.

"This way." I took Elle's hand and her bag and we headed toward the family room, and then up the stairs to the room I was staying in.

Once we were in there, Elle looked anywhere but at me.

My shit was everywhere. I'd only been here a few days since moving out of the Four Seasons and hadn't bothered to unpack anything. I was living out of duffle bags. I reached inside one and pulled out a pair of track pants and a sweatshirt. "You'll be safe here. No one but Tommy would ever come to Killian McPherson's house. And with Miles, his crew, and my father on guard, he'll never make it past the threshold even if he tries."

"I know you wouldn't take me anywhere that wasn't safe," she whispered. I could tell she was scared. I hated that she was.

Wanting to get out on the street as fast as I could, I quickly stripped out of my dress clothes and changed.

Elle walked over to the bureau and picked up the picture that was sitting on it. "Is this you?"

"Yeah, I was around four, and that's my grandmother and grandfather."

"I can see the resemblance."

Dressed, I sat on the bed and put my sneakers on. "The bathroom is at the end of the hall. Ask my old man for anything you need."

She nodded but didn't turn around. She just kept staring at the picture.

"Elle, I have to go," I said, standing and grabbing my hat. As I headed for the door I wanted to go over to her, put my arms around her, and kiss her, but it didn't feel right. Not right now. Not when she was in danger. Not when everything was so fucked up.

Her voice caught me just before I hit the hallway. "Be careful," she said quietly.

I waited a moment, to see if she'd turn around.

She didn't.

Better that way.

Quickly, I closed the door and my mind to the struggle I was feeling between my head and my heart. I'd told her we were in this together, but that was before. Before the note.

Before the one thing I wasn't sure I could wrap my head around—Tommy hurting Elle. That's why I had to focus on removing the threat; everything else would have to wait.

Downstairs, Declan and Miles had already arrived. They were sitting at the kitchen table with my old man. They all looked at me solemnly when I entered the room.

"Is she all set?" my father asked.

I nodded and headed to the coffeepot to pour a cup.

"Who else knows what you did besides Frank and Elle?" He asked this as he walked to the kitchen door. Frank lived next door, but his house was completely dark. He must have been asleep. I doubted he knew anything about the takedown—yet.

"No one, and Frank doesn't really know anything. Only that I needed some empty liquor boxes. But I'm sure when he sees the news, he'll figure it out."

My old man turned around and his eyes were filled with pain. "I've done everything I could to keep you out of this life, Logan, to protect you from the darkness it brings," he started.

I set my cup down and held up my hands. "Not now, okay? Not now."

He dropped his head and ran his hands through his hair. I knew what this was doing to him and I hated it.

Focus. I had to focus on what I had to do. There was no space for feelings in this room, or in this house, or in my life right now for that matter.

"Come on, Declan, let's go," I said, striding toward the door.

He rose but stayed where he was, peering at both Miles and my father.

I kept moving.

I could hear the guys' voices as I walked out of the kitchen door and into the cool night. They were still talking as I stepped onto the driveway but now I stopped listening. I didn't need to hear what they had to say.

Minutes later, Declan hopped in the Rover and pulled

out his phone. "I asked around. The only place Tommy has been seen lately besides Lucy's is down at the docks in Southie."

"Then that's where we'll start." I pulled out of the driveway and drove around for a bit to make sure I didn't have a tail. I was pretty certain the last time I'd left the waterfront I was being followed, and now I was almost certain it was Agent Blanchet who had been on my tail that night. She knew way more about what I'd been doing the past week than I'd let on.

When I didn't see anyone behind me, I headed for the Seaport District. I was going to find Tommy Flannigan if I had to turn over every square inch of the place. The motherfucker could be hiding in an abandoned warehouse like a rat for all I knew. I didn't care. I'd flush him out. He was going to be mine—no matter where he was.

It was still dark when I took the streets one at a time, weaving through them, up and down, all the way from the channel to the river. The ice had melted in the water, but it kept its mucky winter shade. There wasn't much activity this late and there was no sight of him. It was time to hoof it, so I parked near the Boston Fish Pier. "Where the fuck do we start?" I asked Declan.

We had less than three hours before dawn at the most and I knew if I didn't find him tonight, I never would. It was too easy to hide in the city in the daytime. And come nightfall tomorrow, he'd be long gone. It was no use going to Lucy's—the strip club was where the drugs had been found, and the police were swarming there.

Declan's phone had been going off like crazy. He'd put feelers out everywhere. I couldn't believe how well connected he was. Someone said he'd seen Tommy walking down Seaport Boulevard hours ago. We headed down that way, pulling on every warehouse door we could to see if any were loose or had recently been broken into. It was crazy, but as kids, we did this all the time. We'd come down here and wedge open the doors to the warehouses and scare the shit out of anyone who followed us inside. It was a game. I'd played it. Tommy had played it. So had Declan. Back then Southie was also a dump, though, and there were a shit-ton of abandoned buildings. Not so many anymore.

For over an hour Declan and I walked on opposite sides of the streets, up and down the docks, and through alleys. The wind was brutal and it was cold, so I'd pulled my hood up long ago. Lost in my thoughts, I kept walking, searching, pulling on doors, looking behind garbage cans, peering into smaller alleyways, checking out the homeless to see if Tommy was pretending to be one of them.

"Hey, man."

Declan's voice grabbed my attention and I looked across the street at him as he came jogging toward me.

"He's at the fucking Seaport Hotel."

My heart pounded. "No fucking way. I thought he'd checked out."

"Miles just called. A buddy of his in security has been on the lookout and spotted him about an hour ago. Checked in under some alias, but he's there. Room 510."

I started moving backwards and pointed my finger at Declan. "Take the Rover and go back to my old man's. I'll meet you there later."

"No way, man. You're not going there alone."

I shook my head, still pointing. "I don't want you involved any further. You've done enough for now. Don't follow me. Just go."

"I'm not doing that."

"Declan, you have to leave. I can't take the chance of you getting caught up in something dangerous."

He stood there motionless.

"Please, man." My voice was pleading and I think he got what I was saying. My conscience couldn't handle it if he got marked or worse if he got killed in the crossfire.

He said nothing.

I took that as an okay and turned around and started running. The hotel wasn't far, and it would be faster to get there on foot than heading all the way back to my vehicle anyway.

It was almost dawn by now and the early morning sky was just erupting. To everyone else I looked like I was out for a run, not on a mission to confront Tommy Flannigan and—and what? That was the question, wasn't it? Do I sell my soul to the devil and kill the motherfucker? I decided not to go there in my mind right now. One step at a time— first I had to find him.

It was the longest fucking ten minutes of my life, but finally the Seaport Hotel was in sight. I strode through the lobby like I belonged there, hit the up arrow at the bank of elevators, and casually stepped into one when the doors opened. Beneath my calm exterior I was screaming, because my time of reckoning had finally come.

I stabbed the button for the fifth floor and the elevator seemed to crawl up to it. In the hallway, it felt a little surreal. I glanced down and was shocked to see my white knuckles and the ropes of muscle straining against the backs of my hands. I shook off any doubt. I had no choice but to do this. I'd use my fists. If I beat him to a pulp and he didn't recover, I couldn't be charged with premeditated murder. The law was flashing through my mind. Murder in the first degree. Voluntary manslaughter. Involuntary manslaughter. It didn't matter; all would come with a prison term.

If I killed this motherfucker tonight I was going to be without Elle in my life. If I didn't, if I turned around right now, I was going to have to let her go.

It was a lose-lose situation all the way around. But the *come and get me if you dare* note Tommy had sent me was sent for a reason, and I was going to find out what that reason was.

My strides were long. Room 500, 502, 504, 506, 508, and finally 510. Focused on the gold numbers, I reached my destination in less than three seconds.

Without even thinking about it, I lifted my leg and kicked the door in, throwing the entire weight of my body into it. Luckily, this hotel was old and so were the doors.

Barreling into the room, I was shocked when I saw him. I had to remind myself that this time I wasn't going to be held down by three men while he wielded his knife at me.

Yes, it had been a very long time since we were face-to-face, and there he was, looking the same. Like time had never passed. His eyes met mine with a dare, a come-and-get-me, and then he scampered from the bed to the floor in less than a heartbeat. On his feet, he stumbled backwards. "It's been a long time," he snickered.

I clenched my teeth and drew in a breath to calm the fury surging through my veins. "Not long enough."

"You got my note?"

My blood started to pump so fast that I could hear my heartbeat thumping in my ears. "I did. But you already know that. Why else would I be here?"

That grin was back. "A friendly chat between old friends."

"Fuck you," I spat.

He shook his head. "Not one to let bygones be bygones?"

Ignoring the shit spewing from his mouth, I rushed forward and slammed my fist into his face. "What do you want from me?"

He bounced off the wall and I grabbed his shoulders before he slumped to the ground. Kneeing him in the gut, hitting him hard enough to lift his feet off the floor, I then let him tumble down. "We need to talk," he managed.

With his face on the floor, I placed my foot on his back and pressed.

He yelped like a dog.

"Talk!" I barked out.

"Let me turn around."

Easing my foot away, I stepped back but kept my gun pointed.

Slowly, he turned over and wiped the blood from his mouth.

"I'm waiting," I sneered.

Instead of talking, he lunged for the gun that was sticking out from under the mattress.

Motherfucker.

"Freeze!" someone shouted.

"Hands up, now!" someone else yelled.

My eyes darted to the door. Agent Blanchet was standing in the doorway with a swarm of agents surrounding her.

No effing way.

She walked over to me. "I want you out of here."

I stared at her.

"Now, McPherson. Don't make me take you in and then process paperwork to get you out, because that will really piss me off."

Tommy never made it to his gun, but his laughter made my ears ring. He was off the floor in cuffs in two seconds flat. Surrounded by five agents, there was nothing I could do to get to him.

"*Now,*" Agent Blanchet repeated and started shoving me out of the room.

I wanted to deck her but knew that would get me nowhere. With slow strides, I headed for the door.

"Hey!" Tommy hissed.

I turned around.

"Don't think that girl of yours is any safer with me behind bars. If you were a good boy and followed the rules, there wouldn't be an issue. Would there? So for her sake, you *will* stay away from her now because you know I have eyes, and hands, and a few hundred dicks, everywhere."

"You motherfucking piece of shit," I growled and lunged for him.

"Get him out of here." Blanchet's voice was loud as she pointed toward Tommy.

Hands were holding me back and a weird rush of fear washed through me as I watched Tommy being dragged out of the room.

It was like time stood still and I couldn't move.

I had no idea how much time passed or when whoever was holding onto me had released their grip but when I blinked, I realized the room was quiet. I looked around.

Agent Blanchet was the only one in the room and she was staring at the doorway. "You can come in," she said.

As if everything were happening in slow motion, I glanced toward the direction of her voice.

In the doorway was Declan. "Sorry, man, I had to follow you. I wasn't letting you go it alone." He pointed to Blanchet. "Turns out, she'd been following us and she nabbed me in the lobby before I could make it to you. She forced me to tell her what room you were in."

Fuck, I knew she'd been on me. I should have been even more careful.

"Good thing he fessed up quickly." Her voice was like cold steel.

My eyes darted to hers, and they were swimming with that same cold steel.

"Listen, McPherson, you're walking a very thin line. My patience is wearing down."

I scrubbed my hand down my face. "What the fuck more do you want from me?"

She glared at me like I should fucking know.

And I did know. I just hoped to fuck *she* didn't know. Know what I'd done—that I'd committed a felony.

Finally, she spoke. "You should have called me when you found out where Tommy was. I don't want to have to put a tail on you every fucking time I suspect you know more than you're telling me."

I stared at her blankly because thank God, she didn't know that I'd relocated the drugs.

"Next time you pull something like this, I'm going to haul your ass in." She pointed to herself. "I'm the law, not you. Do you understand me?"

I nodded but tuned everything else out.

This whole thing had just gotten so much worse.

Even behind bars, Tommy wasn't going to leave Elle

alone. As if I hadn't already known it, he'd told me so himself. And now there was nothing I could do about it.

Elle and I had just forged some kind of commitment and I was going to be forced to break it.

What had happened tonight?

So much.

Way too much.

It was hard to believe that just hours ago I'd crossed the line an attorney should never cross. I'd tampered with evidence. In truth, I'd committed a felony by relocating a shitload of cocaine that had since been confiscated, and people in connection to it arrested.

Not just people.

My enemies. My foes.

Patrick.

His crew.

Now Tommy.

And I had put them there.

I should be happy.

I wasn't.

I also should be worried about what would happen to me.

I wasn't.

The only thing on my mind right now was, *what am I going to do to make sure Elle stays safe?*

Because I was screwed.

Although a lot of the Blue Hill Gang members had been arrested, not all of them had been locked up. There were too many of them. And besides, some would be out on bail within hours. I also knew Tommy was into something else, something drug related, and those connections would go beyond jail. I was certain he would reach out to them as soon as he could.

The fact was—I couldn't keep Elle safe.

Not always.

Something could happen to her if I stayed with her.

Maybe something bad.

Chills ran through me.

Something like what Tommy had done before to Kayla, a girl I was casually seeing, the girl I made the mistake of bringing back to Boston one weekend, or like what he had done recently to Elle's employee and friend, Peyton. Although I had no proof, I was certain Tommy had caught a glimpse of Peyton and me together on the street and then later attacked her, sending her to the hospital with an *E* carved in her stomach.

An *E* I had wrongly believed was meant to remind me of his dead sister, Emily. Emily, the girl I'd made the mistake of fucking when I was fifteen, which subsequently led to a teen pregnancy and ultimately to her suicide. That event had not only changed my life, but my father's and grandfather's lives as well.

Back then, Emily's father had been the head of the Dorchester Heights Gang, a smaller Irish Mob, and he wanted to be top dog, but my paternal grandfather had held that position in the Blue Hill Gang. The situation I inadvertently created gave Emily's father the ammunition he needed to make his move and ascend his rank.

Patrick Flannigan was ruthless.

The rule on the street was *"A life for a life,"* and he demanded obedience.

Regardless of the circumstances, as a consequence of my actions, my father had been providing his legal services to Patrick for the past twelve years. In exchange for my life my father traded his life in service for Emily's death.

A life for a life.

But that wasn't enough for Patrick. He wanted more. The details behind my grandfather's dissent from power were sketchy, but eventually my grandfather handed over his leadership, his gang, to Patrick.

This went against code. This wasn't a life for a life. But the situation was grave and my family did what they needed to do to protect me.

Patrick didn't follow the rules, and neither did his son.

Where did this leave me now?

Right where I knew it always would. Having to do what I didn't want to do—listen to Tommy's threat and disassociate myself from Elle. It was absolutely the best solution.

"Hey, man, you okay?"

I looked at Declan. Tried to focus. But couldn't. That weird rush of fear I'd felt earlier was suddenly paralyzing.

"We need to go. Agent Blanchet said you had five minutes to get out of here."

I looked around. He was the only one left in the room. "Yeah, yeah, right. Do you think I could crash at your place for a few hours?"

Confusion furrowed his brow. "Yeah, sure, but what about Elle? She's at your old man's."

"Miles will bring her home when she wakes up."

"What are you doing, man? What are you thinking?"

With my heart feeling like it was in sharp, jagged pieces, I forced myself to say it out loud. "I can't be with her. Not right now."

His confusion mounted. "What are you talking about?"

"I can't let her think she's safe with me because the truth is . . . she's anything but."

The disappointed look on his face couldn't be hidden. "So what? You're going to walk away from her just like that?"

I nodded. Yeah, yeah I was.

For now.

chapter
FOUR

Elle

I WAS ON A train.

It was moving fast.

Out the window the earth met the sky, and the two blended together in one giant blur. In the haze, the phrase *Catch him if you can* seemed to etch itself on the glass beside me. The words were so few that you'd think the thunderous sound of the wheels hitting the track would have drowned them out by now. But no, instead they just kept repeating themselves over and over in my mind.

A phrase I couldn't seem to escape.

Catch him if you can.

Catch him if you can.

Catch him if you can.

No matter how hard I tried to block out the words, I couldn't.

It sounded more like the title of a movie than a mantra that had me going on some crazy quest. I could practically visualize the theatrical release poster in my mind. It was as if I had seen it before.

A finely built man with long legs, running, wearing a suit—no, not a suit, a pair of track pants, Converse sneakers, sunglasses, and maybe a knit hat—being chased by a woman. The woman had ginger-colored hair. She was tall but not nearly as tall as him. The image was blurry. It didn't matter, though, because I could still tell who it was—it was me, and I was running after Logan.

Except I wasn't going to do that.

I'd vehemently told myself so.

Told myself I had to let him go.

And yet, somehow I found myself on the train headed to New York City with the events of the past two days replaying in my mind until I felt like they were actually taking place all over again.

The sun shining in his bedroom window wasn't what had woken me. I'd been awake for hours. Waiting. Wondering. Pacing.

Worried, I stared at the faint yellow beams of light.

Where was he?

It took me a minute to gather the courage to get out of bed. It was dawn and he wasn't back. That wasn't a good sign.

I'd spent hours talking to his father during the night. If I thought I understood Logan before, now I understood him so much more. His father had told me a little about growing up the son of the mob boss, and how he'd tried to keep Logan away from that life. Killian had, too. Killian wanted the best for Logan and he knew the life he'd led wasn't it. But then there had been Emily, her suicide, the aftermath, and the attack on Kayla. How Logan blamed himself. He had also told me how happy he was to see Logan with me, caring for someone, letting someone in, but he cautioned me—change didn't happen overnight. The walls his son had built around himself would take a while to come down. And he asked me to be patient with Logan. I had agreed. Change, for either of us, wasn't going to be easy. I'd spent the majority of my life avoiding relationships, not trusting men or my feelings. But what I felt for Logan was compelling, riveting, overwhelming. Fierce. And I didn't want to let it go. Couldn't.

I heard noises from downstairs and hurried to see if he was back.

But it wasn't Logan in the kitchen closing the door. It was Miles. He'd just come inside. All night he'd rotated positions back and forth from his car parked on the street, to the family room, to the kitchen.

"Elle, sorry, did I wake you?"

I shook my head. "Have you heard anything?"

Miles looked anywhere but at me. "Declan just called me—"

"What did he say? Is Logan hurt?" The voice wasn't mine, but it was asking the identical questions I was about to ask. It was Sean's, and he was standing in the pantry alcove with a can of coffee in his hand.

"Mr. McPherson, sorry, I didn't see you," he answered. "Logan's fine. He found Tommy, and nothing happened."

Relief coursed through me and I could see Sean visibly sag in his own relief.

"It seems the DEA was following Logan and he didn't catch the tail. They broke into the room when Logan was with Tommy before Logan could talk to Tommy."

Step by step, I made my way to the table and sat down.

Sean did the very same thing.

Walking toward the sink, Miles spoke. "Whenever you're ready to go, Elle, I'll take you to your townhouse."

I didn't have to ask why. I knew what that meant. Logan hadn't accomplished whatever it was he set out to do. And he had arranged this as his backup plan. The walls had gone up. He wasn't coming back until I was gone.

I had no choice in the matter.

I was too raw from the night's events to discuss anything any further. Sitting for a short while, I made myself get my things and let Miles drive me home.

Once there, I escaped to my room. Just wanting to shut everything out, I lay back on my bed. I had Michael to deal with, but it was too early to call him.

Michael O'Shea was the brother-in-law I never knew I had up until three months ago, and his daughter was the niece I fell in love with at first sight. It was because of her that I decided to leave the gypsy-like lifestyle I'd adopted and move to Boston. It was also because of her that I'd done what I'd done and Michael had done what he'd done.

The catalyst for coming to Boston was my missing sister, Lizzy, who still hadn't returned to her husband and daughter. The last time I saw her was fifteen years ago when she walked away from me. My hope was now that the danger had passed, she'd turn up and maybe we could repair our damaged relationship.

Just as I closed my eyes, my phone started to ring. For one second, I thought maybe it was Logan, but I knew it wouldn't be. Holding a breath, I looked at my screen. It was Michael's name on it.

Nerves rattled me. Did he check with the delivery service and know the cocaine had actually been delivered last night? They were one of those third-party services and my hope was that the fly-by-night guys wouldn't be able to be reached directly. Was I wrong? Did Michael know about Logan? About what he'd done?

"Hello," I answered, trying to swallow my nervousness.

"Hi, it's me. I just wanted to check with you and see if you've seen the news?"

"Yes, I have." I kept my response short.

"I'm glad the delivery never arrived. It seems somehow the DEA got wind of it and intervened."

Details weren't given on where the product was found, so Michael really didn't have a clue. "Does that mean everything will be okay and Clementine is out of danger?"

"I hope so. With the Blue Hill Gang behind bars, I think what-ever Lizzy did will be the least of their concern."

I really didn't want to talk about this. There was so much I wanted to know, but not while lying to Michael. Changing gears, I asked, "Do you think Lizzy will come home now?"

"I don't know, Elle. Listen, I have to run and get Clementine from my sister's. I'll call you later."

"Yes, of course. Give her a kiss for me."

He hung up. That was strange. I was worried about my lies, but he seemed so preoccupied, I didn't have to be.

With that behind me, and while Miles worked on increasing security, I sat on my bed and pondered what I should do about Logan.

I thought long and hard, remembering my conversation with

his father — "be patient with my son." With his words fresh in my mind, I tried to call Logan.

He didn't answer.

I didn't leave a message because I wasn't sure what I wanted to say.

And he didn't call me back, either.

By ten A.M., I knew I couldn't sit around anymore. It was Friday, and I had to get to my newly opened boutique, The House of Sterling.

Logan must have been in touch with Miles, because he insisted on driving me to work and spending the day with me. Knowing that, I was certain Logan would call or text or something.

Nothing.

Miles drove me home, and later that evening after he finished working on my security system, he left assuring me I would be locked safely inside. I was just about to head upstairs and go to bed when there was a knock on my door. Startled, my heartbeat sped up, but then I chastised myself for thinking it would be anyone who'd come here to harm me. It was probably just Miles. Perhaps he had forgotten something. But a peek through the peep-hole told me it was Logan.

Right away, confusion clouded my thoughts. He hadn't called all day. Why was he here now? My heart was already in a tangle and my mind was a web of questions. Seeing him wasn't going to help me figure out what to do.

I should have known Miles had left for a reason.

Staring at Logan, anger threatening to erupt but need over-taking me, I debated whether or not to let him in. I hated that he'd given up on us so easily. I wanted him to fight his fear of what might happen. Don't get me wrong, I understood I could be in danger, but I truly believed Tommy was using that fear to further ruin Logan's life.

"Elle, it's me," he said, his voice low, husky.

Uncertain, I stood behind the door considering my options. I knew what would happen when I opened the door. I'd see him — his knowing eyes, his hard square jaw, his even harder body, and just like that, I'd let him off the hook for thinking I was safer *without him. I'd melt like the schoolgirl I knew better than to be. It would be that simple. But our situation wasn't that simple. It was so much more complicated. And I hated that it was.*

The knocking persisted until I couldn't stand it anymore. I longed to see him, to smell him, to touch him. I didn't want to be apart from him.

"Elle, please." His voice broke.

My heart stilled at the sound of his tone. He was the stronger one, my protector, and yet right now, the dauntless, fearless man needed me and I couldn't shut him out no matter how much I knew I should. The truth was, deep in my heart, I knew there was no way this thing between us was going to end well. He just wasn't willing to accept that he wasn't responsible for my safety, and that fact was going to continue to eat at him and destroy us.

Still, I couldn't turn him away.

All I could do was hope that I was strong enough to make this work for the both of us.

With a shaky hand, I opened the door and there he stood, all male, all need, all hard and yet soft. With his head down and his sorrowful, regretful hazel eyes blazing into mine, I was his. Any sense of self-preservation I had been feeling vanished.

"I'm sorry," he said, stepping toward me and putting his hands on my hips.

Even upset with him, my body flared to life. Lust and love and something that felt a lot like my own fear swirled around me like a mini tornado. I wanted to push him. I wanted to kiss him. I wanted to punch him. I wanted to fuck him. I settled for throwing my arms around him. I needed to touch him. To comfort him, as odd as that sounds. With my mouth unbearably close to his ear, I whispered, "Don't shoulder this situation we're in on your own."

He buried his head in my neck. "I can't think straight. I'm so fucking worried about you."

Oh God, that ache in his voice killed me. My fingers threaded through his hair and as I touched him, I breathed him in. All Logan. All everything I never knew I wanted but now needed so very desperately.

Moments passed. Seconds. Maybe minutes. I knew I had to

push him away. I had to talk to him with a clear head and I warred with myself until I finally did. "Logan, I'll be all right. I can take care of myself."

His sigh told me he didn't believe it.

Clarity set in. "What are you doing here?"

"I was going out of my mind. I had to see for myself you were safe."

"I'm fine, Logan. I'll be fine," I lied. Physically maybe, but emotionally, I didn't think I would.

The doubt in his stare made his hazel eyes look icy.

I chose to ignore it and press on. "Why didn't you come back to your father's this morning?" I asked, even though I knew why. Still, it was a start to the bigger conversation.

His face was worn, his eyes tired. He rubbed his jaw. "I didn't know what to do. I had to figure things out. And to do that I needed, I need, some time alone."

Being alone meant not being with me, which in turn, in his mind, meant I was out of danger. I got that. I just didn't agree with it. I didn't want him to be alone. I didn't want to be alone. But he was worried that if he stayed with me, something bad was going to happen. If something bad was going to happen, I believed it would happen either way. Was he here because he just couldn't fight his need to be with me? Or had he decided we were in this together? I had to know. "And what has changed?" I asked, trying to make him think this through. Hopefully see that we were better together.

Logan stared at me with blankness in his eyes.

I knew right then nothing had changed. I should have asked him to leave—I didn't. Instead I pressed on, hopeful. "Logan, what has changed?" I repeated, hoping for a miracle.

There was a slight shake of his head. His beautiful hair was tousled, his stubble longer than usual. Everything about him screamed that he was lost.

And even though I felt anger that he couldn't see what I saw, that we should fight together, I couldn't fight my longing to take the lost boy and comfort him. Maybe make him see things the way I did. That if anything was going to happen, it would happen *either way.*

"After everything that happened last night, I had to make certain you were okay," he said, avoiding my question.

No matter how many times I tried to reassure him that I would be fine, that I could take care of myself, it didn't matter. I could see the turbulence he was suffering in his eyes—that he didn't see it the way I did.

"And we need to talk. Get our stories straight," he further clarified.

I nodded.

He took the lead, the alpha in him back in action, as he led me to the sofa. Once we sat down, we were only inches away from each other, but it felt like miles. I watched the way his lips moved as he spoke, the way his jaw tensed when I told him about Michael's call. I couldn't turn my emotions off, but I tried as our conversation turned even more serious and we discussed our situation in detail—the delivery, what he'd done, his father, the DEA, Tommy, and what had happened after he left me last night.

Facts. Facts. And more facts.

Nothing that changed our tragic situation.

When the talking had ceased, the what-to-say-if-asked agreed upon, we stared at each other. I was searching for the right way to discuss his fear, but I never found the words.

I don't know who moved first, him or me, just that his lips were on mine and they felt so good I wasn't going to deny the moment.

I opened for him. My mouth, my arms, my legs, and of course my heart.

His hand curled against the back of my neck, possessively, drawing me nearer.

Need so big, so large it was like an ocean, a mountain, the world, consumed us.

Without words, he rose, picked me up, carried me to my bed, and set me down.

My heart was pounding.

He unbuttoned. Unzipped. I tugged my shirt off, my leggings, my panties. Eyes only on each other, both naked, our bodies found one another.

Frantic for each other, we kissed. We touched. We tangled ourselves together.

His hands roamed.

Mine did the same.

Then his lips found my skin and he kissed my mouth, my jaw, my chin, my neck.

The lights in the room were on and I could see everything. All of him. The leanness of his body. The pale, smooth skin that covered his ribs, his stomach, the jut of his hip bones, and his beautiful, long, fully erect cock. I reached for it, and the feel of him in the palm of my hand made my clit pulse with so much dizzying need that I had to close my eyes. "Fuck me." The words slipped from my mouth.

He made a noise and for a second, I wasn't certain he was going to, but then he rolled us over and before I knew it, I was staring down at his handsome face, straddling him.

I drew a line over the scar under his eye. The one Tommy had given him. I wanted to lick it, to kiss it, and to tell him everything was going to be okay, but I didn't want to talk. I didn't want to ruin the moment with words. So instead, I shifted a little, raised myself the smallest of amounts, and then he was inside of me. Ecstasy. With a shudder, I squeezed my knees against his sides and absorbed the pleasure.

After a few moments, he started to move. Slow. Easy. Up and down. In and out.

My hands flattened on his chest.

His body continued to lift and fall, his hands now possessively gripping my hips.

My mouth lowered to his, and gasps of pleasure escaping through open-mouthed kisses filled the room. It was hard to concentrate on kissing him when with every slide of his cock there was a glorious press against my clit.

The pleasure kept building.

Higher and higher.

On the edge, I needed more. I pushed upright and rode him. Faster. Harder.

Eyes locked, he fucked upward and I rolled my hips.
Over and over.
In rhythm.
I arched my back.
My heart beat faster.
My breath rushed out.
And then I was coming.
He was coming.
It was fast.
Intense.
My body quaking in perfect spasms of ecstasy, I looked down at him. He stilled, groaned, and I could feel his cock pulse inside me as he rode out his own release. Once our breathing slowed, he pulled me to his chest and held me tightly. Kissed my head. I didn't ever want this to end but soon, sleep pulled me under.
Early in the morning, too early, I awoke in my bed—alone.
On the pillow beside me was a note:

I had to go to New York City. Not sure when I'll be back. I'll be in touch.

The blood in my veins felt like ice water.

He wasn't going to be in touch. I knew this. I felt it. Hell, I knew it from the moment he set foot inside and told me he needed time.

Still, I couldn't stop the flood of emotions. Anger surged through me. He'd left me—again. He didn't even wake me to discuss things. He made the decision for us to face what might never come—separately.

Suppressing any tears that threatened to spill, I pressed my fingertips to the place where his head had lain last night and said out loud, "Screw you."

Screw ou. Right, I thought with a small huff of laughter, as I was on my way to New York to bring him home.

To be fair, I'd held onto my anger for a good solid six hours after I'd read the note. I'd gone to work, tried to make it through the day without thinking about it. But then the anger began to subside and the tears fell. Somewhere around noon, I rationalized that he was scared, and the only way he knew how to deal with fear was to run. After all, he'd done it his whole life. And so had I. Moving from job to job, from country to country, trying to escape my childhood. But no more. If I wanted him in my life, I had to go get him and make him see it was time for that cycle to end. For him. And for me.

I'd enlisted the help of his father. Sean thought Tommy could be making empty threats, but wanted me to be cautious and reluctantly agreed to give me Logan's address in New York City. He also called the doorman and told him to let me up when I arrived. Miles was much more hesitant about my impromptu trip. Still, he brought me to the station and promised not to tell Logan. In exchange, I promised to call him on my way back so he could pick me up, in case I came back on the train—alone.

That was how I'd come to board the train exactly 215 minutes ago on this Sunday afternoon. The Amtrak Acela Express came to a screeching halt at Penn Station and my heart started to pound. Logan was everything I needed in my life and nothing I'd known I was looking for. Not a white knight or a prince charming but a man I loved fiercely, and who loved me with equal fierceness. He didn't have to say the words *I love you* for me to know that he did—it was in his voice when he said my name, in his eyes when he looked at me, and in the way he touched me with a protectiveness that somehow I'd grown to need.

I exited the train with no luggage in hand but a mission in mind. When Logan and I were together, everything in the world was right no matter how wrong things were. And that was why I was here—to remind him of that.

To catch him if I could.

Walking fast to keep up the pace of the other passengers

wasn't a challenge because it would get me to him faster. The smell of food permeated the air, reminding me just how hungry I was, but my mission didn't allow for stopping.

Madison Square Garden was my point of entry into the city and I quickly hailed a cab. "Eighty-third and Fifth, please," I told the driver.

Even though it was late afternoon, the traffic was still stop and go. It seemed to take forever to get to the Upper East Side and my nerves had started to rear again. When the driver finally arrived at my destination thirty minutes later, my pulse was pounding. I paid, and once I was standing on the sidewalk, I began to second-guess my decision. I'd never been inside this part of Logan's life. This was the elite half, the high-society side he didn't care for very much. But it was still a part of him.

But what if he didn't want me inside this part?

With a deep intake of breath, I decided if I had doubts like that, I should probably find out sooner rather than later.

I looked up at the building he lived in. It was magnificent. The tall limestone structure had solid lines of big bay windows stretching across its façade, beautifully landscaped sidewalks, and large lanterns on either side of the covered steel awning that led to the giant glass double doors.

I felt a little like royalty as I walked beneath it.

"Good afternoon, *Madame*, can I help you with something?" the doorman dressed in classic red asked.

"Yes, hi, I'm Elle Sterling, here to see Logan McPherson."

"Oh, yes, *Madame*, his father called ahead. I'm to send you right up."

I smiled at him but my stomach rolled with worry that Logan would send me away.

Pushing my doubts aside, I followed the doorman. He led me to the elevator and ushered me inside before he pressed the button. "Mr. McPherson lives in apartment 12A," he told me and then he tipped his hat. "Have a good afternoon."

"Thank you."

The ride was the longest elevator ride of my life.

Finally, standing outside his door, I hesitated. Should I just give him what he asked for? Was I being unreasonable coming here? I thought I wanted to save us, but maybe what I really wanted was to save him—from his past, his demons, because I couldn't save myself from mine. And was that really far of me?

Time passed, seconds, minutes.

With the ugly truth coming to light, that this was more about me than us, I turned to head back toward the elevator. I might have taken two steps, maybe not even one, when I heard a lock turn and the door swing open.

Divine intervention?

A cosmic twist of fate?

I didn't know, but I'd take it.

"Elle," he breathed, exhaustion clear in his voice.

The flip in my belly was from the sound of that voice, and that voice alone. No one had ever made by body react the way he did. No one had ever made me feel the way he did. And no one had ever loved me with the intensity that he did.

Slowly, I turned back. With just that one glance, I knew instantly I had to try to make him see things my way. I loved him way too much not to. Dressed in a designer suit, crisp white shirt, and sharp tie, I wanted to lunge for him but settled on staring as I slowly approached him.

His gaze raked down my body and took its time drinking me in on the climb back up.

As always, the air between us was thick. I drew in a deep breath and blew it out. "Logan," I managed as sternly as I could, considering that my entire body was shaking with need from head to toe. "We need to talk."

With a slow nod, he stepped aside to let me in.

My feet moved but I don't remember telling them to do so. I wasn't even sure they were mine.

Suddenly his hand pressed against the small of my back

and my body hummed in delight, making me more than aware of what was mine.

I entered his spacious apartment and felt that just by doing so I had entered his other life. It was a strange yet satisfying feeling. Like he had invited me into his other world, although I knew it was really that I had barged in.

My eyes darted toward the huge expanse of windows. The place was grand in its natural form, yet it reflected who he was. The furniture was sparse, and what was there was simple and functional. There was a lot of black, a whole lot of glass, and not a bit of color, yet the windows were magnificent and the light shining through them more than spectacular. On the walls were photographs of the Brooklyn Bridge taken from many different angles, including an incredible aerial shot. If photos could be sexy, these were super-sexy.

Curiosity rose within me. I was just about to ask him about them when the ding of the elevator from the hall struck me as odd. I stopped looking around. Then, I turned and noticed he hadn't closed the door behind me, which made me wonder if he wasn't expecting me to stay long.

Someone cleared his throat and my eyes darted to my right. That's when I noticed Logan wasn't alone. Oh God, I'd been so involved in him, in his place, that I'd never looked anywhere but at the room in front of me.

My belly flipped again, and this time the feeling was unpleasant.

What if I'd interrupted something important?

A distinguished older gentleman was now standing next to me with his umbrella in his hand, looking as if he was about to leave.

I realized then that Logan had been seeing his guest out when he opened the door. It wasn't some cosmic intervention or crazy twist of fate.

The handsome man was without a doubt Logan's grandfather, the wealthy Logan Ryan. He looked to be almost six feet tall, not as tall as my Logan, but almost. He was long and lean, like my Logan. His hair had gone silver at the temples but remained dark everywhere else. And he was dressed in a finely tailored suit, nothing ostentatious but very professional looking.

My eyes landed on the watch he wore, which was almost identical to the one Logan wore, except his band wasn't made of rubber but rather a fine metal.

Logan's job here in New York was with his grandfather's company, the Ryan Corporation. His title was Associate Counsel, Litigation and Employment. Which meant he pushed a lot of paper—something he really didn't enjoy. About six months ago, he started to go to Boston two days a week to work with his father, whose family law practice was in trouble due to an alcohol problem that was now under control. Working at his father's practice was much more hands-on, and Logan really enjoyed his work there.

Starting sometime last month, though, his grandfather demanded he commit fully to his job in New York. Logan refused and told him that he wanted more time in Boston. That's when his grandfather began to cut him off financially, revoking his access to his trust fund, and most recently putting a hold on his paycheck. Logan's personal savings had just about been depleted. He must have been meeting with his grandfather over his finances. I knew money was of concern to him, but only because he needed it to buy information and hire help to assist in whatever quest he had masterminded in his head.

Glancing between the older gentleman and Logan, it was odd because I could see pieces of him in Logan, just as I had when I looked between Logan and his father. Different pieces, though—these were the more refined ones.

"This must be the lovely young lady you were telling me about," the older gentleman said to Logan.

Logan's hand spread wide against my back and the possessiveness in his touch sent delicious chills up my spine. "Yes, Grandfather, this is Elle Sterling." Logan spoke with a pride in his voice that had my heart swelling. He was talking to his grandfather about me.

"Logan Ryan," the distinguished older gentleman said, offering me his hand.

"Mr. Ryan, really nice to meet you." I smiled, taking my red hat from my head. Suddenly, I became conscious that my attire was anything but appropriate for meeting a powerhouse like Logan Ryan. He was a legend in the business world and here I stood before him dressed for comfort in a pair of black leggings, a white blouse, and a red sweater with matching red ankle boots.

Logan's body seemed to unconsciously drift closer to mine. Like the two magnets we were, we couldn't stay far from each other.

"I was just leaving, but I'd love to take you and my grandson out to dinner one night. How long will you be in town?"

My eyes darted to Logan's beautiful hazel pools. "Not long. I have to get back to Boston. I have a business that I just opened and a niece I've been helping care for."

"I heard about your boutique. On my next trip to Boston, I must stop in. I have a penchant for unique things. Collecting them is one of my many hobbies. Drives my wife crazy."

I knew about his penchant for unique things from my previous life, but didn't mention where I used to work for no other reason than that I needed to talk to Logan and didn't want to start up a long conversation with his grandfather. "I'd love to show you around."

Logan was unusually quiet.

His grandfather squeezed my hand. "Elle, I look forward to getting to know you in the future."

I managed a smile and hoped Logan and I had a future.

Diverting his gaze, he held out his hand to Logan. "Thank you for being honest with me, and take as much time as you need."

When Logan grabbed his outreached hand, he tugged his grandfather in for an almost hug and said, "Thank you for understanding."

They must have discussed his job. I wondered what was decided.

Just as the door was closing, Logan's grandfather said, "Call me once in a while, and your mother, too."

I guessed Logan wasn't going to be working for him.

Logan had no reaction to his comment. Just answered, "Yes, I will, sir."

As soon as the door closed, the air in the room shifted yet again.

My gaze circled the space but then landed on the virile man in front of me. The doubt I saw in his eyes made it hard to breathe. I opened my mouth to speak, but he spoke first.

"You shouldn't be here."

His words punched every last bit of breath I had out of me. "But, I had to—"

"It's too dangerous for us to be together."

A pain in my chest flared. "Logan, listen to me—"

He cut me off again. "We've talked about this."

Reeling from his words, my fists and my jaw clenched in anger. "No, Logan, we didn't. *You* did."

Logan's gaze remained steady. "Then *I* did."

The cold tone of his voice told me his guard was completely up, and that pissed me off even more. I took a breath and said what needed to be said. "You have to stop allowing Tommy Flannigan to rule the direction your life takes."

He pinned me with his stare. "That's not what I'm doing, Elle. What I'm doing is keeping you safe."

I shook my head. "I know that's what you think you're doing but he's been your enemy for so long, you can't see what's real anymore. Don't get me wrong—I get it. He's threatened you your entire adult life and you're scared, but he's behind bars now."

Maybe I imagined it, but I swear I saw him roll his eyes. "Like I already told you, that doesn't mean shit."

I swallowed bitter vile. "Can we at least talk about this?"

For the first time during our conversation, he dropped his gaze. "There's nothing left to say."

Resigned, I knew I couldn't do this anymore. This back and forth wasn't good for me. I had to keep my life stable for Clementine's sake. There was no knowing how long Logan would need to be alone and my mind was already scattered enough. I couldn't live day by day like that. I couldn't leave things between us open ended. I knew if I did it was consume me.

My next words felt like a knife stabbing through my heart. "Then you have to let me go, Logan, because I can't live like this. You want me. You don't. You pull me close and then leave me behind. It's making my head spin and I can't think straight. I can't work. I can't concentrate. I can't do it."

His face went blank and he said nothing in return, but his gaze rose and this time he didn't look away from me.

Looking into those intense hazel eyes, I felt as though I was caught in a swirling storm. I straightened my shoulders and pushed on. Desperation kicking in, I put it all out there. "I mean it, Logan. If you can't let your fear go, then we need to end things."

Vastness stretched between us.

He said nothing.

Pleading now, I said, "You have to know, together, we are stronger. We can support each other."

Stare unwavering, he still said nothing.

Nothing.

Guilt and fear were written all over his face.

I hated myself for evoking these emotions within him, but I wanted so much for him to understand we had to do this together. Looking at him, I could see the turbulence in his stare and I blurted out what was so obvious. "Tommy already knows about us, so what is staying away from me going to do?"

"Save you," he whispered.

"You don't know if he'll actually try to do anything," I

rationalized.

"That's a big if. You weren't there when he attacked Kayla right in front of me. She was petrified and I couldn't help her. I can't go through something like that with you. I won't risk it. I just can't."

Bile rose up my throat.

I wanted to take him in my arms but instead I just stared. This was it.

Self-preservation kicked in. I had to accept that under his strong exterior, he was a runner, through and through. And I couldn't live like that.

In a state of utter desolation, I shouldered past him and flung the door open. One last time I turned to look at him. God, this was so hard. "Together or apart—you choose. There is no in-between."

He blinked as if in shock and opened his mouth, closed it, opened it again. "Don't do this, Elle. Don't make me pick. I told you I needed time to figure things out and nothing has changed."

It had. He refused to even try to see things my way. In truth, I was afraid to be alone. I'd been alone my whole life. I needed him now because yes, I was scared. "Time isn't going to change anything."

Abundant sunlight was like a halo around his lean swimmer's build and I watched with disappointment as he shook his head. "Please, just give me some time."

My emotions had never switched gears as quickly as they did around Logan. Anger gone, heartbreak set in. "Here's the thing, Logan: Time is an abstract word. It could be days or weeks, but it also could be months or even years. I can't live my life in limbo. Not anymore. My emotions can't be up and down. I have to think about Clementine. I need stability in my life for her sake. I hope you can understand that."

"Elle—" he breathed.

This time I cut him off. We'd said all we needed to say. "Goodbye, Logan," I whispered, with my throat tight and the sting of tears in my eyes.

Trapped in that cycle of fear, the atmosphere between us was so fraught, I couldn't stop my entire body from shaking as I closed the door.

In the hall, my knees felt weak. Just standing up was taking all of my energy. I wanted to take the last forty-eight hours back and start all over again. I was a mess. I felt dead inside. I knew I'd never be the same.

As I pressed the down arrow, I looked back. Sadly, no matter how much I wanted to, I couldn't catch him after all.

chapter
FIVE

LOGAN

I FELT REALLY WEIRD all of a sudden . . . kind of like I'd been punched in the gut and kneed in the balls at the same time.

Stunned about what just happened, I couldn't move.

Was I scared?

Hell, yeah, I was.

Living without her and knowing she was alive was a much better outcome than living without her because I'd been selfish and needed her in my life and she'd been killed.

Ding. Ding.

Reality slapped me in the face as soon as I heard the elevator arrive that would take Elle from my life. She had come here with an ultimatum and I had sent her packing.

I ran my hand through my hair. She didn't understand. It wasn't as simple as her protecting herself.

Fuck, I couldn't do this though.

I couldn't let her leave like that.

Grabbing my keys, I rushed out the door but I was too late—the elevator had already closed.

Like a bat out of hell, I ran for the stairs and pounded down them as fast as I could. In the lobby, the elevator door was already open and she was gone. Hustling out onto the street, I spotted her instantly as she crossed Fifth Avenue headed toward the Met. "Elle!" I shouted in a worthless effort to gain her attention.

Even this far uptown, the streets of New York were way too loud. Horns honking, cars racing by, people talking, the wind blowing.

Suddenly, it was all too much.

Not that it mattered, because the light turned red and I was forced to stop. There was a car right in front of me with heavily tinted windows waiting to pass through the traffic, and when I looked into one of them, I saw myself.

What I saw, I didn't like.

Before I met Elle it had been a while since I looked at myself and didn't see a fuck-up. When I was with her, though, everything I'd done seemed to fade into the background. If I stopped her now would it be just another fucked-up decision I'd make in my life? That list was already so long I wouldn't add her to it.

I couldn't.

For a moment I tried to imagine not letting her walk away. Tried to imagine my life with her, but in that blissful picture I was always looking over my shoulder. Always worried. And all I saw was the danger I'd be putting her in.

I had to let her go.

I had to.

What was my life going to be like without her? Would I stay here in New York, go to work at a job I hated, go out with my friends and pretend all was well, act as if the past week was just a blip in my life?

No, I knew I couldn't.

She'd gotten under my skin.

She was a part of me that I didn't want to live without.

Selfishness aside, though, because my need for her was just that, selfish, she needed me to make the right decision.

And I knew letting her go—at least for now—was it.

The car moved forward and I could no longer see my reflection, but the image was still in my head. The fuck-up who made one bad decision after another. But today, I would change that cycle.

The light turned green and as if coming full circle, I didn't move. I'd go after her and hope she'd forgive me, but first I had to take Tommy out of the picture and put that part of my life to rest. I didn't know how I was going to do that, but I had a few ideas.

In order to do anything, I had to get back to Boston. I knew she'd be going there as well—we just couldn't go together.

Sadly, I watched as she walked up the steps of the Met and sat down. I watched as she pulled her phone from her purse and made a call. And then as if I'd been sucker punched, I watched as she hailed a cab and it drove away.

"I'll be there as soon as I can, baby," I whispered.

I knew what she'd said, but I hoped I could end this fast and I more than hoped she'd take me back once I did.

I had to or else I might just crumble.

As it was, I stood here feeling emptier than I ever had in my life.

When I walked back to my building, all I could think about was her face—the hope in her eyes that I'd see things her way and the purse of her lips when I refused. I didn't want to hurt her. I just couldn't give in to her because every time I looked into those green eyes, all I saw was the blood and violence that I'd cause if I stayed in her life.

Once I was in my apartment, I was more determined than ever to bring this to an end. I sat thinking long and hard about the best way to keep Elle safe. Since killing Tommy was no longer an option, I needed some way to both undermine his leadership and sever his ties to the Blue Hill Gang, while at the same time making sure he was locked up for the rest of his natural-born life.

Undermining his authority meant the members of the gang would no longer respect him. I knew that would be easy to do. It wasn't like they actually respected him anyway. Severing ties meant no one on the outside of his prison walls would give him the time of day, even if he tried to give them orders. That wouldn't be as easy to do. Allegiance ran thick in the Blue Hill Gang. My grandfather had instilled that long ago but still, I believed it could be done. And putting Tommy away forever—well, that was a dream I hoped would come true.

The best starting point I had was Lizzy. If only I could find her, then I could figure out what she'd been up to. Find out what kind of relationship she had with Tommy. Who she worked with. Why she did what she did. I knew in my gut she was just the middleman. And I knew from watching the videotape at the hotel that Tommy was very involved, and not in the way he had told his old man. Whatever had gone down wasn't a passing venture. That was the key to bringing Tommy down. Uncovering his involvement and exposing his lies.

What were Lizzy and Tommy up to?

What was their endgame?

How could I find out?

As if a light bulb had just clicked on, I knew where to start—at the top, and then tracing the steps all the way down.

I pulled out my phone and called someone I was hoping could help me get to the top. Help me find out who the source was. Even knowing this didn't guarantee anything but it would be a start. One I hoped would open the can of worms.

The line picked up. "You son of a bitch!" James, my best friend for as long as I could remember, answered in his most typical fashion.

"Hey, man, long time no see."

"Where the hell are you?"

I moved from the sofa to the window in the place I reluctantly called home. The place I never got to show to Elle. "I'm in the city."

"Let's get together."

"I can't. I'm headed back to Boston, but listen, I need your help."

"Yeah, yeah, anything—you know that."

My voice trailed off as I spoke because I knew he was going to jump to the wrong conclusion. "I need the name of someone in the inner circle who has Boston connections."

"That's easy enough. Off my head I can think of Theo Lake, Duncan Scott—"

I cut him off. "Who uses," I added.

"Okay," he dragged out the word, "but I have to ask, what for?"

"I'm hoping to find out who his supplier is."

James stayed silent for a few moments. "Are you—?"

I cut him off. "No, man, I'm not using again. I can't tell you why I need the information, but he won't get in any trouble. I just want to ask him a few questions. Find out who his dealer his and who the supplier is."

The summer after college graduation, the summer Tommy attacked Kayla and me, I had been running drugs between Boston and the Hamptons and making a shitload of money doing it. It wasn't that I needed the money, and to this day I don't know why I did it. At first it was just to get product to my friends, but then word got out and before I knew it, I was selling to everyone I knew. The supplier had long ago dried up and had replaced ten times over, I was sure but still I knew there was one.

That same summer James and I had also taken using a bit too far. We vowed at the summer's end, after way too much shit had gone down, to stay away from the blow, and I was pretty certain we both had—so I got why he was concerned.

"Logan, you're not lying to me, are you?"

I looked around. It had been a long time since I wanted to lose myself in oblivion and even though I really wanted to right now, I knew I had to stay focused. "Come on, James, you know me."

"Okay. Give me a day. I'll ask around and get back to you."

"Thanks, I'll owe you one."

"If I were counting, you'd owe me way more than that," he laughed.

"Fuck off. You're the one who owes me."

"Your memory is warped."

"No, no, no. I think it actually dates back more than ten years ago."

"What are you talking about?"

I couldn't resist taunting him. "Remember that time you were jonesing to get back together with George?"

"Fuck, don't remind me. How is it that you never made me see that she really did have a mouth like a monkey?"

It felt good talking to my old friend. "You can't be serious. Who do you think named her after Curious George?"

"I'm pretty sure that was me."

"Are you kidding me?"

"Lindsay," he yelled. "Come here—you have to hear this story and tell me who you think is lying."

Lindsay was James's wife, whom he met on a Friday night and married on a Saturday, the following day. Love at first sight. Turns out she was the right one for him, because I'd never seen him happier. She, of course, was a model, but he claimed that's not why he loved her.

"Hey, Logan, how are you?" she said into the phone.

I sat back. This might take a while. James hated to lose. "Good, Lindsay, and you?"

"I'm great. So tell me how this one goes," she said with a laugh.

As I started to relay the story from years gone by, I couldn't help but think this time I believed James . . . He loved this woman and she was perfect for him.

The thought of finally finding *the one* fucked with my heart even more. I'd found the perfect girl for me when I hadn't even been looking. And I had to let her go.

In my head I kept saying . . . *for now.*

That I was going to get lucky on this one.

But who knew?

Luck had never been on my side.

chapter
SIX

Elle

ENERGY SURROUNDED ME.

The burst of flames in the open kitchen of B&G's was intensified by the brilliant white marble bar that circled them. Walls painted in shades of blues and grays zapped charm into the place. Small balls of fire hung above my head, providing ambient lighting. The staff was dressed in all black and they were moving quickly.

Energy seemed to live everywhere.

Yet, I had none.

Not even a spark.

I couldn't seem to find my center.

I was off balance.

It was as if the world was at an angle and I was trying to walk in a straight line but finding it more difficult with every passing minute.

What doesn't kill you makes you stronger. Isn't that what they say?

My heart was ripped from my chest when I walked away from Logan and although it almost killed me, it certainly didn't make me feel any stronger.

Just the opposite, in fact.

I missed him.

Everything about him.

So much I could feel it down to my bones.

And I was starting to regret what I'd done.

I knew I shouldn't be. I wasn't wrong. I had a life now that didn't have room for maybes. I knew this. Still, I was just so unhappy. And I didn't understand it because here's the thing—two weeks ago I never wanted a man in my life, and then along he came and hijacked me. Gave me a glimpse of something I'd never had, and now I wasn't sure I could live without it. Without him. Yet, I knew I had to—for Clementine. For her I had to stay strong. Keep my mind healthy. Not let it wander with wonder.

"I'm sorry I'm late. I hope you got my text," he said softly.

Blinking out of my daze, I looked up and tried to smile. "I did."

Lips brushed my cheek in a way I didn't feel entirely comfortable with. "I got a call at the last minute that I had to take."

"It's fine, Michael, relax. I ordered for the both of us."

The Saks Fifth Avenue bag in his hand slid under the table. "Thank you for meeting me like this. I know it's last minute, but I really needed to talk to you."

Mild curiosity as to what was in the bag distracted me for a moment.

"You look tired. Are you sure everything is okay?"

Forcing myself to stop thinking about Logan was difficult, but I had to concentrate on the conversation at hand. "I'm fine. I've just had some trouble sleeping. But honestly, Michael, meeting you for lunch isn't a problem. I wasn't doing much today anyway. Peyton took care of the entire inventory restocking at the boutique yesterday and everything else was already done."

Michael and I hadn't talked since his early phone call Saturday morning and I found that strange. Usually, he called me for dinner on Sundays but he hadn't called yesterday, and since I was in New York City, I hadn't called him either.

He sat down. "Good then, I don't have to feel guilty about dragging you out on a rainy day."

It might be a cold, rainy spring day outside, but it didn't matter because even in here I was chilled. Nothing could warm me. I was cold, sad, and tired. I hated feeling like this. I blinked away my thoughts and focused on Michael. "What is it you wanted to talk to me about? It sounded urgent. Is everything okay with Clementine's new nanny?"

Unfolding his napkin, he set it on his lap. "Yes, they're both fine. This meeting isn't about Clementine."

"Oh. From the urgency in your voice, I just assumed it was."

Actually, I had come here with two trains of thought. One—he knew I'd lied about the cocaine being delivered to my boutique; or two—he had changed his mind about who he was appointing as Clementine's guardian and had invited me here to let me know.

My heart started beating so fast.

This had to be about the delivery.

I was so screwed. I tried to remember what Logan had told me to say under this circumstance, but nerves got the better of me and my brain felt frazzled.

A small sip of his water on his part alerted me that he was nervous too.

I wondered why.

Finally, he spoke. "First of all I want to apologize for involving you in that entire mix-up last week. I never should have put you in a position like that."

Phew, he was completely unaware of not only the delivery, but also Logan's involvement. Another attempt at a smile I just couldn't seem to form failed. Instead, I tried to be as upbeat as I could. "Please, Michael, I think we're past all the pleasantries. I understand why you had to ask me for help. Sending the packages to the boutique and not the house or your office made sense. No one would have had any idea. I'm just glad the people who were threatening you and Clementine are now behind bars and we can put all of this behind us."

I hoped that was true.

Dark circles below his eyes couldn't hide how tired he looked and I wondered if something was still worrying him. "Good then, we can agree to put that behind us."

I nodded.

"You're certain everything is okay?" he asked again.

No, everything was not okay. I was heartbroken and downright upset over this entire situation I'd allowed myself to be put in, but I couldn't tell him that. He knew nothing of my brief affair with Logan. I drew in a deep breath and found some inner strength. "Yes, I'm fine." This time I managed a smile that had to look as fake as it felt.

"Okay then, I have a favor to ask you."

Before I could think of what to say, because the last thing I wanted to do was another favor for him, the waiter arrived with our food. "Lobster rolls," he said, placing our plates in front of us. "Can I get you anything else?"

Michael looked over at me and I shook my head. "No, I think we're good. If you could just bring the check, I'm in a bit of a hurry today."

"Yes, certainly, Mr. O'Shea, no problem."

Michael was a regular at B&G Oysters. He's the one who turned me on to the restaurant and to lobster rolls. Both of which I loved, but neither of which pleased me today.

I looked down at my rectangular plate of food—the sandwich on one side, the sea-salt-seasoned fries on the other, and in the middle pickles and a small silver container of ketchup.

Ketchup.

Even the stupid condiment made me think of Logan, and my mind drifted back to the first night we'd met.

Logan had been sitting across from me at the table and I couldn't get the ketchup to come out of the bottle. He took it from me and magically poured some onto my plate. Those hazel eyes lifted seductively. "The secret is knowing where the sweet spot is," he'd said. That was the first time my stomach had ever done a full belly flop over a guy.

Michael cleared his throat.

Pulled from my thoughts, my eyes darted across the table.

"I have this fundraiser Wednesday night that I was hoping you would attend with me."

Shocked, I tried not to let my mouth drop open. "What kind of fundraiser?"

After taking a bite from his sandwich, he wiped his mouth. "Political."

I blinked. "The fundraising for next year's elections starts this early?"

He nodded. "I'm a little behind the ball and I have a lot of ground to make up."

"I don't know, Michael. Politics aren't anything I know that much about."

"Please, Elle, I could really use as much support as I can get."

Not at all wanting to go, I felt like I should. "Can I think about it?"

Michael took another bite of his food. "Sure. My hope is that you'll say yes. It's at the University of Massachusetts and it's a big one. We're hoping to raise $250,000. A friend of mine was able to arrange for a well-connected alumnus to speak. He's sure to attract a deep-pocketed crowd."

"That's great. I'm certain it will be a success. What is the dress code should I decide to attend?"

Reaching under the table, he pulled the bag out. "I hope you don't mind, but I took the liberty of buying you something to wear. You look like you're close to Elizabeth's size, so I went with that."

I wasn't certain how to take that. On one hand it was nice of him; on the other, was he worried I wouldn't know how to dress? I took the bag from him. "Thank you. I'm not sure what to say."

He looked a little sheepish. "It's not meant to offend you in any way, so please don't take it like that. I just didn't know if you'd have anything to wear to a black-tie affair and I didn't want you to stress out about spending the money to purchase something. If you don't like it or if it doesn't fit, you can take it back and exchange it. Or if you have something you prefer to wear, you can keep it or return it."

The sincerity in his voice pushed away any animosity I might have had. "No, I appreciate it. I don't actually have anything formal and I'll let you know by tomorrow. Let me look at my schedule."

His phone beeped and he glanced at the screen. His face instantly paled. "I have to go." He grabbed the bill that the waiter had discreetly placed on the table and then peeled off some twenties from his wallet before setting them inside the leather folio.

"What is it?" I asked.

He leaned forward and whispered, "The men who were supposed to deliver the product to your boutique were found shot to death in their van this morning."

"What?" I felt ill. "Why? What's going on?"

"That's all I know."

"Who told you?"

He ignored my question and sent a text message before he finally looked up and answered me. "A news text alert. I'm late for a meeting. I really should be going."

For some reason, I didn't believe him. I pushed my plate away. "It's fine. I'm done."

"Are you sure?"

I waved my hand. "Yes, go."

"I'm sorry. I just can't be late for this meeting with my br—" He stopped before finishing.

"I'll be fine," I said.

That was another lie.

I wasn't sure I would be fine ever again.

I sat there, watching the rain out the window for the

longest time. Something was going on. Something more than I had imagined. Would Logan have eliminated the deliverymen so as not to expose the fact that the product had actually been delivered to my boutique? I just didn't think so. If not him, then who did? It was way too coincidental to be a random crime. I pondered it for a long while before leaving to go home in the pouring rain.

Later that evening, I was lying in my bed, my mind a web of tangled lies, lost love, and incoherent thoughts, when my phone rang.

I grabbed for it, hopeful, yet knowing I shouldn't be. I was in the very state of mind that I wanted to avoid. I hated feeling like this. Glancing at the screen, the number attached to the call was blocked, but I answered anyway. "Hello?" I said quickly.

"Hello, Elle."

"Who is this?"

The voice was deep. "Someone who wants to help you."

"Who is this?" I asked again, this time louder.

"That's not important but what is important is that you understand your role and understand that sometimes the toughest decisions are also the easiest. If you doubt you should say yes, just think of the little lives God has created and go forth wisely."

Chills ran down my spine.

Say yes?

Say yes to what?

chapter
SEVEN

DAY 13

LOGAN

THE GENERAL ETIQUETTE IN black-tie dressing was that there should be no watch on your wrist. The unwritten rule stated that if a timepiece had to be worn, it should be a pocket watch, but if one absolutely must wear a wristwatch, it should be a slim dress version thin enough to hide underneath French cuffs.

My big, sporty Patek didn't really meet the qualifications, but then again most of the time I doubted I myself met the qualifications.

I hated going to events like this because of all the social niceties one had to abide by, but at least this time I wasn't being forced to attend by my mother or grandfather. This time I was on a mission that would bring me closer to getting Elle back in my life.

The campus was all too familiar. After I'd fucked up and gotten kicked out of Harvard at orientation for stupidly thinking I could sell drugs on campus and get away with it, my father pulled some strings of his own and got me into the School of Law at UMass. My mother was so disappointed in me that she didn't talk to me for almost a year, and my grandfather Ryan was equally as upset and only talked to me a dozen or so times during my entire law school stint. Like I'd come to realize, they were two peas in a pod.

As I parked and looked out over the harbor, my mind was anywhere but here. It was on Elle. It had been since I saw her get in that cab. How was she? What was she doing? Did she miss me as much as I missed her? Fuck, just standing there, I could still remember the way she tasted.

Shaking my melancholy off, I forced myself to focus and headed inside to find Pierce Foley. Pierce was a thirty-something Upper East Sider whose wife was connected to the Kennedys, and that relationship had the couple rallying among the political fundraisers all up and down the East Coast.

James had called me back as promised with five names of guys who he had heard the elite grapevine used cocaine and were also highly connected to the Boston social circle. I couldn't believe it when I called Foley's New York law office and they said he and his wife were in Boston for a fundraiser.

Maybe luck was on my side.

A quick sweep of social media informed me that I was looking for a man of average build, a little on the husky side, with thinning brown hair deeply parted on the side. I hoped it wouldn't take long to find him, and then I hoped even more that it would take even less time to befriend him and find out what he knew. From what James had told me, I was certain pumping a few drinks in him would help me with that.

The place was jammed with people, and even at a cost of a grand per ticket, it didn't surprise me. The rich always loved things that were expensive. In my monkey suit, I moved around in the way I'd been groomed. After having to stop to talk to the few people I knew, I tried to sideline any more familiar faces. I grabbed a quick glass of water with a lime wedge from the bar and was finally able to start my search.

Through the crowd it was hard to spot anyone who didn't look like Pierce Foley. I walked the perimeter of the room, moving closer to the center with each lap. Thirty minutes later I still had not found him. This time I started in the center and worked my way outward. I was almost to the wall of windows that overlooked the Boston Harbor when I spotted him.

At the bar.

Bingo!

Casually, I made my way over and sat beside him, setting my glass down. I leaned in toward the bartender and ordered a gin and tonic, which I had no intention of drinking, and then looked toward a very bored-looking Pierce. "I'm on my third, what about you?" I lied.

He swirled what I guessed was a scotch and raised it. "My third as well. Long fucking night."

I smirked. "You're not kidding. I swear having to be on good behavior always makes time pass even slower."

His roar of laughter told me I was in. "What do you say we do a shot?" he whispered.

I pretended to look around. "I'd better not. If the fiancée catches me getting out of hand, I'll be in the doghouse for a week."

Just saying *fiancée*, making up another woman, made the words burn in my throat.

"Good point. If my wife, Sarah, sees me drinking too much, I won't even tell you what will happen to me."

My grin came easily. "What's it like?"

He arched a brow.

"Being married, I mean. I'm supposed to get married next month and I have to be honest, I'm not really feeling it."

"Cold feet. I get it. I went through the same thing. Marriage is hard. I'm not going to lie. Of course, it has its ups and downs. I've been married for almost seven years, and I have to say I've been feeling the seven-year itch for a while now. But on the whole it's worth it."

The bartender set my drink down. "My friend here needs another."

Pierce held his hands up. "No, I shouldn't."

"Come on, one more, and you can give me some honest advice. No one ever wants to be honest about marriage."

With a quick gulp of his drink, he set it down. "Sure, one more."

As he glanced around the room to be certain his wife wasn't anywhere nearby, I poured half my drink into my water glass. Last thing I needed was to fog my brain. Fuck only knew what I'd be saying then.

By the time he'd finished his fourth, he'd practically told me his life story. He had two kids, worked for his father-in-law, and had a nagging wife. A variation on the very picture I had in my head of marriage.

It was my parents' life all over again minus one kid.

"How do you do it every day, man?" I pretended to slur.

"Escape."

"Escape?"

His shoulders rose and he sniffed through his nose, holding one nostril closed.

"And your wife doesn't care?" I asked.

"Oh, she'd care."

"She doesn't know?"

Chewing on an ice cube, he shook his head. "Clueless."

I lowered my head a bit. "I'm new in town. If one was looking for *an escape*, where might one find it?"

"The Priest," he whispered.

"The Priest?"

"Well, not him directly, but he's the one you'll be getting it from."

"How do I get in touch with him?"

"That, my friend, I can't tell you."

"Come on, really?"

"Sorry. He has rules, and he's ruthless if any of them are broken. Besides, I've never actually made contact. A buddy of mine takes care of it for me."

"Pierce, there you are, I've been looking everywhere for you," a woman's voice called.

He shoved his drink toward me. "Pretend you don't

know me."

My smile couldn't have been more genuine. "Not a problem," I said and turned the other way.

"You're not drinking, are you?" his wife asked when she got closer.

He stood. "No, I was just getting you that glass of water you asked for."

"That was an hour ago."

"Are you certain it's been that long?"

I peeked at them and saw her tuck her arm around his. "Come on, there are some people I want you to meet."

"Yes, dear," he said, and turned and gave me a wink.

Poor bastard was all I could think.

My time with him was up and if you discounted learning Pierce Foley was an addict in every sense of the word, I'd learned one real thing. The drug supplier in Boston's high-society circle went by the alias "the Priest," and I doubted that was Lizzy, or O'Shea or Tommy for that matter. Neither seemed like the religious type to me.

I didn't know how to reach him.

Didn't know his connection to Lizzy.

Wasn't even sure if finding him could help me find Lizzy.

Still, knowing the kingpin's street name made me feel like I was one step closer to getting Elle back.

Standing from the bar, I glanced around for the nearest exit. Something caught my attention. Narrowing my eyes, I focused on a group of boisterous men deep in conversation with one lone female among them. Not just any female. A beautiful woman with ginger-colored hair standing way too close to Michael O'Shea.

My gut twisted.

My body stiffened.

My vision blurred.

It was Elle.

My Elle!

Elle

WHENEVER I THOUGHT OF political fundraisers, I pictured old men standing around outside smoking cigars, women in stodgy long dresses clustered together gossiping, and glasses of cheap wine everywhere.

That was not the scene I was currently immersed in.

The grand ballroom was beautiful in a roaring twenties kind of way. The ceilings were gilded with a golden hue, the chandeliers were gleaming crystal, the carpet red, and the linens black. And right in the middle of it all was a giant champagne fountain that was absolutely gorgeous.

After thinking about it, I'd said yes to Michael. The voice on the phone had rattled me and I wasn't sure what the call was about, but I was almost certain whoever was on the line might have been threatening Clementine. It was after that I decided Michael wasn't being truthful. There was too much that didn't add up. Going to this fundraiser might help me figure out what it was. I longed to discuss it with Logan, but I'd already burned that bridge.

In the midst of all the chaos, I'd been worried about the dress Michael had selected for me to wear. It was a long black silk, almost classic-style A-line with a deep vee in the back, but the matching deep vee in the front brought it to a whole new level.

It was a bit too sexy for me.

I might not have seen my sister in fifteen years but there was no way her breast size had shrunk that much, therefore there was no way she'd have been able to wear a dress like this without spilling out of the sides.

"Can I get you anything?" Michael asked, pressing his hand to the small of my back.

He'd been talking to the same group of gentlemen for the past twenty minutes about the Suffolk County crime rate statistics and I was out-of-my-mind crazy. With a smile I said, "No, I'm good, but if you'll excuse me for a moment, I need to use the ladies' room."

"You're bored, aren't you?" he whispered in my ear.

His concern seemed genuine, but I wasn't taking anything he said at face value. "No, not at all. Watching you at work is fascinating."

The smile that lit up his face made me wonder if I'd taken my attempt to be upbeat a little too far. "The least I can do is walk you to the restroom."

"No, Michael. Stay and network. You're doing such a great job."

He moved a little closer. "It's you who's doing the great job."

Without pretense, I gave him a return smile. "I'll be back."

It was odd, but I couldn't tell him about the threatening call I'd received. I was too suspicious of him. Although I wanted Michael to succeed in his bid to be nominated to run for the Suffolk County District Attorney position, I had to wonder what the big push was right now when his life was so completely turned upside down.

With each passing day, my doubts about Michael's sincerity kept mounting. How was he going to keep my sister's drug dealings out of the press? And if it did come out, would he be implicated? Because if I knew he was somehow involved, and Logan knew he was involved, someone else must surely also know.

Like the deliverymen, I thought.

Chilled, I couldn't help but think about how they ended up.

The restrooms were near the bar and I took my time walking the short distance to them. My feet were killing me in the heels I was wearing and I couldn't wait to kick them off. In truth, I couldn't wait for this night to end. All this hobnobbing was exhausting. It didn't take more than one night of this to know the political arena wasn't exactly my cup of tea.

As soon as I opened the bathroom door, I found it to be equally as impressive as the ballroom. There was a lounge area with a few comfortable-looking chairs, a perfume bar, and stacks of black washcloths next to bottles of luxury soap. Obviously it had been decked out for the evening.

The perfume bar drew me to it and I looked at the various bottles. Jo Malone was among them, and I picked up the lavender scent and sprayed it on each of my wrists. Once I'd rubbed them together, I lifted them to my nose and closed my eyes to enjoy the fresh, clean scent.

There was a crinkle, a tickle, a tease on the back of my neck. I didn't need to open my eyes to know who it was. His own fresh scent gave him away. I gasped as my body betrayed me, my toes curling and my stomach fluttering at just the hum of his body near mine.

Lips brushed my neck and I couldn't stop myself from trembling in need.

"You look incredible."

That voice was raw. Husky. Sexy. All Logan.

My eyes snapped open and I found his hazel ones staring back at me in the mirror with more lust in them than any one human should be allowed to convey in that manner. "What are you doing here?" I somehow managed to ask, albeit in a squeak.

His hands gripped my hips and pulled me back toward him. I melted into his hard body and felt how much he wanted me.

Fire flamed through my veins, giving way to lustful

desire that I couldn't suppress.

I missed him.

I hated not being able to talk to him.

Hear his voice.

Touch him.

Feel his body against mine.

Yet, I knew I had to stick by my decision. My life wasn't my own anymore and I had to remember that girl needed me.

His hold on me was possessive and he urged me to tilt my head to the side. "I'm the one who should be asking you that question."

My pulse was beating wildly and even though I knew I shouldn't, I gave in to his unspoken command and tilted my head.

Those lush lips skimmed down my neck.

And I couldn't resist him.

In my red-hot haze, I allowed myself only a moment to absorb the feeling. While doing so, I admired him. I couldn't help myself. Dressed in an expensive tuxedo, he screamed class, sophistication, and all things money. Pressed white shirt, black bowtie, and dropping my eyes I noticed he was even wearing expensive-looking shoes. He fit in at events like this so well, while all night I'd felt so out of place. That had to be another sign of why we shouldn't be together. When I lifted my gaze and found his eyes, I knew I had to push him away. We were over. "I don't think it's any of your business."

His hands started tugging my dress up. "Everything about you is my business," he growled.

It was then that I realized he must have seen me with Michael and he was jealous.

Jealous!

Was he trying to make his mark, stamp his claim on me? Well, I wasn't his. He'd had a choice; he'd chosen not to be with me. I turned around and shoved him away. "No, Logan, you're wrong. We're not together anymore and nothing about me is any of your business."

My words were cold and they killed me to speak them, but for the past few days I'd been just barely holding myself together. If this little *tête-à-téte*, or whatever this was in the bathroom, went any farther, it would surely make me crumble when he was finished marking me and then left me alone—again.

Logan grabbed my wrist. "Don't say that, Elle."

My breath caught when I looked at the real him, not the reflection of him. His eyes were wide. Pupils dilated and dark. So intense. And his lips were slightly parted, the lower one wet from where he'd just swiped his tongue. So delicious looking.

The urge to kiss him was too much to bear and I had to close my eyes to try to find my center, but I couldn't. The sexual tension between us was off the charts and quickly causing my control to shift.

His hand was still holding my wrist and he let it slip lower. Before I knew it, he was tugging me into a bathroom stall and I was going willingly.

Saying nothing, he pushed me against the door, hard enough to rattle it. He moved closer until we were face-to-face, chest-to-chest, hip-to-hip, and then his hands were lifting my dress.

I shuddered when his thumb moved back and forth against the inner skin of my thigh. Slow, even strokes. This small touch was enough to electrify me and the shudder of my breath echoed in the small space.

He leaned even closer and his lips brushed my earlobe. "Tell me you'll wait for me."

I turned my head the tiniest bit toward him. I felt like I was going to break in two right there, I was so torn.

But I had to keep my stability—for Clementine.

My lips barely moved when I said, "I can't do that."

"You can."

I shook my head. "I can't, Logan. I can't put my life on hold for something that might never come."

The air around him crackled dangerously. "Don't say that."

"It's the truth."

His lips skimmed down my neck. "Do matter what you do, you're mine, Elle. Mine. You'll always be mine."

Torn between giving in to him and holding on to what I knew was the right path for me, I had to get away from him to think clearly. In a split-second decision I reached behind me and unlocked the latch, causing the door to swing open. I didn't deny that I was his. He already knew I was. My body's reaction to him alone was enough to confirm that, but I did say something I knew would make him dislike me, or maybe even hate me. Keep him from following me and tearing me apart. "I have to get back out there. Michael will be wondering where I am."

"Michael," he spat.

Guilt set in and I had to push it away. I was doing what I had to do. Still, I tried to ease the burn of my words. "Logan, I'm here with him to support him politically, not that I owe you any explanation."

His expression cleared. I couldn't read him at all. But then he leaned back against the sink and gripped the edge tightly, and I knew he was hurt.

I hated this. All I wanted was to be with him, but our separation wasn't my choice.

His jaw twitched.

My eyes were glued to him. Under his clothes, I could see the impressive muscle tone of his arms and chest that I loved to have pressed against me. I could hear the way he breathed. I could almost taste his lips on mine.

"Don't, Elle. Just don't," he said.

"Don't what, Logan? Go on with my life?"

His eyes were flat, his expression lifeless. "You know why we can't be together right now. All I need is some time."

I was shaking my head and lashing myself at the same time. I felt physically sick. "I gave you a choice and you didn't pick me. There is no in-between. Not for me. There can't be."

His gaze remained steady, unblinking; his mouth was straight, almost a frown. "This is our story. There can be whatever we want."

My fists and jaw were clenched. When it came to us, he wasn't right. "How does that work? The in-between, I mean. We call each other on the sly, maybe meet up to fuck in secret, in a bathroom, a backroom, someplace where we are with other people so no one knows we're together?"

The look of pain and despair he gave me was one I'd never seen.

The ache in my chest flared, but I didn't stop. I had to put an end to this before I couldn't. "Tell me, Logan, in this in-between, do we not only fuck each other but fuck other people too, to make the sham all the more real?"

Red seeped into his face. "Fuck you, Elle."

His words punched the air from my lungs. I wanted to fall to my knees right there and say I was sorry, but I had to stay strong. I had to end this between us for good, because I knew he would keep going with the back and forth. "We shouldn't be seen together. Do you want to be the first to walk out of here or should it be me?"

He pulled his bowtie loose and unbuttoned the top button but didn't answer me.

Everything in this small space was suddenly too bright and my heart was beating way too fast. I couldn't be near him for one more minute because I knew if I was, I was going to launch myself at him and give him what I knew he'd take. And I couldn't do that. I was here for a reason—to spy on Michael. Find out what he was up to, if anything.

With a quick pivot on my heels, I made the decision for him and turned and started for the door.

"Elle, don't leave things like this between us," he pleaded.

I had to.

Nothing had changed.

A quick fuck wouldn't make me feel any better tomorrow or change the fact that we had no future.

Realizing this, I thought I might just hate him.

But as soon as I left the room, left him, the hole in my heart told me I didn't hate him.

Instead, it told me I would love him forever.

chapter
NINE

DAY 14

LOGAN

THE PAVEMENT WAS WET as my feet pounded against it. I sprinted faster, arms working, fists flying up beside my body. Faster and faster I went, until my legs cramped and my stomach knotted, but that wasn't enough to make me stop. I didn't even falter. I just kept running.

The rain came down harder, but not hard enough to drown out the sound of her screams. They were everywhere.

I was running in the very early hours of the morning, trying to clear my head—to erase the nightmare I couldn't seem to shake. It was so real. I had gone to her. Brought her back into my life. And then soon after she was in a dark place, alone and afraid. I saw the image of her frightened face, heard the sound of her shrilling screams, and felt her warm blood on my skin.

Running wasn't erasing it—I could still see it.

Nothing was working.

I couldn't shake it.

The haunting image surrounded me.

It was to my left.

To my right.

In front of me.

I just ran faster.

Miles and miles seemed to pass in mere minutes, but

then my legs began to burn. I didn't care. I kept going. The knot in my gut felt more like bricks. I didn't care. I ran faster. But no matter how fast or how far I ran, it wasn't going to change anything. Whether I was with her or without her, she could still be in danger, and I didn't have a big enough army to save what my gramps would call my Helen of Troy.

Gasping for breath, I finally stopped.

Fuck, what had I done?

Was she with him?

No, I knew what she'd said last night was her way of coping with what I'd done to us. But knowing that didn't stop the ache in my chest.

With my hands gripped around the back of my neck, I looked around, hoping to latch onto anything that would stop the constant noise in my head.

I couldn't stand being without her.

The very early dawn created a purple haze that enveloped the surrounding area like a shroud. The sky was still dark. The air was thick and moist. And I could feel sweat running down the side of my face.

Flashing lights down at the waterfront caught my attention, and something about the situation drew me closer to the chaos.

An unwanted feeling I couldn't shed.

Long strides brought me toward it. The closer I got, the louder the sounds became. The whoop of a chopper along the riverbank, the chatter of reporters, a Channel 7 news truck. It was utter madness for the early morning dawn.

"Stay behind the tape," the cop said, pointing his flashlight at me.

Hey, I knew that cop.

"What's going on?" I asked him, hoping he didn't remember me from the night he introduced me to Blanchet, the she-devil DEA agent who coerced me into helping her bring down Patrick Flannigan.

Turned out that wasn't all she wanted. She also wanted a lead on the source of the drugs that were hitting the streets of Boston in monstrous proportions. She'd tracked Flannigan and knew he wasn't the kingpin in Boston's cocaine operation, but he was still vital enough to hunt down. He had his hands in many illegal things, but drugs weren't his most lucrative venture. Numbers and prostitution were more his game. What he didn't know was that his son had upped their involvement in the drug market, and that was why they were both behind bars right now.

Blanchet had spoken to my gramps and gotten all she needed from him. Hence, my father was still a free man. She had yet to pull him in. And my hope was she wouldn't.

"I said, stay back." The bite in his tone wasn't strong enough to indicate he recognized me.

Someone behind me spoke up. "A body was found. They think it's been in the river for a while."

Something told me I had to edge closer. Something else told me to keep running.

I watched the cop as his rubber boots squished along the mucky riverbank and then when he was out of sight, I maneuvered myself around the mob of people to where I could better see what was going on.

My sides were cramping; my skin felt tight, my throat dry. I needed water. My vision was slightly hazy and I had to squint to see that far, and finally I did.

Oh fuck!

There it was.

A body.

A woman's body.

My lungs were no longer burning, but still I felt myself gasping for air.

The body wasn't just a body.

Inconspicuous in the brush, I took another step forward and heard my sneakers squish in the mud.

Fuck!

I glanced around. No one was paying any attention to me.

They were focused on the body. And now so was I. Her

arms seemed bare, although her torso appeared clothed in black. Her legs were covered in what had to be streaks of mud. Her feet and legs were hidden in her leather boots. And then there was the halo of fiery red hair floating grotesquely around her limp body.

That knot that had been in my gut twisted even more.

Fuck! Fuck! Fuck!

Maybe, just maybe it wasn't her.

The body was facedown and splayed among the underbrush of the slimy riverbank, so really, it could be anyone.

Suddenly, a spotlight shined down, and that's when I saw the glint. An icy chill swept through my blood, because right then I knew for certain who it was.

In her hand, tangled between her fingers, was a red ribbon with a large silver rattle beside her. The object was Clementine's Rosie.

And the dead woman was Lizzy O'Shea, Elle's missing sister.

My stomach lurched. The only time I had seen that rattle before was in the hands of Michael O'Shea, back at the garage where Elle's car had been towed.

The man who Elle was with last night. The very same man she was entangled with in a way that there was nothing I could do to untangle her.

What if all of this shit wasn't just about Tommy?

Maybe there was a bigger picture.

That had to be it.

Like a lightning strike, I knew I had to be with her.

That being apart didn't mean shit anymore.

There was so much more to all of this.

The stakes just got higher.

Tommy Flannigan was no longer the only man I had to protect Elle from.

My mind was reeling.

I had to come up with an even bigger and better plan.

I had to build my own army.

I had to be with her.

Fear took a backseat.

Strength puffed up my chest.

Determination racked my brain.

I knew what I had to do to keep her safe.

First, go and get her, begging on my knees if I had to, and then . . .

Crush Tommy and figure out what O'Shea was really up to.

No matter what.

chapter
TEN

Elle

NINE VERY UNSETTLING MINUTES with him and my world was more upside down than ever.

Would it ever be right again?

This morning I just didn't think it would.

The spring drizzle trickled down the outside of my bedroom window and I found myself sitting in a chair and staring out at it. It was already dawn and I hadn't slept much.

I couldn't stop thinking about him.

How could I have been so cruel?

I hated what I'd said.

I'd made a huge mistake.

I should have put the same trust in him I wanted in return. I had been wrong in pushing him away—in thinking that my emotional health would be too uneven with us in a state of limbo, and that I wouldn't be able to navigate my life reasonably. The truth was, without him I was in a state of complete instability anyway. I was uneven. I was unhappy. And I didn't think it would ever go away.

Oh God. I needed to apologize. I wanted to talk to him so much I couldn't stand it. But how could I fix anything between us now? I'd said the most horrible things to him last night.

Tears clouded my sight and I pressed the heels of my palms to my eyes. When the sobbing subsided, I wrapped my arms around my body in a sad attempt to comfort myself.

Drop after drop I watched the water until I couldn't anymore. Finally, I closed the blinds and then padded over to my bed and tried to make myself go back to sleep.

I was just tired.

So tired.

My phone was beside me and I thought about calling him. But would he answer? And if he didn't, would I feel worse? If he did, would talking change anything? No. No it wouldn't. How could it be that my life felt so empty without him in it? I tried reminding myself it was no fuller before I met Logan but that didn't help. The difference was— there was a hole in my heart that wasn't there before. And it hurt. It hurt so damn much.

Thank God for Clementine.

She was the only light in my life.

I needed sleep.

After that, I could determine better what I should do.

Perhaps my sadness was simply a function of lack of sleep.

Just as I started to drift off, my cell phone began to ring. I anxiously grabbed for it. *Blocked caller* flashed on my screen. I refused to answer it, but that didn't stop my heart from pounding faster and faster.

It had to be the same person who had called me days ago.

Fear.

Fear like I've never known seized me.

For some unknown reason, this caller scared me more than anything.

A minute later a text message appeared. It read, *You made the right choice. Keep on the correct path and little lives will remain safe.*

My hand flew to my mouth.

Oh God.

He was threating Clementine!

What did he want?

Ding dong. Ding dong. Ding dong.

My body began to shake.

Ding dong. Ding dong. Ding dong.

I was so afraid.

Who was here?

Was it the caller?

Was it someone on Tommy's behalf?

Was it the Irish Mob?

Knock, knock.

My pulse was racing.

Knock, knock.

Heart hammering against my ribs, I jumped out of bed—it felt like I was jumping out of my skin.

I didn't know what to do.

Where was the security team Logan had arranged to watch my townhome?

An adrenaline rush kicked me into gear.

They had to be here.

Terrified, I grabbed my gun from the bedside table and hurried to the window to see if their car was still parked out front. My hand was trembling so much as I peeked out the closed blinds to the street below that I could barely pull them open.

The incessant ringing of my doorbell and the pounding on my front door wasn't stopping.

Then, as I looked down, my terror ceased immediately.

Relief set in.

The Rover was parked right in front of my house, haphazardly squeezed in between two cars and partly up on the sidewalk.

It was Logan at my door.

I didn't know what he was doing here but I didn't care.

I needed him.

Right now, I didn't care about anything other than him.

Him being here was all that mattered.

Needing to see him, feel him, hold him, I put my gun

away and quickly grabbed a blanket off my bed. Wrapping it around me, I rushed for the door. "I'm coming!" I yelled from the top of the stairs. As I ran down the steps, the doorbell was still ringing and the pounding was still occurring. Faster and faster I went. I wanted to get to him just as much as he wanted to get to me.

In his arms, I knew I'd feel safe.

I reached the foyer quickly and without looking, I turned the alarm off and swung open the door. The streetlights were still on and shone behind him in a way that highlighted everything he was.

Strong.

Dauntless.

Confident.

Sexy.

My protector.

A feeling of intoxication overcame me as I drank him in. There he stood in his track pants, long-sleeved T-shirt, and sneakers, soaked to the bone. Noticing this, I was suddenly alarmed. "Logan, what's the matter?" I asked.

"I need to talk to you." He stepped in without being invited and I didn't care.

Still shaking from the text, I had a hard time focusing.

He closed and locked the door, reengaged the security system, and then turned to me.

I watched as the water dripped off him in excess. As it puddled on the floor, as it flowed beneath my bare feet. With a tug of my arm he moved me away from the cold water.

I couldn't help but stare at him. Had he known how much I needed him right now? Or did he need me? "What is it? What happened? You look shaken," I asked all at once.

His eyes were so intense as they stared back at me. "Together, Elle, I pick together."

That didn't answer my question, but it told me what he was doing here.

My emotions wouldn't register. They were all over the

place. I'd asked him to pick, and when he didn't pick me, it left me more than a little shattered.

But now, now he was picking me.

He'd picked me.

That's why he was here.

In my time of need.

My emotions were a conflicting mess.

Shock.

Elation.

Love.

Confusion.

My heart forgot to beat. My lungs forgot to breathe. My eyes forgot to blink. So many feelings were flowing through my veins that I wasn't certain which one I should be feeling right now, or if any of this was even real.

With a slight hesitation in his movement, he took a tentative step toward me. "I want to move forward with you. I pick you, Elle. I pick you over being cautious, being scared, or trying to figure things out alone. I pick you."

Unguarded, I was hopeless to answer him. I didn't know what to say, but then I looked up and saw so much pain and regret in his face. I had a choice. I could turn him away or I could take a leap of faith. I didn't know what to do. What I did know was that I loved him, and of all the crappy things I might have known about love, I knew for certain that it was never perfect. People made mistakes and people hurt each other. Sometimes on purpose, sometimes not. Life didn't always have a happily-ever-after, but maybe together we could try to make one.

"Am I too late?" Logan asked.

It was then that I realized I hadn't said anything.

Tears threatened to spill from my eyes as I took one step closer to him. And then another. And one more, and finally my bare toes were touching his wet sneakers. I shook my head and nodded at the same time. "I don't understand. What's changed?"

Linking his fingers between mine, he answered, "I want

you. Me. Us. I know we have to be cautious but I want to face the future with you, not without you. Will you let me pick you?"

I was finding it hard to breathe. I didn't know what to do. But the way he was standing there looking so uncertain, I knew there was no way I could turn him away. He needed me. And I needed him like I needed air to breathe. I had to have faith he wouldn't leave me again, and I did. My heart felt so full. I believed every word he'd just told me. Without any doubts, I smiled and said, "Yes," and then to make certain he understood me, I repeated myself. "Yes, yes, yes."

His hands grabbed my face and he brought his mouth to mine. Slow, burning kisses with feather brushes of his lips on mine made my stomach flip, but then when he pressed harder and slipped his tongue inside my mouth, I felt those beloved butterflies take flight.

I thought I might be dreaming, but the cold wetness of his hard body told me I wasn't. "Take this off," I demanded, tugging at his T-shirt.

His answering grin was utterly charming and adorable. It was the look that said sex was on his mind. It was the look I had missed so very much.

The blanket slid off my shoulders and impatiently I helped him strip his wet shirt over his head.

When it fell to the floor, he gripped my hips and tugged me flush to his body. "Do you have any idea how much I've missed you?"

Every part of me had an idea, because it must have been as much as I'd missed him. "Logan," I breathed.

His hands roamed my body, over my hips, stopping to finger the elastic of my sleep shorts, up the torso of my camisole, and stopping again to cup my breasts. "Yes," he responded with a nip at the sweet spot on my neck he knew drove me wild.

"You have to promise me that was the last time you'll leave me. No matter what. I can't go through this again."

He toed his sneakers off. "I can't either, Elle. And I never want to."

My fingers went to his waistband and I pushed his wet track pants down. "Promise me, Logan. Promise me."

Standing in his boxer briefs with his wet clothes surrounding us, he wrapped his arms around me and held me tightly. "I promise you, Elle, I promise."

The honesty in his voice was all I needed to hear. Words were for later. Right now all I needed was to feel him. All of him. And I was going to start with his mouth. I kissed him until my face was numb. Until my lips tingled and my skin burned from the stubble of his jaw. And even then, that wasn't enough. I wanted to reacquaint myself with every inch of him from his head to his toes. "Let's go upstairs," I said, wanton and breathless.

His roaming hands stopped their movement, but only to pull me closer and hold me tighter.

With my arms around his neck, I rested my head on his shoulder and held onto him just as tightly.

Our hold was fierce.

Warming.

Loving.

Forgiving.

Comforting.

And I hoped everlasting.

I tried to undo myself from his hold, so we could go upstairs. "Come on," I managed.

He didn't move. Just held me tighter.

Beneath my fingertips, I could feel his body tense. "Logan, what is it?" I asked.

Finally, after a few moments, he pulled back, and I nervously watched as he picked up the blanket and wrapped it around the both of us. "Let's go sit on the couch. I have something to tell you."

chapter
ELEVEN

DAY 15

LOGAN

"WHAT ARE YOU DOING here?"

My head jerked up from the stack of papers on my desk. "Um . . . I work here."

My old man perched himself on the corner of my desk. "Don't be a smart-ass. I just thought you were taking a few days off to be with Elle."

I shook the glower off my face. "She had to go with O'Shea to Lizzy's viewing."

"Arrangements were made quickly."

I gave him a solemn nod. Elle had told me O'Shea seemed in a hurry to put all of this behind him. *Odd way to put it.*

My old man folded his hands together. "And let me guess, by the look on your face I'd say you weren't invited."

I leaned back in my chair and pointed my finger at him. "You're good."

He shook his head. "Well, I can also guess you're not happy about it, either."

"I wouldn't say that. I didn't know her and it's not my place to be there."

"But?"

I shrugged. "I would have liked to be there to support Elle."

"And?"

He was smart. "I don't know. I can't explain it. Don't get me wrong. I understand this is a tough time for them both. It's just weird that they'll be spending so much time together."

Understanding sparked in his eyes. "You're jealous."

Maybe I was wrong about the understanding. "No, I just don't like Elle anywhere near him."

He raised a brow. "It's okay if you are, son. It makes sense. She's a beautiful woman and he's a man. Just remember he's also a man who just lost his wife. Regardless of the situation surrounding her death, I'm certain he must be grieving."

I'd decided not to say anything to my old man about O'Shea and my suspicion that maybe he had something to do with Lizzy's murder just yet, or about the strange messages Elle had received. Only two to date, but that was the real reason I didn't go today. She just felt they were warnings and had something to do with her relationship with O'Shea. I agreed. Since we had no proof of anything, I didn't want to add more to the pile of shit my old man was already dealing with, so I answered smoothly but honestly. "Yeah, yeah, I know. I still don't trust him. The smoke screen he conjured up about his wife's disappearance has too many holes in it."

"Logan, listen to me: I know you're concerned about Elle's safety and so am I, but I think there are some things better left alone. And at this point O'Shea and Lizzy's involvement with Tommy and Patrick is one of them. The old saying *Don't poke a sleeping bear* might be one that applies in this case."

I completely disagreed but nodded in agreement anyway. "Yeah, you're probably right. Well, I had some stuff to get done today, so it all worked out fine." I looked at my watch. "Where have you been, anyway?"

"I went to an AA meeting down the street and then was going to head home early, but I saw your car when I was walking back so I came in to check on you. What do you say to letting your old man buy you dinner?"

I stood and rounded my desk. "Sorry, Pop, I'll have to take a rain check. Elle said everything should be wrapped up by five, and I think I'll try to catch up with her and take her out to dinner. Do you need a ride, though?"

He shook his head. "No, I'm good."

"You sure?"

He nodded.

"Then can I ask you a quick question?"

"Yeah, sure."

"Have you ever heard of anyone on the street referred to as the Priest?"

His brow creased. "No, I haven't. Why do you ask?"

I shook my question off casually. "No reason really, I just heard someone refer to the Priest and had no idea what they were talking about."

"Church maybe," my father laughed, rising from the desk and patting my shoulder. "A place you might want to visit once in a while."

It was then that the thought struck. The call and message Elle received spoke of God. Was the Priest the one contacting Elle?

Holy shit.

No, it couldn't be, or could the connection be that easy?

"Logan?"

I snapped out of it and gave my old man a shake of my head. "What can I say? I follow the lead of my old man."

"I probably should have done a better job on that one."

I laughed. "You know what they say about hindsight."

"You got me there." He looked at his watch. "I think I'll catch dinner with Killian. Give Elle my condolences."

"I will," I said, and couldn't help but notice that his shoulders were slumped. "Hey, is everything cool with you?"

Like a bat out of hell, he averted his gaze. "Yeah, I'm good."

"No you're not. Talk to me."

With a sigh, he turned to look out the window. "It's nothing I want you involved with and I mean it, Logan, but Patrick has me pulling financials for all his businesses. He's looking for something and I'm fairly certain it's what we already found."

"How? He's still in jail. I thought his bail was denied?"

"It was. His trial attorney contacted me."

I should have known. "What's he looking for?"

"My best guess—to verify his son's involvement."

"The Tommy connection to the drugs. The reason they're in jail," I commented.

My father nodded. "And the money clearly leads back to Tommy and I knew about it. If I act like I didn't know Tommy was stealing money, I'm fucked, and if I tell him I knew, I'm even more fucked."

"Then don't tell him anything. It's not your fucking job to look out for his tweaker son."

He turned back around. "No, but it is my job to make sure the money-laundering process runs efficiently."

"Patrick is behind bars, and hopefully will stay that way. Can't you stall? Ride it out and stay clear of him."

The smile on his face was anything but genuine. "He owns me, Logan, you know that. I do what he says, when he says, regardless of where he is."

"Maybe it's time you talk to Gramps. See if he knows anyone that can help get you out of this. With Patrick behind bars, there has to be a way. Someone out there willing to cut a deal."

Wide steps brought him close to me. "Yeah, I'll do that."

I wasn't sure he would. "Call me if you need anything."

He patted me on the shoulder before he left. "I will."

Following the impromptu discussion with my father, I felt both better and worse. Better about O'Shea and Elle having to spend the day together, and worse because my old man's situation should have been getting better with Patrick behind bars, not worse.

When the brief for a client that had to be filed in federal court on Monday was complete, I glanced at my watch. I had a shit-ton of other work to do but decided to spend some time researching scripture to see if what the caller had recited and texted to Elle had any context. After finding nothing that made sense, I concurred with Elle: it was this man's, whom I'd concurred could possibly be the Priest, own words.

Before closing out, a local advertisement online caught my eye. Taking the bull by the horns, I decided to quit waiting around for Elle to be finished and text her.

Me: Everything go okay today?

I knew Elle felt torn. She hadn't seen her sister in fifteen years, and all she knew about her was that she had abandoned her family and somehow put them in danger. On the other hand, she was her sister. I didn't push her to talk about it. I knew if she wanted to she would.

When she didn't answer, I quickly sent another text.

Me: Can you meet me somewhere?

Then, like a chick, I sat back in my chair and waited. Unable to concentrate on anything, I paced my office, cleared some papers off my desk, then stared at my phone screen. It was just as I was about to head out and go meet up with my old man at the nursing home when my phone buzzed.

Elle: Yes. We just finished eating. Where?

Dinner was out of the question since she'd already eaten, but that was okay because I had something better in mind. I wanted to take her on a real date, but it would be dark if I went to go pick her up first, so I settled on a pseudo date.

Me: At the George Washington Statue in the Public Garden.

Her response came in the way of a smiley face: " ☺ "

I'd never texted nor written a heart, smiley face, or anything like that in my life. My fingers hovered over the keypad until finally I just did it: " ☺ "

Lame.

I felt incredibly lame.

I almost looked around and wondered if this was me sitting here. Shaking off what James would surely call the secret Romeo within me, I grabbed my keys and got ready to go.

The Internet had notified me that today was opening day at the Swan Boats, and I'd always seen people riding in them during the spring and summer months but never thought about going on one myself. It was like the carriage rides in Central Park; I'd always seen people taking them but had never actually ridden in one of the carriages myself.

With Elle, I wanted to do things I'd never wanted to do before.

Stupid, dumb things. Things couples did.

Chances were small that anyone would see us together there but just in case, I shoved my hat on my head and slid my sunglasses onto my face. It was still slightly cool outside, so the knit hat didn't look that out of place. Hopefully I wouldn't have to worry about being seen with Elle for much longer. I'd put in a request to meet with Tommy and although my request had been denied, Miles was working on a way around that.

The area of the park where the statue was located was under construction, as was almost everything in the Garden this time of year. Winter damage was harsh, but I was certain by the end of April there would be no sign of it.

I leaned back against some of the scaffolding that surrounded the at least forty-foot height of the eerily lifelike bronze George Washington on his horse. With my tie removed and sleeves rolled up, I looked like a resident out for a stroll after work.

A text from Miles told me Elle had arrived and he was off for the night. Miles and a crew of hired security men had been watching out for her since we'd gotten the note from Tommy in the hotel. Surprisingly, she'd never objected.

Scanning the area, I spotted her before she saw me. She was rolling some of that lip balm in a small silver tin that she seemed to have in multiples on her lips. She'd changed since I'd seen her this morning. No longer in a black skirt and blouse, she was wearing black skinny jeans, a gray sweater, her red hat, and a pair of boots.

I was practically frozen in place she was so beautiful.

It was hard to believe there was ever a moment when I thought being apart was the best choice for us.

This stupid fucking situation we were in wasn't going to be easy to navigate, but I knew if I could just keep my shit together and think clearly, I'd get through it. I had two things to do—eliminate Tommy as a threat for good and figure out what O'Shea had or hadn't done.

Maybe it was jealousy that had sparked the change of mind.

Maybe it was the fact that no one was safe.

Maybe it was because this wasn't just about me anymore.

But I now felt confident I could accomplish those two things while keeping Elle safe and in my life at the same time.

She put the tin back in the purse that she wore strapped across her body and scanned the area with an almost blank expression on her face.

I pushed myself up just as she spotted me and I saw her entire face light up.

My legs moved fast and I smiled at her the entire distance it took to reach her. "Hey," I said.

"Hi," she said, smiling.

"Everything go okay today?"

She half nodded. "Only a handful of people showed up and none seemed to know my sister at all. It was sad, really."

"Who were they, then?"

She shrugged. "I think they were people Michael knows from the courthouse. I'm not entirely certain. I saw one or two of them at the fundraiser. At least Michael's sister stopped by for a few minutes. It was strange, though, that no one else from his family came."

My hands went to her waist. "I'm sorry I couldn't be there for you. I'm sure it wasn't easy."

"Thank you. I know you wanted to be but it's not possible right now," she said, and to lessen the burn, she placed her hands on my chest.

"Is everything all set for tomorrow?"

She sighed. "It is. Michael is going to keep it small."

I nodded, having nothing else to say.

For the next few moments we gazed at each other, lost in each other's eyes, and then I broke the connection only because the pull of her lips to mine was too much to put off for another second.

That mouth. I needed it.

Those lips. I was hungry for them.

That tongue. All I wanted was to taste it.

I was greedy for her.

Before I got as carried away as my thoughts in a public place, I broke the kiss. "Come on, we don't have much time."

"For what?"

"Just follow me."

She accepted my outstretched hand.

Loving the feel of having her by my side, I squeezed her small hand. "You're sure you're okay?"

She nodded. "Distract me. Tell me what we're doing here."

"I'll do better than that, I'll show you." I led her over the Lagoon Bridge to the Swan Boats. "See those?"

"The boats?"

Apparently not everyone knew how famous these boats were, so I paused halfway across the bridge and turned so we could lean over the railing. "Those aren't just any boats. They are the Swan Boats."

Her husky laugh was contagious. "I can see why they're called that, but what is the significance?"

"Good question. In the late 1890s everyone wanted to ride across the lagoon, but obviously allowing anyone and everyone wasn't feasible due to its small size. A really smart guy named Paget was the first to apply for a license for what he called a boat for hire. He wanted something to draw people in, to want to pay the cost of the small excursion, so he selected swans."

"Why swans?" she asked.

I'd done my research and grinned at the fact that I knew the answer. "They were inspired by the opera *Lohengrin*, in which real-life swans pulled a boat carrying a knight on a mission to rescue a beautiful maiden. Paget couldn't use the real swans, so he decided to camouflage his boat operators with the shape of a much-larger-than-life swan made from copper."

"I love the romantic notion behind it."

Romance was never my thing, but if she thought this was romantic, who was I to tell her otherwise? I pointed to the platform of waiting people. "Riding on one is a rite of passage here in Boston."

"Then by all means, lead the way, my knight."

More excited than a boat ride should have made me, I smiled at her. "I'm not sure I'm a knight by any definition."

She tugged on my hand. "Well, you're mine."

I didn't respond to that. I couldn't. I was no knight. I still wasn't sure I would be able to protect her in the way she needed protecting. A change of topic felt best. "So it's probably best that I confess right now that I've never ridden on one."

The corners of her mouth quirked up. "You said it was a rite of passage."

My shrug might have been a little cocky. "It is, but I'm a half-breed Bostonian so it doesn't apply to me."

She got a little flirty and took the lead, leaping in front of me. "It doesn't apply to me either then, but I'm still going to board first and beat you to the title."

I laughed. "I'll let you have this one."

"Last call," the operator yelled and we both picked up the pace, speeding to the pavilion, where I quickly paid the nominal fee and we crossed the wooden platform.

We were the last ones on, so we had to sit in the back row. That was fine with me. With my arm around her shoulder, the boat started toward the southern end of the lagoon and then slowly circled the edge. It was quiet and relaxing, almost making my life feel a little normal.

"Can I ask you something?" Elle whispered.

Calm and steady for the first time in so long, my gaze slid her way. "Yeah, sure, anything."

"When I was at your apartment in New York, you had photographs of the Brooklyn Bridge on your walls. Why?"

An emotion I'd buried deep within myself long ago wormed its way up. I leaned forward and rested my elbows on my thighs. "It's stupid really."

Her chin was on my shoulder and her breath was a whisper. "Tell me."

I turned my head to see her. "When I was a sophomore in college, I took a photography class and one of our assignments was to photograph something that represented hope to us. I picked the Brooklyn Bridge. Having grown up being shuffled between the Upper East Side and Beacon Hill, my hope was that someday I'd find a place I could call home."

The feel of her hand on my back was comforting as she rubbed it. I'd never had this from any other woman, not even my mother. "That makes sense. But why Brooklyn?"

I loved that she cared to ask, but I shook my head. "It's stupid."

"Tell me."

My eyes met hers and I felt like I could share anything with her. "My college roommate in my freshman year was from there and he used to take me home with him once in a while. His family had a huge loft and they seemed really happy there. Everything appeared so simple. I guess I kind of envied that kind of life."

She kissed my cheek. "I think we both yearn for the stability we never had in our lives. For me, my hope came in the prospect of visiting a new place, like maybe this would be it, a place I could call home; for you it came in the form of a bridge. I get it."

Straightening my back, I pulled her to me. "Yeah, I guess we are a lot alike."

The rest of the ride was nothing earth shattering, but being beside her and doing something out in the open that new couples do made it feel like so much more.

Just as the boat began to pull back to the platform, I placed my hand on her thigh and then whispered, "Can I follow you home and bid you a proper good night?"

She snorted laughter, either at the old-fashioned way I asked the question or the fact that I asked at all. "I'm not sure."

My fingers squeezed her thigh and my other hand cupped her shoulder as I leaned even closer, close enough so that I was touching her ear with my lips. "What aren't you sure about? How good I'm going to make you feel or waiting to get home to have me?"

She shifted in her seat, and I leaned back and watched as her cheeks flushed. "Logan!"

"What?" I shook my head as if innocent, giving her a sideways smile. Before me, Elle wasn't big on sexual innuendos or anything to do with sex for that matter, other than the act. She hadn't allowed talking and didn't do repeats. We were both very similar and very different in that respect. I didn't do repeats, but the only way I had of connecting with women was by talking during sex.

Her tongue snuck out and licked her bottom lip. "Be a gentleman."

With a shrug, I smirked, "I tried that, but when I asked if I could see you home and it got me nowhere, I had to up my game."

The boat docked before she could say anything and as we were in the last row, we were ushered out first. I passed by her, and stepped up and then offered my hand.

She smiled at me. It was a sexy, playful smile, but it still revved me up. When her feet were on the platform and we were safely out of the way of others, she grabbed me by my belt loop and tugged me flush to her. "Being a gentleman isn't getting you nowhere, not by a long shot," she purred.

My smile was wide and I could feel every heartbeat in my cock.

It looked like I'd be seeing her to her door, and inside her door, and up her stairs, and then all the way to her bed.

Who knew—just maybe I was a gentleman after all.

chapter

TWELVE

DAY 16

Elle

MY HEAVY LIDS FLUTTERED at the incessant singing of birds outside my window.

Squinting, I pried my eyes open.

It was early, but I knew I wouldn't be able to fall back asleep. I had way too much on my mind. Still, today was a day to dread and I wished sleep would pull me back in.

With a small sigh, I rolled over and then couldn't help but smile when I saw the man I had come to love in such a short period of time sleeping soundly beside me.

Our relationship hadn't had a conventional start. We'd met under less than ideal circumstances. A situation neither of us had chosen to be involved in.

At first when we met, I thought we were on opposite sides, but I soon found that wasn't the case. And in the midst of the turmoil, we were drawn to each other in the most intimate of ways. Although we tried to fight the magnetic pull, we couldn't. Shortly after meeting, we sought comfort in each other, and soon discovered it was a comfort we'd never felt with another.

The man I silently called my protector, my white knight, stirred at my slight movement but didn't wake. Exhaustion must have taken its toll.

The sight of him, all long, muscled limbs and smooth

skin, curled my fingers in anticipation of touching him. Guilt held me off. I knew he hadn't slept through the night in days. Worry over me had consumed him. Sure, he played a good game. Made like everything was going to be okay, but I could see beneath his tough exterior to the gentle, terrified man beneath.

Logan McPherson had been raised in two worlds. Shuffled between the wealthy elite of New York City and the brutish Irish Mob of Boston, he had become a man with two sides. The one seen by most was the dauntless, strong, confident man who knew how to take care of himself and everyone around him.

The protector.

The other side, the one he camouflaged, was a man who was drowning in the sins that surrounded him. Only through small glimpses had I seen the toll the violence that surrounded him had taken over the years.

The victim.

All I could do was be there for him and hope that with Tommy Flannigan in jail, all the chaos would soon be put to rest so he could begin to heal.

Placing a soft kiss on the scar beneath his eye, I carefully slipped out of bed. As soon as I tugged his white button-down on, his clean, fresh scent assaulted me and I had to turn back for another glance.

Hair the color of expensive milk chocolate that he wore brushed forward looked slightly more rumpled than usual. Where normally his beautiful hair feathered against his forehead and cheeks, now it was sticking out everywhere.

Bed head suited him, though.

The sheet had fallen away and my eyes greedily scanned his body from the twin dark circles of his nipples, to the ridges of his ribs, down to the narrow cut of his waist, and then stopped on hip bones that jutted out beneath the sheet.

Long and lean.

Powerful and strong.

Dauntless.

Covered by the soft cloth was all the rest of his magnificence, but also covered was the scar that ran down the inside of his thigh. That one, along with the scar under his eye, was a constant reminder of the danger he faced when in the presence of a woman, which was the source of his constant worry over me.

My worries were on many things, that included, but I tried to downplay it for his sake. Although I was confident I could take care of myself, I was also certain Logan would keep me safe. Besides, the state-of-the-art security systems Miles had installed in my house and boutique made them both seem impenetrable.

With those grounding thoughts in my mind, I tiptoed out of the room. The house was quiet, with pearly dawn light peeking through the blinds as I made my way down the stairs.

The row house, which had been in foreclosure when I first laid eyes on it and then managed to purchase with Michael's help and by mortgaging it to the hilt, backed up to a small park, and it was a place I had to have. To me it was the first place I could call home.

In the early hours of the morning everything around me was peaceful and quiet. The soft gurgle of the coffeemaker was the only sound to break the silence. As I waited patiently for the pot to brew, I stared out the kitchen window into the small park behind me. My eyes drifted to anything that might take my mind off what today was. The dread was beginning to loom and I wanted to lose myself in something else, even if only for a little while.

The dew that coated the grass.

The trees that were starting to sprout leaves.

The purple horizon with a small yellow glow popping over it.

Strong arms gripped the lip of the sink on both sides of me, caging me in. The feel of his stubbled cheek against the sensitive skin of my neck sent tiny fissures of excitement through my veins. "Good morning. You're up early," he said in that sleepy, sexy voice that made my stomach flip in excitement every time I heard it.

With the air around me suddenly feeling thicker, I leaned back against his strong bare chest and twisted my head so I could kiss him. "Good morning. I tried not to wake you up."

His lips brushed mine and electricity flared through me. "You shouldn't be up either. Come back to bed."

Not a question, a command, laced with a whole lot of promise.

I found myself licking my lips. "I don't have a lot of time. I need to be at the police station at nine and then to Michael's by ten so we can ride to the service together."

His hands whisked under the hem of my shirt and went right between my thighs. "We don't need a lot of time."

Oh, God.

His hands, his fingers, they were magic. The shudder of my breath officially became louder than the residual dripping of the coffeemaker. "What did you have in mind?" I teased. This distraction was more than welcoming before the start of what I knew would be a dreadful day.

Hot breath blew in my ear. "I want to make you feel good," he paused as he pressed his palm against my sex, "right here."

My eyelids fluttered for the second time this morning, but this time for an entirely different reason. He knew how to rev me up. That was for sure.

When we first met, I had two rules when it came to sex—no talking and no repeats. One failed relationship had left me burned and I wasn't interested in another. But with Logan, everything changed and those rules went right out the window. It might take me a while to truly push through my childhood issues, but Logan was being patient. The memories of hearing my father tell my mother he had to be inside her almost every night for years was strong within me. However, the memory of how much she disliked the act was stronger. And the truth was, what Logan and I were doing was mutually pleasurable. We both gave as much as we took.

Knowing this, I was trying to compromise and found myself more than okay with the way Logan chose to let his emotions out. I sometimes found it embarrassing. I called it dirty talk. He preferred the term *communicating*. The simple fact was that even though I'd come to embrace this part of who he was, Logan knew my limits, and after learning about my aversion he had been careful never to say those words my father said to my mother. His efforts to tread lightly warmed my heart. I found them endearing and charming and sexy as hell all at the same time.

Fingers fondled me in the most delicious way, and then he slid one a little lower. "And right here."

The stroke of his flesh against mine, and the rumble in his voice, sent my body into overdrive. "Go on," I whispered breathlessly, pressing myself back against his hot, thick erection.

His breath caught and he had to suck in air before he said, "I don't think I need to explain any further—you're already dripping wet." On his last word, he plunged that single probing finger deep inside me.

The tension in my lower belly coiled so tightly, I thought if he moved a little more or added one more finger, I just might come right here.

But he didn't. Instead, he kept teasing me.

Unable to withstand the torture another moment, I turned around. For a moment, the world stopped spinning and it was just he and I, and what we felt for each other.

With a smile that I couldn't help, I ran my hands up his bare, smooth chest. He was standing there in black boxers, body ripped with strength, lids heavy with desire, eyelashes thick, those hazel pools bright and those lush lips parted. My hands reached his shoulders and then my nails dragged down his back. I thrilled at the feel of his rock-hard muscles under my fingertips. I never wanted to stop touching him.

Logan pressed against me. Backing me up against the

sink, his leg eased between mine. My heel hooked around his leg, drawing him even nearer. His mouth was greedy on my neck, sucking, licking, kissing. My fingers were in his hair, caressing, tugging, pulling. We were all mouths and hands and tangled limbs.

"Take me back to bed, unless we're staying down here," I demanded impatiently.

His smile was wicked and wild, and without hesitation he took my hand and led me back up the stairs.

My guess was fifty-fifty as to whether he'd fuck me on the counter or on my mattress. There were times he was soft and gentle and we made love. And there were times he was wild and raw and we fucked like animals. Most of the time, I allowed his mood to determine the pace we took and at other times, I directed it.

Today, I was leaving it up to him.

We passed the threshold into my room and he kicked the door shut behind us. As soon as I heard the click of the latch his mouth was on mine. Our bodies melded in the perfect way that only we fit together. Not holding back, he started backing me up. Our kisses were hungry, deep. Delicious.

Slow steps were taken in sync until my knees hit the bed, and then somehow the two of us made it onto the mattress without either of us crashing down.

At first he was hovering over me but within moments we were rolling, and then I was on top of him and my knees were straddling his hips, squeezing them, letting him know just how much I wanted him. Moving quickly, he unbuttoned my shirt—*his* shirt—and discarded it. And then his hands were on my breasts, pinching my nipples, rolling them between his thumbs and fingers in a way that made them instantly hard.

Leaning down, I let my tangle of messy hair tickle his bare chest as I kissed my way up to the curve of his jaw. Stopping along the way to nip and bite where I saw fit.

With a hiss, he growled, "Watch it. Two can play at that game."

I sat up straighter and grinned at him. The upward curve of my lips was an undeniable, come-and-get-me smile.

At thirty, I'd only recently come to learn just how affected my body could be by small things, like how a little bit of pain could make the pleasure all the better. Small things, nothing too extreme. If I was sitting on the lip of my old-fashioned tub with his face between my legs, the tighter I gripped the rim, the more the lip rubbed against my skin, the more intense my orgasm. Or if Logan held my hands over my head while he fucked me, the inability to move and the tight grip around my wrists sent me spiraling. And then there was the way he could bring me to the edge and deny my tipping over it until I thought I might go crazy. I wasn't looking to use whips and chains or anything like that, but a small bite here or there certainly was fun.

His hiss morphed into a groan when I struck first. Inching back, my hands drifted to the black fabric that separated us and I pressed down on it. With the feel of his erection beneath my fingertips, I stopped playing around and rocked forward.

Logan's eyes shined with desire. He, too, had obviously decided to abandon the games, because he shot up and pulled me on his lap.

"You have too much on," I whispered and rose on my knees.

Doing the same, he tugged down his boxers with quick efficiency, kicking them off and onto the ground in no time. Finally, both of us were naked and ready for this.

Heartbeats apart, we were both on our knees gazing at each other. When my eyes cast down onto his perfectly erect cock, I licked my lips.

He noticed my response and then in one of the most erotic moves I'd ever seen, he took his cock in his hand and held it for a beat of two.

My heavy breathing gave way to how much it turned me on.

His eyes watched me as he gave himself a little stroke.

"You like that?"

I nodded, my breathing coming way too fast—I was practically panting.

Logan dipped his chin to look down, and then he stroked himself again, this time pushing his hands forward and thrusting his cock into his fist.

In a rush, I moaned his name. "Logan."

With a desperation only I understood, he quickened his pace.

Fascinated, I watched, taking notice of the way his muscles corded in his arms, the smooth skin of his cock and the way his hand easily glided over it, the pre-cum that glistened on his tip.

But my show was not for long because before I knew it, he'd stopped stroking himself and started stroking me with that cock, that delicious cock that was still in his hand. My clit pulsed and my muscles clenched in response. Full of need, my eyes found his.

"Come closer," he said, and I did.

Lowering himself so his knees were now beneath him, he grabbed my hair as soon as I leaned in, pulled me onto his lap, and then captured my mouth with his. Giving me hard, wet, breathtaking kisses that made it impossible to breathe.

When I pulled back, my hands moved to his face. His hair had fallen forward and he looked rakish—impossibly sexy—as I pushed it from his eyes.

Logan didn't waste any time as he gripped my hips.

My desire for him was so fierce I was wet long ago. There wasn't any need for any further foreplay. Rising slightly on my knees, I lowered myself down onto his lap. Onto his cock. Slowly. Inch by inch. A little at a time. Exquisite pleasure started to surge all the way from my core. I didn't stop until he was fully inside me. For a moment, I didn't move, wasn't sure I could without coming.

Logan took over for me, surging his body upward and taking control of mine with his hands on my hips. I drew in a shuddering breath and wrapped by arms around his neck. He pumped slowly at first and I found myself leaning in to kiss his mouth. I kissed him hard, and he returned my kiss with the same strength. We were all lips, teeth, and tongue. Wild. Frantic. And soon the energy transferred to our bodies. He started to fuck into me, faster, faster still. Abandoning the kissing, I pushed myself upright and began to ride him, matching his pace.

Cries of pleasure sputtered from his throat, rough, gravel-like, filled with a rumble. "Oh, shit. Oh, fuck. That's so good. That's it. Oh, fuck, I'm going to come."

Words that sent me right over the edge.

He pumped faster and faster and I followed in that rhythm that existed only between us. Unable to hold on any longer, I arched my back and closed my eyes. Pleasure filled the space in my head where my mind no longer was. In the space that should have held thoughts was nothing but flickering lights, small bright stars in a far distance, and colors of the rainbow. I rode out my orgasm in that place, not allowing coherent thoughts to reenter my mind until I had exhausted every ounce of pleasure that was coursing through my body from head to toe.

He murmured my name. My heart, which was already pounding, skipped a beat. Without opening my eyes yet, I answered with his name. "Logan," I breathed.

In response, he rolled onto his side and his hands found mine. Lacing our fingers, he pulled me flush to his chest. "Come here."

At the sound of his voice again, I opened my eyes and looked at him. If it was possible for your heart to be so full of love for someone that you felt it might explode, that's how I was feeling. We hadn't expressed our love in words since that dreadful night, but we both knew how the other felt. Those three little words didn't always have to be spoken for someone to know it. Besides, how many times were those words spoken among people in an empty, meaningless way? "I love you" could be said without really meaning it. But showing it, that meant everything.

Satisfaction filled the air. We were both breathing loudly when Logan propped himself up on his elbow. I turned as well, folding my arm under my pillow.

Gently, he ran his fingers through a stray piece of my hair that had fallen to the side. When he tucked it behind my ear, he sighed. "I want to come with you today to your sister's funeral."

Treading cautiously, I grasped his hand tighter and brought it to my lips. "Logan, you know you can't." It wasn't that I didn't want him there—I did. But those calls frightened me and I didn't know what they meant but knew they had something to do with Michael and I. For now, Logan and I would have to remain a secret.

Taking his hands from mine, he flopped onto his back and put them behind his head. "I want you to tell him."

I moved closer, stroking my fingers over his chest. "You know I want to, but the calls are freaking me out. What if they have something to do with Michael? Or what if when I tell Michael that I'm involved with someone, with you, it doesn't go over very well?"

Logan was quiet at first, and I wasn't sure what he was thinking.

"Hey," I whispered.

Instead of answering, he looked over at me with a blank expression on his face.

"Michael not knowing about us doesn't change anything. You know that, right?"

He scowled. "Yeah, sure I do. It's just, it's bad enough we have to be concerned about being seen in public. I hate that you have to tiptoe around him because you're worried about him finding out."

"Logan, even if the calls weren't an issue, it's too soon to tell him. Too close to everything that has happened. Think about it: what if I did tell him and then he started thinking about the drug bust? He's not stupid; he could figure things out."

Logan ran his hand down his face. "Even if he did, what does it matter? It's not like he's going to go to the cops."

I willed my racing heart to slow down as I sat up and pulled the sheet with me. It was time to be honest. "Logan, I haven't told you everything that happened those first three days we were apart that first week."

He frowned. "What are you talking about?"

I swallowed the lump in my throat. "The threat of Clementine being kidnapped wasn't the only reason I agreed to help Michael."

Practically his entire body went taut. "What did he do to you?"

"Nothing," I said quickly enough to keep his anger at bay. "It's not what he did. It's what he said earlier that same night he asked me for his help."

"You mean the night when he asked you to commit a felony," Logan said through gritted teeth.

"Logan, we've discussed—"

He held up a hand. "Just go on."

I flinched at the coolness in his tone. "Well," I stuttered before pulling myself together and just spilling it. "He alluded to the possibility that he could cut me out of Clementine's life, forbid me from seeing her. And Logan, I can't allow that to happen. You have to understand, I can't do anything that might jeopardize my role in her life."

Logan sat up abruptly. "What the hell are you talking about? He knows how much you love her. Why would he do something like that?"

Emotional warfare, I thought but didn't say out loud. That would really send him reeling. My fingers curled into my palms as I spoke. "Before he told me anything about his plan, he let me know he was going to report Lizzy missing and then file for divorce. Then he said he thought it would be a good idea with everything going on if he named Erin as Clementine's guardian."

"His sister, the one with four kids? Not you? I don't—" He stopped, narrowed his eyes, and clenched his fists. "Did he blackmail you?"

I shook my head. "No, not exactly. He was much more subtle about it. He started with the guardianship and then moved on to what he really wanted. He tried to convince me that Clementine's safety was in jeopardy and that was why I needed to help him. But I saw through his words. The reason he told me about possibly naming his sister as Clementine's guardian was so that if the kidnapping threat wasn't enough to make me say yes, the hope of ensuring my place in Clementine's life would be. And it worked, because I did help him. I had to. For her."

Logan was up and out of bed faster than I could blink. Punching his legs into a pair of track pants that were folded on top of my dresser, he yanked them up and then started pacing the room. "You understand for any guardianship to be invoked something would have to happen to Michael, so all of his talk is a bunch of presumptive bullshit."

The lawyer in him was taking over.

"I do understand that, but it was more than just the dangling of awarding me possible guardianship. There was an undertone to his words."

Logan narrowed his eyes. "What do you mean?"

Tangling my fingers together, I admitted what I hadn't even really admitted to myself. "I just got the feeling that he was giving me a choice to make and if I made the wrong one, he was going to cut me out of Clementine's life altogether."

Logan slammed his fist against the wall. "Motherfucking piece of shit. That's it. I'm done with this charade."

"Logan, calm down. Please don't do anything stupid. Don't jeopardize what I have with my niece," I begged.

The pacing started back up. "And the fundraiser, did you go to that under the duress of a threat as well?"

I shook my head. "No, he asked me to go with him as a favor. I didn't say yes until I got that first call."

The muscle in Logan's jaw twitched.

"This is why I didn't want to tell you in the first place. I knew how you'd react."

He stopped at the foot of the bed and ran his hand through his hair. "Knew how I'd react to the man you're spending so much time with threatening you? Using an innocent child as a pawn? A man who might be a killer? How *should* I react? Sit down and have a drink with him?"

I threw my hands up. "Logan, stop it. You have to calm down. Michael has all the cards. I have to play by his rules. And if you do anything that pisses him off, makes him doubt my loyalty to him, he will cut me out of her life, I know he will."

Hands on his head, he paced. After a few moments his breathing seemed to relax. "So you did what he asked. Has he done what he underhandedly dangled before you and named you her guardian yet?"

I shook my head. "That wasn't something he actually said he would do."

"Did he name his sister?"

"I'm not sure. We haven't discussed any of this since that night."

"Fucking son of a bitch." His mouth quivered, that's how angry he was. "You have to trust me when I tell you, he's dangerous."

My feet reached for the floor and I stood on the rug that used to belong to my mother. "No, he's not dangerous. He's manipulative. There's a difference."

Logan took the two steps between us in one stride and gripped my arms. "No, Elle, in his case, there's not."

I sighed in exasperation. "Please don't start with the *you think he killed my sister* talk again. He might be many things, but he's not a killer."

Logan drew in a breath and huffed in frustration. "I know how important Clementine is to you and how important keeping her in your life is, Elle, but you have to start thinking more clearly."

This conversation was going nowhere. "I have to get ready," I said and started to walk toward the bathroom.

Logan grabbed my wrist. "I'm going with you today."

Determination showed in my face when I spoke. "No, Logan, you're not."

With certain gentleness, he let go of my wrist and grabbed some clean clothes. "Fine. I'll stay out of sight but I'll be there, and then tomorrow I'm going to see Tommy to find out what the hell he, Lizzy, and O'Shea had going on."

"Logan, no, you can't go see him. It's too dangerous." My pleas went unheard.

The door was slamming behind him before I could even voice my concern. Two seconds later I heard the hallway bathroom door slam as well.

I hated this.

I wanted to talk reasonably.

But we both needed to calm down.

Listening to the water run, I knew he'd be showered and out of the house before I even took my bath.

Talking would have to wait.

chapter
THIRTEEN

LOGAN

I LEANED DOWN ON the reception counter. "Where's he at today?"

The nurse behind the desk pointed to my right. "Ahhh . . . big poker game in the rec room."

My huff of laugher couldn't be helped. "I hope he's not taking everyone for all they've got."

She laughed at that and moved her chair closer to the window. "I think its penny-ante, so you never know."

Amusement still in the air, I glanced around. When I saw no one in the vicinity, I slipped her two C-notes. "Make sure he gets what he needs this week, will you?"

Without hesitation, she took the bills. Folded one and slipped it into her top. Folded the other and put it in the desk drawer. When they were both out of sight, she looked up. "I always do. Last week it was Jack Daniel's for his chocolate ice cream and jelly beans to put on his pudding. God only knows what it will be this week."

Standing straight, I thumped the counter. "Thanks for taking care of him, Judy. I really appreciate it."

A slight blush crept up her cheeks. "It's really no problem. I don't mind at all. Besides, he's a real sweet talker, that one," she said before quickly turning back to her computer screen.

With a shake of my head, I headed toward the

high-stakes poker game. The halls of Brighton House, the top facility for elderly care in Boston, were like any other nursing home in the area. White, drab, and if they didn't smell like piss, they smelled like Lysol. The only difference, this place cost a fuck-load more.

Having taken a shower, dressed, and given myself an attitude adjustment, I had an hour before the funeral, and decided it was time to stop avoiding my grandfather.

The room wasn't that far from reception and I reached it quickly. When I did, I leaned against the door and couldn't help but smirk at what I saw. The place was filled with people. Some playing chess, others watching TV, a few reading, and even a handful at the computer stations against the back wall. But Gramps wasn't anywhere near those traditional forms of entertainment. Instead, there he sat, at a large round table with a bunch of women playing poker. Women had always been his weakness. My grandmother had been the love of his life, and when he lost her, he never remarried, but that didn't mean he didn't chase anything with a skirt, and even at seventy-seven he hadn't changed.

"Shit," he said as he threw his cards on the table.

One of the women, the only one with jet-black hair, grinned and raked in the pot of pennies.

"I was so close," he whined.

Killian "the Killer" McPherson was many things. Predecessor to the current Blue Hill Gang's Irish Mob boss. Outlaw. Fighter. Lover. Gambler. Card shark. And card shark had to be ranked pretty high on the list.

I slapped my gramps on the back. "Damn, you lost?" I taunted.

He turned in his chair and gave me a wink. "I certainly did. Can you believe it?"

I shook my head. "No, I can't," I said, and then I turned my attention to the table. "Hello, ladies," I greeted.

In response, they all spoke at the same time. I had no idea who was saying what. It was a cacophony of, "Your grandson is so sweet. How handsome your grandson is,

Killian. He's such a nice young man."

My grandfather twisted his head once again and grabbed my hand. "Where have you been?"

I leaned down. "There's been a lot going on. Can we talk?"

Glancing back at the woman he had just let win, he said, "Gloria, meet me for dinner tonight at five. I'll arrange for us to eat alone in my room."

Gloria brought her hand to her rose-colored mouth. "Oh, that would be lovely."

In his most charming way, my grandfather reached across the table and squeezed her other hand. All the ladies giggled. "Ladies," he said, dipping his chin.

"'Bye, Killian." They waved.

Unlocking his wheelchair, he rolled it back. "Come on, Logan, we'll go back to my room and talk."

My hands gripped the handles of his chair. "Are you sure? Sounds like a pretty popular spot."

His head jerked around. "Take your hands off this damn contraption. I'm not a complete invalid. Not yet, anyway."

Raising my palms in surrender, I let him take control of the wheels and strode up beside him. His mind was sharp as a tack. But sadly, it was his body that was giving out. After years of fighting, I don't know how many gunshot wounds, and endless broken bones, he had a hard time getting around. Which is why he was here. After his last fall, he broke his hip and required extensive rehab. My uncle Hunter, who lives in New York City, thought it was best if he had assisted living care. My father agreed. I didn't, but my vote didn't count.

My grandfather stayed silent the entire way to his room. As soon as he unlocked the door, he impatiently motioned for me to move. I had planned to help him in, but obviously that wasn't his plan. "What are you waiting for? Christmas?"

Not so charming, after all.

I moved my ass forward, and he followed. Once inside

his suite, he transferred from the wheelchair to the chair he always sat in.

Having learned from experience, I took the chair over near the table and moved it closer to him.

Those dark eyes stared at me. "Well, what do you have to say?"

There were times when I was around him that I felt like that ten-year-old boy again, worried I'd upset him because I wanted so desperately for him to be proud of me. This was one of those times. In a very uncharacteristic manner, I rubbed my sweaty palms on my pants. I never let my nerves get the best of me.

"Don't be nervous. Tell me what happened."

Okay, it was time to do this, so I manned up and did it. I told him everything from the simple—like the security tapes I watched of Lizzy, who was at the time supposedly missing but was for some reason with Tommy at a hotel, to finding the drugs in Elle's boutique, to what I'd done with them, to Lizzy's death—to the more complex: my theory that O'Shea had been lying about his lack of involvement when it came to the missing drugs and money.

"So you're telling me O'Shea somehow managed to magically get his hands on half of what was needed to satisfy Patrick's demands?"

I shook my head. "Not really, because there's still the issue of the missing five mil."

"Yeah, yeah, I know, but I'm still on the drugs. How the hell did he get them? I mean, come on. What? Did he pull one hundred and twenty-five kilos of cocaine out of his ass? "

I had to laugh.

"Something isn't right, kiddo."

"Glad you see it my way."

Finishing up the O'Shea conversation, and having agreed he knew more than he let on, I stopped there. I didn't tell my gramps about the note I'd received threatening Elle. I didn't want to upset him. He'd go crazy just knowing Tommy had broken the order given years ago for us to stay clear of each other, because I'd have to tell him that so had I. Yeah, for now, it was best to leave those violations unspoken. I knew I'd have to tell him soon enough; I just needed some more time—I needed to see Tommy first.

When there was nothing more left to say about the shit storm that had become my life, his big palm landed on my shoulder. "It's okay, Logan, you don't have to feel guilty about anything. You did the best you could in the shitty situation you were in and you kept her safe. That's all you can ask for."

"Did I do what was best?"

He nodded. "She's your Achilles' heel. Mine was my Millie, and I'd have done anything, and I mean anything, to keep her out of harm's way."

Relief was all I felt. I'd stayed away from him because I thought he'd be disappointed that I didn't follow through with the plan that would have, without a doubt, put Tommy and Patrick away for life, and in doing so, eased the hold Patrick had over my old man. I feared he'd think that I'd pretty much fucked it all up by picking Elle. Sure, Tommy and Patrick would still do prison time, but nothing like the life sentence they would have been given had the transaction been witnessed by the DEA and the source of the cocaine identified.

"How do you feel about this girl?" he asked, his voice going soft, quiet.

Done trying to deny anything, I admitted, "I love her."

"Does she prefer winter or summer?"

I shrugged.

"What's her favorite movie?"

I shrugged again.

"Does she like chocolate?"

I raised my brow. "I'm not certain. What's with the twenty questions?"

He blinked a few times. "Come here," he said, reaching for me.

I eased forward.

"If you love her like you say you do, then you'll find out even the smallest details about her. It's your business to know what her favorite flower is, her favorite smell, color. If she likes a table or prefers a booth. Would rather stay home and watch a movie or go out. Remember, Logan, it's the little things that matter the most. And always, always, say good morning and good night. Never let a day go by without that."

More wisdom.

"Well?" he prompted.

"I don't know all of those things yet, but I love her."

He leaned closer and took my head between his hands. "I know you do. I know you do. Now the hard part begins—showing her every day that you do, no matter what."

He was choking up and the emotion was overwhelming. He wasn't an affectionate man and when he became emotional, it was usually out of anger. In that regard, I was a carbon copy of him. The change in demeanor compelled me to hug him. As I started to wrap my arms around his big body, he bear-hugged me so tight I almost couldn't breathe. For nearly thirty seconds we stayed that way and then we broke apart.

My grandfather cleared his throat. "I'm so proud of you for so many things. I don't think I tell you that often enough. But I want you to know, there's not a day that goes by that I don't regret having kept you in Boston. I should have made your father move to New York City when your mother asked him to after you were born. Or I should have at least made you start high school there. If I hadn't been so selfish, you would never have been a part of this fucked-up world of mine."

I shook my head back and forth. "Don't say that, Gramps. You're one of the best things that ever happened to me in my life. If it weren't for you, I wouldn't have known what was real. I wouldn't have understood what it meant to be grounded. I am who I am mostly because of you."

Tears streamed down that old man's face.

"I mean it, Gramps. I love you."

With a lift of his hips, he took a hankie from his pocket. "Enough," he said as he blew into the white cloth. After he stuffed it back in his pocket, he said, "Over in the top middle drawer of my dresser is a silver box. Bring it to me."

The emotional litany having affected me as well, I was thankful to be able to get up and walk around. The box was one I remembered from the house. It had been in his room and I was pretty certain it belonged to my grandmother. I'd never really paid much attention to it but as I picked it up, I noticed that although it had a very slim shape it was heavy. And the box itself was quite ornate. Scrollwork embellished the sides, and in the center of the top was an oval with a coat of arms.

Suddenly curious as to what it was, I handed it to my grandfather. "Here you go."

He took it with both hands and carefully set it on the table beside him. "Do you know what this is?"

"No."

With great care, he set his hand on the top of it, like it was precious. "This box was given to me by your grandmother's father. Millie and I weren't even eighteen when we got married. We were so young, but we were determined to leave Ireland. Her father had no money to give us and he knew going to America was going to be a hardship on his daughter. I tried to reassure him that I would take care of her, but he wanted to ensure that she would be okay. That's why he gave me this. In case I ever needed something so badly, and had no way of getting it."

My brows bunched.

With his hand still on it, he went on. "It's a snuff box and it belonged to his great-great grandfather. I'm not sure what it was worth in 1956 when it was given to me, but I had it appraised in the seventies when all the violence on the streets got out of hand. At the time I was thinking of taking my family and disappearing and wanted to see how far it would take us."

"How much was it worth then?" I asked curiously.

"One-point-one million."

Shocked, I gasped. "And you leave that in your dresser? Shouldn't you lock it up?"

"Na, everyone thinks it's just a cheap box."

I couldn't believe it. I'd had no idea.

Moving past its history, he opened it up and took out two key rings. With shaky fingers he managed to pocket one of the keys before holding the other up to show me. "This key is to a safety deposit box at the Chase Bank over on Washington Street near Franklin Park. Do you know which bank I'm talking about?"

"Yeah, I know where it is. The one on the corner of Park Avenue."

"That's the one. Inside that safe deposit box is your grandmother's engagement ring and our wedding bands. I want you to take them and when you're ready, you give that diamond to that girl of yours."

I stared dumbly at him.

He put the key ring back inside the box and handed the box to me. "I don't have as much to give you as your grandfather Ryan does, but I want you to take this. Use it if you ever need to. Think of it as a security blanket, like I did."

Unease washed through me and I shoved it back his way. "What's all this about?"

Sensing my worry, he reassured me. "It's something I've wanted to do for a while, and now that you found the girl you're going to spend the rest of your life with, it seemed like the right time."

The box had somehow transferred into my hands. "Gramps, Elle and I just met. We're nowhere near ready to get married."

He patted my hand. "Time isn't what matters; knowing she's the one is the only thing that does. Sure, take some time to get to know each other, but don't wait too long, Logan. Life can pass you by so quickly."

"Are you sure you want to give me Grandma's ring?"

He eased back in his chair. "Millie wanted so much to see you grow up. And when she found out the cancer was going to take her, she hated that she was going to miss it. She made me promise to give the ring to you when the time was right."

Words stuck in my throat.

"Promise me you won't wait too long. Promise me, Logan."

For him, I found the words. "I promise, Gramps. And I'll bring her by next week."

His dark eyes glinted with contentment. "I'd like that."

"Is there something going on?" I asked.

He shook his head.

Somehow I managed to convey what I'd always felt in my heart and gestured between the two of us. "Gramps, this means more to me than all the money in the world."

His smile was bright and prideful as he looked at me. Then he closed his eyes, and shortly after that he dozed off.

I left his room with another knot in my gut—something just didn't seem right.

chapter
FOURTEEN

Elle

S PRING WAS IN EARLY bloom this year.
     The breeze was light and cool.

The air fragrant.

The landscape almost indescribably beautiful.

From the rich, vibrant colors of azaleas, rhododendrons, and tulips bursting across the adjacent meadow to the fence separating this holy ground from the wildness beyond, with its overabundance of yellow daffodils growing against it.

The grass, too, was picture perfect. Although barely green, it was still soft and welcoming. And each building had planter boxes outside its windows filled with hundreds of purple violets.

Then there were the pathways. They were made of smooth gray stones that peeked out beneath a mat of leggy clover and dandelions. The dandelions. The reason I picked this location over so many others Michael had suggested.

Green Meadows was a small cemetery on the west side of Boston in Watertown, and although Michael thought it was too small and too far, I thought it was perfect. It reminded me of my childhood, of my sister and me running through the fields, picking dandelions and blowing on them.

Perhaps sensing in a way that I knew what Lizzy would

prefer, Michael had conceded, and Green Meadows was the place we'd laid my sister to rest. The funeral gathering was small and nondenominational, the sermon short, and the gravestone marker was simple. It read:

Elizabeth Sterling O'Shea
In loving memory

Anything else would have been hypocritical.

To say *loving wife and mother* would have been a lie. Lizzy had deserted her husband and child for a life she had somehow found more fulfilling. A life filled with drugs, sex, and money.

To say *loving sister*, well, since we hadn't spoken in fifteen years. That said it all. The last time I saw my sister was when my mother died and I was lying in a hospital bed. She came to say goodbye and left me alone with our father, who by any definition was a monster.

And to say *loving daughter* would have been a joke. I hadn't talked to our father in twelve years, and when I finally found the strength to track him down and call him to let him know Lizzy had died, he told me, "She has been dead to me for years." When I hung up, I knew that would be the last time I'd ever talk to him.

After the casket was lowered, we all began to leave the cemetery. Michael took my hand and I tried to pull it away, but he just seemed to grip it tighter. I couldn't wait to see Clementine, to hold her to me. Michael and I had both agreed she was too young to attend.

Coming to a halt, I glanced back. I knew Logan was somewhere in the distance watching me, but that wasn't why I stopped. I had a few things I needed to say and do. "Go ahead. I'll catch up," I said to Michael.

"I'll wait in the car," he told me and headed that way with the dozen or so other people who had attended. Aside from his sister and her husband, and his father, I didn't know anyone there.

With the delicate silver bracelet I'd recently found gripped tightly in one hand, I closed my eyes. The bracelet was the one that my sister had given me on my tenth birthday. It was meant to bring me comfort on those nights my father would insist on having sex with my mother when it was clear she wasn't interested. It was also the same one I had thrown at her when she told me she was leaving me alone with our father. The same one I'd found in her car. The dainty silver chain was a lot of things, but right now it was a keepsake I'd hold on to. I'd save it and give it to her daughter one day when thoughts of her mother might surface.

My sister's daughter would never know her mother. Never know she'd been abandoned. Never know the things mothers and daughters should share. I'd paint a pretty picture for her, though, of how wonderful her mother was, because there was a time she was. Still, I was certain there would be days she'd cry for her mother. And that broke my heart. At the right time, I'd give her this, and tell her a happier version of the story of how it came to be.

Letting my tears fall, I picked a dandelion from the ground and clutched it in my other hand. With a gust of breath, I turned toward the heavens and whispered, "Blow, Lizzy, just blow."

As I walked toward the car, I breathed in a deep lungful of the spring air. The sweet scent of the just opening cherry blossoms was poignant, and I was content with the place my sister would lie forever more.

"Are you okay?" Michael asked, handing me a tissue once I'd gotten into his car. He had driven himself, opting to forgo the formality of limos and the procession of cars following the hearse to and from the cemetery.

I drew in a deep, cleansing breath. "Yes, I am. What about you? Are you okay?"

He looked at me. "I have no idea. Elizabeth seems like the wind, she blew into my life and out so quickly."

I wasn't sure what to make of that.

Remaining silent, he eased out of the parking lot and onto the main road. Once his tires were no longer on the gravel, he glanced over at me. "I will be . . . okay," he said, reaching for my hand and squeezing it. "I just want all of this to be over, so I can focus on my daughter. She's what's most important to me."

Easing my hand out of his grip, I pretended to tuck a stray piece of hair behind my ear. "She's going to be fine, Michael."

He nodded. "I know she will."

Catching the worry on his face, I had to ask, "What's next?"

He hesitated and then said, "We take one day at a time."

Whether purposely avoiding what the real question was or caught up in his grief, I couldn't be certain but I had to know. "I mean about the drugs. Is all of that over? Are you and Clementine free from danger now?"

With a thoughtful expression, he glanced over at me. "You know, I think we are. With the five million dollars' worth of drugs now in the possession of the police, there's nothing left for anyone to go after."

I blinked. Shocked that he was lying to me. "The news reported cocaine worth about *half* that was found."

"That's what I said."

The blatant lie threw me for a loop. That was *not* what he'd said. Was he testing my knowledge of the situation? Did he know where the rest of the cocaine was? Was he hiding it? Did he have it? Was he keeping it for himself? And if so, what the hell was he going to do with it? Was Michael even more involved than I had thought? For Clementine's sake, I had to hope not. Still, I had to put my faith in him that he'd do what was best for her. I didn't have much of a choice. If I didn't follow his rules, he'd cut me out of her life, and I couldn't let that happen.

From this point forward, though, my eyes would be more than wide open.

We rode the rest of the way back to his house in silence. With my eyes focused out the window, my mind started to drift.

I had two men in my life. Both had earned my trust. One was regurgitating the police's theory that my sister's death was the result of a fall after a self-induced drug overdose and, rather than dealing with the fallout, whoever she had been with at the time tossed her body in the river. The other believed my sister was murdered . . . by her husband . . . the very man sitting beside me.

I didn't know what to believe anymore.

The police were still investigating but with no solid leads, their theory would hold true and the case would be closed in no time.

Michael O'Shea was no longer my sister's husband; he was now my sister's widower. I wasn't sure what I was. My sister and I had been estranged, and up until three and a half months ago, Michael and I had never met. Still, he'd been the one to call me upon Lizzy's disappearance. Concerned, I came to Boston. Once I'd arrived, I met Clementine, my one-year-old niece, and after that I knew there was no way I was leaving. I fell in love with her the moment I laid eyes on her, and I wanted to be a part of her life. And Michael, not even knowing me, had let me into his daughter's life. Something he didn't have to do.

Then there was Logan McPherson. He had entered my life just over two weeks ago by way of accompanying his father to deliver a threatening message to Michael concerning the missing drugs. My sister had somehow gotten herself involved in a drug ring in which the Irish Mob played some kind of part. The details were sketchy, the facts unclear. What wasn't confusing, though, was Logan's concern for me.

We were drawn to each other in the strangest of ways, and we came together in a way I'd never known with another man.

I'd since come to trust him. To love him. It wasn't that I thought Logan was lying about Michael; it was just that I thought his theory may have been a little tainted. He hated Michael for some reason, and I couldn't help but wonder if that hatred was what was leading him to believe things that just might not be true. Until I could be certain, or, of more concern, in case Logan was correct, I had to focus on convincing Michael to appoint me as Clementine's guardian.

"We're here," Michael said, parking in front of his stately brick home.

"I need to give you the spare garage door opener back. It's in the Mercedes," I said, snapping out of my reverie as I opened the car door.

Stopping me, his hand went to the black hose below the hemline of my dress. "I need to talk to you about that."

In an obvious attempt to remove his hand from my skin, I moved toward the door and turned sideways to look at him. "Sure, what is it?"

"I hate to do this to you, but I'm going to need Elizabeth's car for the new nanny. Unfortunately the engine in Heidi's car died, and she'll need a vehicle to be able to take Clementine places."

Surprised, I said, "Sure, of course. When did you need it by?"

The careful politeness that had developed between us since the night he asked me to do the unthinkable seemed to be thick in the air. "No rush. Just as soon as you can figure something out. I have to go to work on Monday, but I can shuffle back and forth if I need to, and Heidi said she's trying to figure something out. I wouldn't ask, but I'm just worried that if something happens to Clementine, Heidi won't be able to get her where she needs to. I really hate to throw this at you."

He had a point. Besides, I didn't really need a car. The weather was nice and I lived close enough to the boutique to walk. The only issue would be coming to see Clementine, and of course, taking her anywhere, but I'd figure that out later. "No, it's fine. Let me see if Peyton can pick me up later tonight and if so, I can just leave it."

"You're not spending the night?"

"No, I wasn't planning on it."

"Oh, I just thought with everything going on today, you'd want to be close to Clementine."

That horrendous ache in my chest for that sweet girl who'd lost her mother seemed to be moving to all parts of my body. I had to shake it off or it would overpower me. Without explanation, I opened my door and then turned to him. "I'm sorry, Michael, I need some air."

The sound of my door shutting coincided with his door opening. "Elle, wait," he called.

"Michael," someone who had parked behind us called at the same time. I turned back to see a man and a woman who I had seen at the cemetery walking toward him, with a younger man who looked to be around eighteen, possibly their son, between them. The woman had long black hair, the color of licorice. The man had dark brown hair, almost black as well, like Michael's, but it was graying at the temples. His eyes, even from here, looked icy blue. The younger man was a cross between the man and woman, but he had dark brown hair like the man. All three of them were carrying armfuls of flowers.

"Seamus, you didn't need to come," Michael responded in a clipped tone.

Stepping up my pace, I tossed over my shoulder, "I'll see you inside."

My body was trembling and I felt like the sky was falling down on me. But then as soon as I opened the door, I heard the pitter-patter of tiny feet and I felt like I could breathe again.

"Mommy!" Clementine shrieked as she toddled toward me.

My heart went into full-on arrest and panic wrapped around me. Snapping my head back, I saw that Michael was still outside and hadn't heard her. The nanny, on the other hand, was standing in the entrance to the kitchen with a narrowed gaze.

Clementine had been calling me that for almost two weeks now, but never had she done so in front of Michael.

I wasn't certain how to handle it. A part of me loved the very idea that I would get to call this beautiful, precious little girl my daughter. Another part of me knew she wasn't mine, and that Michael wouldn't approve. But the biggest part of me was worried he would approve, and that name would come with a price I couldn't possibly pay. Not now that Logan had entered into my life.

Keenly aware that I would most likely have conceded to such terms before Logan made me feel unbalanced in a way I couldn't wrap my head around, I never wanted to have to choose between Clementine and Logan. I hoped it would never come to that. I'd tried to explain this to Logan this morning but I just couldn't get the words out. If he had even an inkling that Michael had expressed interest in me, I wasn't certain how he'd react. Or maybe I *was* certain. And I couldn't take that chance.

Besides, I rationalized, Michael had never openly made a play for me, or told me directly that he wanted me, *Not yet*, that small voice inside me stressed.

Guilt pricked me for not mentioning my concerns to Logan. I'd been trying to shake my thoughts off as preposterous, but I just couldn't because they simply weren't.

As of late, Michael's desire had been written all over him. It was in his eyes and the way he looked at me, in his lips and the way they parted when he saw me, in his words and the way he spoke them. I think Logan had sensed Michael's interest in me from the first time we met in Michael's office, even though at the time, I was completely unaware of Michael's feelings.

Before now, I had the illusion of his marriage to my sister to hide behind. Now that Lizzy was dead, though, I was worried that once the grieving widower was done mourning, the subtleties would be done, too.

God, I hoped not.

For now, I could handle this. I just had to keep Logan and Michael apart. As much as I wanted to tell Logan how Michael made me feel, it wouldn't help anyone; in fact it could jeopardize my relationship with Clementine, and she was the one thing I couldn't bear to lose.

"Up," that sweet little voice urged.

More than happy to comply, I lifted her and cradled her in my arms. "Have you eaten your lunch, sweet girl?" I asked.

"I was just preparing it," the new nanny, Heidi, said in her German accent.

Heidi was in her mid-twenties and at almost six feet tall, she looked like she should have been a supermodel, not an au pair from Germany who'd just moved in with Michael and my niece.

"Great, I'll sit with her."

As I walked toward the kitchen, I glanced at the photos around the house. Michael's mother, his sister and her family, him and Clementine, just Clementine, but there were none of him and Lizzy, or Lizzy and Clementine.

Out of nowhere, but not for the first time, it struck me that Michael and Lizzy might not have been happily wed. I'd never asked. Yet, there were no pictures of the two of them in the house, no wedding mementos anywhere, and he very rarely talked about her. When he did, she was Elizabeth, a name I know she'd have never allowed, as that was the name our father called her.

"Where's my girl?" Michael called from the front door.

I looked over at him and pushed all of my craziness aside. Today was a day to mourn my sister. Tomorrow, I'd worry about what came next.

"Daddy. Daddy!" Clementine yelled in a burst of excitement.

Right there was the problem. The hex to all the negative theories I had about Michael. He loved his daughter and she loved him. No matter what he was, he was a good father.

And what I wouldn't have given to have had a father like him.

chapter
FIFTEEN

LOGAN

I HAD A TEACHER in the sixth grade who used to nag me about my lack of focus.

If only she could see me now. Every fiber of my being was focused on figuring out what the fuck had happened to not only the rest of the stolen cocaine, but also where the hell the five million dollars in cash was. Gaining this knowledge would help me prove or disprove that O'Shea was way more involved than he let on.

In addition, I still had to figure out what Patrick was really after when he made the demands on O'Shea.

The money?

The drugs?

Lizzy?

The connection?

Everything?

If he was after Lizzy, she wasn't in the picture any longer. Had he taken her out, not O'Shea?

Or was my gut right and there something—*someone*—else also involved?

Obtaining this information was key to keeping Elle safe, on all fronts. It would not only take Tommy and Patrick out of play for the rest of their natural-born lives, but could possibly implicate O'Shea. Fighting fire with fire was my game, and my hope was that Tommy and Patrick were the ones who would get burned. It was also going to help me see just how involved O'Shea was.

Agent Meg Blanchet had gone freezer on me. She hadn't spoken a word to me since she blew a gasket over the hotel fiasco. Of course, she was still also pissed about my lack of delivery and follow-through in the cocaine bust. I wasn't certain whether that was good or bad news. Sure, part of the drugs had shown up right in the Blue Hill Gang's back-yard, and as hard as they tried to deny the connection, the evidence was hard to negate, but still the pipeline was un-known. The source a mystery. The kingpin missing.

My cell rang.

"Yeah," I answered.

"Hey, you're never going to believe this," Miles said excitedly.

"What is it?"

"One of my guys at the BPD said a gang member has agreed to turn state's evidence."

"RICO?"

"Yes, sir.

I slammed the wheel in excitement. "No fucking way."

"Keep it to yourself but I wanted you to know the charges will be filed soon, and then Blanchet will be able to try Patrick and Tommy for the crimes they ordered other members of the gang to commit. Murder, torture, robbery."

"Best news I've heard in a while."

The Racketeering Influenced and Corrupt Organizations Act allowed the DEA to gather enough circumstantial in-formation on someone for him to be formally charged for crimes not directly committed by him but linked through his assistance. If a gang member spilled Tommy and Patrick's outlaw behavior, it would be a huge win for the DEA.

"I thought you'd think so."

"Yeah, thanks again for the heads-up. At least I know for certain they won't be getting out anytime soon."

"Right. I think they'll be locked away for a good, long

time. I'll talk to you later if I hear anything else."

"Thanks again," I said. "Miles, wait, what about—" I called, but he had already disconnected. I tried him back and got voicemail. Hopefully Declan had taken care of the Tommy visit arrangements with Miles.

I downshifted the Rover to take a turn. God, I loved this vehicle. Loved to drive it when I had steam to burn. As long as I was moving fast, I wasn't overthinking everything or doing anything stupid.

Right now, my life felt like it was spinning out of control, and it scared me. Not because I needed to be in control of those around me, but because I wanted to be in charge of my own destiny for once in my life. And that call might have put me one step closer.

Slamming down on the accelerator, I hit the turnpike at high speed. I weaved in and out of the traffic. Faster and faster I took my speed until I was forced to slow down. The exit ramp had a sharp turn and I needed to get to my destination in one piece.

I pulled into the parking lot of the boxing gym around the corner from Declan's coffee shop, Mulligan's Cup, and not much farther from Elle's boutique, The House of Sterling. As I eased my Rover into a spot, I couldn't believe how helpful Declan Mulligan had been. When we were kids he'd hung with Tommy's crowd. He was even the driver the night Tommy attacked me. Somehow he managed to turn his life from shit to something decent, and I think helping me was his way to atone for his sins. And that was something I not only got but also respected.

He'd started seeing Peyton, Elle's employee, and they seemed happy together. Both were artsy and seemed like a good match.

Were Elle and I good match?

For a moment, I just sat there, listening to the engine hum as I tried to pull my thoughts together. I wanted to talk to her. Tell her the news. To atone for my own sins, I guess. But I knew she wouldn't be able to talk and calling her would only piss me off. It had been a long fucking day, though, between the argument I had with Elle this morning, seeing my grandfather and our more than weird conversation, and then watching Elle with O'Shea. Seeing him take her hand to comfort her. That should have been me.

With a shiver, I gazed out at the brick buildings that surrounded me and took more than one calming breath. When the ill feeling passed, I rolled down the window to let the fresh air whisk away the jealousy I couldn't shake.

I was in bad shape.

I just wanted this fucking day to be over. Saturday. All day. Who the hell held a funeral from practically dawn to dusk? I knew I sounded like I was whining because I couldn't be with my girl, but I couldn't help it.

Right then I told myself to stop being a pussy.

Manning up, I grabbed my duffle and moved like lightning out of my vehicle and into the gym. Declan was already at it, punching the bag with a force that told me his mood wasn't much better than mine. I stopped for a moment. Watching him in action made me grin.

Feeling like a caged tiger, I approached him. "Hey, man."

He jerked his chin in response and threw one last punch before tossing me his gloves. He'd called me right after I left my grandfather and told me to meet him here. I didn't have my gear, but I didn't really need it.

Arteries pumping with adrenaline, muscles bunched, ready to punch anything that got in my way, I got to it.

I would have thought all the sex I was having would wear me out. But instead it was having the opposite effect on me. I had more energy and drive than ever. Or maybe it was pent-up frustration I was feeling. Whatever it was, I was going to take it out on the bag.

I let loose a thundering punch.

Declan whistled. "That bad of a day, huh?"

I nodded. "Did you talk to Miles?" I asked.

"Just got off the phone. He said he had just hung up with you when he got word."

"What is it?"

"He can get you in early in the morning, but that's all he can guarantee. Tommy might be moved by afternoon."

I pounded into the bag. "How long will I have?"

"He said fifteen minutes at the most. Go in and tell the guy behind the desk you're Flannigan's new attorney. He'll bring Tommy up and let you in."

My teeth were grinding together, the sweat pouring down my back. I knew gaining visitation wasn't going to be easy. Even as an attorney I hadn't been able to arrange it myself. Luckily, it turned out Miles still had deep connections, and my little upcoming "sit-down" had been arranged courtesy of him.

"Yeah, okay. No one will block me once I pass the desk?" I asked, pulling off my gloves.

"Miles assured me that not a single sheriff in lockup is on the Flannigan family's payroll. He also told me to tell you there's a dark corner in the basement with no security cameras, and for the right price, Tommy could easily be dealt with down there."

Raw punches to the bag were going to leave my knuckles bruised. "If only it were that fucking easy," I muttered. I wasn't a killer, though. I may have crossed the legal line when it came to the drugs, but I wasn't going to cross that line.

"Miles also got one of the cokeheads to talk, but he didn't know much."

I turned for a moment to catch my breath. "What did he say?"

"He doesn't remember exactly where he was buying his product. Just that it was a tall skyscraper down on the waterfront."

The bag once again became my outlet for my anger. "How the fuck doesn't he remember the address?"

Loosening up, Declan reached for the gloves I had tossed and put them back on. "He'd moved on. That was two dealers ago. Miles is going to walk him down there tomorrow night and get him to point the building out. He needs five hundred, though."

I slammed the bag over and over. "Yeah, okay, I'll drop it off when I leave here."

Declan started punching again and we each took our pent-up frustration out on the bag.

I wasn't sure how much time passed, but I was drenched in sweat before my hands began to ache and my muscles burned—this was what I needed.

Declan pointed under the bag. "Hey, man, I think that's enough."

I looked down and sure enough, blood was dripping on the floor. "Probably time to hit the shower."

In the locker room, I let the water sluice down my body. I had to get my shit together. This anger, rage, frustration, or fear, whatever it was, wasn't healthy. I couldn't change the situation Elle and I were in, but if I kept up the way I was, I might just drive her away.

Having realized this, I emerged, feeling like I could handle things better. My goal was right in front of me—bring them all down and close the door behind me.

"Want to talk about it?" Declan asked as he tied his boots.

I slipped a T-shirt over my head. "I was a dick to Elle this morning."

He stood straight. "That's what's bothering you?"

I shook my head. "Yeah."

"Look, man, that's the one thing that has an easy solution."

I furrowed my brows.

"You do what all groveling men do when they fuck up."

Shoving my feet in my sneakers, I glanced over at him, "And what would that be?"

He crossed his arms over his chest and laughed. "Come on, man. Don't you watch the movies?"

My look was one of question.

Declan shook his head. "Buy her candy and flowers."

This time I raised a brow. "That's a little cliché."

"Then do something sweet and romantic. Women can't stay mad at a man for long when he gets all romantic on her."

I shrugged. "Not really my thing."

His quirked smile wasn't making me feel any better. "Well, if you fucked up, you better learn how to make it your thing or get used to sleeping on the couch."

I winced at the thought.

"Trust me, man, and do it. Take it from someone who has way too many ex-girlfriends, if you don't, she won't be your girl for long."

With a sideways glance, I considered what he said.

chapter

SIXTEEN

Elle

I WAS READY TO scream.

The day had been an endless parade of casseroles, neighbors, Michael's colleagues, and I didn't know who else.

It just all seemed so fake.

None of those people knew my sister.

Erin seemed to be doing a good job as hostess and was talking to just about everyone.

At seven thirty, I read Clementine a story and put her to bed. And then when I felt like I couldn't take another moment of "I'm sorry for your loss" from another person who didn't know my sister, I excused myself.

My fingers were just reaching for the handle of the door in the kitchen that led outside when a hand grasped them. "You're Michael's sister-in-law?" a man asked. It was the same man I'd seen with all the flowers in the driveway earlier.

Something about him seemed off and I didn't look up. "Yes," I answered.

"He is very fond of you."

My eyes stayed trained to the floor. "We have a common goal of making sure Clementine is happy despite the sadness surrounding the death of my sister."

"Hmmm . . . yes, the child."

I didn't like the way he'd said that. "Clementine," I reaffirmed.

"Yes, Clementine."

Chills ran down my spine. I didn't like the way he'd said her name.

"Are you going outside?" he asked.

"No, I was just making sure the door was locked," I lied and then stepped back, not sure why but knowing I didn't want to be alone with him.

"Seamus." Michael's voice sounded like a warning.

The man turned and walked toward Michael. "There you are, we need to talk."

With a deep breath, I tuned them out and went back into the living room, where I sat on the sofa and watched Michael and this man discuss something heated. When they went out the back door, I took advantage of the coast being clear.

Frazzled and done, I slipped out the front door without saying goodbye to anyone. Peyton was waiting for me outside and I didn't want to chance another uncomfortable conversation with anyone today. I'd call Michael tomorrow and explain. Mental exhaustion had long since set in and I just wanted to go home. I needed to see Logan.

Peyton drove a silver Prius, and she had parked as close to the house as the trail of cars would allow. I walked down the sidewalk in my black pumps that were demanding to be taken off, and when I saw her flash her lights, I was thankful I didn't have much farther to go.

Bracing myself for an onslaught of questions I didn't want to have to answer, I swung open the passenger door and collapsed into the seat.

"Are you okay?" she asked.

The concern in her voice was hard to deny and it eased my agitation. "I will be. I just want to get home and out of these clothes."

She pressed the gas and started driving. "Do you want to talk about it?"

I looked down at the new black trench I had bought—guaranteed to repel the rain—and surprisingly found myself wanting to tell her everything. "I do, Peyton, just not today."

"Okay. No pressure from me," she said.

Mascara came away on my fingertips when I rubbed my eyes, suddenly more tired than I'd felt in a very long time. To avoid the awkward silence, I simply said, "Like I said in my text, the new nanny's car broke down and Michael needed his back."

She nodded. "Yeah, I get it. He's still an asshole."

"Peyton, he's not. He wants the nanny to be able to take Clementine where she needs to go. I get it. And besides, it feels wrong driving my dead sister's car."

The traffic was light but still she eased up on the gas, perhaps to give us more time. "As opposed to driving your drug addict sister's car?"

I hated that I couldn't tell her the truth. Tell her that Michael had told everyone my sister was in rehab when in reality, he had no idea where she had been. But that information was linked to the missing drugs, and the fewer people who knew about that situation, the better.

Michael and I had gone to the police station separately this morning. We were both told trace amount of drugs were found in Lizzy's system but there was evidence of long-term addiction. This only reaffirmed the preliminary police report that she was, more than likely, a victim of a drug deal gone bad.

During his visit, Michael had to fess up to not knowing her whereabouts for the past three and a half months, and that didn't sit well with him. It was on record that Lizzy wasn't in drug rehab, and now he would have to watch what he said during his campaign so as not to contradict what he had already told others. Of course, he wasn't talking about it to me.

That was all I knew.

However, I was certain he had to be a suspect.

He hadn't told me that, though.

He hadn't told me much.

Peyton's eyes were on me. "Elle, did you hear me?"

When I turned to look at her, out of nowhere, I found myself laughing so hard I couldn't even get my words out in one cohesive sentence. "When you . . . put it . . . that way . . . I guess it shouldn't really matter."

Peyton reached her hand over and took mine. It wasn't until then that I realized I was crying. It was the laughter that prevented me from speaking; it was the sobs that had gotten stuck in my throat. "It's okay, Elle, let it out."

If only she could really understand, but then again, I wasn't even certain I did.

My life had changed so much in the past three months. Before coming to Boston, my biggest worry was what take-out restaurant to eat from and what television show I wanted to accompany the meal. With everything that was happening around me, my life should have felt tilted, off balance, but instead it felt more right than it ever had. And I knew why. I also knew I had to tell Logan everything. I'd intended to tell him about how broken I was the night he came back to me, but then he told me about Lizzy and I just couldn't.

Sitting here, thinking through everything, I realized Logan was the only real thing in my life. Maybe the only real thing I'd ever had in my life, and I couldn't lose him. I had to have faith in him. I couldn't continue to keep secrets from him—not about Michael and not about me.

Tomorrow would be the day of reckoning.

"Are you sure you don't want me to come in?" Peyton asked when she pulled up to my place.

"No, I'm fine. It's been a long day. I'm exhausted and just want to go to bed."

"Okay, call me tomorrow if you need anything. I'll be at the boutique for a few hours in the morning doing inventory."

"Peyton, I don't want you going there alone. I finished

everything yesterday. There's nothing left for you to do."

"There's always something to do and you know it. Besides, I refuse to let some asshole scare me. But if it makes you feel better, Declan doesn't have to work until the afternoon and he's coming with me."

I put my arms out and hugged her fiercely. "I'm so sorry."

She returned my hug. "Stop saying that. It wasn't your fault and I'm fine."

I drew in a breath and tried to give her a smile. "Thank you, for everything."

As I got out, she yelled, "Don't forget, call me if you need anything."

My eyes landed on Logan's vehicle and my heart started to thump wildly. "I will."

The Range Rover was parked under the trees across the street, but I still saw it. He was here. Waiting for me.

The squeak of my front door made me jump. When I turned around, it was open and Logan was standing there watching me, one shoulder pressed against the doorframe. His beautiful hair was slicked back and I knew he must have recently showered. Wearing a pair of black track pants, a white T-shirt, no shoes or socks, and with his hands in his pockets, he couldn't have looked sexier. My pulse started to race with each step I took closer to him. I had really missed him today despite our earlier argument.

All I could do was hope he wasn't still upset. As I got closer, I just wasn't certain. There was a blank look on his face, but that was all I saw. The brooding side I'd seen this morning was definitely gone.

"You're home," I said with a smile.

A slight nod acknowledged what was obvious and a hand on the small of my back guided me inside.

As soon as my feet hit the wooden floor of the front entrance, I reached back and took one, then the other, shoe off.

I could feel his eyes on me and once my shoes were off, his hands were on the front of my coat and unbuttoning my trench with an energy that electrified the air. "I'm sorry about the way I left things this morning," he whispered in my ear.

A thrill of excitement ran through me as his warm breath swooshed down my neck.

Like a whirlwind, I turned and flung my arms around his neck, all but collapsing against his strong body. "No, I'm the one who's sorry. I should have listened to your concerns."

In that way he knows how to make me feel like I'm the only thing that matters, he took my face between his strong, powerful hands. "Hey, talk to me. What's going on? Why did Peyton drive you home? Did the Mercedes break down? Why wouldn't you have called me?"

My tears were like a waterfall and although I tried to speak, my words were utterly incomprehensible. It had been such a long day, and I thought I would be much stronger about today's events than I actually had been.

Logan clutched me to his chest and gently stroked my hair. "Shhh . . . don't cry. I know how hard today must have been for you. That's why I wanted to be there for you. That's why I was there at a distance. It wasn't because I thought you weren't safe, but because I wanted to be able to comfort you if you needed it."

If that just didn't make me cry even harder. "I love you. I can't lose you."

He pulled back and gripped my upper arms. "Hey, where's this coming from? You're not going to lose me."

"Besides Clementine, you're all I have left in this world. Without you, I'd be practically all alone." The thought made me shudder and I squeezed my eyes shut. I didn't want to be alone anymore.

"Hey, look at me."

I opened my eyes to see those hazel pools gazing at me. I felt like it had been so long since he'd held me.

"I love you. I know I don't say it enough, but I do."

I nodded. I knew he did, but would he still when I

confessed what I had yet to tell him?

His fingers went back to unbuttoning my coat. "Let's get this off."

My coat peeled off easily, but the revelations from the day would stay with me forever. Out of his arms, I could think more clearly. It was as if my emotions were running on high octane. Recognizing this, I went to sit on the steps to talk to him from a distance. I wiped my tears away with the back of my hand. "About the Mercedes, Clementine's new nanny's car is in the shop and Michael is going back to work Monday, and he needed it so Clementine wasn't left at home stranded."

Sugarcoating the issue by not telling him that Michael had asked for the car back wasn't the smartest idea but I didn't want to upset Logan, and I knew explaining the situation the way I had with Peyton would. Tomorrow I'd tell him everything; tonight I needed him. It was selfish, but for once that's what I wanted to be.

He stepped forward and crouched down in front of me. "It's not that big of a deal." He wiped a stray tear away with his thumb. "You hated that car anyway. You can drive mine until we go get you a new one."

My voice was still shaky with tears. "What will you drive?"

"My old man's license is still suspended, so I'll take his car."

Distance had sounded like a good idea a minute ago but now that he was so close, I just couldn't keep my hands off him. My palms slid from his chest to his well-defined shoulders. "Are you sure?"

That long, lean body eased forward and I found myself lying back against the stairs with him hovering over me. "There are a lot of things I'm not sure about, Elle, but you aren't one of them."

Breathless, I found it hard to talk, to think. "I meant that you love that Range Rover."

"I know what you meant," he said, his mouth moving

close to mine.

"I was thinking of getting a Prius like Peyton's," I babbled. "It's really cute."

"Whatever you want. Give me a few weeks to get the money together, and we'll go pick one out."

I shoved him back. "You aren't buying me a car. That's not what I meant. I meant as soon as I can save some money."

Ignoring my little outburst, he stood and reached out a hand. "Come with me, I want to show you something."

Butterflies swarmed in my belly as I took his hand.

Connected, he led us up the stairs, through my room, and then stopped at the closed bathroom door.

Perplexed, I waited for him to turn around.

When he did, his smile alone practically seduced me.

I had no idea what we were doing outside my bathroom door but with the way he was looking at me, I didn't care if we were fixing the rattling pipes.

Dropping his hold on me, he grasped the old glass knob and pushed the door open to my tiny bathroom.

I couldn't believe what I saw.

The old-fashioned black-and-white tile floor was aglow with dozens of small red tea candles carefully placed around the perimeter. The claw-foot tub was filled with water and red rose petals were floating on the surface. There was a bottle of wine with a single glass beside it on the marble counter that held the sink.

My hands flew to my mouth. "It's beautiful."

A shyness crossed his face. I'd seen it a few times, but it wasn't until right now that I figured out what caused it. He was nervous when he did anything even slightly romantic. And, God, if I didn't find that utterly adorable. "You think?"

"I know."

Those magical fingers started to unzip my simple black shift. "I wanted to do something to make you feel better."

A shiver rocked my body as his hands glided up my

back to my shoulders to slip the fabric of my dress down. One, then the other, and then it fell to the ground and left me standing in my bra, underwear, and hose.

It felt like the room was spinning, but it was me. He'd spun me back toward him and we were moving in a small circle. My head on his shoulder. His arms around me. Mine around him. No, we weren't just moving, we were dancing. Dancing right in the middle of my bathroom.

There wasn't any music, but we didn't need it as we danced to the beat of our own thumping hearts.

As if the song was about to end, Logan stopped our movement and unclasped my bra, making my heart race even faster. "The water will be cold if you wait much longer," he whispered.

I looked up into heavy-lidded eyes. "Then I'd better get in," I said as I stepped back. Feeling seductive, I ran my hands down my body to my thighs and began to slide my hose down, slowly, seductively, leaving my skimpy panties on.

Logan sucked in a breath as he watched me. He had drifted over toward the small vanity and was leaning against it.

Nine at night and I found myself doing my first quasi striptease. My thumbs hooked into the sides of my panties and I eased them down even slower than I had with my hose before I stepped out of them.

Logan's track pants did nothing to hide the sign of his arousal. Knowing I could do that to him made me feel powerful and I wanted to see just how far over the edge I could take him.

My pulse racing, I stepped into the lukewarm water of the tub. The water temperature was irrelevant because it was about a million degrees in this small space. I slid down at what normally would have been the foot of the tub, but I wanted Logan to have a bird's-eye view of me and I also still wanted to be able to see him.

Once I was fully submerged, I let my legs drift apart as

seductively as I could. "Aren't you coming in?"

His lips parted and his tongue snuck out to lick around them. "The plan was to pour you a glass of wine and let you relax in private."

I bit my lip. "I'm not thirsty and I don't want to be alone."

Logan leaned back and gripped the counter.

I let my hands roam my body.

His eyes were on me like a hawk's.

My hands drifted down a bit farther. "See something you like?"

He nodded. "Yeah, I do."

"Come in."

He shook his head. "I want to watch you make yourself come."

His command was as much unexpected as expected. I knew I was headed that way the moment I took my hose off, but actually touching myself was another thing. It's not that I hadn't masturbated before. I'd done that and a whole lot more. But every first time with Logan made it feel like my first time all over again. And in a way it was. With him I felt everything. Every ounce of pleasure, every intense touch, every small kiss. Whereas before him I felt like I was removed from the act, with him I felt like the star.

Sometimes the best way to do something is just to drop your insecurities and plunge forward.

He whispered my name, "Elle."

My gaze swung to his.

"Touch yourself," he clarified in a guttural tone.

I didn't make him wait. My fingers drifted down my belly, the water lapping over my breasts with the slight movement.

His eyes started fluttering closed, his lashes dark on his cheekbones. "Not there. Not yet. Your beautiful tits. Start with those."

The rasp in his voice thrilled me. I had never actually fondled my own breasts. I couldn't imagine I'd feel anything by doing that, but I complied and palmed each of my breasts with my hands.

Logan's cock had jutted straight out by now and there was no denying how much this was turning him on. I was going to do this and more. I was going to push him right over the edge.

"Use your thumbs." His voice was hoarse. Low.

My thumbs passed over my nipples as the water rippled around them and when they became small hard peaks, I started pinching them. A little pain. Just a little.

Tiny pricks of pleasure radiated around them and I couldn't believe it.

His eyes were watching my every movement. His breathing was ragged. I could see the rise and fall of his chest.

I wasn't sure if it was his reaction to what I was doing or the act itself that was turning me on, but I supposed it didn't really matter. I knew if I had been doing this alone, I wouldn't feel a smidgen of what I was feeling now.

Feeling bold, I left one hand where it was and let the other drift down and find the nodule of my clit. Working them in the same manner, I began to feel the same small fissures of pleasure below my waist that I was feeling above it. Sparks tingled along my entire torso.

"Does that feel good?" His voice shifted again. It was a little huskier. A little lower.

Such an incredible turn-on.

Working both small, tight buds at the same time, I found myself almost panting when I answered, "Yes."

His eyes were trained on my pussy. "Tell me what you feel."

I pushed my thighs apart as wide as I could, slipping the leg farther from him over the edge of the tub.

His gasp sounded like a growl.

Soon, I needed more and inserted a finger inside myself. "I feel your cock inside me, moving, in, out, in, out."

The face he made was utterly sensual.

My hand was moving faster and the water splashed out of the tub.

"Fuck," he muttered. He moved closer and sat on the edge of the tub. The end where the water controls were, at my feet. I thought he might come even closer. Put his hands in the water, his fingers inside me, but he stayed where he was.

My heart skipped against my chest.

"Are you going to come?" he asked.

It took some effort to speak. I had to lick my lips first. "I might. I'm not sure."

He spanned the distance between where he stood and the tub and took hold of my foot, kissing it before submerging it back into the water. "I want you to stop before you do. Can you do that?"

My pace, up until he had come so close, had been steady and even. With Logan this close, I wanted to speed it up, to feel even more, but I knew if I did, I just might come. "I can try. Can you do something for me?"

Everything about him at the moment was serious but at my question, the corners of his mouth tipped up. "I can try."

My hand stopped manipulating my breast, but the hand below the water continued moving at the torturous slow pace. "Take your clothes off. I want to see you naked."

His answer came in the form of a low groan as he removed his clothes with quick efficiency. He must have known I was watching him because he stood there for a moment and let me stare at his naked form. His cock was beautiful. Long, thick, and ready for me. The rest of him was equally magnificent. Abs ripped, muscles lean, thighs just right.

I had all but stopped what I was doing, but my tripping heart hadn't figured that out. Pulse pounding, heart thumping, I sucked in a breath. I must have blinked because when I did, I opened my eyes and he was sitting again, much, much closer this time.

Something flickered in his gaze. Hot. Intense. Sexy. His hand slid around to the back of my neck. One by one, he tugged out the pins holding my hair up and they fell into the water. Once they were all out, my hair tumbled to my shoulders. With it down, Logan easily threaded his fingers through my hair. Then he pulled, tilting my head back and exposing my throat.

Everything about the two of us was gasoline and a match. One touch and we were on fire. Ablaze. Flames out of control, unable to be doused.

His lips brushed mine as he whispered, "I don't think I even said hello yet."

The water had started to cool, but I didn't care.

I bit down on his lip. "Hi."

He smiled. "Hi."

Those lips slid along my jaw to behind my ear, where he pressed them. His mouth didn't stop there. He trailed his lips lower, grazing my skin with his teeth along the way.

"Do you like this too?"

"Yes," I gasped.

His hand was under the water and he was doing what I had done, thumping my nipple. It didn't feel the same. It felt so much better. His touch spiraled through me, causing my body to arch and water to lap around the edge of the tub.

"I got you wet," I purred as I tried to reach for his cock, but he wouldn't let me.

Instead he leaned down lower, his hand sliding lower too, right to the place my hand had been moving moments ago. "I can take care of that," he said, and then his hand left the sanctuary of my pussy.

It was then I noticed bruising on his knuckles. "What happened?"

He shook his head. "Nothing to worry about. I went to the boxing gym without my gloves."

"Logan, why?"

His gaze held me in a trance, and I knew I should drop it

or what we were doing just might come to a dead halt. So, I did.

Logan pulled the plug and then was back. His hand resumed its previous position, and it was as if the sound of the water echoing in the bathroom matched the rhythm of his skilled fingers.

Magic fingers plunged inside me and I felt my clit swell under his touch. "Oh, God."

"Do you like that?" The grit and huskiness in his voice made my stomach flip.

"Yes," I moaned, pressing my feet to the bottom of the tub and thrusting upward.

The movement of his had stopped and he leaned down to kiss me. "Tell me you want to come."

"I want to come." My own voice was hoarse.

His lips were at my shoulder and he bit it. "Tell me I'm the only one you'll ever allow to make you come."

I gasped and my heart started to race in anticipation. "You're the only one who will ever make me come."

The last of the water sluiced down the drain and as if on cue, his fingers started to move again. The bath oil from the water acted as a lubricant and allowed them to slide in and out so easily. It felt so incredibly good.

His thumb stroked me and his fingers moved at a punishing pace. "Tell me you're mine," he whispered in a guttural voice.

With the thrill of those words, my orgasm rolled through me like a storm. "I'm yours," I called out as my body started to unravel and I lost myself to the sweet pleasure of nothingness. Like thunder and lightning, the storm consumed me, pounding throughout my body in sweeping waves. When it started to calm and seemed to reach the vast horizon, I opened my eyes to see his looking back at me.

Desire was written all over his face. He reached a hand out, "Come here."

I took it and launched myself at him, wrapping my arms around his neck, and holding him tightly. He needed to know Michael meant nothing to me. I hadn't seen that. I'd been blind to the fact that it was killing him for me to spend time with another man, even if it was only because of that man's child. "I don't want anyone but you," I reassured him. "Forever," I added, and wondered if I shouldn't have said that.

Logan had his arms around my waist and he lifted me out of the tub like I weighed nothing. "Forever," he repeated.

Something a little giddy shook inside me, because there was absolutely no denying I was his and he was mine.

As soon as my bare toes hit the tile, Logan grabbed a towel and wrapped it around me.

I let it absorb some of the water and then slipped it off. Barefoot, I had to tilt my head to look at him. "Take me to bed and make love to me," I whispered.

Fire burned in his eyes. "There's nothing I want to do more."

Our mouths met, ravenous and devouring. Hungry for only each other.

When I was with Logan like this, there was just him and me, and everything that wasn't quite right around us disappeared.

We spent the rest of the night making love over and over. It was the best way we had of communicating with each other. Of letting our feelings for each other truly shine. Words just didn't seem to be enough. Not in the midst of the craziness that surrounded us, anyway.

When we were both sated and spent, he pulled me to him. My back was to his front, in a spooning position.

Finding comfort in him, I molded my body to his as tightly as I could and then turned my head. "How did you know to get red candles and red flowers?"

Logan let out a breath and kissed my forehead. "Because red is your favorite color."

Overwhelmed that he had figured that small detail out on his own, that he paid enough attention to me to notice, I started to weep.

"It's nothing to cry about," he soothed.

"I can't help it."

"Come here," he said, turning me toward him.

Tangling in the sheets, I rolled my body to face his. "Do you want to know why red is my favorite color?"

Logan used his thumbs to brush away the tears sliding down my cheeks. "If you want to tell me."

I did. This was something I'd never told another. "Because it represents the warrior inside myself."

His voice was soft. "Red is definitely a color of strength."

My eyes on his, I opened up even more. "It's more than that, though."

"Tell me," he whispered.

I nodded. "We were living in France and I was going to school on base since I didn't know the language. They were having an eighth-grade father-and-daughter ball, and I was so excited. I'd never gone to a ball and I'd never gotten to be a princess. I was twelve, but I still loved Disney movies. My sister thought it was ridiculous. I didn't care, because I knew just what I wanted to wear—a red dress. *Mulan* had just come out and I wanted to be just like her. I was determined to be a legendary princess warrior."

Logan leaned toward me and kissed the corner of my mouth where the tears had accumulated. "I can believe that."

I took a deep breath and blinked away the blur. I wasn't crying over what I was about to tell him. The incident had long ago passed. I was crying that he cared enough about me to figure things out no one had ever even attempted. "My father didn't like us to spend money on needless things but my mother thought that occasion deserved a new dress, so she took me shopping and I found the most perfect red satin dress. It was almost identical to Mulan's. When I put it on I felt strong and brave—it represented everything I wanted to be. My mother did my hair and I got all ready and then waited for my father. He was late, as usual, and beeped the horn for me to come out when he arrived. I had my coat on already and ran to the car."

Logan was softly caressing the bare flesh of my shoulder, and I had nestled myself farther into his chest as I continued to speak.

"Needless to say, my father didn't see my dress until we arrived at the dance. As soon as I took my coat off, his nostrils flared. I knew he was angry but had no idea why. The night went on and I had fun walking around. When it was time for the fathers to dance with their daughters, mine was nowhere to be found, so I stood alone in the corner where no one could see me. As soon as the dance ended, my father grabbed my arm and told me it was time for us to leave. By then he smelled of alcohol and I knew he was drunk. We got in the car and he turned toward me and said one thing, and one thing only to me. It wasn't how pretty I looked, or how proud he was of me, though; he simply told me only whores wear red."

"Fucking asshole," Logan muttered under his breath.

I lifted my head. "Without another word, he took me home and ordered me to my room to take my dress off. Once I did, he took it and locked the door. He and my mother argued for a long while, but I don't really remember what was said. What I do remember, though, is the next day my dress had been shredded like pieces of red silk ribbon and was laying all over my parents' entire room. I vowed not to cry for that dress. And I didn't. Instead, I vowed to be stronger and to not allow him to crush my spirit. Ever since that day, red has been my favorite color. He might have had a need to control everything in our house, but I knew I'd never let him control who I was."

Logan pulled me to him and held me tightly, stroking my back with his fingers. "I can't even tell you how sorry I am that you grew up with a man like him for a father. You're beautiful, Elle, inside and out. Despite him."

There was probably something more to say, something profound, like that my inner warrior blossomed under his tyranny, but exhaustion had taken hold of me and I closed my eyes.

His voice was soft when he spoke. "Hey, I have to leave early in the morning. Miles arranged for me to see Tommy, and then I need to run by Brighton House and check on my gramps. Do you want to drop me off at my old man's first thing tomorrow, or can you wait until I get back and we can go pick up his car then?" he asked quietly.

My sleepy eyes had just begun to fall into slumber but now popped open. I turned to look at him. "Why are you going to see Tommy? Nothing has happened. Why can't we just leave things alone?"

He swiped the hair from my face. "It doesn't work that way. And I don't want us looking over our shoulders, waiting for something to happen. I can't live like that."

With a sigh, I turned back and laced my hand in his. "I'll wait until you get back."

He squeezed me tightly. "It'll be all right, Elle. I promise."

I think I nodded.

"Good night," he whispered.

I closed my eyes again and dreaded the coming of tomorrow for so many reasons.

chapter

SEVENTEEN

DAY 17

LOGAN

THE FUCKER WAS SMILING like he'd just gotten a *get out of jail free card.*

His arms were tatted up, half-sleeves to his elbows. His eyebrow was missing a ring that the Suffolk County Sheriff's Department must have confiscated. His dark blue eyes, mousey brown hair, and sharp jawline were staring at me, daring me to set foot inside.

No dare was necessary.

He had no idea.

I was more than ready for this.

Just seeing him unfurled a lifetime of hatred. I could feel my jaw clench and my fists ball at my sides.

Easy, I thought.

Control.

Focus.

Stick to the plan.

Don't act like you did the last time.

Just get in, get what you need, do what you have to, and get out.

Fifteen minutes was all I had to get enough to make it look like he was a rat. And in doing so, set myself free. You see, a rat would be extricated from his power faster than lightning would strike a pole in a storm.

Tommy Flannigan might have thought he was untouchable, but he couldn't be more wrong. His coveted status as the son of the Blue Hill Gang's boss didn't mean shit to me, and soon enough it wouldn't mean shit to anyone else.

The number two, second in command, son of the boss—soon none of that would matter.

I couldn't wait.

He was pure evil.

Vile.

Ruthless.

Scum of the earth.

No one was off-limits to him—but me.

And if that didn't put a smile on my face.

He hated me.

It was mutual.

Blamed me for his unwed pregnant sister's suicide.

I blamed him for so much more.

Unfortunately for me, he also held the key to my kingdom in his hand. He was everywhere, even locked up, and I knew it. That's why I was doing this. I just hoped my plan worked.

The Nashua Street Jail was a maximum-security facility in Boston and it was no playground. But I wasn't looking to play. That note. That note that read *The letter E wasn't meant for Emily* was a threat. A threat I wasn't going to push under the rug or cower down to. This time, I was going to fight, tooth and nail, with anything and everything I had.

"Ready?" the voice behind me asked.

Snapping out of my thoughts, I couldn't help but admit, "Ready isn't even close."

The uniform laughed like he hated the motherfucker sitting at the steel table almost as much as I did. Gave me hope that Tommy's stay would be anything but pleasant despite any connections his father might have.

The door opened into the small room. All the furniture was bolted to the floor, the overhead light had a cage around it, and security cameras were in every corner. A malfunction with the sound couldn't be helped, but courtesy of Miles there would be lots of pictures. Lots of proof that Tommy Flannigan was turning against his father, against the Blue Hill Gang. Or at least that was how it was going to look before I finished with him. First a visit from me, then one from the Attorney General's office, on a Sunday nonetheless, the big favor Miles had arranged, should do the job. No doubt Tommy wouldn't say anything to either of us, but no one else had to know that.

Dressed in his prison uniform and shackled in chains, I found myself hesitating for a moment before stepping into the same room as Tommy Flannigan. Old instincts died hard. Last time I saw him our face-to-face wasn't so civilized. But this time, I reminded myself, it would be. It had to be.

"Just knock on the door if you need anything," the corrections officer told me.

I gave him a nod. "Will do."

Tommy was positioned directly in the middle of the table with his cuffed hands on its surface. He didn't look up when the door closed or at the sound of my feet on the linoleum floor. Instead, his eyes were trained on the tabletop.

With steady strides, I eased toward him, taking my time, rehearsing my words in my head. My nerves were locked down deep inside me. To anyone on the outside I looked rock solid. The fabric of my slacks hid the quivering in my legs. Just before I reached the table, I forced my knees to steady.

My shadow loomed large over his small body as I strode toward him. When I came to a halt, his head snapped up and lifeless eyes stared back at me in a suddenly expressionless face. Something had shifted in the sixty seconds since he glared at me through the window.

I placed my palms on the table, leaned down, and stared back at him, my expression just as flat as his. "What's the matter? Cat got your tongue?"

His lips twitched into a dangerous smile. "McPherson."

And then, there it was, the hatred. The one thing no one can keep locked inside.

My hands stayed steady on the table as I leaned down. "Flannigan."

"I knew you'd come see me."

Every muscle in my body went taut. "I want to kill you with my bare hands."

"Come on. You don't really mean that, do you? I saved your ass by never telling my old man Emily was pregnant. You owe me."

My teeth clenched. "I don't owe you shit."

Fire seemed to light in his eyes. "It wasn't for you anyway. I wasn't sure if it was yours and if my old man looked into it, he might not like what he found out." He shrugged his shoulders. "Had to protect my boys."

I didn't believe him for a minute. He'd never let anyone touch his sister. She was the only thing he ever cared about.

Ignoring his poor attempt to goad me, I leered at him. I was here to make it look like he was turning against the Blue Hill Gang. My way of protecting Elle. I had to remember that. I had to keep my shit together.

"Sit down." He motioned with his chin to the only other chair in the room. "We have a lot to discuss."

Controlling my urge to fling myself over the table and choke the life out of him, I remained where I was. "I think I'll stand."

He shrugged. "Then I think this visit is over. And here I was hoping to have a heart-to-heart about your girl. Elle, isn't it?"

My fingers pressed the table so hard my knuckles were turning white. Still, I knew I couldn't give him the upper hand. If I did, he'd see through my real reason for this visit. That it was a show. A picture to present to the world. A lie. A well-thought-out lie. He'd asked me here. Had something he needed to tell me. Why me? Who else did he have to turn to that wasn't on Patrick's payroll? I was fucking perfect. Thoughts back in the game, without a word, I slid backward and started for the door, hoping his need to taunt me would far surpass his need to flex any control he thought he might have over me.

"Hey," he called, the quiver in his voice giving him away.

Triumphant, I turned around.

He was sitting up straighter and that smile had slipped from his lips. "Come back here. You're going to want to hear what I have to tell you."

My lips twisted. "What exactly do you think you have to say that I want to hear?" My tone was light, breezy. Very *I don't give a shit* because I really didn't give a shit.

"I know things you're going to want to hear."

"I doubt it."

"About Elle's sister."

"Like what?" I practically spit.

"Like who killed her."

That got my attention, and in three strides I was back at the table. "What are you talking about?"

Those hard eyes narrowed on me and then toward the chair.

Not playing, truly curious, I lowered myself into the seat. "Explain to me what you're talking about."

"I know who killed her." His voice broke.

The motherfucker had feelings for Elle's sister—it was written all over his face. You had to be shitting me. "You know who killed Elizabeth O'Shea?"

He nodded his head.

"Why are you telling me this?"

"Because she deserves justice."

I had to laugh. "And I'm supposed to believe you care . . . why?"

"Because I fucking loved her."

Noises of disbelief escaped my throat. I couldn't help it.

"You have to go after him."

"I don't have to do shit."

"You're the only one I've got, man."

The hairs on my neck stood up. Desperate. He was desperate. I didn't have to put on a show after all. He really was going to talk. "And who exactly is *him*? Who do you think killed Lizzy?"

"It's not who I think killed her. It's who I *know* killed her."

"Who?" My voice rose.

He leaned forward. "Her fucking husband did it." He practically spit the word *husband*.

I might have thought that too but with him telling me, now I wasn't so sure. How could I believe him? "Are you sure it wasn't you?"

His cuffed hands gripped the table and his face turned red. "I told you, I loved her."

"Like that means shit to me."

"Listen to me. He stole the drugs from us and later he killed her."

Something in my mind scrambled. I knew Michael had to have been playing some kind of game with the drugs. I just didn't know why he'd put everyone around him in jeopardy if he had them. "What the fuck are you talking about?"

That taunting smile was back. "Oh, did I get your attention now? Worried about your precious Elle being around him?"

"Don't say her name," I fucking growled.

He remained silent.

Pulling my shit together, I inched back in my chair. "Yeah, you got my attention, but not for long."

"I'm not fucking around with you. I've told the guards at least a hundred times that I know who killed her and not a single fucking one of them will pay any attention to me."

My heart was racing but I remained calm. We weren't buddies and he wasn't looking to help me out. "And you think I will?"

"Yeah, I do. You're smart enough to know, once a killer, always a killer. Extrapolate from there, Silver Spoon."

I didn't let him rattle me. "What do you think I can do with this information?"

"Make the motherfucker pay!" he seethed.

My cough couldn't disguise my laugh. "You want him to pay? Are you fucking kidding me? What about you? What about *your* sins? You're the one who should pay."

He was shaking his head. "This isn't about you, McPherson."

Now I laughed out loud. "No, it's not. But for some fucked-up reason I'm the one who's here. Why didn't you just send one of your crew to take care of him, like you did me? Oh wait, that's right—because you can't be there to watch, you sick fuck." My emotions were taking over. *Reel it in, McPherson. Reel it in. The plan is going better than expected. Don't fuck it up.*

With his hands, he tried to shake the table. "This isn't about you. Or me. I'm in here; what more do you want?"

Focus. I had to focus. He was right. "I know that," I seethed. "But like I said, I'm the one who's here. So tell me, why not use your crew?"

"You really don't know what's going on, do you?"

I stared at him flatly, giving nothing away.

"I don't have a crew left."

My brows popped. "What the fuck are you talking about?"

Tommy eased forward. "My father put a hit out on me. As soon as I get out of solitary, I'm a dead man."

Holy shit!

My worries about Elle's safety, when it came to Tommy anyway, might just be over. Looked like my plan to remove Tommy from the equation was going to be taken care of courtesy of Patrick Flannigan, fuck him very much. I should have left right then and there, but I didn't. "Why would your father put a hit out on you?" I asked, trying not to sound triumphant. I still wasn't entirely buying what he was feeding me.

"He found out what I was doing. That I was trying to

break free of him. And that I'd been using his money as capital to buy drugs. Found out I had a part in losing the two hundred and fifty kilos of coke. Found out I'd fucked everything up."

My head was spinning and still back at the lost crew. "So you can't hurt Elle?"

That sinister laugh was back. "Aren't you fucking listening to me? I don't give a shit about her. I want Lizzy's death avenged."

I narrowed my eyes on him. "Then why did you send me the note?"

He laughed. "That note I sent you was just to make sure you ended up finding me. When I sent it Lizzy had gone missing again. At the time, I thought you could help me find her. I didn't know she was already at the bottom of the fucking river. You can rest assured your little girlfriend is safe, from me anyway. I promised Lizzy I'd leave her sister and her kid out of this."

Relief crashed over me.

Could I really trust him, though?

Was he playing a game too?

My jaw twitched. "What about the girl you attacked outside the boutique?"

"She was collateral damage."

I pushed against the table. "What the fuck are you talking about?"

"I thought she was Lizzy's sister. She was wearing the same red hat I'd seen her sister wearing."

Anger ripped through me. "You just told me you promised Lizzy you wouldn't hurt her sister. Now you're telling me you thought it was her when you carved up her skin. Make up your fucking mind and stop feeding me a line of bullshit."

"It's not like that. The night before, Lizzy had gone missing, and I needed to keep you away from her sister in case she was somewhere out there waiting to talk to her. And the only way I could think of to make sure you stayed clear of her sister was to leave my mark."

I found myself in a haze of needing to know what the fuck he was talking about. "You have less than three minutes to make any sense out of all this bullshit. After that I'm walking."

He sucked in a breath. "It all started when Lizzy and I had decided to take off. We were going to grab the kid and leave Boston. Disappear. But in the midst of making out plans, I got this call with an offer I couldn't turn down."

"What kind of offer?"

His smile was sly. "One that would make me more powerful than my old man."

"What kind of offer?" I repeated. Like I cared about his power trip.

"To be a wholesaler for the biggest drug supplier in Boston. Me. To be one step under the top of the cocaine chain. It had the potential to be a fucking gold mine."

"Who was the supplier?"

He shook his head.

I rolled my eyes. "Okay, so what happened next?"

"I told Lizzy that we couldn't leave. That I was going to make so much money it would be worth staying. She agreed and even offered to help me unload the product. We started pushing the coke and just like I thought, were making money hand over fist."

He said the last part with a pride that nauseated me.

"It wasn't long before I was able to increase my buys. The supplier was happy. I was happy. I was doing a fucking great job. But Lizzy wasn't happy. She still wanted to leave town. She didn't like her life and she was ready to start over somewhere else. The thing was, I wasn't."

"Who was the supplier?" I asked again.

He laughed, but this time he answered. "Come on, you have to know. The Priest."

"What's his fucking real name?" I demanded.

He shook his head. "I don't fucking know."

Doubtful, I narrowed my eyes at him. Was he feeding

me a bunch of bullshit? Maybe. Still, I didn't stop him. I wanted to hear what he had to say. "Go on."

"One morning when I was about to make my biggest buy yet she shows up. Said she couldn't stay in that house one more minute. I was in a hurry. She had parked behind me. We took the Mercedes and the five mil and went to make the buy."

Five mil. *The missing money.* It was beginning to make sense. "But," I interjected.

"The shit storm that followed is still a blur. The exchange went off without a hitch. On the way back to my place, I was out of cigarettes and asked her to stop at a corner store. When I went inside, she fucking took off with the drugs and left me there."

Doubt coated my brow. "Let me get this straight—she stole two hundred fifty kilos of cocaine from you?"

"She called me as soon as she took off. Told me she was going home to get that kid and then it was time for us to leave town."

"So she blackmailed you?"

"No, she'd just had enough of that husband of hers."

"Why not just leave the guy?"

"Come on, she had a record. She was a drug addict and a prostitute. She knew no court would award her custody of that kid and for some reason she wasn't willing to leave her behind. Her only option was to run."

I shook my head. "Okay, so then what happened?"

"Then she never showed up."

"Why?"

"Because the fucker hijacked the drugs."

"And what happened to Lizzy?"

"The Priest took her."

"Took her?" She'd been taken? Hadn't she disappeared on her own? That I wasn't buying.

"Aren't you listening to me? O'Shea sabotaged the whole fucking thing. He took the drugs and arranged for her to disappear."

Surprisingly, the events were making more and more sense. Patrick was demanding both the money and drugs as retribution, which I always found odd. How could both disappear? Obviously, just the drugs had been stolen. Oddly, I got the feeling Tommy wasn't feeding me a complete line of bullshit except for one thing—I'd seen Tommy with Lizzy, and recently. I kept that to myself. "So what happened next?"

"I went to the Priest, told him what had happened. Hoped he'd help me, and instead he laughed in my face."

"Not a surprise I suppose."

Tommy narrowed his eyes at me.

"What did you do next?"

"I sat on it for a while, waiting to see if Lizzy showed up."

"So you weren't sure she'd actually been taken then?"

He looked annoyed. "She had been taken. I just didn't know it at the time. I found out later what had actually happened to her after she escaped."

I still wasn't buying it. "Okay, so you sat on it. Then what?"

"When I couldn't take it anymore, I told my old man what I could without cutting my own dick off. I knew once he found that the money used was his, he'd make something happen. But he fucking sat on it forever."

"Why did he wait?"

"How the hell would I know?"

"Maybe because he wanted to see you squirm?" I taunted.

"Fuck you. He told me it was because he wanted me to handle it, but more than likely it was because he was afraid of stepping on the wrong toes."

Skeptical, I raised a brow. "Whose wrong toes?"

"Like I said, you don't have a fucking clue."

"Then enlighten me. You want my help. Tell me."

Hatred seethed from his pores. I could practically smell it. "He took his time deciding because he was afraid of starting a war. Word on the street was that his old gang, the Dorchester Heights Gang, was reassembling, and that they were about to step up their game. He was afraid if he got involved in the drug side of things, they'd have reason to go after the Blue Hill Gang."

Anger rising at his lies, I shouted, "The Dorchester Heights Gang has been out of play for years. Stop bullshitting me."

"You, your old man, and even the DEA are in the fucking dark. They've been gearing up for years and they're about ready to reemerge bigger and better than they ever were. Probably even stronger than the Blue Hill Gang ever was, even in your grandfather's day. Rumor has it they have political ties."

"How the fuck would you know that?"

"Have you not been listening to a goddamn word I've told you?"

My mind spun. "The Priest is the mob boss of the Dorchester Heights Gang?"

He gave a huff of laughter. "You're a smart one."

Made sense that Patrick would be fearful. Drugs were the most lucrative venue for mob business, and being in that business would put a huge bulls-eye on his back. "And you're trying to tell me you were involved with them. Why would they want you?"

His expression became pure hostility. "Because I'm an asset."

"A pawn," I mumbled.

His lips pursed. "You have no fucking clue what's happening out there, and neither did your grandfather when he made that worthless deal with Patrick."

Something twisted in my gut and I jumped to my feet. "What worthless deal?"

That fucking smile was back. "To end his legacy. His shadow was too large for Patrick to live under, especially from inside here. So Patrick had to get rid of him. Killian gave his life for the return of your old man's."

Oh God, I thought I might be sick. My old man was in-dentured to Patrick's service because of my fuck-up, be-cause when I was fifteen, I may or may not have gotten his daughter pregnant, and then instead of telling her father, she killed herself at my grandfather's house, in his bath-room. And instead of me giving my life, which is the way it should have gone down, my father took responsibility for her death and gave his unlimited legal service and whatev-er else the Blue Hill Gang, or Patrick himself, needed.

A life for a life.

Dead or alive.

Tommy glanced at the clock on the wall. "Your old man should be free right . . . about . . . now." He clicked his tongue in the most chilling way. "Tick tock."

Anger boiled in my blood and before I knew what I was doing, I soared across the table and slammed his head down on the metal, over and over. "What do you mean? What are you talking about?"

Words were sputtering out but I couldn't understand what he was saying.

That's when I stopped the pounding. Switching gears, I wrapped my hands around his neck and brought his face right up to mine. "What the fuck are you talking about?" I screamed in his face.

His eyes were like flames of hatred. "Now you'll know how it feels to lose someone you love," he laughed as blood gushed out his nose.

"No, no, no!" I kept squeezing.

He was sputtering, choking, gasping for air, but all of my control was gone.

The doors burst open and I found myself being peeled off Tommy. "I'm going to fucking kill you!" I screamed.

"Hey, you need to calm down," the corrections officer said to me as he shoved me out of the room.

Even in the hall, I lunged for the door. My plan had gone to shit. There would be no visit from the Attorney General's office now. But really, that plan had gone to shit the minute he started talking. We weren't buddies. I wasn't going to help him. This was never going to end well.

The officer shoved me against the wall. "You need to leave, now."

Leave.

Yeah, I needed to get the hell out of there.

Hyped up, I moved quickly. My shoes slapped the pavement until they reached the parking lot. Hopping in my truck, I gunned it. Slamming on the gas. *Go. Go. Go.* I opened the window so I could breathe. *Go. Go. Go.* A sharp breeze whipped around me and jolted me out of the crazed reality I was swimming in. My hands gripped the wheel and my foot slammed on the brake as I skidded to a stop at the traffic light. *Change. Change. Change.* That burning red circle felt like a hot poker searing my skin.

Change. Change. Change. My eyes were shifting. Looking for signs of the oncoming traffic slowing. That's when I caught a glimpse of myself in the rearview mirror. My shirt and face were splattered with blood. With one hand on the wheel, I yanked off my tie and wiped my face.

That's when it hit me.

Killian can't be dead.

Killian isn't dead.

Killian will not be dead.

But even as I said it, I had a sickening feeling in my gut.

No. Tommy was fucking with me. This was a game to him. This whole thing was a fucking game. My frustration was escalating. My desperation to get to my grandfather felt so crippling that my hands were shaking.

The light changed and I didn't hesitate to pound the gas. Back on the road, I pulled out my phone and hit speed dial.

"Brighton House. How can I help you?"

My voice was shaky. "Can you connect me to Killian McPherson's room?"

"One moment please."

It started to ring. One, two, three times.

Come on, answer the fucking phone.

Four, five, six.

Answer the fucking phone.

Seven, eight, nine.

No answer. I threw my phone at the windshield.

Weaving in and out of the lanes of traffic, speeding as fast as I could, I finally arrived at Brighton House.

My head was swimming as I bolted out of the car and ran into the building.

"Judy, have you seen him?" I asked, trying not to sound as panicked as I was.

She smiled. "Yes, he had a breakfast date with a nice younger gentleman." She looked at her watch. He arrived over an hour ago."

There was no time for niceties. I took off like a bat out of hell toward his room. *Fuck*, I left my gun in the truck. No time to turn around. My breath was coming in short, ragged bursts and my eyes were stinging by the time I reached his door.

I froze with my hand on the knob.

Somewhere deep inside me, the spark of hope I'd held onto the entire drive over here died.

What replaced it was a really bad feeling that Tommy wasn't lying about anything and my blood felt like ice in my veins.

Images flickered through my mind.

A little boy in a Red Sox cap walking down the street and holding the giant palm of a man he wanted to be just like. "Understanding what it's like down here will help you make better decisions from up there," he said, pointing to a high-rise office building.

A child sitting next to a much-respected older man learning what a flush was, what it meant to fold, and what it meant to bluff. "The bluff is key," he told me.

A young teen at the top of a mountain named Wildcat who had decided to walk down the mountain instead of ski down. "You have to conquer your fear, Logan—it's the only way to survive in this world."

I drew in a deep breath and pushed the door open.

My stomach heaved.

My body swayed.

My vision blurred.

Lying on his bed with his bloodshot eyes wide open was the lifeless body of my grandfather. On the floor was a pillow. Someone had smothered him to death.

I wanted to scream louder than I ever had in my life, but I knew I couldn't. It had to look like he'd died of natural causes. The last thing he would want was a police investigation into his death—he'd had enough of those during his life.

It was my turn to take care of him.

Thoughts hummed in my head. My heart slammed against my chest. A sound leapt from my throat. I picked up the pillow. Made sure everything was in place. And then I threw myself beside him, pulled him onto me, and closed his eyes.

No. No. No.

No. No. No.

No. No. No.

chapter
EIGHTEEN

Elle

KNOW WHAT THEY say about secrets.

That nothing good can come from keeping them. That they'll eat you alive. That they destroy even the strongest of relationships.

All of which worried me because I was keeping one from both of the men in my life and the time had arrived to come clean.

The secret I had yet to share with Logan would reveal just how broken I am, and then, as with my first boyfriend, it might just tear us apart. I could only hope it wouldn't. To be fair, I should have told Logan before I ever let those three little words slip from my mouth. I should have learned from my mistakes. But everything that happened between us happened so fast and it never felt like the right time.

And then there's my brother-in-law. Michael held all the cards when it came to my niece. If he decided I shouldn't see Clementine again, there was nothing I could do about it. So pissing him off wasn't something I wanted to do. But after yesterday, I thought it was time he knew I was involved with someone. No, not just someone—Logan McPherson. I wasn't sure how he would react, but I hoped he knew me well enough by now to know that my relationship with Logan wouldn't impact my relationship with Clementine in any way.

My mind was a web of worry, sorrow, and confusion. And I took the quiet of the morning to contemplate everything in my life. The good, the bad, and the ugly.

It was well after eleven before I drifted into the bath to let the steam and heat take away some of my hesitation about the confessions I planned to make today. After a long while, I submerged myself and allowed the scented water to wash me clean. I took my time shaving my legs and rinsing the soap from by body.

When I finally emerged from the tub, I felt much better about what I had to do. My secrets were eating at me and I had to get them out. Telling Logan about Michael's advances didn't rank high on my priorities, and I figured once I told Michael about Logan and me, that issue should naturally put itself to rest.

That was if there was something to tell him—if Logan stayed with me.

My skin was a warm shade of pink and the steam in the room was still thick. I wrapped a towel around myself, patted my wet skin until it was dry, and then I ran a comb through my still damp hair.

The door creaked loudly when I opened it and stepped into my darkened bedroom. I had yet to open the blinds and let the sunshine in.

The dark figure in the room caused my heart to stop and I screamed at the top of my lungs. Its beat didn't even jump-start during that one moment it took me to realize it was Logan sitting on the end of the bed, cradling his head in his hands.

At the sound of my scream, his head jerked up.

"It's just me." His words were barely audible.

Even in the darkness, I could see right away that something was wrong. A flip of the light switch confirmed it. I'd never seen him like this before. His face was drawn, his eyes red-rimmed, and his body looked utterly defeated.

With my heart in my throat I ran over to him and fell to my knees, taking his hands in mine. At first I recoiled. Blood stained his shirt, his neck, and his fingers. But I pushed my dread aside and focused on him. "What happened?"

"He's dead." His voice was scratchy, not his own. He cleared his throat like he, too, knew it sounded weird.

My heart was now thumping hard. "Who's dead, Logan? What are you talking about?"

"A life for a life," he mumbled.

Frightened beyond belief, I took his face in my hands. "What are you talking about?"

"Patrick had my grandfather killed."

A chill ran through me and my entire body began to tremble. The shaking in my arms caused my hands to fall to my lap. "Why? I don't understand. He wasn't a threat."

Logan's head was moving back and forth. "Patrick saw him as one. He offered my grandfather a choice: his life for my father's eternal freedom. And he took it. The stupid old son of a bitch took the offer to free his son."

"But Patrick's in jail."

Logan dropped his head and his voice was low. "Elle, I've told you, the Blue Hill Gang still functions no matter where the mob boss is, or who he is for that matter. My father's servitude was for life, indentured to the Blue Hill Gang. My grandfather freed his son by trading his own life."

I had to swallow, hard, before I could force myself to speak without my voice crumbling. And even then, "I'm so sorry, Logan. I'm so sorry," was all I could manage.

"I knew something wasn't right when I went there yesterday. I should have pushed him more. I should have seen this coming."

I shifted to sit beside him and I drew him to me. "It wasn't your fault." I stroked his hair the same way he stroked mine when I was upset.

"Yeah, it was," he said, his voice flat and sounding very far away.

"No, it wasn't."

"I told you how it—" he started to say but before he

could finish, he bolted off the bed and ran toward the bathroom, slamming the door in his wake.

In a rush, I hurried after him. When I turned the knob, it was locked. The sound of solid splashing against liquid could be heard through the door. A flush. More splashing. Another flush. Dry heaving.

I knocked lightly. "Logan, let me in. I want to help you."

Silence.

"Logan, please, let me in."

The sound of water running.

I flattened my palm to the door and pressed my forehead against it. "Logan, please," I said softly.

"I need some time, Elle."

I closed my eyes. "Oh, Logan."

A soft shuffle on the other side of the door made me think he was standing directly opposite me.

"Open the door, let me help you," I whispered again.

Time passed, seconds, minutes, I wasn't sure.

I spoke again. "Let me help you, Logan, please," I pleaded.

Finally, slowly, the door creaked open. So many emotions cascaded over his expression as he looked at me. "He's dead because of what I did."

I flung myself at him and threw my arms around his neck. "No, Logan. That's simply not true."

When I pulled back to look at him, I could tell my words weren't even registering. His mind was somewhere far off in the distance.

I smoothed his hair back. "Does your father know?" I asked, wondering if I should take charge.

He blinked as if he just remembered something. "Yeah, he met me over at Brighton House earlier. I should go. He'll be alone at the house until my uncle arrives."

"We'll go together, but first you have to take a shower." I attempted to take his arm to lead him through my bedroom to the hall bathroom where the shower was.

"I'll do it." He flared his palms out.

"I want to help you."

His eyes gained focus as he looked down at me. "I don't want Tommy's blood on you."

"What?" I asked, my throat going tight over my own surge of nausea. For some reason I just assumed it was Killian's blood on him. My eyes roamed over his shirt again as if the spackling that coated him might have been altered in some way. "Why is Tommy's blood on you?"

He was watching me and I knew he noticed my reaction. "Because he's the one who told me what my grandfather had agreed to."

There was no need for him to explain any further. I nodded in understanding, my voice stolen by emotion I wasn't sure I was ready to face, and questions I wasn't ready to ask. Like, *what else did he tell you?*

Death seemed to be all around us. I felt like we'd just gone through this, and we had. I didn't want to know anything else right now. Besides, I had pushed Logan away from me by not allowing him to accompany me to my sister's funeral. I wasn't going to let him do that to me. I wasn't going to let anything like that happen again between us. I was his, and he was mine, and that meant we took care of each other. It had taken me some time to realize that, but I did now.

I reached out my hand, "Come on."

His eyes questioned me.

I didn't hesitate as I grabbed his hand.

My towel was still around me as I took the lead and walked us to the hall bathroom.

Twisting to turn the water on, I took a deep breath and blinked away the tears that had formed in my eyes. Once the blur cleared, I focused on the buttons of his white shirt and avoided looking at the red stains.

One. Two. Three. Four.

He stood stoic as I opened the flaps and pulled each sleeve down. Balling the shirt up, I tossed it into the corner. I'd get a garbage bag and throw the clothes away later.

Next, I undid his belt and then the zipper of his slacks. I got on my knees to slide them down, urging him to lift his feet so I could remove his shoes and socks at the same time.

Logan watched me the entire time, every move, every breath. He was stiff, uncertain, but still he let me. And when he was naked, he stepped into the already steaming shower and hung his head.

The defeat I'd witnessed in his body when I first saw him on my bed and that I saw right now frightened me. He was the strong one. The one who always had a plan. The dauntless warrior I could only hope to be.

When he pressed his palms to the wall, it occurred to me that it was my turn to be the strong one in our relationship. He'd taken control and protected me from the very beginning. This would not crush him; I'd make certain of that.

Sensing how much he needed me right now, I took my towel off and stepped into the shower with him. At first I only wrapped my arms around him and settled my cheek against his back. It struck me that the biggest difference between Logan's loss and mine was that Logan had an incredible bond with his grandfather. In fact, if I had to guess, I think Logan was closer to Killian than he was to his own father. I found myself whispering to him. "He loved you, Logan, remember that."

More whispers.

More water sluicing down on the two of us.

Time passed

I kept whispering.

Something got through to him because finally he turned around and grabbed me, pulling my body as tight as he could to his, and when there was no more space between us, he buried his face in my neck.

We stayed like that, under the spray of the shower in each other's arms until the water started to cool. And when it did, I took the soap and washed him. Sexual stirrings weren't what I had planned, but with each one of my gentle touches, his cock grew thicker and harder.

Just as I set the soap down, he pushed me against the shower wall and once again buried his face in my neck. "I need you," he whispered.

"I'm here, Logan. Right here."

His body radiated heat as his erection pressed against my thigh and I knew what he meant. "Turn around."

I did.

His hands gripped my hips.

Tight.

Mine flattened against the tile wall and I bent forward, offering myself to him.

His groan was muffled but his actions spoke clearly. He slid a finger inside me, plunging upward, then another. Wet. Wild. When he removed his fingers he plunged his cock inside me. He slid in easily. A cry leaked from my throat when he was all the way in. He moved, thrusting faster and faster. I could feel my clit swell as it accepted all he had to give. He moved faster still, bucking wildly. I pushed back against him, and the wet slap of my skin against his belly made me moan.

Logan clutched my hips harder. His fingertips pushed against my bones and his thumbs pressed into my skin, all the while his cock was filling me.

Although this fuck wasn't meant to be about pleasure, it still felt delicious.

Solace took over.

Water made us slippery.

Still, we fucked.

Wanting to connect with him even more, I reached back to wrap an arm around his neck and I held him as tight as I could. He kissed my neck and moved at his own pace. I shifted my hips to meet each and every one of his thrusts. Before I knew it, my stomach was practically flat against the wall and both my arms were wrapped around his neck. One of his hands was bracing the wall while the other began to rub my clit without mercy.

As I embraced him with everything I had to give, he

anchored me, giving me his strength. Together we formed a perfectly aligned union in the face of despair.

His breath quickly became ragged and he ground his hips into me as he took up the pace. Harder. Faster. Wilder. He wasn't rough, though. He moved at a tempo that helped ease his pain and I gave in to that. When I felt my body approaching the edge, I deliberately held myself back, wanting this to be for him.

"Let yourself go," he demanded, his thumb rubbing circles around my clit.

"No," I whispered.

"I need this," he insisted.

So I did. I gave it up for him. My clit was pulsing out of control under his touch and his words were all I needed. I went tumbling into a climax fierce enough I thought I could see the heavens. My screams were loud. Filled with sorrow for everything we'd both lost.

Behind me, Logan let out a series of low groans filled with the same I was certain.

And very unexpectedly we came together. In the shower. In his time of need.

A heartbeat later he turned me around.

Needing stability, my hands went for his biceps, where the muscles bunched and tightened. Fingers gripping the powerful force that he was, I realized something. Beyond being long and lean and physically strong, Logan also had a strong mind and soul. It felt good to remind myself of that—that his strength wasn't only physical in nature.

He'd get through this.

We'd get through this—together.

Whatever it took.

When he was ready, he eased himself back and turned the water off. This time he took my hand and led me out of the shower. We dried ourselves in silence and when I went to tuck my towel inside itself to hold against my body, he finished the job for me.

His eyes fluttered closed, then opened to meet mine.

"Thank you for being here for me, but if all this craziness is too much for you I understand. I wouldn't blame you if you walked away right now, because fuck knows you should be running."

There was no hesitation in my reply. I took his face in my hands. "I'm not going anywhere that isn't next to you."

His eyes remained on mine, as if he were waiting for me to change my mind.

I wouldn't.

Or maybe he was waiting for me to include a "but."

There wouldn't be one.

Ever.

chapter
NINETEEN

LOGAN

EVERYTHING ABOUT THIS WAS wrong.

And I knew it.

We were in between viewing hours at my grandfather's wake, for fuck's sake.

Yet, I couldn't resist her. She was like a drug, an addiction, and being with her was the only way I could keep from spiraling out of control right now. I needed Elle in a way I couldn't explain. It was like she was the glue keeping me together.

And she knew it.

She had followed me into the bathroom. Locked the door behind her. Then kicked her shoes off. She didn't have to say a word. I knew why she was in here. I should have sent her away.

A gentleman would have.

We already knew—I wasn't one.

Just looking at her eased the tension inside me right away.

"Logan, talk to me," she whispered.

I took a step back until I hit the sink. "Elle, I'll be fine. I just need a few minutes."

I'd just found my father out in the parking lot with some guy from the neighborhood and a bottle of Jack Daniel's in his hand. He was about to shove the neck in his mouth when I saw him. As soon as he saw me he started shaking so much, he dropped the bottle.

"Don't, Pop," I'd said. "Don't do this. Killian wanted you to be whole. That's why he did what he did. Don't make it all for naught."

"Sean," my uncle Hunter's voice boomed. "That's not what Dad would want."

I jerked my head around.

Uncle Hunter, my father's older brother, had moved to New York to get away from the shadow of the Irish Mob. He approached my old man. "Let me take you home for an hour," he said, and then he looked at me. "I need to have a talk with him and then I'll bring him back at five for the final viewing hours. Will you stay here until I get back?"

Irish tradition mandated that the body of the deceased not be left alone until burial. It was just one of many traditions that didn't make much sense. Still, I stayed at the funeral home.

My old man hadn't taken a drink, but I knew he was close to losing his months of sobriety. The thought cut me like a knife. He had been on his way to living a life free of addiction. I was going to be the one to cut the ties that bound him to Patrick as soon as I figured the whole cluster-fuck situation out. Killian didn't have to go and do what he'd done. And besides, my old man wasn't the one who should feel the blame for what Killian had chosen to do, I should. I was the one who started this whole fucked-up thing.

I was the fuck-up.

"Logan," Elle said, pulling me back. "I know you'll be fine but I want to be here for you. To help."

Feeling every sound she made in my cock, I stepped closer to claim her mouth. I knew this was not the place to be doing it, but I needed a hit of something to take the edge off and she was it.

Still, I should have fought my animalistic need. I just

couldn't. My willpower felt as drained as my life.

Our open mouths came together almost savagely and my tongue thrust into her mouth the instant we made contact. This kiss was short, hard, and anything but elegant.

Five seconds or more passed and then she unzipped my pants and started to slide down my body, taking my pants with her.

Again, I should have stopped her. "Elle," I groaned, trying to protest.

She ignored me and didn't stop until her face met my cock. By then it was too late to stop her, because I wanted nothing more than to feel her warm mouth on my throbbing dick.

My pants were at my ankles. "Oh, fuck."

She was licking me like a lollipop from the tip of my cock, which was soaked in pre-cum, all the way to my balls, and then she took me in her mouth as much as she could.

My hands went to her hair, and even though it was pulled back neatly, I still had to hold on to her.

Sounds left my mouth that I tried to hush but couldn't.

Her hands were jerking me off fast, her lips gliding up and down at the same time.

I thought about pulling her up, lifting her dress, and plunging deep inside her, but I couldn't move.

Teeth slid, lips sucked, tongue licked, and I let myself go in the pleasure of it all. Let all the shit around me fade away.

When my toes clenched inside my shoes, I had held on to sanity for as long as I could. My thumb was in her mouth and I lifted her chin. "If you want to stop, now is the time."

She knew what I meant. I was going to come in her mouth if she didn't stop and if she didn't want that, she had to stop now.

She didn't.

My thrusts were frantic. This was it. What I needed. It felt so incredible, and everything that was fucked up around me was gone. "That's it. Don't stop. Oh fuck, don't stop."

There was no stopping. Her hands were on my ass now, her back arched, and her mouth working magic on me.

My hands were on her head and I felt my orgasm as the sensations began at my feet and traveled up my body. Coming while standing up takes an orgasm to a whole other level. "Fuck!" I shouted.

Her eyes looked up at me and whatever she saw in my own caused her to take me even farther into her mouth. My cock plunged inside her mouth over and over as my body spasmed until I had nothing left. Until all the grief and remorse was drained from me.

This was what I needed in order to face tonight.

And she knew it.

And later tonight she would do the same—she'd spread her legs wide for me and let me fuck her until I was exhausted. Until sleep took me.

And in the morning, I'd lick her to orgasm and then plunge inside her, and I hoped that would give me the strength I needed to make it through the funeral.

It just had to.

chapter
TWENTY

Day 22

Elle

WISE MEN SAY WOMEN can be thoroughly fucked.
Well, I now know guys can be too.

I'd made sure Logan had been. It was the only way I could make him feel any better. To help ease his pain and suffering. And I think it worked . . . for a little while anyway.

This day, though, had been extremely long for him. First the church, then the cemetery, and now the reception. Everything had taken its toll on him. I could see it on his face even from across the room.

We were at Molly's. The place had been closed to the general public. Frank, who owned the pub that had been turned into a club by his daughter, Molly, was Killian's next-door neighbor for years, and he mourned Killian's death along with everyone else. Perhaps as a way of showing his condolences to the family or perhaps because he just wanted to help, he had not only volunteered to host the after-funeral affair, but also to cook for the almost one hundred people who had shown up to say goodbye to Killian.

Faces I'd never seen had come and gone, all within a five-hour time span. I worked in the morning and met Logan here after the funeral. I needed to stay away from the public eye in case someone who knew Michael saw me.

There was no way I could explain being at Killian's funeral that would make any sense.

Obviously, I hadn't gone through with my plan, and I had yet to confess anything to either Michael or Logan. I had gotten sidetracked by the death of Killian. And the more time that passed, the more scared I became to talk to either man. Both outcomes were just so uncertain.

Finally, the funeral reception was coming to an end, and all that remained were Logan's friends from New York City.

Logan's mother and maternal grandfather did not come and Logan said it was for the best. In fact, he had asked them not to. I guess he knew they didn't care for Killian and didn't want to have to deal with them today of all days.

Since Logan, his father, and uncle had arrived in a limo, Logan's uncle had taken the Rover that I used to drive to Molly's and brought Sean home a couple of hours ago. Being around all these people drinking wasn't a great idea for Sean, but I guess at Irish funerals booze couldn't be avoided.

"How long have you known Logan?" Phoebe St. Claire, one of Logan's best friends from New York City, asked from across the table.

Both our feet killing us, we had retired to a dim booth in the corner. The sound of her voice caused my gaze to shift from Logan over to her. "Three weeks."

Phoebe took a bite of her Irish soda bread. "That's all? The way he talked about you I would have thought it was much longer."

My hands on my coffee mug, my smile couldn't be contained. "He talked about me to you?"

"Well, not to me but to Jamie, who in turn mentioned it to me."

I glanced back over to where Logan sat at the bar with the group of people I had learned were a very close-knit circle of best friends. There was James Ashton and his new wife, Lindsay; Phoebe's husband, Jeremy McQueen; Emmy Lane; Lily Monroe; and Danny Capshaw. They all had come this morning to be beside Logan and help him through this tragedy in his life.

It was touching.

Strangely, I realized I yearned for something like that in my own life. How had I gone through thirty years with not even one single person to confide in? Had my past shattered me that much that I couldn't connect to anyone?

God, I hoped not.

Sipping my coffee in contemplation, I burned my tongue it was so hot and winced.

"You okay?" Phoebe asked me.

I blinked. "Yes. The coffee is really hot, so be careful. What about you? How long have you been married?"

She laughed and glanced at her protruding belly. "Less time than I've been pregnant. Jeremy and I met over five years ago, but we just reconnected last year. Logan actually helped us find our way back to one another."

"Logan is a matchmaker?" I couldn't believe it.

"No," she admitted, "but he did take me to a launch party for Assassin's Creed that Jeremy was attending."

Games?

Logan?

"You're kidding. Logan plays video games?" I laughed.

"Oh, yes. Jamie and he claim to be masters at all things video."

Ripping open a packet of sugar, I added it to my coffee to help subdue its bitter taste. "I had no idea."

"No idea about what?" Logan asked, sliding in beside me. I'd never seen him drink, but tonight he most certainly had indulged. Slightly drunk, he found my thighs as soon as he set his glass down and pushed them apart. His fingers were cold, and tingles traveled up to my sex and down to my toes.

"That you're a Guitar Hero master," Phoebe said with a laugh.

Logan rolled his eyes while at the same time, under the table, his hand snuck beneath the hem of my dress. "That was a long time ago."

"Not that long ago," she countered.

I shifted in my seat as fingers found the inside seam of my hose and traced up it.

Thank God Jeremy slid in next to his wife and took Phoebe's attention off us.

"Logan," I warned quietly through my teeth.

My warning went unheard as his hot breath blew in my ear. "What?" He chuckled.

My gaze shot across the table, trying to focus on anything but the pleasure radiating from my core.

Jeremy placed his hand on Phoebe's cute belly and whispered something in her ear. A strange pang of envy ripped through me; not at the loving couple I was looking at but at her belly, carrying a human being.

Phoebe nodded at him and looked over to Logan. "We need to get going. We have to be back in the city early for a meeting."

"Thank you for coming," Logan said. There was a quick press of his thumb right to my clit and then his hand was gone. "Meet me in the bathroom in five minutes," he ordered hot in my ear.

The words seared through me. Meet him. I didn't think I could move. Tension had already coiled tight in my belly and the feel of his hands between my thighs was the only thing I could think about.

Jeremy had stood to help Phoebe out and Logan quickly followed.

Phoebe threw her arms around Logan as best she could with her bump and I watched as he stiffly hugged her back.

When she pulled away, she patted his chest. "Sorry."

His friends must have known he had a hard time showing affection.

Surprising me, he put his hand on her stomach. I couldn't hear what he said, but it ripped my heart in two. The way he looked at her stomach, I just knew he wanted to have children of his own some day.

I forced myself up on rubber-like legs as he took my hand, and together we said goodbye to most of his friends. Oddly enough, they had made me feel like I was part of the inner circle.

"Come on, man, time to toast Killian. You and me and a bottle of Jameson should just about do it," James shouted unnecessarily to Logan since he was standing so close.

James and Lindsay had stayed behind and it was just the four of us now. They were spending the weekend in Boston.

Logan was standing across from me and he tossed me an apologetic glance. Looked like the bathroom rendezvous would have to wait. "Rain check," he mouthed.

Butterflies took flight in my belly when I looked at him and I couldn't help but nod. He was, as always, breathtakingly handsome. It didn't matter that alcohol had dilated his pupils. In fact, tonight they looked wide and dark. Languid. Sexy. Maybe even luminous as they burned into me with a desire I craved. His gaze seemed to have a glow in it that was only for me. And his scrumptious hair was a beautiful mess, different shades of light and dark brown sticking up everywhere because he had been running his hands through it all day. It looked like just-fucked hair and I had yet to fuck him tonight. Free from intoxication myself, I still licked my lips at the thought of what was to come.

Seeing him, knowing what we were like together, just being with him lit me up from the inside.

"You're a fucker," Logan laughed and pointed to James.

I was glad to see the upbeat effect his friend had on him, even though their maturity was lacking. It was obvious their boyhood friendship was emerging the more alcohol they both consumed. It was okay, though. Logan needed this.

James drank from his beer bottle and then looked at me. "You'd better keep him in line, Elle. Whips and chains if need be."

I hadn't heard the conversation but answered him nonetheless. "Bondage? I'm not certain he'd be willing to give up control."

James looked at Logan. "Hey buddy, that would mean you gave a shit enough to take control." James laughed. "I'm proud of you."

"Cold, man. Cold." Logan drained his drink.

Insults flew back and forth. One worse than the other, and each time they both laughed.

More than five minutes later, James slung his arm around his wife, kissed her sloppily on the lips, and then patted her ass, whispering something to her that I knew had to be sexual in nature.

She smiled at him submissively, and the term *alpha male* came to mind. I remembered calling Logan that when we first met. Made me wonder—was he one? James was for certain. I'd spent enough time with him to know this and I didn't have a doubt that Lindsay knew it too. Not that I was judging their relationship. They seemed very happy.

James then clapped Logan on the shoulder. "Come on, you fucker, time to hit the bottle."

Logan glanced at me.

"Oh man, don't be a pansy-ass."

Logan threw James the finger.

James shoved Logan's hand playfully out of his face and said, "I prefer the real thing."

Lindsay laughed at them both. She'd seen this behavior before; I could tell when she threw me a *just wait and see what's to come* look.

I laughed too. Really, these two men were just too adorable together.

In the midst of the antics, Lindsay turned to James. "Mind if I get some air? It's a bit stuffy in here."

He nodded at her. "Only if Elle agrees to go with you," he said, and then looked toward me. He was charming in a caveman sort of way. It seemed to suit him.

Lindsay was right, though. The room was smoky. Earlier, a few older men had been puffing on cigars and the air smelled stale. I didn't seek Logan's approval when I said to Lindsay, "Come on, what do you say we go for a walk?"

Her smile beamed. I could see why she was a Victoria's Secret model. Besides being tall and thin, she had a quality about her that radiated beauty. Oddly, I wondered how many women like her Logan had fucked. Dozens was my guess, since James and he appeared to have many similar qualities and had traveled in the same circle for many years. I hated the insecurity being around his friends had drawn out in me. It wasn't like me at all, but then again, it had been only the two of us in our own private bubble since we met, and this was more realistic. A shroud of guilt began to consume me for my dark thoughts.

A hand wrapped around my waist and a hard body pressed against mine. "Did you forget something?" His breath tickled my neck.

I leaned back and played along. "I don't think so."

"Are you sure?" His voice dipped, low, husky.

"Oh, right, I probably should leave a tip on the table," I joked.

"No. Not that."

I tipped my head back even farther. "Help a girl out and tell me."

He spun me around.

That grin. The look. Heat. God, I loved him, every piece of him. Happy or sad. Right or wrong. Dressed or naked. Sober or drunk.

"I can do better than that," he growled, and then his lush lips were on mine, parting, demanding, seeking.

Breathless, I pulled away. "Oh, if you wanted a kiss goodbye, all you had to do was ask," I said with a wink.

In the midst of all the sadness surrounding him, he gave me a heart-stopping smile that I would remember forever. "I shouldn't have to ask," he teased.

On my toes, I gave my own alpha male another kiss, not like his but memorable nonetheless. Wet. Wild. With a little bit of tongue. "Was that better?"

"That's enough, Romeo." James's big hand was on

Logan's shoulder, yanking him back. "It's my turn."

He pretended to go in for a full-on mouth kiss, but Logan shoved him away before he got too close.

Laughing, Lindsay and I left the pub.

Being free of Miles felt good. I appreciated the protection he had provided for me but was more than thankful when Logan called it off. After everything, Logan knew the one thing Tommy hadn't lied about was leaving me alone.

Also, I hadn't received any more blocked calls or messages, for which I was also thankful.

Outdoors, it was still light. Although inside it seemed like midnight, it was actually only six o'clock. Since Michael's office closed early on Fridays, I was confident that even though it was right around the corner, he would have left already. Still, to be safe, I took Lindsay down the side streets.

We walked down one and up another, passing store after store. Soon, the light started to drain from the sky. "We should probably head back," I suggested.

It was then that she spotted a stationery store called Love Notes and clapped her hands together. "Oh, let's go in."

I shrugged. "Sure, why not."

Myself, I'd never been into cards. Then again, I'd never had anyone to give one to.

Inside she found the section she was looking for immediately. It was in the back and designated by a sign that read naughty.

"Porn cards." I had to laugh.

"Erotic cards," she corrected. "Haven't you ever given one to Logan? I give them to James all the time."

Rather shocked such a section even existed, I shook my head. "No, I haven't." Surprised she gave them to her husband, I had to ask, "How long have you and James been married?" Logan hadn't spoken of his friends much, so I knew little about them.

She laughed. "Not long. The same amount of time we've

known each other."

Eyes wide, my mouth dropped open.

She glanced at me. "We got married the night we met, or maybe it was the next day."

Perplexed, I had to ask, "How does something like that happen?"

With a head shake she answered, "It was a Friday night and I was out with my friends. Next thing I know I'm on a private jet headed to Vegas with about twenty people, and then I'm in a chapel saying 'I do.' Sounds crazy, but it was love at first sight and we both knew it, so since we were in Vegas, we decided to do the deed."

"Sounds almost like a fairy tale."

She gushed, "He is my Prince Charming."

My eyes wandered the section in front of us. There was a card with two cherries and a tongue between them, one with a woman stepping on a man's ass in high heels, and another with a woman in a garter belt sitting forward on a man's knees while he had his hand inside her panties.

Lindsay browsed for a few moments and then she picked one up. On the front was a picture of a woman bent over a man's lap, his hand on her bare ass. The card read, "I've been naughty. Punish me." She handed it to me. "Do something bad and then give this to Logan. I guarantee you'll like the results."

I didn't take it. "Oh, Logan and I don't have that type of relationship."

She shoved it toward me this time. "Trust me, Elle, all men like a woman to be submissive once in a while. I doubt Logan is any different."

I took the card and stared at it.

Did I want him to spank me?

Did he want to?

I remembered what he'd said to me the first day we'd met with a gleam in his eyes when we talked about the sex toys I was selling, "My friends from New York would love these," or something like that.

She picked up another card, this one of a woman's arms and legs bound to a bed frame and a man's head between her legs.

My face must have registered my unease. Too many ghosts from the past.

She looked at me and simply said, "The best orgasms come when you give up control. I was never submissive with a man until James."

Inserting my card back into its sleeve, I was interested as to what changed her. "What made you decide to be submissive with him, then?"

She set her card down and picked up another. "It's what makes us work. It was what I needed and what he needed. I had a mother whom I always had to take care of and my entire childhood and teen years were full of decisions she should have made for me, but instead I was the one making them for her. James, on the other hand, had a very controlling mother and I think because of that, he needs to feel in control himself. It just happened naturally between us."

"And you're happy?"

"More happy than I've ever been in my life. I like that someone else makes the decisions for me. With the hecticness of my job, it's so much less stressful for me. I ask permission and he decides if I should receive it. I need something and he takes care of it. Sometimes, I let him bind me and he gives me earth-shattering sex. And once in a while, I misbehave just so he can punish me."

Her honesty didn't shock me but it did surprise me. I was glad she felt comfortable enough around me to admit her feelings. Before I could say anything, her phone started to ring.

"Here, hold this," she said, and handed me the card she had just picked up so she could dig in her purse. On the front was a picture of man holding his erection, and the caption read, "Talk dirty to me, baby. I need to get off."

I stared at it and an unwanted memory flashed before me.

The surgery had been arranged.

My sister had reluctantly agreed to donate one of her kidneys to my mother. They were a perfect match. I was a match, but not as well matched as my sister.

Both my sister and mother were to arrive at the hospital early in the morning. It was the night before and I was sitting at the kitchen table, doing my homework. My mother was sitting beside me, watching me. She was weak, feeble, but optimistic she would get better.

My sister was supposed to have come home for dinner but never did.

It was just after ten when the door opened. Boots clunked inside and my heart fell. It wasn't my sister.

My mother scurried from her chair to get my father's dinner.

"I'll get it, Mom. You sit down."

She smiled at me. She had allowed me to do more and more for her over the past year. Grocery shopping, dinner, dishes, cleaning. All of her duties that my father expected but she had a hard time keeping up with.

He came into the room and set his gun on the counter before he looked around.

"Where's Elizabeth?"

"She's not home yet," I answered quickly.

Anger flared in his eyes. He turned around and went back toward the door. I heard him lock it and latch the chain. Lizzy would have to call and apologize before he'd let her in. I hated nights like this.

His steps were louder this time as he came back into the kitchen. "What are you still doing up, Gabrielle?" he asked, his tone stern.

"I had to finish my homework, sir," I answered, as I removed the foil from his carefully covered plate.

"Leave it. I already ate. I need to talk to your mother. Go on to bed."

I couldn't tell if he'd been drinking.

My eyes shot to my mother.

She nodded.

With that, I covered the plate and put it back in the refrigerator before I went to my room.

When he locked my door, it was a surprise. It had been a while since he'd done that.

"Susan," he called.

Her steps were feeble as she came down the hall.

"I'm going to take a shower and then I want to talk to you."

Doors opened. Closed. And then silence.

I lay on my bed, squeezing my eyes shut, hoping, praying, he was going to leave her alone tonight. All I heard was silence. I must have fallen asleep because I awoke to that god-awful thudding of the headboard more than an hour later.

"Talk to me, Susan. Tell me you like what you see."

If my mother was responding, I couldn't hear her.

"That's it. Keep talking. Tell me you like to see my hands on my own cock. Tell me it turns you on. Gets you wet."

Again, if my mother was talking, I couldn't hear her.

"That's it, baby. I'm so close. Tell me to move my hands faster. Fuck myself harder. Talk dirty to me, baby."

At fifteen, I was so much more aware of things than I had been years ago. I knew he was jerking off in front of her. And sadly, I was just thankful he wasn't making her have sex with him.

The phone started to ring.

"Ignore it. She'll call back. Keep talking to me, baby. I need this. I need this from you."

The phone kept ringing.

His moans told me he was starting to climax even through the incessant ringing.

Soon, though, all was quiet. Even him.

I had fallen back asleep.

The phone started to ring again and woke me. This time when I looked at the time it was close to three A.M.

"Yeah," he barked into the phone.

Silence.

"Fuck. I'll be right there."

My eyes flashed to the card again. Maybe it was because

my sister's death was still fresh in my mind that I had to fight back the urge to cry. My family was such a fucked-up thing. And my daddy issues would never allow for me to be submissive with any man.

"Yes, baby, I understand. Sure. I can do that. Have fun," Lindsay said.

Her words drew my attention.

Silence.

Her cheeks flushed. "Me too."

With her phone in her hand, she dug into her purse again, and this time pulled out her keys and looked at me. "Molly's is closing so it can reopen to the public later tonight. James suggested you and I take the car back to the hotel and he and Logan will take a cab back later."

"Oh," I said, a little surprised that Logan hadn't called me to tell me himself, but then I remembered why. "I have to go back there—my purse is locked up in the backroom along with my phone."

She grimaced a little. "Let me tell James to get it for you. I guess Logan is more than a little drunk, and James thinks it's best if he sobers him up before they rejoin us."

"Oh," I found myself saying again. "Maybe he needs me."

"Nonsense, he'll be fine with James. James was very fond of Logan's grandfather and I think they want to reminisce and have some boy time." She plucked the card from my hand. "Let me pay for this and we'll have a girls' night in. We can rent a movie and raid the candy in the minibar."

Worried about Logan, I found myself saying yes just so I would know what was going on. Besides, I didn't seem to have any other choice without my purse, and I also wasn't about to leave Logan alone.

Lindsay and James were staying in a very familiar Four Seasons suite. It was the same suite Logan had been living in when we met, before his grandfather blocked his access to his trust fund and his own money started to run out.

It was after ten and the movie Lindsay and I were

watching had just ended, but no guys had come to the hotel yet. I was more than a little worried about Logan.

Lindsay jumped up. "Let's go find a store that sells Ben & Jerry's. I'm still hungry."

My eyes skittered over the candy wrappers littered on the table. "You're going to get a sugar high."

She laughed. "I'm already on one. I need to keep it going. Besides, I'm going to go stir-crazy waiting for them."

Standing up and stretching, I conceded. "I think there's a store around the corner. But I'll go only if you call James when we get back and find out where they are."

She nodded. "Okay, deal."

The expedition on foot to find the small convenience store took longer than I'd anticipated, and by the time we got there it was closed.

With no ice cream but a few bags of chips from a vending machine, we headed back to the hotel. I had to work in the morning, but sleep wasn't what was on my mind. Logan was.

We passed a strip bar and she bumped my hip. "We could go in and when we get back, I could call James and tell him I watched naked women dance. I guarantee that would bring him back fast."

Shaking my head, I was horrified at the thought, but at the same time, I laughed a real, genuine, from-the-belly laugh. I liked Lindsay. She was free-spirited about sex in a way I'd never been. She was also a nice person. I could see myself being friends with her.

The coolness of the night air had begun to set in. With the suddenly harsher wind, we both felt the chill and even in our heels, we hastened our pace.

As soon as we walked into the hotel suite, I was assaulted by the tang of a sticky, sweet scent. It was the smell of pot. Never one to try it myself, in my travels I'd come across many people who had. Moldy grass was how I'd always described the smell.

Lindsay shot me a glance and confirmed my suspicion.

Hard rock blared through the open space. The patio doors were open and I saw the back of two heads flopped on the lounge chairs. Even over the music, I heard laughter rumbling into the room. I was glad that at least Logan was upbeat.

Lindsay started for them and looked at me. "Shhh."

I followed, keeping my mouth shut.

We both approached, eager to see our men, but stopped at the edge of door to watch them. They were playing cards and a baggie of pot was on the floor.

James had changed and was now wearing sleep pants and a T-shirt. He had a cigar gripped between his teeth while he tossed two piles of cards onto the table between them.

Logan was still in his suit pants but had removed everything else. Everything. Outside in his pants only, I wondered how he wasn't freezing until I looked up and saw the heat lamps were on.

"Baby, you're going to stink," Lindsay said loudly, breaking the silence.

Both men jerked their heads back.

The smile that spread across Logan's face was slow and seductive.

Sexy.

The sight of him dried my throat and made my heart pound. Right then I didn't care about anything but comforting him through kisses.

Lindsay was still talking, saying something about the rancid smell of the cigar.

Me, I was already leaning over Logan and placing my lips very close to his. "Are you okay?"

"I am now."

"You sure?"

He nodded and said, "Don't listen to James. He likes to be a drama queen."

"I heard that."

Ignoring James, Logan gave me a single tug and pulled

me onto his lap. I found myself provocatively straddling him. His cards fell to the floor, but I heard no one complain. And then his hands anchored my hips as his mouth attacked mine, while my hands gripped his shoulders for support.

"Where are your clothes?" I managed to ask.

The corners of his lips tilted up. "We had a small wrestling match and my shirt took the brunt of the action."

I laughed.

Boys will be boys.

My dress had ridden up and if anyone was looking, they could see my panties. I just didn't care enough right then to see what James and Lindsay were doing.

I should have cared. I should have cared just how inebriated or high Logan was. I should have, but his primal response to my presence did something to me that made me want to be what he needed. Made me want to be wild and free for once in my entire life.

Maybe it was the Lindsay effect.

His kiss traveled from the corner of my mouth, along my jaw, to my throat.

My hands moved higher to toy with his hair behind his neck.

His teeth were sharp as they skidded across my skin, but the soft heat from his tongue soothed the burn.

I turned my head to give him full access, and that was when I saw Lindsay's head moving towards James's lap.

Again, I should have cared, but I just didn't.

I wasn't sure if Logan noticed, but he turned my chin to look at him. "We should go home," he slurred. The way his eyes flickered over me so intensely made the idea of waiting for a cab and then riding home in one seem like it would take a lifetime.

With my hands flat on his bare chest, I found myself scooting up his body, stopping only when the soft fabric of my wet panties aligned perfectly with the tented fabric of his slacks. "I want you now," I whispered.

Logan's tongue flicked out to wet his lips. "I'm drunk, probably not the best idea."

I raised myself ever so slightly and lowered my body, making the most exquisite contact with his erection. "I'm not and you seem just fine."

His hand stroked my hair and pulled out the clip holding it up. "You want this? Here?"

My breath was wild. My nipples taut. My clit was pulsing. I realized I was excited. "Yes, I want you to take me here."

His gaze slid to the side and so did mine. James was thrusting into Lindsay's mouth. "James!" Logan shouted.

A grunt was his only reply.

"Hurry up and get the fuck inside, will you."

Again, a grunt was his response.

Logan's attention back on me, his hands threaded through my hair and slid over my shoulders and down my arms to capture my hands. He pressed our palms together so that our fingers were linked and drew in a shuddering breath. "You're so beautiful. You know that?"

"I love you." I'm not sure why I felt compelled to tell him that, but the way he looked at me when I did made me feel like we'd both found true love in each other, and all the worries that messed with my thoughts evaporated as his gaze flared. All that mattered was him. Comforting him. Getting him through this. Being here—for him.

He brought me to him with a hand to the back of my head, holding me in place while he kissed me breathless, maybe hard enough that he might have bruised my mouth.

Again, I didn't care.

The kiss went on and on and when he finally pulled away, I hadn't had nearly enough of him. It was when my eyes fell to the bag of joints on the ground that I realized Logan did not taste of thyme or moldy grass or smell like skunk, and I was a little glad that he hadn't gotten high. I had a feeling he had struggled with drugs during his life and with my own father being an alcoholic, I was all too familiar with the claim that addictive habits were hereditary.

Another sideways glance on his part had my gaze following. "Finally," he muttered. The lounge beside us was now empty, as was the living area. James and Lindsay must have gone into the bedroom. Logan must have been waiting for them to leave.

Knowing we were alone, lust won out over good sense and I stood and stripped myself naked.

Logan drew in a shuddering breath and stood as well, shedding his pants and underwear quickly.

I stared at him, naked and beautiful, and licked my lips. That card I'd seen in the store came to mind. Just because my issues might never allow me to be submissive didn't mean I couldn't be the dominant type.

He held out his hand for me to take it and instead I pointed to a chair next to the lounger. "Sit down."

"Don't you want to go inside?" he asked.

I shook my head. "No, sit down."

He raised a brow.

I kept my finger pointed.

No one could see us up this high and with the heat lamps on, something about fucking outside felt incredibly erotic.

A slow, seductive smile spread across his lips, and as he sat his eyes looked like dark flames. The hazel was gone, replaced by dilated pupils that bled pure lust.

Since I was already drenched, he easily slid inside me as I sat on his cock.

The sensation of him filling me made me shout out, and Logan wasn't exactly quiet himself. I heard pleasurable groans escape his throat.

This was what we both needed.

Each other.

I just hoped it would be like this forever.

My hands were not bound but they gripped the chair, my back was to his chest, and my legs were spread wide. I was open to him. Fully and completely open to him. In this position, I was his to do with whatever he pleased.

It was then I realized that in our relationship we didn't need a dominant or a submissive. We only needed each other.

And as his palm found my breast and his fingers pressed against my clit, I closed my eyes and relished what I had with him.

For us . . . give and take was all we needed.

chapter
TWENTY-ONE

Day 30

LOGAN

"LET'S GO TO NEW York."

"What?" she asked in surprise.

"Let's go to New York," I repeated.

"Why?" she sputtered.

Perched high on top of a ladder, I took the nail from my mouth and set the hammer down. "To get away. We can stay at my apartment in the city, go out to dinner with James and Lindsay, hang out with the gang, and do mindless tourist things I can't stand even thinking about. You know, like going to the top of the Empire State Building or taking the ferry over to the Statue of Liberty." With a wince, I added, "We could even see a Broadway show."

"Logan, it all sounds wonderful, but you know I can't leave the boutique. Rachel has Tuesday and Wednesday off and Peyton can't manage things alone. I also have a schedule with Clementine that I like to keep to as much as possible. Routine is important for her right now."

I picked the nail back up and pounded it into the wall. "I know all of that. I was thinking we could leave tonight after you close up and come back late Monday night, in time for the boutique to reopen on Tuesday. That way we won't impact your work and your schedule with Clementine won't need too much altering. It's just one weekend away."

She pulled her lower lip between her teeth. "It could work, but what about you? Don't you have appointments?"

"I already checked and I don't have any on Monday—my schedule is clear."

Elle handed me the twin to the cuckoo clock that was already on the wall. "Do you really think it's a good idea right now?"

I eyed the clock with disdain and then hooked it on the nail. "This? No." I grinned. "But a weekend away with you, yeah, I do."

She stared up at the clock. "That's good, right there. And you know that's not what I meant."

I double-checked to make sure the clock wasn't tilted and then waved my finger between them. "Are they going to go off at the same time?"

She nodded with a playful grin.

"Fuck."

Her laugh sounded good. "I think you secretly want me to bring one home."

I shook my head and caught her eye, seriousness taking over. "Elle, I'm fine. I know I've been in a bit of a funk and preoccupied with getting to the bottom of this drug ring over the last two weeks, but that's why I need to get away. Everything is spinning and nothing is making sense. I just need to forget about my grandfather, Tommy, Patrick, about everything . . . even if it is only for a couple of days."

Those green eyes, whose magic had spilled out into my life and changed it from a world of black and white to one where color actually seemed possible, looked contemplative. "It's just that I don't know if now is the right time."

She'd been worried about me. That I wasn't going to recover from my grandfather's death. Sure, I'd been distant. Quiet. Gone a lot. Tracking endless leads taking me nowhere. Going on wild goose chases that only brought me back to the starting point. In my defense, my mind was constantly thinking and my body had to keep moving. It was how I coped. But I was Killian McPherson's grandson, and he'd roll in his grave if he even sensed I'd let his death keep me down for too long. I looked over at her. I couldn't believe how much I needed her. I couldn't lose her. "I'm fine, or I will be as soon as all of this is over. Just hang in there with me. Give me some time to figure it out." I was determined to find out who the Priest was and what his connection to O'Shea was. I felt like it was a big puzzle and all of the pieces fit in there somewhere.

Tears seemed to fill her eyes. "I'm not going anywhere. And it's not time that worries me. It's you, going out there alone. Let your friends help you." Her worry over me was evident. She didn't like me going out on the streets on my own. Neither did Miles. Or Declan. I got it. Still, it was something I thought I should do by myself. But looking at her now, and after two weeks of getting nowhere, I knew it was time to stop being reckless and start being smart.

Climbing down the ladder, my grandfather's voice came to mind. *It's not how you fall, Logan,* he used to say, *it's how you get up that matters.* Distancing myself from everyone hadn't been on purpose, but his death had been a shock. The funeral was brutal and ever since, I'd been on a rampage to get to the truth. Every day I'd had to face the daunting reality that he was gone—because of me. It was harsh and tough to face. But my determination to make his death mean what he wanted it to mean—the freedom of my old man—was what had kept me grounded. Freeing my old man from the DEA was still on the table and that was what kept me moving forward, searching, looking, forging through all the shit. Even when it got me nowhere.

My old man surprised me. He was stronger than I'd ever thought he was. Somehow, he managed to stay away from the bottle. I knew it would take time for us both to truly accept that Killian wasn't around anymore, but we both would in our way. We were the blood of a very strong man, after all.

As for why Patrick offered the swap of lives in the first place, that was pretty evident. Now up on RICO charges, his power was quickly dwindling, and getting rid of Killian was a power-play move. I'm sure in his own twisted way it somehow made him feel stronger, even behind bars, to have the authority to order a hit on the ex-mob boss. I'd made sure to put a crack in his shield, though. Let information slip on the streets that both Patrick and Tommy were going soft, turning state's evidence against the gang. It was as much a lie as it was the truth, but I didn't care. I wanted him out of play. Over the past two weeks the Blue Hill Gang had dismantled—every guy taking what he could and leaving town, or at least laying low. There had been no activity from any of them. Blanchet owed me one because chances were good that the Blue Hill Gang would completely dissolve very soon.

The information Tommy had told me about O'Shea still couldn't be validated in any way. I had no idea if Tommy was telling the truth about his relationship with Lizzy, but my gut told me that it was at least partly true. Still, there were holes in his story. Mainly, how did Tommy know about the hit on my grandfather if he was out of the loop? Why would Patrick have told him? To gain his trust? To test him? Or was it possible someone in the organization leaked it to him? I had to find this out. It was key to trusting what Tommy had told me.

Then again, if I really thought about it, more than likely Tommy had killed Elle's sister and wanted me to spend my time chasing something that wasn't there. He wanted me to lose my mind thinking about Elle with Michael and wonder if he might do to her what he'd done to his wife. That was much more his game than the fact that a woman had stolen his heart and he wanted to avenge her death. No, he knew that was more my thing.

Regardless, I needed to get back inside to talk to him. See what I could find out about this Priest, but Miles couldn't make it happen. I guess Tommy had spent a good two days in the clinic, and the explanation that it was a self-inflicted injury wasn't holding up well with the higher-ups.

The only lead Miles had on where the Priest was located was where the drug deals were taking place, and that turned out to be a dead end. The cokehead Miles had found pointed out three buildings on the waterfront where the deals might have gone down. They all looked alike. No specific location could be identified. Absolutely no fucking help at all.

I wanted more. I wanted to know who the Priest was because (A), if I provided that information, Blanchet would remove my father's name from all of her files, and (B), now this was personal and I just fucking wanted to know.

The problem was that he was a ghost. The Priest was known on the street, but no one knew his true identity or where to find him.

It was early Saturday morning and Elle was trying really hard to make sure I stayed off the streets, so she'd asked me to help her do a few things before she opened the boutique. The ulterior motive was clear, but I didn't care; I liked helping her and just being with her made me feel better. Besides, I'd already decided it was time to ask Declan and Miles for more help in finding the Priest.

As I glanced at her, I couldn't help but feel she, too, had been preoccupied over the past two weeks. I could sense something more was on her mind that she wasn't telling me. I took the last rung of the ladder and turned to her. "Well?" I asked, vowing to get to the heart of what was eating at her this weekend.

She raised a brow and pointed to the ladder behind me. "Do that again, will you?"

I laughed and for shits and giggles, played along and turned back. My cell vibrated in my pocket and I ignored it. The fun between us had all but been zapped with Killian's death, but maybe this was the start of something even more. The flirtatious, sexy side I knew she had somewhere deep inside her was blossoming. And I really wanted to nurture what was emerging. Up on one rung, I twisted around. "You want me to go up and down the ladder so you can stare at my ass, don't you?" I said coyly.

She flushed.

"Well?"

She stepped closer. "It is a great view from down here."

Overjoyed, I yanked her to me and gently pulled her mouth to mine. "Answer me."

Her body melded to mine instantly. "What was the question?" she asked, a little breathless.

Lip on lip, a gentle brush meant to be a small kiss. "You know what it was. Say yes," I murmured with our mouths pressed together.

"Yes, I'll go." Her voice was low and I felt uncertainty in her tone.

I pulled back. Looked at her. Knew something was there. Waiting until tonight to talk about it sounded great in theory, but I couldn't. "Why do I feel like there's a 'but' in there somewhere?"

Elle took a deep breath and stepped off the ladder.

I followed.

She was wearing tight black skinny jeans, a gray sleeveless top, and a pair of boots. She looked sexy as fuck. "Logan," she said quietly. "There's something about myself I should have told you before we let things get so serious. But we went from zero to sixty and I never found the right time."

My brow creased. "Okay."

She drew in another breath.

My cell vibrated again, but I was too busy trying to untwist the knot that just formed in my gut to even think about answering it. "Hey, just tell me, because right now I'm thinking all kinds of weird shit, like maybe you have a husband out there and you want to go back to him."

She shook her head and the corners of her mouth tugged up slightly.

"Phew, okay then, anything else I can handle."

"There's no easy way to say this, so I'm just going to say it. I can't get pregnant."

I opened my mouth to speak, but I wasn't sure what the correct response to that was. An *"I'm pregnant"* might have shocked the shit out of me, but an *"I can't get pregnant"*? I wasn't sure what to do with that.

"Let me explain," she added.

Good, because I was standing there dumbfounded.

She seemed a little lost, and the breath she sucked in tore at me.

"Take your time, Elle. I'm here when you're ready."

She blew out the breath she was holding. "Okay, I'm ready."

I stepped a little closer.

She stopped me from getting too close. "When I was fifteen, my mother started to go into renal failure and needed a kidney transplant. My sister and I were both matches, but my sister was the better match. The surgery was scheduled, but the night before my sister swallowed a bottle of sleeping pills and had to have her stomach pumped. Because of this she was no longer a viable donor, and I took her place. During the surgery there was a complication. Once I was closed up my vitals weren't recovering. The doctors discovered I was hemorrhaging internally and the surgeon had to go back in."

Step by step, I slowly inched toward her. My heart was beating faster as she revealed more of the horrific childhood she'd had to endure.

She was shaking as she relived what must have been a nightmare. "I was bleeding severely and somehow in the midst of the trauma, my uterine wall had been torn. The doctors tried to fix it, but in the end they couldn't. Now, I can't get pregnant."

I wiped her tears away with my thumbs. "I'm sorry, Elle. That was a terrible thing that happened to you."

She pressed her face against my hand. "I'll understand if you want to end things."

My breath caught in my throat. Was she kidding me? "How can you even say that?"

"Because I'm broken," she whispered.

"Broken?"

"Yes, I'm barren. And if we stay together, I can't have your children. I should have told you a long time ago and I'm so sorry I didn't." She said it with such sadness in her voice that it hurt to hear.

Everything about her suddenly became very clear. I understood now more than ever her connection to Clementine. I took her hand. "I'm not him, Elle. I'm not your father, and I'm not your old boyfriend. I'm not going to leave you. I'm not either of them."

She squeezed her fingers around mine. "I know you're not them, Logan, and right now it might not seem like a big deal, but it is. You're younger than I am, don't forget, so maybe you're not thinking about a family right now, but someday you will. And this is especially important for you because you're an only child and it means your last name won't have a legacy. There will be no one to carry on your family name."

All I could do was stare at her. She was broken, but not in the way she thought. Actually, I preferred to think she was bent and I could straighten her out the way she was doing it to me. I brought my hands to her face. "If the day comes that we decide it's time to have children, we'll adopt."

She shook her head.

"Elle, it's done all the time."

Tears were in her eyes. On her cheeks. Sliding down her face. "Logan, don't you understand? I can't have your children and you know this now. You should walk away and find someone else. Someone who can give you a family."

Taking her other hand, I tugged her closer to me. "Just like you once said, I'm not going anywhere. I'm sorry, Elle, but I really don't see this as a roadblock in our relationship. Not in the slightest bit."

"You're not mad I didn't tell you before?"

My hands cupped her face. "No. This obviously means a lot to you, and finding the strength and courage to finally tell me makes me proud of what we have together. It means you trust me, you really trust me."

Relief. Hope. Admiration. A myriad of images passed over her features.

The butler bell on the door chimed, surprising me, and I quickly turned around.

"Hey, man, I've been calling you," Declan said, walking in with Peyton and a tray full of coffees.

I leaned in and whispered into Elle's ear, "We'll finish talking about this later."

This time she took my face in her hands. "Think about it, Logan, really think about it. It's a much bigger deal than you realize."

With a hug and a kiss to her on the forehead I whispered, "I don't have to. What you told me doesn't change anything between us."

"It should."

"Stop it," I scolded. Thinking she was being ridiculous, I kissed her on the lips and pulled away. Then I turned to Declan. "You got me now. What's up?"

"Miles just called me. Tommy Flannigan was found dead in his cell this morning. Knife to the throat."

The girls both gasped.

A chill ran through me. Not because the motherfucker was dead. Not because I felt a huge sigh of relief that the shadow that had loomed over me for years was finally gone. But rather, because if his death actually occurred as he predicted, the chances that he was lying about O'Shea killing Lizzy were pretty slim.

"Crazy shit. Right?" Declan said.

My mind was thinking in overdrive. I kissed Elle one more time and then focused on what came next. "Are you busy right now?" I asked Declan.

"I have to go in to work and do inventory, but I'm flexible. Why? What's on your mind?"

I looked at my watch. It was almost nine.

Elle looked at me warily.

I had to be careful. And I would be. I wasn't going to go this alone anymore. Still, I knew she'd worry, and telling her my thoughts wouldn't ease her mind at all. I didn't want to lie, but I couldn't blurt out the truth just yet, either. "I wanted to hit the gym before it got too busy. Saturdays can be crazy in there."

Saturdays were always dead in the morning and he knew that. Too many hangovers for the guys to show up that early and start pounding the bag. "Yeah, sounds great."

The boutique opened at ten, and it looked like Elle was happy with my response and was starting to get ready. She was behind the cash register, counting the money in the drawer. I walked up behind her and put my lips to her ear. "I'll pick you up at six. We'll run back to your place and grab a few things, and then jet. We can even take my old man's car if you want."

I felt her shiver under my touch, and I knew if we were alone and I could slide my hands between her legs that I could reassure her everything was fine. She must have had the same thought because she pushed her body back against mine. "Are you sure?" she asked.

I turned her around and pulled her flush to me so I could kiss her harder, more passionately. "I'm sure . . . about everything," I said, stressing the last word.

She squeezed me tightly and I knew she felt relieved about telling me. I wasn't lying to her about my feelings. We'd be just fine, and we'd deal with the child situation when the time came.

Declan was busy tongue-diving into Peyton's mouth and I thumped him on the shoulder. "Come on, man, let's go."

He pulled away from Peyton and I heard her sigh.

Guess they liked each other.

When we stepped out onto the sidewalk, the sky was bright enough that I had to pull out my sunglasses. I stopped just out of sight of the boutique. "Can you call Miles and see if he can meet us at my old man's in an hour?

We need to regroup."

Declan squinted against the sun. "Yeah, sure. What are you thinking?"

"That there's a possibility Tommy wasn't lying about O'Shea killing Lizzy or about the reemergence of the Dorchester Heights Gang."

Declan tilted his head.

"What?" I said.

He eyed me. "Scary shit, that's all."

I started to walk backwards. "Maybe, maybe not."

Using his hand as a visor, he shaded his eyes. "You have a plan?"

When I reached the Rover, I hopped in. "Yes. See you in an hour."

Elle had driven the Rover once but after the first time she drove in my old man's beat-up Porsche 964, she fell in love with it. Why, I have no idea. The black 1989 Porsche looked like it needed a shower even after it rained—the paint had no gleam left. But like my old man, something about it charmed her.

Either way, she had two options, and it hadn't gotten by me that she was still borrowing Peyton's car when she visited Clementine, which means she hadn't told O'Shea about us yet. I hadn't pressed the issue, either. And now in light of the fact that Tommy might not have been yanking my chain after all, it was probably best she didn't tell him about me.

For now.

It would more than likely just piss him off.

But Elle had a point. She didn't see O'Shea as a killer, so if Tommy was right, there had to be more to all of this.

I put the car in drive and took off.

The house in Dorchester Heights had belonged to my grandfather for more years than I'd been alive. With its small front porch, narrow driveway, detached garage, and side door that got used more than the front, I wondered if my old man would keep it now that Gramps wasn't around, or sell it and move somewhere else.

Maybe even out of this godforsaken town.

Something felt different when I walked into my old man's kitchen. The memories of what had happened here would never truly fade from my memory, but with Tommy gone, I felt like I could breathe.

A huge burden had been lifted from my shoulders. Not only was Elle no longer in danger—from Tommy, anyway—but my old man was free. No more mob ties that bound him.

"Pop!" I yelled, walking toward the family room, where I expected to see him horizontal on the couch watching sports highlights.

Perfectly groomed hair, wearing a pair of jeans and a Red Sox T-shirt, my old man appeared on the landing of the stairs. "Logan, what are you doing here?"

Freedom seemed to be good for him.

I raised a brow. "Came to bend your ear. Where are you going?"

His grin was wide. "At the last minute your uncle Hunter somehow snagged two tickets to opening day at Fenway."

"Is he here? I didn't see his car."

My father looked at his watch. "Should be here any minute."

"That's awesome," I beamed.

He was tucking in his shirt as he came down. "Do you want to come? I'm sure we can get you a ticket. The scalpers will be out in full force today."

I plopped down on the couch. "No, I'm good. But is it okay if I hang out here?"

"Yeah, no problem. What did you want to talk about?"

Everything about him was so calm, I didn't want to ruin that by bringing up Tommy or the threat of a possible underground gang. "Cars. I wanted to discuss cars. Elle needs to get one soon. You get your license reinstated in a couple of weeks, right?"

The smile on his face made me feel like he was going to be okay. "That's right. May first, and you no longer have to be my driver."

I ran a hand through my hair. "It's about fucking time," I joked.

"What are you thinking?"

My brow creased.

"About a car for Elle. Any thoughts on make or model?" he asked.

Beep. Beep.

He grabbed his wallet. "That's Hunter."

"Go, we can talk about this later."

"You sure?"

"Yes, there's no rush."

"Do you want to run out and say hi to your uncle?"

I shook my head. "No, you guys go on. I'll catch him next time."

My father looked at me as if he knew I was lying about something. "How about dinner tomorrow?"

"Can't, I'm taking Elle to New York for the weekend. We won't be back until Monday night."

Beep. Beep.

"I think that's a great idea. The last couple of weeks have been difficult on us all. Relax, son, and try to have fun. I'll talk to you when you get back."

I gave him a nod. "Oh, hey, one more thing. What's that guy's name over at Tobey's Automotive you use to tune up the Porsche?"

"Dwayne. Why, is something wrong with it?"

Beep. Beep.

"There's a hum in the engine that sounds off. I want to see if he can look at it today before I leave."

He was halfway out the door. "I'll give him a call." He glanced toward the driveway. "Where's it at?"

"Elle's. I drove her to work."

His spare set of keys to the car was on the hook near the door and he grabbed it. "I'll stop by the garage now. I'm sure he'll be able to send someone over to her place to pick it up this morning and have it done by the end of the day."

"That would be great."

Beep. Beep.

"He's an impatient motherfucker."

"Like his younger brother." I grinned.

My old man gave me a shake of his head and then he was out the door.

It was strange not telling him about Tommy, but there was time. I would call him once the news was released, which depending on the circumstances could be as late as next week. But for now, he could use the peace and quiet. For the first time in over twelve years he wasn't bogged down with the life of the Blue Hill Gang, and I just wasn't going to pull him back into all the shit. Especially with my uncle Hunter in town. He had kept his distance from that life and preferred to be kept completely out of the loop.

The remote was beside me. I clicked the television on and turned the channel to World News. Stretching my feet out on the coffee table as I caught up on what was happening in the world outside of Boston, my mind started to free itself of everything that was threatening to swallow me whole.

Just as the haze of mindlessness settled in, there was a knock on the kitchen door.

"Come in," I called.

Keys hit the counter. "Where are you?"

"Family room."

Miles strode in and Declan right behind him.

Declan, wearing torn jeans and leather braided bracelets, waited for me to move my feet to let him pass.

"Finally ready to do this as a team?" Miles asked, taking a seat in the chair my father always sat in.

I sat up straight. "Yeah, I am, but why do you want to help me?" I asked them both.

"That's what friends do," Declan said.

"I want to see justice served," Miles replied.

"Right. A little too emotional," I joked, then laughed.

"So what's the plan?" Declan asked.

"Flush the Priest out."

"How?"

I looked toward Miles. "You must know some cops looking for him."

The grin on Miles's face was wide. "Oh, they're looking for him. The guys on the beat tell me they've definitely been hearing rumblings of emerging underground activity and they're looking to squash it. It seems Blue Hill's downfall is leaving the city wide open and they're worried."

My brows popped. "Any of them say whether it's coming from the men in Patrick's old crowd? The former Dorchester Heights Gang members?"

Miles crossed his leg over his knee. "Nope. The gang was small and no one has names. The only name they've heard on the streets is the Priest."

Declan kicked back and put his arms behind his neck. "Let me ask my old man. He'll remember who was involved."

"You sure he'll tell you?" I asked as I stood. "He's been out of it for so long."

"He'll tell me."

I gave him a nod.

"Get me the names, I'll slide them over to the BPD and let them look into it."

We all nodded.

Declan shifted in his seat. "Moving forward. I just don't get why Patrick would have his own son killed unless he stood to benefit somehow. I mean, I know he's a heartless bastard, but he kept Tommy as his number two for all this time, even through all of his fuck-ups. So why now?"

Miles shook his head in agreement. "I'm with you. Why? It's true we all know Patrick didn't keep Tommy around for his brains. He fucked up time after time, each train wreck worse than the last, so how is it Tommy stealing money and selling drugs under Patrick's nose is any bigger of a crime?"

"A life for a life," I muttered.

"What'd you say?" Miles asked, his ears perking.

"A life for a life. It's the code on the street."

Declan shot to his feet. "That's it. Patrick had to have given up his son as retribution."

I started to pace. "But for whose death?"

"That's what we have to find out. If we find out who has Patrick by the balls, who Patrick gave his son up for, we'll be one step closer to uncovering this entire mess."

"You think it could be the Priest?" Miles asked.

"I do, except he has to be relatively new in town. I don't see him having the pull to get Patrick to agree to off his own son." Glancing out the window at the clouds that had started to take dark form in the sky, I hated to rain on their parade. "Then again, what if Patrick simply ordered the hit on Tommy for the drug deals he was making behind his back? What if that's all there was to it?"

Miles was shaking his head. "We talked about this. It makes no sense."

"I agree," Declan added.

"Okay, I agree too. So what next?"

Miles pointed at me. "You lay low. You've caused enough chaos on the streets. Playing off of the life-for-a-life thing, let me ask around and see if anyone of importance was one of the Blue Hill Gang's victims. Coming from me, no one will question it. Coming from you, it might just get you killed."

I conceded. He had a point. I had gotten in a little over my head. "What about O'Shea?" I asked.

"Seems clean. Can't find anything linking him to his wife's disappearance before her murder."

"And Tommy? Any solid links to Lizzy or O'Shea?" I asked.

"Well, we know she worked at Lucy's. As for Tommy's claim that Lizzy and him were an item, nothing solid to prove that other than the tape where we saw them together at the hotel."

Declan cleared his throat.

"You got something?" I asked him.

"Not much, but I talked to a few guys who've gone to Lucy's for years. One remembers her from about two years ago. He said, and I quote, she was a chick who really knew how to suck his dick in the backroom. Another dude said he thinks he remembers seeing Tommy with her more than any of the other girls but when he paid her a hundred to blow him under the table, Tommy was cool with it. Anyway, if Tommy was tapping Lizzy, he didn't mind her blowing others while he was hitting it."

"Maybe they weren't together. Maybe he lied," I noted.

"Either way, he sounds like a real scum bag," Miles remarked.

"Did either of the guys you talked to know O'Shea?" I asked Declan.

"Not sure; I didn't ask. What are you thinking?"

"Maybe he had met Lizzy before he represented her on that pro-bono prostitution charge, like at a strip club, and that's the connection between the three of them. I mean I'm really reaching here."

"Like maybe at Lucy's?"

I was leaning against the wall. "Exactly."

"Let me check into it," Miles said as he rose to his feet.

Declan was already in the doorway. "Let's get together Tuesday and go through everything again. See if we can come up with anything new."

"Sure. Let's talk to Frank, too. He was around in the Dorchester Heights Gang days. Molly's, Tuesday at seven?" I suggested.

"It's a plan," Declan said.

"Sounds good," said Miles.

I followed the two of them out to the kitchen. After they left, I stood there for a bit, listening for ghosts.

None.

I pulled my wallet out of my pocket and took the newspaper clipping of Emily's death I kept there from it. It was time to let that go. I crumpled it and threw it in the trash.

With a deep breath, I thought about whether I should be kicking a possible hornet's nest. Tommy was gone and nothing around me showed signs of upheaval. Yet, there was something about O'Shea that had nagged me from the moment I laid eyes on him.

My gramps, too.

Blanchet aside, that was reason enough to dig further.

But not today.

Today was a day of celebration. With the threat of Tommy no longer hanging over us, it felt like a fresh start for Elle and me.

Hopping back in my truck, I decided to go to the bank and get that ring my gramps wanted me to have. I didn't know when I'd give it to Elle, but I wanted to have it cleaned and sized so when the time was right, it would be ready.

I hightailed it back to Elle's place first to get the key out of the silver box. I'd told Elle about the box but not the key. And like my grandfather, I didn't go to much trouble to hide the box. It had always worked for him. While I was there, I picked up my shit that was all over her room. Elle had been cool about it, but it was time to get my laundry done. While I was at it, I also packed a few things for the weekend. I didn't need much since we'd be staying at my apartment.

My apartment.

I needed to figure out what to do with it.

My current financial status dictated that I should sell it, which didn't bother me. It wasn't like I was attached to it or anything. It was nice, though. Located in a ritzy, white-glove building directly across the street from the Metropolitan Museum of Art, it was prime real estate. The problem was my grandfather owned the building and he had insisted that I live there, which meant I bought it for next to nothing. I wasn't sure what he'd think about me selling it.

Then again, he was much cooler with the news of my leave of absence from the Ryan Corporation than I thought he would be. I think he was finally coming to understand I preferred working on my own. I have no idea what brought about his change of heart, but I accepted it at face value and figured it was time to terminate my employment now that I knew I'd be staying in Boston.

Although Elle and I really hadn't discussed where I'd reside, I knew she wouldn't leave Clementine, which meant either I moved to Boston or our relationship turned long distance. The thought of not seeing her every day twisted my gut and the answer to where I would live was an easy one—anywhere she was.

After I shoved everything in the back of the Rover, I jumped in and headed for the bank. The dark clouds had multiplied and there was no doubt rain was coming.

For some reason it made me think about the first night I met Elle. It was raining and she was so wet when she walked into Molly's. Even then I thought she looked beautiful. *Exquisite* may be a better word. There wasn't anything about her that didn't make me want to give her as much of myself as I possibly could.

Just as the rain started to pound the pavement, something in my rearview mirror grabbed my attention. Someone was following me. My mindless driving had me looking around, trying to figure out where the fuck I was.

I hadn't been paying attention.

Okay, I was on a small side street, just having crossed over Dorchester Avenue. With another glance in my rearview mirror, I saw flashing blue lights. The sound of the siren immediately followed.

Fuck, how fast was I going? I hadn't been paying attention.

I pulled over and then yanked open the glove box to retrieve my insurance card. As I was reaching for my wallet, I noticed another cop car pull behind the one already parked.

Suspicion started to loom.

The rain was falling, and as one officer got out of the first car in his rain gear, another leaned out, holding a transmitter in his hand. "Get out of the car with your hands up."

Fuck me. Not this again.

Slowly, I opened the door and heard my sneakers squishing in the water as I stepped away from the car and turned around. It wasn't Blanchet's goon squad, though, like I thought it might be. These cops were from Patrick's neighborhood, which meant more than likely they were on Patrick's payroll.

Fuck me.

The officers approached me and this time there was no pretense. "Logan McPherson, you're under arrest."

"What for?" I yelled over the drowning sound of the rain.

"Aiding and abetting a known felon with possible terrorist ties."

Cuffs were being slapped on me before I could even draw a breath to think. "What are you talking about?"

The cop from the second car got out and strode over toward us. He popped the hatch to the back of the Rover. "Call impound and have them pick up the vehicle."

"Why? What's going on?"

No answer.

One was in front of me. Another one behind me. The third was now inside the Rover. "I got a weapon," he said.

"It's registered," I bit out.

"Move it," the one from behind drawled.

Sandwiched between two of them, I was being shoved toward the police car. "You have to read me my rights."

"Law enforcement has the ability to question suspected terrorists without immediately providing Miranda warnings when the interrogation is reasonably prompted by immediate concern for the safety of the public . . ."

I struggled against the hold on me. My legs stopped moving. My body became rigid. My shoulders squared.

No. No. No.

This wasn't happening. This couldn't be happening.

I started to dig my heels in. That's when I saw the baton. Felt it against my rib cage, my thighs, my back, and then my legs. The one cop kept speaking. The second cop was now dragging me to the car.

They could keep me in isolation for a prolonged period of time by marking me as a potential terrorist. Twenty-four, forty-eight, or even seventy-two hours wouldn't be blinked upon.

Up to three days I could be MIA.

Elle.

Elle.

What would she think?

Oh, God! Fuck no.

"You have to let me make a call," I pleaded.

Their laughter was loud and the echo of it carried over the rain.

There weren't going to let me do shit.

At that point I tuned out.

I knew the law. I knew what this meant. The only way to gain latitude when it came to Miranda Rights was for the DEA to have turned to the FBI.

The DEA knew. Somehow they knew I'd moved the cocaine. They had to.

And now they'd involved the FBI.

I was fucked on so many levels.

chapter TWENTY-TWO

Elle

THE CLOCK ON THE wall read six twenty.

It wasn't like Logan to not call if he was going to be late. I pushed the door open and stood outside. Time passed slowly as I gazed around. At the sidewalk that was wet from the rainstorm that had just passed. At the spring leaves that blew in the cool breeze and stuck to the ground. At the birds singing in the sky.

When the streetlights switched on to illuminate the impending dusk, I glanced at the time again.

Six forty.

A dark and terrible thought pushed to the front of my mind as I pressed end on the call I'd just made. It was something my mother had always said, and it had been in my mind ever since Killian's death.

Things come in threes.

Was this the third?

One last time I tried to call him, but Logan's phone was still going directly to voicemail. I left a short message: "Logan, it's me. I'm going to go ahead and walk home. In case we miss each other, meet mc there."

I could call Peyton and ask her to come back and pick me up, but the walk to my townhouse was short and I hoped it would help unravel the unease I was feeling in the pit of my stomach. I refused to think the way my mind was headed.

Logan and I had simply crossed wires. Miscommunicated. He was probably at my house waiting for me and hadn't realized his phone had died.

Yet, deep within, I knew that wasn't the case. He was always beside his phone. Always answered every single one of my calls.

Nonetheless, I pushed that aside until I couldn't any longer.

As soon as I turned the corner onto my street, I noticed the Porsche was gone. Picking up the pace, I started to run down the street. I felt like it was Charlie all over again. Charlie was my first love. The only person I had said "I love you" to besides Logan. At the time I was young and naïve, and I mistakenly thought love conquered all.

I learned the hard way—that couldn't be farther from the truth.

Charlie and I were inseparable.

We were such a perfect pair with such similar interests.

We'd been living together for a while when one day, he came home and announced, "My family is coming to visit."

I was shocked. "When?"

"Next month. They're going to adore you, love."

Nervousness was the only thing I felt for the next week. When I came home from work one night, out of the blue, he started talking about marriage.

Marriage? Was this because of his family coming?

I felt sick. I couldn't discuss marriage until he knew everything about me. "Charlie," I interrupted as he was going on about how perfect we were for each other.

"Yes, love," he said.

"I have something to tell you."

Right then and there, with no preparation at all, I was forced to tell him I was unable to have children.

Charlie did his best to accept that hard truth but as the weeks passed leading to his family's arrival, I could tell he wasn't doing well processing the information. He was from a large family and I had come to learn he, too, wanted a large family.

All talk of marriage had ceased and he began to pull away from me. More time passed and we were no longer inseparable. I had thought about ending things before he eventually did, but I just couldn't. I didn't want to be alone, so I held on to hope. Hope that I shouldn't have had.

Three days before his family was to arrive, I had to go out of town. It was a Wednesday and I had to travel from Paris to Monaco. The back-to-back meetings and seven-hour commute had me returning just in time to meet them on Saturday. But by some stroke of luck, on Friday morning I had finished my work and decided to hop on an earlier train.

Feeling stressed about our relationship, I knew Charlie and I needed to spend some time together and just talk before his family arrived, so I stopped at the store and bought what I needed to make a nice dinner. My arms were loaded with bags when I burst open the door to our flat and found it practically empty. Everything that Charlie had brought into our relationship was gone, and so was he. He'd left a note on the counter that said, I'm sorry. I just can't.

Approaching my townhouse, it felt like déjà vu as I reached my door and swung it open. "Logan!" I yelled.

There was no answer.

I knew there wouldn't be. The Rover wasn't parked out front and the Porsche was gone. Still, who knew? Maybe something had changed.

Hopeful, I hurried up the stairs and into my room. "Logan," I said hoarsely.

There was no answer.

That's when I knew there wasn't ever going to be one. His things that had been scattered around the room for weeks were gone. I'd told him the truth about myself and like Charlie, he couldn't handle it and had packed up and left.

"Logan," I whispered, and crumpled to my knees.

No tears fell, though. Somewhere in the back of my

mind I knew this was how things would end for us. There was no other way. Love really never would conquer all.

My father hadn't talked much about the future with me, but he had told me I'd end up alone. Taking charge of my own life, I'd set that course all by myself, but then with Logan, things had changed and I thought maybe my father had been wrong. In that regard, he wasn't.

That horrid memory started to materialize.

Huge and overpowering, he stood at my bedside. "I begged your mother not to go through with this, Gabrielle. I knew you weren't a strong enough match. We should have waited for your sister to be cleared."

"No, we couldn't wait. The doctors all said time was running out."

"Nonsense, they didn't know what they were talking about. Your mother was doing fine. She would have held in there. She was tough, like me."

He was delusional. Had he always been?

I think he refused to see my mother's physical weaknesses. "You're wrong," I dared to say out loud.

His eyes narrowed on me and his jaw twitched. "No, Gabrielle, you were wrong for agreeing to do this. For encouraging your mother. It was selfish of you to want to take your sister's place. Now, your mother is dead and I'll be stuck with you forever."

His words stung, but I kept on. "It wasn't about me. She was my mother and I loved her. I only wanted her to get better."

"And she was my wife."

Anger roiled in my gut. He'd said that as if it trumped anything I'd said. "She was just another one of your soldiers. Someone to command. You never loved her," I spat.

He grabbed my chin and jerked it toward him, slapping me hard. "You don't know what you're talking about. You should have listened to me. And because you didn't, she's gone and you have no future. Don't you see? No man will want you now."

Although frightened, I wouldn't let him see it. Instead, I jerked away. Even with tears in my eyes I refused to look anywhere but at him. In his face I saw many things, and I think he might have even had a tear in his own eye. We stared at each other until that one tear slid down his cheek. When I finally looked away, I wondered whether he was crying over my mother being gone or being stuck with me.

It was the only tear I ever saw him shed.

The shrill ring of my phone startled me. Tiny flicks of hope bloomed beneath my skin as I practically skidded for the purse that I'd thrown onto my bed. Fumbling to get it out, I couldn't help but think I had been wrong about Logan. My hands were shaking as I looked at the screen. The name *Michael*, not *Logan*, was what flashed before me. And just like that, all of my hope diminished. But then, what had I thought? That it was Logan, and even though he'd cleared out of my life, he'd miraculously changed his mind?

And what, that I was going to be okay with that?

The thought weakened my knees because yes, I would have been.

"Hello," I answered as I sat on the still tangled sheets where Logan and I had lain a mere twelve hours ago.

"Elle, hey, are you home?"

Five seconds of silence.

"Elle?"

I composed myself as best I could. "Yes, I am."

"Great. I just picked Clementine up from Erin's and she's been asking for you."

"Is everything okay?" I asked.

"Yeah, why wouldn't it be?"

"Where's Heidi?"

"I thought I told you. She quit. She was moving her things out today and I thought it would be best if we weren't around."

Concern for Clementine made my chest tighten. "Why? What happened?"

"It just wasn't working out. The live-in thing isn't for

me. I have someone new starting Monday. I know it's last minute, but it is Saturday. Any chance you haven't eaten yet and would like to come over for a late dinner? We can talk about it then."

The rain had kept me from taking Clementine on our Friday afternoon walk so I hadn't seen her since Wednesday, and I did miss her. Besides, getting out of here wouldn't be a bad idea. I tried to control the tremble in my voice. "As a matter of fact, I haven't eaten. Dinner sounds great." I had absolutely no appetite, but I did have a need to see Clementine. She was the only stable thing in my life.

"I'm about ten minutes away from your place. I can pick you up."

"That would be great. I'll be ready."

"And Elle, if you haven't arranged to purchase a new vehicle yet, you can take the Mercedes back until you do."

Although I knew better than to rely on anyone but myself, I also knew right now that I shouldn't turn it down. "I'd really appreciate that, Michael, but this time I promise it won't be for long."

My hands were still shaking when I hung up the phone. Heartbroken, I absolutely hated what was happening in my life right now. It felt out of control. For so long, it hadn't been. For so long, it had been just the way I'd planned it. Right now, I felt like that teen under my father's rule—lost and alone.

Soon enough I'd have saved enough money to make a down payment on a car and could stop relying on other people. Depending on others never ended well.

How had I ever allowed myself to become dependent on Logan? I was stronger than that.

Moving quickly to avoid letting my feelings take over, I hurried downstairs and grabbed some clean clothes out of the laundry room. I think I was in a state of shock over Logan leaving me, because what should have been sorrow was beginning to feel more like rage.

When Charlie left me I had been sad. Right now I was

mad.

Coward!

I'd thought I knew Logan. I'd thought he was different. That he really, truly loved me. Me. But I had been wrong.

Staying away from here for a couple of days would probably be best. And I knew Michael wouldn't mind. If I were alone, I didn't know what I'd do. Thoughts of hunting Logan down and telling him how I felt were top on the list, though. His father's and Molly's were two more-than-likely places he'd be. But a psycho ex-girlfriend was nothing I wanted to be.

No, I'd leave things the way he did.

Silent and broken.

Tossing some extra clothes into a bag was all I needed to do. I'd left toiletries at Michael's from my nights of staying over before Logan.

Beep. Beep.

Compartmentalizing my anguish was something I knew how to do well. I drew in a breath and headed for the door. Whenever I went to Michael's I had to leave Logan behind, and this time would be no different.

The cool night air felt good on my skin but as I walked toward Michael's car, I just couldn't let go of Logan. I told myself to squelch the sadness that was looming over me. He was gone. The faster I could accept that, the better off I'd be. Still, I couldn't help but remember how I thought he was different. How I thought he loved me in a way no one ever had.

That our love could conquer anything.

Mindlessly, I opened the door.

"Mommy!" Clementine shrieked as soon as she saw me.

All things Logan disappeared as panic set in. With my heart in my throat, my eyes darted to Michael.

He was shaking his head. "Clementine, Daddy told you, that's Auntie Elle. Your mommy's in heaven."

"Mommy," she called again, waiting for me to turn around and greet her.

My eyes were still on Michael as I got in and closed the door. "She keeps referring to you that way. I'm sorry, but I don't know how to get her to stop."

It was odd, but a feeling of relief coursed through me and I turned around. "Hi, silly girl." I clutched her kicking foot. "I missed you. How are you today?"

Sputtering sounds escaped her throat and my broken heart felt a little more whole at the pure excitement this little girl felt at seeing me.

She was what I needed.

Michael pulled away and a piece of my heart was left on the curb.

"So how's business?" he asked. "We haven't talked much lately. It's keeping you pretty busy, I take it."

The boutique was the other bright spot in my life. "Business is booming. I can't believe how people have taken to the idea of the finest things in life. To be honest, I'm having a hard time keeping the shelves stocked. I'm trying to buy up as much inventory as I can."

The rain started up again and he took the corner with caution. "Not a bad problem to have."

Everything with Michael seemed more at ease tonight. Our conversations were slowly getting easier with each passing day, like they had been before that night that changed everything. The night he, in the most roundabout way, told me that if I didn't help him I'd be banned from Clementine's life. Stress had a way of impacting people, though, and maybe he hadn't meant it the way it came across. He was obviously worried about his daughter. And for good reason. Understanding that, and even though I knew I had to stay on my guard, I was happy things felt more back to normal.

"What do you think?" he asked as he pulled into his garage.

I blinked, realizing I'd tuned him completely out for most of the ride.

He laughed. "I thought I lost you somewhere on the

highway. I was talking about dinner. I picked up every-thing I need to make chicken stir-fry."

I raised an impressed brow. "You're cooking?"

"Yeah, it's been a while since I turned the stove on and I felt it was time. Erin fed Clementine, so if you want to give her a bath and put her down, I'll start chopping."

Something felt off about this. I hoped this wasn't a date and I'd misconstrued what he'd meant by dinner. Grabbing a bite to eat was one thing, but Michael cooking for me felt like something else.

"Elle, are you sure everything is okay?"

I plastered a smile on my face. "Yes, it was just a long day. That's all."

"If you're too tired, I can take care of Clementine."

Realizing it sounded like I didn't want to, I spoke quick-ly. "No, I'd love to put her to bed."

He opened his door. "Great, I'll grab the groceries. You grab her."

Before he questioned my behavior anymore, I did as he said.

Whenever Clementine spent the day at Erin's, she came home exhausted. Nap time there was spotty, and she was used to getting her full two hours each and every day. Without complaint she let me give her a quick bath. She usually liked to play in the water, but not tonight. Within twenty minutes we were in the rocker in her pink fairy-dec-orated room and I was reading her *Goodnight Moon*.

The sparkle on the walls was supposed to look like fairy dust and every time I was in here, I wondered if my sister had come up with the idea. In a way, it looked like dande-lion weeds blowing in the wind. I'd never asked Michael about it. Sharing that part of my past was too intimate. I already knew he was very unaware of what Lizzy's and my childhood was like because when I first arrived in Boston, he asked me if my parents had heard from my sister. Lizzy hadn't even told him our mother had died.

"And good night to Clementine," I said, putting our

special spin on it as I tried to reel in my scattered thoughts.

She clapped.

Closing the last page of the book, I hugged her tightly. "I love you," I told her.

She wrapped her little arms around me in a hug that melted me. She was what I needed to help ease the ever-growing gap in my chest. Logan's abandonment of me was starting to settle in, the anger wearing off, and grief becoming a screaming wound opening deeper and deeper.

After a long while, I brought her to her crib and settled her beneath a blanket. "Good night, sweet girl," I whispered and kissed her, not once, but twice.

Her eyes were closed before I even backed away from the crib and I had an overwhelming urge to go bury myself under the covers and go to bed myself, but I knew I couldn't.

Quietly, I tiptoed down the hallway. The house was old, but all the rooms had been remodeled with a distinguished elegance. Michael had owned the house for a few years and although I'd never asked, I was certain it had been decorated before my sister moved in. With its parquet wood floors, white walls, and different shades of blues throughout, it looked like something out of Martha's Vineyard.

My sister had been more wild child. The sixties "peace, love, not war" was her philosophy. Her drug use went along with her disposition. It was just who she was. How she rebelled, I used to think, but maybe it was more how she coped.

As I passed Heidi's former room, something about its disarray caught my attention. This room had navy drapes and a white bedspread with blue doves embroidered all over it. It was typically kept neat, as was every room in the house. Today it was anything but. The bed was unmade and the blue-and-white striped carpet was thrown back. I found that strange.

Inside the room, it was apparent that Heidi had left in a hurry. The drawers were all pulled open. And as I glanced around, everything seemed slightly disheveled—not just the rug or the dressers, or the bed, but the closet door was wide open, with hangers on the floor.

I kicked the rug back into place, and that's when I saw a yellow piece of paper in the wastebasket. It was from the type of pad Michael used all the time. With a quick glance behind me to make certain I was still alone, I uncrumpled it. It read, *Pick one.* Below those words was a web address: *www.evanmarks.com.*

That was all.

I'd never heard of the site.

Didn't know what it meant.

But I'd seen the words before in Michael's ex-secretary's drawer.

I was curious and continued to glance around looking for something else.

Footfalls on the stairs alerted me that Michael was coming up. Tossing the paper back into the trash, I began to straighten the bed.

"What are you doing?" he asked.

I pretended to be startled and grabbed my chest. "Oh, you scared me. Sorry, my OCD kicked in. Heidi seems to have left a mess. I thought I'd straighten up a bit."

Michael stepped inside the room and glanced around.

My heart was pounding.

His eyes landed on me, and for a moment I thought he might have seen how perplexed I was by the way Heidi had cleared her things out, but then he shoved a drawer closed. "She wasn't the neatest houseguest."

I tugged the corner of the bedspread. "No, she wasn't."

He was behind me, his arms around me reaching for the spread. "Another reason she didn't work out," he whispered in my ear.

I smelled liquor on his breath. Images of my father came to mind, and I tried not to shudder as I ducked out from under his body and made my way to the other side of the bed to straighten it.

Michael walked toward the door and stopped just short of it. He held out his hand. "Come on, dinner's ready."

After a few seconds of silence, I stepped toward the dresser, not him. "Let me just finish."

He let his extended hand drop. "Traci will take care of this mess when she comes on Monday. You know she lives for cleaning."

Even though I forced myself to laugh, he wasn't wrong. Traci, Michael's housekeeper, certainly did love to clean. She spent more time here than she needed to. I think she preferred to be here during the day than at home. Her husband worked long hours and she was home alone a lot.

Michael stood at the door and waited for me to pass him. As soon as I did, he closed the door behind me. "Did she go down okay?"

The hallway was wide. Shaped like a square, it had six doors. Four were for the bedrooms, each with its own bathroom; another led to the attic, and the last to a terrace that overlooked the backyard. I glanced toward Clementine's room. "She was exhausted. Poor little thing fell right to sleep."

"I thought she might. Erin didn't give her much of a nap." His hand went to the small of my back as he guided me toward the stairs I needed no help locating.

Each step I took, it remained in place. By the time I got to the first step, I considered grasping the doorknob to the attic because the walls were beginning to blend into the floors. I wondered how much longer I could hold my breath.

The answer came soon enough when his hands shifted. "You feel so tight."

My breath was still in my lungs.

His fingers began massaging into the knots that had to be spreading throughout my entire back by now. This was the time to tell him to please keep his hands off me. That I wasn't interested in him in any way other than as a friend. Yet, I knew I had to be careful. Do it with tact. He held my future with his daughter in those hands.

"Michael," I tossed over my shoulder, very unsure of what I was going to say and how I was going to tell him that not only was my heart in a thousand shattered pieces right now, but I wasn't the least bit attracted to him.

The smell of something burning wafted through the air and had him rushing by. "Shit, I must have left the rice on."

Relief whooshed through me.

I was wrong—things weren't back to normal between us.

A very unsavory feeling struck when I began to fear this might just be the new normal.

chapter
TWENTY-THREE

Day 32

LOGAN

IT WAS HARD NOT to wonder what would have happened.

If I hadn't gone to the beach that day twelve years ago, if Emily hadn't looked so innocent wearing shorts and a T-shirt when all the other girls were wearing bikinis, if I would have left when the guys wanted to leave, or if I would have just listened to them and not gone after her.

The problem was, in the parallel version of my life, everything would be different. I probably would have ended up like most of the guys I went to prep school with, James excluded. Unhappily married with two small kids, having dreams about girls on their knees and blow jobs that never came, and then waking up next to a Stepford wife in training who closed her vagina after her last pregnancy.

In this alternate future, I wouldn't be sitting here staring up at the green-painted steel frame of an empty bunk in a place that smelled like perspiration and disinfectant for two fucking nights wondering about what might have been.

I also wouldn't have met Elle.

So fuck the might-have-beens.

Deal with it, McPherson, I found myself saying. I was talking to myself now. But then again I had no idea how long they were going to keep me, and I had to find a way to keep my sanity because I really felt like I was going insane.

It's not as if I didn't know the law inside and out. I was well aware of my rights. None of that mattered in here, though. I was stuck with no communication to the outside world and no one knew where the fuck I was. I was about ready to lose my mind. I wanted to claw my way out of here so I could get to Elle. I couldn't even think about what must be going through her head.

The South Bay House of Correction was a place I'd been to almost as many times as the Nashua Street Jail, yet I never knew they had an isolation wing for possible terror-ist-linked inmates.

And here I sat.

Minutes ticked by.

Hours.

Days.

It had to be Monday morning by now. How much longer were they going to keep me here? The weekend was one thing, but how could they keep me under wraps during the week? Then again, I was in isolation in some unknown wing God knew where deep within the prison walls.

I closed my eyes and tried to push the ache in my heart out of my mind. I had to think. Use my head to get them to let me use a phone. Bribe the guards if I had to. Patrick's goon squad had to be off duty by now. I might have a chance with a new crew.

"McPherson," one of the guards called as he opened the door. "Get up."

I did. I was done resisting. It wasn't getting me anywhere.

Sure enough, new guards had taken over and none of them seemed to know or care who I was. They were just doing their job. I did the best I could to be whatever the hell it was I was supposed to be.

I was led down a hall, through a number of doors, around a corner, and through another door. It had taken two days, but I was finally sitting in the attorney's room.

The problem with this little scenario is that I had yet to be allowed to make a phone call.

A quick glance in the mirrored window told me I looked like shit. I ran a hand over the top of my head. The sons of bitches in processing decided to shave it before taking my mug shot. The ones in holding complained I was mouthing back, so my black eye was owed to that. But none of that mattered. What mattered was the tightness I felt in my chest because I hadn't been able to contact Elle. She'd told me she was unable to have kids, and in truth, I didn't see that as the end of the world, but I knew she saw it as a failure. And then I up and disappeared on her. I couldn't imagine what she must be thinking. Actually, I could, and that's why I couldn't breathe. She probably thought I'd abandoned her. And there was nothing I could do about it.

The very thought was enough to bring me to my knees.

My gaze shifted around. Here I sat in my wrinkled orange jumpsuit, handcuffed, waist chained, and shackled around the ankles, waiting for someone to grace me with his or her presence. The million-dollar question was—who was it going to be?

FBI?

DEA?

Someone else entirely?

Voices carried down the hall. Someone was shouting at someone else. It was a female voice I heard getting louder.

Suddenly, the door burst open and the she-devil herself came waltzing in. She had a suit on, and her trademark red heels, but her face wasn't plastered in that frown she always wore.

Today, she looked genuinely pissed. "Get those off him," she barked.

Two cops came scurrying in and unlocked the chains and undid the cuffs.

"I'm sorry about that," she said to me, looking truly upset.

I shrugged. "Want to tell me what this is all about?"

"Out," she ordered the two cops who were now standing beside me.

"Ma'am, protocol calls for us to stay with the prisoner."

She narrowed her eyes at them. "If you don't want me to put your balls in an envelope and mail them home to your wife, you'll leave us alone. Now!"

They were out of the room in two seconds flat.

Agent Meg Blanchet with her red hair, red nails, and red shoes came and sat across from me. "I gave the orders on Friday for you to be placed under surveillance and then picked up Monday morning for questioning. The local cops assigned to tail you saw you packing your vehicle. They thought you were fleeing the country, so they picked you up Saturday."

"I wasn't fleeing. I was going to New York City for the weekend."

"Not that I don't believe you, but how do you explain the wire transfer of over five million dollars into one of your accounts?"

My brows popped. "My maternal grandfather must have released my trust fund."

Dark brown eyes looked unexpectedly amused. "Well, whatever the purpose of the transfer, since there was no passport found in your possession, I don't believe you were planning on fleeing the country. Unfortunately, an error in the chain of command delayed my notification that you had been detained."

My anger was well past any explanation. "Tell me why I'm here and what this bullshit terrorist charge is about."

"The terrorist threat charge had nothing to do with me. According to the local PD, a call was traced back to you. One in which you were threatening to burn the entire courthouse down if Flannigan didn't get life behind bars."

"When I was picked up, the officers claimed I was aiding and abetting a known terrorist. Now you're saying I made a threat. Which bullshit claim is it?"

She shrugged. "Does it really matter?"

I shook my head. "No. I guess not. You know I'm smarter than that. Why would I ever do something so stupid?"

She held a hand up and ticked at her fingers. "Because Patrick had your grandfather killed and everyone is claiming he died of natural causes, even the facility he was living in. Because you were the one who arranged for the cover-up. Because you wanted vengeance." She lowered her hand. "Any of those reasons could be why. Are you going to admit it?"

I pushed from the table and ignored her question. She fucking knew what I'd done, I didn't have to admit it, and why the fuck did she care? I couldn't have everyone investigating his death. And I couldn't have Flannigan basking in the glory of Killian's death. I wasn't going to let him flex his power that way. "You know the terrorist charge is total bullshit. Those cops are on Flannigan's payroll and just wanted to fuck with me."

She pursed her lips. "Yes, unfortunately I'm afraid you might be right about that. I'm looking into it."

I narrowed my eyes. "Get me the fuck out of here then and I might not take down the whole fucking place with the lawsuit I'm going to shove so far up your ass, you'll be lucky to be pushing paper behind some desk."

Her grin was wicked as she slid a folder my way. "Take a seat and calm down. You're not here for terrorism, but you are here for a very good reason."

I didn't sit, but I did open the folder.

She tapped her fingernails on the table. "I'm not going to beat around the bush, Logan. You're our prime suspect in the murder of Elizabeth O'Shea. That's why you're here."

My head jerked down. I hadn't even read the first line of the report yet. I was having trouble wrapping my head around the pictures of Lizzy's dead body spread out on the table. "What?"

"We've got your fingerprints on an item found at the crime scene. I have a statement from you claiming you never met Elizabeth O'Shea, and yet a mechanic has identified you as the man with Elizabeth O'Shea on March twenty-first when her car went into the shop."

"Did he identify Elizabeth?"

"No, he said he'd met her inside a bar and it was too dark."

Whatever. I started to list the other facts. "My fingerprints? On what?" I asked quietly, suddenly very concerned.

"A baby rattle. An elephant's head." She pointed to the folder. "It's all in there."

I slammed the folder down. "You know I didn't kill her. Just like the terrorist charge, that's not why I'm here. So what's the real reason?"

She shook her head. "Believe it or not, Logan, what I think is irrelevant. It's the evidence that tells the story, and the evidence in this case is very convincing."

It would be easy enough to clear up the identification of Elizabeth with a few more photos. The messy part would be explaining why Elle was pretending to be her. And I didn't want to bring her into this at all. I sat down. Not. One. Fucking. Bit. "What do you want?"

"I want to know where you got the drugs. Who had them before you moved them to Lucy's."

Fuck.

Fuck.

Fuck.

I knew it.

She knew.

Fierceness tightened my features. "I had nothing to do with that."

She picked up the folder. "You and I both know that's bullshit."

I stared her in the eyes.

She opened the folder and pulled out a piece of paper and handed it to me.

I glanced at it. I knew I was looking at compounds, but what the values meant, I had no idea.

"You can keep that," she said with a smile.

"What is it?"

"Evidence."

"Okay, I'll bite. Evidence for what?"

That smirk wasn't fading. "To convict you of a felony. We found traces of an acidifier compound on the bags of cocaine that were picked up at Lucy's, and traces of the same agent were found in your vehicle during a recent forensic search."

My brows drew together in concentration. "An acidifier compound? What the hell are you talking about?"

The bricks of coke were in bags of salt.

"Flora Crystal Clear is what it's called. It's a salt compound used to increase the life of fresh-cut flowers."

No fucking way.

A light bulb went on in my head at the same time a conversation I had with Killian presented itself in my mind.

"'Shea, he's Mickey the florist's boy?"

"Yeah, that's him. He's an attorney."

My gramps raised his brows. "And young O'Shea's claiming he isn't involved?"

"That's what he told Pop, but I'm not so sure."

Gramps shook his head. "I'm with you. Not sure I'd believe him."

The tiredness in the back of my eyes faded at the realization I might be right. "Why do you say that?"

Shifting on the bed, he brought his large frame to the head and settled back. "I can't say, really. It's a feeling based on what I know of his old man. When Mickey O'Shea was a teenager, he was a small-timer hoping to hit it big. Always doing stupid things. I warned your father to stay away from him in school. And it was a good thing I did. At nineteen, Mickey did a five-year stretch for hijacking a fleet of trucks. His first big job and he gets caught right out of the gate. Fucking idiot. When he got out, he started up his own gang. Some shit went down with his wife and after that the gang folded. Lucky for him, his mother had passed and he took over her flower shop. He seemed to give up on making his fortune and settled for domestic life. Then his wife was killed in some gang-related crime and I haven't heard his name since. But if the young O'Shea is anything like his old man was, he's a dreamer hoping to hit it big the easy way."

Holy fucking shit. Mickey O'Shea was the Priest, and that's the connection to Michael O'Shea.

It has to be.

Holy.

Fucking.

Shit.

Blanchet eased her body forward on the table. "What is it?"

My enlightenment must have registered all over my face. "We've been missing a huge piece of the puzzle. The source of the drugs is the unknown. Right? The reason we haven't been able to make heads or tails of this."

"No shit. That was your job. Remember? We thought we'd get to the source the night the drugs just miraculously turned up outside a strip club."

I ignored that comment. "If I tell you what I know, will you let me out of here?"

Doubt was written all over her face. She didn't think I knew what I was talking about. "Depends if the info is good or not, McPherson."

I had to trust it was, and also trust that she was going to let me out of there. I decided to keep the name "the Priest" to myself for now. It could be leverage for later. "Ever hear of Mickey O'Shea?"

She nodded.

"Then you know there was a time years ago that he operated his own gang."

She looked bored. "I know the story. Small gang. Gang wars. It folded. Patrick branched out on his own after that."

"Did you also know that he's a florist?"

She tapped her pen on the table as if excited. "Go on."

"This is just a theory. Other than the compound you mentioned, I have no proof. But what if he's been trying to resurrect Patrick's old gang . . . and what if he's the source?"

That got her attention and she slowly nodded her head. "Why not his own gang?"

"Some kind of payback?"

"Very plausible lead, McPherson."

That might have been a pat on the back. "Good. Now are you ready to drop the bullshit trumped-up murder charges?"

Her huff of laugher had to be admired. "You're pushing it. I never said that."

"Come on. You know it's bullshit. It will take me all of two minutes out of this room to convince anyone I didn't do it. Yeah, I was in Elizabeth's O'Shea's vehicle and I moved some things around; the rattle must have been one of them. And you know Elle Sterling was driving her sister's vehicle. She was the woman with me that night. I didn't lie. I never met Elizabeth O'Shea."

She shrugged. "Then why worry about it?"

I narrowed my eyes and came clean. "I don't want Elle involved."

"Very admirable of you, Logan, but I'm afraid the law doesn't work that way."

My ability to remain calm was surprising even myself. "Look, there's a much bigger picture here. You have Patrick Flannigan in custody for a long stretch, but that isn't going to put an end to the mayhem in the streets. You need the source of the drugs. What I'm giving you, what I can give you if you let me out of here, will help you do that as well as bring down a possible gang that you weren't even aware existed."

Her lip twisted and I could tell she was hungry to dig into the information. "Okay, I admit the murder charges are bullshit." She took a piece of paper from the folder and tore it in half. "And I'll even let the small detail of similar compound traces on the drugs and in your car get buried." She took another sheet of paper and stuck it in the middle of all the others in the folder. "For now."

I leaned back in my chair and crossed my arms. "This is what I can do . . ." I told her how I planned to get to the source. It was sketchy. I had to lay the whole thing out, but if it was Mickey O'Shea, and on the surface it looked like it was, how hard could it be? I knew Blanchet wasn't going to be able to uncover the truth alone, and so did she. She didn't have enough. Not yet. And she needed me. I had connections she would never have.

The clock on the wall read eight thirty when she slid the keys to the Rover my way. "You're free to go."

"Just like that?"

She shrugged. "You were never formally booked or charged. In fact, there is no record of you ever having been here. I've also already let the FBI know the terrorist charges couldn't be validated."

I shook my head in disgust.

"It's a task force, Logan, that I'm in charge of. I have certain leeway not everyone has. And letting you go is one of the things I can do."

I got to my feet.

"But, Logan," her voice was stern, "don't screw with me, because I may be new to Boston but I'm not new to the streets. I know what you did. The thing is, I can see the bigger picture, and in it, what you did is irrelevant. But that doesn't mean I can't and won't bring you in and book your ass if the need arises."

As I stood beside the door, all I could think about was Elle. I didn't care about anything that had happened in here, and I didn't care what the fuck the bigger picture was. There was time for that later.

All I needed right now was to get to Elle, so I calmly answered, "I understand," and walked out the door.

Just like she said I could.

Elle

MARY POPPINS DIDN'T HAVE anything on Mrs. R. Rebecca Reeves was Clementine's new nanny and I couldn't be more pleased. Michael had broken the mold and hired an older, more experienced woman. She seemed completely competent in childcare and took charge right away.

Finally confident that Clementine was in good hands, I was packing my things to return home. My nerves over her care had gotten the best of me. She'd gone through three caregivers since I'd arrived in Boston and with the death of my sister, I wanted her to have some stability during her days.

Knowing that besides Michael, I might be the only anchor in her life, I'd spent Saturday and Sunday night here. Logan was never far from my thoughts, but with Clementine to occupy my time, my heartache didn't seem so catastrophic.

Aside from the incident where Michael had put his hand on my back, nothing in his behavior the rest of the weekend had pushed me to feel the need to say anything to him about it.

Just as I was zipping up my bag, the house phone rang. "Hello," I answered.

Michael had to leave unusually early for work and I had

agreed to stay until the new nanny arrived so I could introduce her to Clementine. Things had gotten off to a great start and they were busy getting acquainted in the nursery.

"Elle, is that you?" The familiar voice shouted my name.

"Yes, is this Heidi?" I knew by the German accent that it was.

"Is Michael home?"

Michael? Not Mr. O'Shea. Interesting. "No, he left for work early."

With a huff, she said, "I'm at his office and his secretary has informed me he won't be in until later today."

I set my bag down. "Can I help you with anything?"

She sighed. "I need my paycheck. I've been staying at a hostel, but I have to be out in a few days. Could you tell him to please leave it for me at his office and I'll come by again in the morning?"

Curiosity took control of me. "I'll let him know. Do you mind if I ask why you left so hastily?"

She laughed. "I didn't leave. He ordered me out."

Stunned, I didn't hold back. "Why?"

"You must know what he's looking for."

My skin bristled. "I know he wants someone competent to look after Clementine."

"Right, that's what he wants."

I flinched at the tone of her voice. "Did your departure have to do with a disagreement over Clementine?"

Her laugh was dry. "Not at all."

"Then what?" I was pushing it and I knew it.

"I didn't want—" She stopped. "I said no, and he ordered me to leave—Never mind, I'm not looking for any trouble, just please tell him I'll come by his office in the morning."

Once she hung up, I stood there at the night table near the bed, reeling. What was going on with him? I didn't like what I was thinking. Why had he lied to me about Heidi quitting and also about having to go into work early?

The website I saw on the piece of paper in Heidi's former

room came to mind and I found myself back in there. Traci hadn't arrived yet, so everything was the way it had been left. First thing I did was look at the crumpled paper again. It had been cut to about a quarter of the size of a normal piece and I could tell it had been folded down the middle. I'd seen one like this before in Michael's secretary's desk. The secretary he fired over a month ago.

Tossing it back in the wastebasket, I glanced in the open drawers and then under the bed. Nothing. I went into the bathroom. Nothing. I hurried to the nightstand and when I pulled it open, I found nothing there either.

What the hell was going on?

What was Heidi alluding to?

I had to know. Before I knew it, I was in Michael's office and at his computer before I could stop myself. My phone battery had died and I couldn't wait until I got home. I had to know what this meant now.

The screen saver vanished and I was prompted to enter a password.

Crap.

The first word that came to mind was *Clementine* and I entered it. That didn't work. I was no hacker, but I kept going, this time entering her birthdate, and what did you know? It worked.

In the address bar, I typed *www.evanmarks.com.* The site loaded immediately. What came up were pictures of professional-looking men, as if Michael were searching for a law partner. The site was very nondescript. Its name was across the top, with the images scrolling down.

Pick one, the piece of paper had instructed. Was it possible Michael had wanted Heidi to pick a man? What on earth for? I clicked on one of the images to see if the profile would load beneath it.

"Did you need something?" The question was asked in a cool and strong tone, like that of steel.

My hand moved quickly and the shaking caused me to click in the wrong place. A list of files filled the screen and my eyes landed on a video clip labeled *Elizabeth*. With no time to look at it or even blink, I somehow managed to close the window and then glance up within a reasonable amount of time. "I hope you don't mind that I was using your computer, but I needed to check my inventory and get my orders placed before nine." My own tone was calm, but I was anything but.

Michael stood in the doorway with a bouquet of beautiful mixed flowers in his hand. "Not at all, but you've been keeping something from me."

My hands began to shake and I had to dig my nails into my palms to tame their quivering.

"You're a hacker," he said with a grin.

I snatched air into my lungs. I realized that I'd been holding my breath. "No, not really. After Clementine's name didn't work I tried her birthday. Sorry about that, but I was desperate to catch an auction before it ended."

He gave me a casual shrug. "It's fine. In fact, I came home hoping you'd still be here."

I pushed the chair back and felt the sweat on my palms as my hands slid down the wooden arms. "You just caught me. I was getting ready to leave."

Michael strode into the room looking effortlessly powerful and set the flowers on his desk.

I stood, my heart fluttering like a bird in a cage. "Here, take your seat."

His grin seemed to widen as he approached me.

Willing my nervous trembling to stop, I circled the desk in the opposite direction. "What did you need?" My tone was eerily calm considering he'd just caught me at his computer and could very easily discover what I said I had been doing was a lie.

"Sit," he commanded.

I bristled at the command but did as he said and sat in one of the two chairs facing his desk.

The flowers were spilling out over his legal pad and he pulled out a rose. "I've been thinking about something and it makes complete sense."

My nerves were getting the better of me, and I had to clear my throat to make certain I didn't squeak when I spoke. "What would that be?"

Michael's suit was perfectly pressed, his dark hair expertly combed, and his eyes were an icy, icy blue. "I want you to move in with Clementine and me."

"What?" I couldn't contain my shock.

Those eyes seemed colder and more calculating than I'd ever noticed. "Elle, I think we need to give up this pretense."

I sat up straighter, not liking the tone he was using with me. "I'm sorry, Michael, but I don't know what you're talking about."

His grin was almost wolfish. "You want to be a part of my daughter's life. I think we can even go as far as to say you want her to call you Mommy. You made quite an impression at the political fundraiser. I need a confident woman in my life to help me rise up within the social circles I've been trying to break into for years. As you know, I hope to be elected district attorney and then possibly move up to judge or even mayor. In order to do so, I need a more stable home life." With the rose in his hand, he fingered the thorns. "And Elle, you are the perfect woman to help me build that."

My body was screaming "No," but Heidi's words, *I said no and he ordered me to leave*, were echoing through me at the very same time. If I flat-out said no right now, would he cut me out of Clementine's life just like that? I couldn't risk it. "Your wife was my sister, Michael. What would people think?"

He brought the rose to his nose and sniffed it. "They'd think a grief-stricken man found solace in a beautiful woman. Of course, we'd wait a respectable amount of time before going public, but I don't think anyone would think badly about the situation. After all, I was a man burdened by his wife, left to raise our child, and you were there for me."

My eyes were anywhere but on him. Sparkling crystals in the early morning light drew my attention to the floor. It was salt, like what I had seen that night I opened the bags with the cocaine in them.

Odd.

I knew half of the missing drugs were in the possession of the DEA.

My gaze wandered, and it was then I noticed a missing tile in the façade of the fireplace that I always thought was just a decorative listello. The three others were in place, but this one displayed a keypad. It had to be for the panic room. I knew the entrance was in his office but had never really paid attention to where.

I wondered why there was a trail into it or from it. Did he have the missing drugs in his possession? Here? And if so, what was he going to do with them? I didn't like where my mind was headed. Had he left everyone in danger, including his daughter, for a profit? No, he wouldn't. I pushed those dark thoughts away and wondered what the room looked like inside. I wondered about anything except what he was proposing, because what he was proposing to me—it didn't sound so crazy right now, especially if he was involved with something illegal. Clementine would need me.

We both wanted something and his proposal was a way for both of us to get it. Most importantly, if I lived here, I could assure Clementine's environment was safe. Of course, there were many other issues and I threw one out there. "I just bought a place of my own. What would I do with it?"

He set the rose down and fiddled with his mouse. "It was mostly my money. The rest of it was mortgaged. It's not like you have money in it."

"That doesn't mean I want to let it go."

"Well, you live in an area of high demand. We could rent it out in no time."

My heart was racing. Was he going to catch me right now? Know what site I'd been on? I stood up. "I don't know, Michael. I need some time to think about it."

Michael lifted himself from the chair and circled the desk. He stopped directly in front of me and reached behind himself for the rose. With the stem in his hand, he offered it to me. "For you," he said with a satisfied smile.

I took it and brought it to my nose. It smelled of his coercion and my discomfort, but that was okay, because what else did I have in my life? Did it really matter what price I had to pay to have Clementine a part of it? My initial thought was—no, it didn't. Yet still, I couldn't answer. The words were stuck in my throat.

"Take the week and consider my offer. We can discuss you being involved in Clementine's life by moving in with me further next weekend. There's no rush."

I swallowed. "Okay."

His grin felt more genuine as it softened. "Okay," he agreed.

I turned to leave but twisted back. "Oh, Michael, Heidi called."

His face froze on that grin.

"She asked if you could leave her final paycheck at your office and she'd pick it up in the morning."

He nodded. "Of course, I should have thought of that."

My nails were biting into my palms. "I have to run. I have a lot to accomplish today. But thank you for this weekend."

"I enjoyed it too," he responded, and went back to his computer.

I was breathing so hard my entire body was shaking as I started what had once been my sister's car. As soon as I got out of the garage, I opened the window. The air was crisp and cool. I breathed in. I pushed the air out. My panic was mounting. I knew how to defend myself physically, but emotional warfare was nothing I was prepared for. Michael was using that precious little girl to get what he wanted, and what he wanted was me.

Michael just suggesting it sounded crazy enough, but me considering it was insane.

I plugged my phone in to charge and started driving. A few minutes later, the sound of my cell ringing broke my concentration. I looked down and saw *blocked call*. Fear seized me. I shoved it away. For the next five minutes it just kept ringing, but I refused to look at it again.

I feared who it was. Was it the same blocked caller again with some scary message, or was it Michael with more ways to make "us" work? I refused to look and hit ignore.

When I was far enough away from the house, I opened the window wider and tossed the rose out of it. With that anchor away from me, I let my mind go free. I'd held it tightly captive over the last two days and couldn't stand it any longer.

Logan was gone from my life.

Sadness suddenly washed over me. I'd been alone for many years, but I'd never felt more alone than right now. I missed him desperately. I wanted to call him. Hear his voice. Feel his body against mine. Talk to him. Ask him what I should do.

Over the past two days I had saved my tears for late at night when I was in bed and wished I could feel his arms around me. The great loss of him in my life came barreling at me as I drove home. This time I didn't try to push the tears away or keep my sobs at bay; the minute I let go, the memories of our time together flashed before me.

Sitting across from him eating a hamburger, walking through the park with him, sitting beside him as he drove us through Boston talking about nothing and everything— our favorite foods, places we'd been, running, the Boston Marathon that we'd missed this year but vowed to train for together and run next year. Even in the midst of the craziness, being with him over the past month was the happiest I could ever remember being.

My fingers had gone stiff from gripping the steering

wheel by the time I exited the highway. Crying wasn't going to bring Logan back. I had to worry about myself—no, not myself, that little girl. In my head I replayed what I knew about Michael. The way he was around me—mostly kind and considerate, at times manipulative. Then I thought, everyone has flaws. Could I be with him? For Clementine? Was his proposal even real? I knew it was. What kind of woman traded herself to a man to have his child in her life?

Never in a million years would I have thought me. Yet, I found myself seriously considering Michael's offer.

And if that didn't make me want to cry even more, because I knew he was going to take her from me if I didn't say yes and I couldn't let that happen. What if there was more to Michael than I knew? What if he did have a dark side? I wasn't going to let Clementine grow up like I had. I didn't care what I had to do to stay beside her. What I had to sacrifice. Was that what my mother had thought, too, I wondered?

When I finally pulled up in front of my house, the thought of not living there anymore widened the crack in my chest even further. It was that old familiar ache that came every time I had gotten attached to our new home when I was a child, only to be told it was time to move again.

By the time I unlocked my door, all I wanted to do was crawl into my bed and sleep the day away. My world felt like it had tipped on its axis and would never be right. Feeling off balance, I tossed my bags to the floor and then hurried up the stairs to get out of my jeans and slip on a pair of sweats.

My closet doors were closed and I opened them to throw my dirty clothes inside. When I did, I froze. Logan's things were still hanging in the place I'd cleared for him weeks ago. I'd never checked the closet on Saturday.

In a frenzy, I ran into the bathroom. His toiletries were all still there. Toothbrush, razor, and the bar of soap he preferred to my lavender body wash.

I glanced around the room and nothing had changed since I'd left. He hadn't been back. Everything must have been as it was on Saturday. Worry flickered in my chest.

Things come in threes.

Had something happened to him and I misread the situation?

Oh, God.

I rushed over to the dresser, and that's when I heard the front door open and close. Blood swooshed between my ears and my pulse raced at the sound of footsteps coming up the stairs. I knew the sound his sneakers made on the steps.

Creak. Creak.

The louder those footsteps grew, the harder my heart beat.

I began to lose my stability. The dresser I was clutching became the only reason I was still standing. My legs had gone limp, my knees weak, my feet numb.

The more audible the creaking, the closer he drew, the more intense the aching pang in my chest grew, and then suddenly the air in the room felt thicker.

"Elle," he said with that familiar rumble in his voice.

Like always, my body responded to his tone, but I didn't turn around. I couldn't. The high and the low that came with his arrival was hard to bear. It meant he was okay, but it also meant he had left me. I took a breath so deep it lifted my shoulders. "Why did you come back?" I asked.

"Elle," he repeated, but this time he sounded pained.

It didn't matter. My heart was in pieces, splintered and shredded. I just couldn't look at him. "You should have taken everything when you left, or at least come back for the rest of your things when you knew I wasn't home."

The floor creaked from behind me and I knew he'd stepped inside my room.

I couldn't stand it. Didn't know what to do. I opened the drawer I had cleared out for him expecting it to be empty, but it wasn't. Everything was still inside it, and so was the small silver box his grandfather had given him. The one he never would have left behind. It meant the future to him, not in the monetary conversion it could provide, but in the hope he saw in it. The hope that life could possibly be normal for him someday. All the air was sucked from my lungs. Something wasn't right.

"Elle," he said my name again and it was like a plea. "Please look at me."

Ever so slowly I turned around, and I quickly glanced away. He was standing in the doorway, unmoving. For no good reason, the world seemed to right itself, no longer tipping and throwing me off balance.

Light and shadow painted him as he always had been. I didn't have to see him to know what I was looking at. Broad shoulders, chiseled jaw, and the strong lines of his face were the first things that came into view. His face, with the scar just below his eye, was both a warrior's face and beautifully exquisite, at the same time. And his eyes, those ever-changing sometimes brown, sometimes green eyes, were eyes I wanted to get lost in. If he smiled at me they would crinkle ever so slightly, and everything hard and rough about him would instantly soften.

I made sure to keep my eyes anywhere but on him. "Why did you come back? I told you the last time that I wasn't going to do this back-and-forth anymore. I want you to leave."

"I never left." His words were a whisper.

"Don't lie. You did. You couldn't handle the truth and you left."

"That's not true. I told you, your inability to carry a child doesn't change how I feel about you."

My chest constricted and pain stabbed my lungs. I couldn't breathe. I wasn't certain my heart was even beating, as many pieces as it was in.

"Look at me."

At his command, I had to raise my eyes. My head snapped up to completely take him in. And when I did, for a moment, just one, the room went black. I wanted to die. I knew I had been so wrong, and that I should fall to the ground and beg forgiveness. Pinching my eyes closed, I tried to stop them from stinging, but that was useless. I had to see him. I opened my eyes and stared at him through blurry, wavy vision. Before me was a bone-weary man. Logan had a black eye, his head had been shaved, and he was wearing the same clothes he had been wearing on Saturday.

Yet still, when I met his gaze, the heat in his eyes was so intense I thought it would burn right through me.

He took a tentative step my way.

My knees buckled and I had to grab the dresser. "Logan, what happened?" I tried to ask him, but my throat tightened so much my words would only come out as fragments of a whisper.

His voice was gruff as he spoke. "I'm so sorry. I would have been here if I could have. I never would have left you doubting me. You have to believe me."

The tone in his voice told me nothing he was saying was a lie.

I clenched my hand to my heart and let my painful sobs convey what I couldn't at this very moment. I didn't know what happened to him, but I knew he was telling me the truth. Something had happened that had kept him away from me. And here I thought he'd left me. The reality of how wrong I was shattered my already broken heart.

As if reassured I wasn't going to turn him away, he rushed to me and fell to the ground. He was on his knees and his arms were wrapped tightly around me. "Elle, I'm so sorry. I'm so sorry. I'm so sorry."

Tears rolled down my cheeks before I could stop them and I, too, crumpled to the floor. "I thought you couldn't handle what I'd told you and you left me."

His hands went to my face. "No, no, no. I would never, ever leave you. I love you more than I love anything in this world."

"Oh, God, Logan, I love you too," I whispered, and then buried my face in his neck. I let my sobs rise from my belly, and I cried for everything that was happening in my life, and in his. I wanted this man so desperately and I knew he felt the same about me, yet I'd let my own insecurities drive me to doubt that.

"Don't cry, baby, I'm here. I'm here," he whispered in a soothing tone.

We stayed like that, in each other's arms, for a long, long time. When I felt strong enough to pull away, I did. My fingertips traced the discoloration under his eye. My palms caressed his head. Somehow I managed to speak around the painful feeling in my throat. "What happened to you?"

His lips sought my forehead, slid down my temple, eased over to my ear. "Later, can we talk about it later?"

I threw my head back in answer so he could kiss down my neck.

Soft, velvety-smooth lips grazed my skin and left wetness in their wake. As they grazed back up, butterflies swarmed my belly and it felt like they might escape.

When his mouth found mine, he sighed, and his arms went around me as tightly as they could. "I should take a shower."

"I'll come with you," I offered. I just couldn't bear to be without him.

He shook his head. "I'll only be five minutes."

I started to protest, but his finger brushed my lips in the most soft and sensual way so that I knew it wasn't rejection. But what was it? We'd never been shy about getting naked in front of each other. And for that matter we'd never really cared where we fucked. On the floor, on a table, on the couch, or against the shower wall, unless we were making love; then Logan preferred to be in the bed.

All sense in my mind was gone. Completely demolished by the events that had taken place, and his refusal to allow me to join him made my stomach twist. It was evident something was going on in his head and that didn't soothe me in the least.

Logan kissed me deeply before he got to his feet. I touched my lips with my fingertips and felt them tingling where his lips had just been. Once standing, he walked over to the open blinds and closed them. Before he left the room to shower in the hall bathroom, he grabbed some clothes out of his drawer.

While he was gone, I settled on the bed and leaned my head against the pillows. The last few days had been a roller coaster of emotions. In the dark of the room, I reflected on my actions and chastised my behavior.

Why hadn't I looked for him?

What had happened to him?

Where had he been?

Did his disappearance have something to do with the Blue Hill Gang?

It must have, and the thought sickened me.

The bed dipped, and I was surprised I hadn't heard the creaking of the floor. Logan crawled up to the top of the bed and lifted the sheet. "Come here," he beckoned.

My skin tingled and I didn't hesitate to join him under the safety of the soft fabric. "Logan, are you okay?" I asked, still wondering and still worried.

Without hesitation he scooped me in his arms and kissed my head. "I am now. I just need to feel you for a little while, just like this."

He kissed me again.

And again.

And one more time before he pressed my head to him.

I stayed like that for a long while, and then I couldn't stand it any longer and lifted slightly to look at him. It was dark and all I could see were shadows of his face. His hair was gone and even without it he was breathtaking, or maybe without it he was even more breathtaking. I couldn't tell, nor did it matter. All that mattered was that he was here with me. "I'm sorry I doubted you."

His head began to shake. "Shhh . . . no more talking

about it right now, please." The tremble in his voice told me just how wrecked he was. Not one to cry, his emotional outlet came in different forms, and right now I knew that form was me.

I straddled him and ran my palms over his now short hair, and then I found his face and his mouth with my lips and kissed him all over. I found myself whispering to him in the dark. "I need you so much, Logan."

He was silent but his hands roamed my body, pulling my shirt off, and then tugging my jeans down.

Naked on top of him, I couldn't stop kissing him. I needed to feel him against my lips to believe this was real.

His hands found my slick flesh, already wet for him, and his fingers teased the folds of my clit. Soft. Gentle.

Slowly, I lifted his T-shirt over his head.

His fingers continued to tease me and I reveled in how good it felt.

Through the material of his sweatpants I could feel his cock swell, and I slid down his body so I could kiss him there too.

My lips left wet marks on the fabric all along his hardness, and then I pulled down his sweatpants and kissed the bare skin of his cock. My hands and my mouth worked in tandem down its length to his balls, and back up. When I took him in my mouth, he made a mewing sound like he was home, and everything came crashing down all around me. The enormity of our time apart felt like a weight I couldn't bear. I needed to see him. To hear him tell me how he felt with his eyes and his mouth.

Abruptly, I stopped what I was doing and crawled up the bed to turn the light on. When I did, I knew immediately why he hadn't wanted me to shower with him and why he'd closed the blinds.

"Oh my God, Logan," I gasped.

He reached for the light. "Turn it off, Elle."

I shook my head. "No, tell me what happened. Where did you get all of these bruises?"

Logan reached for me and rolled us over so he was hovering over me. "I didn't want to do this now," he sighed. "I was pulled over and detained by some cops who I'm pretty certain are on Patrick Flannigan's payroll."

I gasped. "Why?"

"For Agent Blanchet and her task force, although she claims she knew nothing of my extended stay and poor treatment while there."

The squeak that left my throat was completely incomprehensible. "Treatment. Oh, my God. Logan. Are you sure you're okay? Should we take you to the emergency room?"

He smoothed my hair. "I'm fine. I really am. And I told you, I'll tell you everything, just please, not now. I just can't think about it right now. I just want to be with you."

I believed him and I understood. I wanted to be with him too. I wanted to touch him. To feel him. Every beautiful inch of him. "Turn the light off," I told him.

There was no hesitation in his compliance.

"Logan," I whispered.

"Yeah."

"Talk to me."

"Please, Elle, not right now."

"No, not about what happened to you. Tell me how you feel about me?"

He fell back onto the mattress with a sigh that sounded so erotic it made my own body tremble. "That's easy," he said. "Ever since I met you, you're all I can think about. It's like you're the air that I need to breathe. The reason my heart beats. Being with you makes me feel like everything in this fucked-up world we live in is right side up instead of upside down."

"Oh, Logan, I feel the same way. I was so lost without you this past weekend."

He sucked in a breath that I knew was one of guilt.

I didn't want him to feel that way. I wanted to make him feel good. To relieve the suffering. I went farther. "What do you feel when you kiss me?"

"Like you're the universe giving me what I need."

I loved that. I pushed my boundaries even farther. "How do you feel when I touch your cock or wrap my lips around it?"

He groaned a noise that reverberated through my soul.

And after hearing it, I was done talking. He could show me how he felt. I sat up and shifted my body so that the smell of him intoxicated me. When I was right where I needed to be, I pushed my hands under his ass to lift him closer to my mouth and then I took him all the way in.

"Oh, fuck, Elle, that feels so good. Take me as far as you can. All the way."

I did as he told me and took his cock down my throat as far as I could. Over and over. Tip to base, my mouth sucked him, my fingers stroked him, my lips and teeth and tongue moved together.

Soft words and louder groans told me how much he liked it and I kept going. I wasn't going to stop until all his pain was overtaken by pleasure.

When I sensed he was close, I asked him, "Do you want to come in my mouth or inside me?"

His hips thrust upward. "I want to come inside you," he whispered, as if worried his words would trigger an adverse reaction.

They didn't. This kind of dirty talk was how Logan connected with me, and it had become one way in which I connected with him too. Sure, we communicated outside of bed, but in this way I knew what he felt for me was exactly what I felt for him. Today we both needed this.

I sat up and pulled him up with me. "That's good, because I need you to be inside me," I whispered into the dark.

He had me on my back and was sliding his cock in me within moments of my words. "You're so wet for me."

I ran my nails down his back. "Only you."

In and out.

His cock moved.

Slowly at first.

And that deep shock of connection only we shared was the first thing I felt followed by a sizzling awareness that there would never be another for me in my lifetime. Logan was it. He was the man perfectly made to fit me.

"You're so tight. You feel so good," he growled.

Feeling his body all over mine was what I needed. I let go of everything except making sure my hips met his over and over. His pace picked up steadily, yet still, it wasn't too fast or too slow.

Flesh on flesh.

Frantic.

Grasping.

My moans couldn't be contained. It felt way too good.

"You like that?" he asked.

"Yes. Don't stop," I pleaded and then, out of nowhere, trembling spasms of pleasure started to sweep over me. My fingers clutched his shoulders as the tremors kept coming.

Over and over, like electric shock waves that felt way to good for any one person to be able to enjoy.

Logan groaned at the slight gouge of my nails in his flesh.

I couldn't help myself.

The sound only tipped me farther over the edge. My orgasm continued and my entire body started to shake.

He drove himself deeper, moved faster, and my pussy responded by clenching around his cock.

"Oh, God, Logan. Don't stop."

The sweet pleasure rippled through me again as he pounded harder, faster.

"Fuck!" he called in a shout that matched my cry, and I knew then that he, too, was coming. He murmured my name, over and over, a little louder each time.

Hearing it made me feel like my blood was singing.

Once we were both spent and gasping, he shifted his weight off me and rolled onto his side.

I turned to face him.

We stared at each other for at least five minutes.

My hand caressed his cheek. "Talk to me," I said. "What are you thinking?"

He kissed my fingers, each of them, and held my hand tightly. "Do you trust me?"

There was only one answer to that question. "Yes."

Without hesitation he gathered me close and breathed into my hair. "I don't think Michael or his family are who you think they are."

I didn't miss that he called him Michael and not O'Shea, as if to soften the blow. "I know," I whispered.

Logan shot up. "Did he do something to you?"

I shook my head. I couldn't tell him about Michael's proposition. Not in the state of mind he was in right now, but I did tell him about Heidi and the note I'd found in her drawer.

"You need to stay away from him."

I took his hand. "I can't do that, Logan. I'm worried about Clementine."

"Do you think he might hurt her?"

Panic started to creep into my soul. "No, not physically. But emotional scars can be just as devastating, and I couldn't live with myself if I allowed that to happen. We have to find out what's going on."

"We will."

"Do you promise?"

Logan gathered me close once again and brought us down to the pillow. "Whatever it takes."

Whatever it takes, I repeated to myself, and then I leaned in to kiss him but found myself rubbing my face against the stubble on his jaw. I wanted to memorize every single thing about him. The angle of his jaw. His scent. The feel of his skin. His touch. The way his mouth curved at the corners. His lips. The things I'd struggled with trying to visualize exactly right the last two nights—I knew I'd never allow myself to forget again.

Whatever it takes.

chapter
TWENTY-FIVE

Day 33

LOGAN

THE WORKDAY WAS OVER, but at the same time it was also just beginning.

I'd already removed my jacket and was loosening my tie when I pulled open the boutique door.

Elle was deep in concentration, sitting on the stool behind the cash register, counting the money in the drawer. She glanced over and held a finger up. "Would you turn the 'closed' sign around?"

I did as instructed and made my way across the wooden boards with slow, deliberate steps until I reached her. "I think you've forgotten something," I whispered in her ear from behind.

She nudged me with her elbow. "Two hundred, one, two, three, four, three hundred."

"Like a hello."

I couldn't see her face, but I knew she was grinning.

The pull and surge of sexual tension was thicker than ever between us. Yesterday we'd made up for the time we'd lost over the weekend. We also probably had one of the most candid discussions about O'Shea we'd ever had. I thought she was finally on the same page as me when it came to the kind of man he really was. If she wasn't yet, I was pretty certain she would be after tonight. We'd agreed we were both all in, which meant I wasn't going to try to protect her from the cold, harsh truth, and the reverse was also true.

Tonight would be her first hands-on experience with the investigation that was already well under way. I was meeting with the guys and we were going to discuss what came next. I'd already told them about Blanchet and the acidifier. I also told them about what Elle had seen in O'Shea's study. There was a very likely chance the missing drugs were in his possession, but we needed proof before Blanchet would make her move. There was also the issue of Clementine. Elle was worried about what would happen to her and asked that I wait before saying anything to Blanchet until she'd secured her role as Clementine's guardian. That was a tall order, because who knew what he'd do? At the same time there was more to all of this, and waiting until we could figure it out wasn't necessarily a bad thing. There was something bigger here—I just didn't know what.

My patience wore thin as I waited for her to finish. My need for her attention seemed to mount with every passing second. Who the hell she had turned me into I didn't know anymore, but at the same time I felt more alive than I'd ever felt in my life.

Dropping her off this morning to go into work wasn't easy. After everything that had happened, I wasn't ready for us to be apart. I drove her to the boutique since we had something to do after work. It made sense, and I really wanted to be with her as much as possible.

When I couldn't wait any longer, I nipped at the soft skin of her neck. "I don't like being ignored," I growled.

Elle switched from the stack of twenties to the stack of tens, but I knew she was very aware of my presence because the wobble in her voice gave it away. "Five hundred, ten, twenty, thirty, forty, fifty, sixty, seventy—"

Her stool was a red leather swivel one from Italy. The showroom had become populated with leather items similar in nature. She kept counting, but as soon as she set the pile of tens down, I snagged her wrist before she could pick up the fives and turned her toward me.

She swatted me across the ass. "Now I have to start over."

"Hey now, don't tease," I warned.

Those emerald-green eyes almost gleamed when she looked at me. "Hi, you're early."

She was incredibly beautiful, and for a few moments I couldn't believe she was mine. Long enough that I had to pull in a breath, because I'd forgotten to breathe. "I have a lot of making up to do," I confessed, instantly turning the moment from flirty to serious.

My guilt about what I'd put her through over the weekend wasn't going anywhere. I did have a lot of making up to do.

She looped her arms around my neck. "Stop saying that. It wasn't your fault."

I leaned down and kissed her long and hard. I loved the taste of her, not just the cherry flavor of her lip gloss but also the actual taste of her tongue and her mouth. We were both breathless before I pulled away. "I want to take you to eat before we meet the guys. What do you need help with?"

"I just need to finish the deposit and turn everything off."

Something caught my attention in the case beside us and my eyes darted to it. The glass cabinet held the sex toys display and the shelves were completely full. Diamond dildos, platinum vibrators, strings of pearls, and some things so exotic I wasn't even sure what they were called. "You received the snakeskin handcuffs from Singapore?" I asked, raising a suggestive brow.

She glanced toward the case, chewing on her lip. "Yes, everything arrived early this morning."

Three steps and I was in front of the unlocked case and opening it. One reach and the cuffs were in my hand. I turned around with a rueful smile on my face. "I'd like to purchase these."

She gave me a contemplative look and bit her lip. "Sorry, I've already closed out the drawer."

I took the one long stride that separated us and closed the distance. "Surely, there must be a way I can pay for these." I dangled them in the air.

A weary aspect had entered her eyes but I tried to push her past it.

"We could barter."

Another smile prodded my lips. "Barter, as in trade?"

She breathed very close to my mouth. "That's what the early traders intended the word to mean."

Amused, I replied, "I'll bite. What are you looking to receive in return for the goods in question?"

"Funny you should ask, because we also just got these." She turned on her heels and opened the glass case. On one of the shelves there was a stack of silk pieces of cloth in different colors. She picked up the red one and held it in her fingers. "Control."

I raised a brow. "Control?"

She gave me a slow nod. "Control."

I laughed, almost sardonically. "Christ. I don't think I can do that."

Elle gave me an impassive shrug and took the cuffs from my hands. "Okay then."

Just as she was putting both items in the case, the click-clack of high heels told me either Rachel or Peyton was coming up the stairs.

I snatched them from her fingers quickly and searched for her purse. It was where it always was, under the cash register. I shoved them inside.

"Do we have a deal?" she asked.

"I'll think about it."

Again the impassive shrug and I had to admit, my cock twitched. She was turning me on and I hadn't even agreed.

Peyton was standing at the top of the steps just as I tucked Elle's bag back in place. Her coat was on, her purse was on her arm, and I thought maybe, just maybe, the conversation about my new look would be bypassed. But in case it wasn't, I had my story down. After all, I did have to recite it with my pop's friends and my clients numerous times throughout the day.

As soon as she hit the main floor her jaw dropped. "Logan, your hair!" Peyton exclaimed in shock. Today her own hair was tinged blue, which matched one of the shades in her multicolored coat and earrings. She looked a little Smurf-like, but what did I know about fashion?

With one hand tightly gripping Elle's, I rubbed my head with the other. Declan hadn't informed Peyton about anything that was going on. It was safer for her that way. "I lost a bet," I said with a slight forced grin.

"You look like Jax Teller when he got out of jail."

If only she knew how close she was. Still, I had no idea who she was talking about, and I gave her a puzzled look. "Sorry, Peyton, but I'm not sure who he is."

"Charlie Hunnam from *Sons of Anarchy*."

My look remained the same.

She shot a glance toward Elle, who also shrugged.

"Never mind. I guess neither of you are a fan," she said, almost exasperated.

A mirror was on the counter near me and Peyton pulled out her lipstick and came a little closer. "Oh my God, Logan, your eye. What happened?"

Elle squeezed my hand and then turned around to finish counting. I knew she didn't like lying to Peyton, even if it was for her own good. "A boxing gym mishap. Nothing to worry about. I'm fine," I told her.

"Same day you made the bet?"

"Yep." I kept it short.

"Looks like you lost all the way around."

I said nothing, just grinned.

Beep. Beep.

"That's my mother. We're on the hunt for the perfect wedding dress."

"Wedding dress?"

"Her mother's getting married," Elle laughed.

And if that news didn't make me feel completely out of it! I knew I had disconnected over the last couple of weeks, but I hadn't realized just how much.

"In like two weeks," Peyton said, rolling her eyes. "Nothing like short notice, but when love hits there's no denying it." She shifted her gaze to Elle, who was done counting the day's receipts. "Isn't that right?" She winked.

Elle actually blushed, which I found adorable.

Beep. Beep.

"I'm coming. I'm coming! She's so impatient. I have to run. Have a good night, you two."

"You, too," I said.

"See you tomorrow," Elle called.

Like a flash, Peyton opened the door and was gone.

"Are you ready to go eat?" I asked, rubbing my stomach. I was starving.

Just then the bells chimed and a young man wearing a news cap came in carrying a bouquet of roses. "Delivery for Elle Sterling."

"That's me." She smiled, and I could tell she thought they were from me.

They weren't.

The kid walked over to her and handed them off. "Sorry I'm so late. You're the last delivery of the day. Have a great night."

"You, too," she said still smiling.

"God willing," he said, and I found his response completely odd.

As if he knew what I was thinking, his eyes found mine, and he stared at me his entire trip back to the door. His eyes were icy blue and he had a familiar look about him, but I couldn't place him. Under his cap, I could see he had dark hair. A black Irish, as my gramps would have called him.

Elle picked up the card and when she read it, her face fell.

"Who are they from?" I asked, suspicion in my voice

that even I hated to hear.

She slid the small card back into the envelope and set the flowers down. "Michael," she said. "He just wanted to thank me for helping him with Clementine last weekend."

A noise escaped my throat and I couldn't stop the wave of nausea that seemed to run through me. I took a deep, steadying breath.

"Logan, don't."

I looked away. "Don't what?"

"I can see you shutting down. You know he and I are going to come into contact with each other. It's impossible to avoid him. Not if I want to keep seeing Clementine."

Infuriated, I tried to push the anger away. I pulled in another deep breath and tried to think of things differently. She didn't ask to get the flowers.

Okay, it still irked me, because she did get them.

And I didn't send them.

Different take.

She didn't want him. She wanted me.

And that was the truth.

I let the air seep from my lungs.

Elle crossed the room to the display of handheld satellite radios shaped like small purses from Japan that could really jam. Instead of turning off the one that was playing music, she turned it up. "Do you like to dance?" she asked out of the blue.

I didn't want to let her distract me, but I was tired of arguing about him. I had decided to trust her and until O'Shea could be sorted out, either as bad or worse, I had to stop my shit. I made a conscious decision then to let this go.

For now, anyway.

I leaned back against the antique counter that once sold tickets for a carousel in Vienna and watched her hips sway in the short black dress she was wearing. It made her legs look a mile long. "When I was in college I spent my summers in the Hamptons and my friends and I used to hit the clubs, but I haven't done that in a while."

Her hands went above her head and her entire body started to move slowly.

I pushed off the counter and made my way over toward her. I didn't know the song that was playing, but it didn't matter. When I got close enough, I offered my hand. "May I have this dance?"

She smiled at me and her smile reached her eyes when she extended her hand. "I didn't mean you had to dance with me."

I pulled her close to me, right up against my body. "I don't have to do anything. I want to."

She bit her lip.

My hands anchored her hips and we danced slowly in a circle, our feet moving half an inch at a time. She'd told me one time that she hadn't gone to her prom. I could give her the prom. If someday she wanted something grander I'd bring her to the Met Ball. Fuck, I would give her everything she'd missed. I wanted her to experience it all.

We moved well together, those two pieces of a puzzle that fit just right.

After a while, I took it up a notch, changing moves from slow dancing to more dirty dancing. My thigh slid between hers and we continued to move together. Everything around us disappeared and it was just the two of us in our wonderland.

Her hands slid from my shoulders up to cup the back of my neck. She rubbed the spot where once she'd been able to run her fingers through my hair. My hair was gone, but her touch was hot. I felt branded. Like she knew I needed to know we belonged only to each other.

Heat flared where my groin rubbed against her lower belly. I had to kiss her. I slid my hands up her back to tangle in her hair, and then I tipped her head back so I could slide my lips down her neck.

She made a noise that had my hands skirting the hem of her dress, but I stopped myself. I didn't want everything we did to end up in sex. I wanted to show her we could be together and not end up naked. It just seemed like the mature thing to do when one was trying to have a real, grown-up relationship.

But fuck, it was hard to stop my fingers from twitching. She, too, was fighting the driving desire. I could tell. Her eyes were squeezed closed. Her lips were parted. And her nipples were like small diamonds protruding from the fabric of her dress.

My lips found her ear. "When we make it to New York, I'll take you to the Rose Bar. It's a great place to go dancing."

She kept moving. "I think I've heard of it."

"Jeremy owns it. It's a Jet Set property."

The lace of her dress flapped with our movement and somehow I managed to keep my hands at bay. "I had no idea he was that famous," she joked.

I laughed. "Not famous, just a friend."

"I liked all of your friends who came to be with you for Killian's funeral. The way you talk about them I know they mean a lot to you."

They did.

But then so did she.

"And they liked you." I slid one of my hands up to the center of her back between her shoulders and then dipped her low. I had to stop before I wasn't going to be able to. I kept her there for a few moments and then pulled her back into my arms. "I hate to end this, but we should probably get going."

She was still gazing at me, biting her lip.

My body was starting to react to hers and I felt my own lips part. I quickly let go of her and shook my desire off. "Come on, we don't have much time to eat before we have to meet the guys. Where do you want to go?"

Elle looked flushed. "How about the Hornet's Nest?"

I gave her a little tap on her ass. "Sounds great. Now let's get moving."

Many choices in my life have been hard to make . . . none harder than passing on sex. Great sex. Sex with Elle . . .

Elle

"**S**O IT'S DECIDED THEN?" Miles asked quietly.

Logan was glaring at everyone. He was all coiled power as he stood over the table in the break room at Molly's. With his tie removed, his sleeves rolled up to his elbows, and the first couple of buttons of his white shirt undone, his muscles seemed to flex with his every movement. "No, it's not," he barked.

Declan cocked his head and looked toward Miles.

In response, Miles slid a piece of paper across the table and Declan picked it up and read it out loud. "Compound agent found on outside packaging is a perfect match to compound agent found in vehicle registered to Logan McPherson."

"I know what the fucking report states," Logan muttered, flopping down in a chair beside me and grabbing my hand. He laced our fingers together and I rubbed his skin, hoping it might calm him down. Agent Blanchet had given him a copy of the report with the information she had on him before she released him. He could be in a lot of trouble. This was my fault and there was nothing I could do to help him. I felt guilty. I felt helpless. I hated it. I had to do something.

"Then you know we don't have much of a choice because I don't care what that bitch told you, this is some persuasive evidence that you committed a felony, and you know as well as I do, she'll use it if she has to."

I shivered at the thought of what Logan had done for me. How he'd risked his entire future for the choice I'd made. And even though I'd do it again as long as it meant keeping Clementine safe and out of harm's way, it didn't temper my guilt.

Logan's eyes burned into me and I knew he could see my despair. With a squeeze of my hand, he gave me a small smile. I gave him one in return to reassure him I was fine. Even so, he still flung Miles a filthy look.

Just then, my phone rang. I let go of Logan's hand and quickly reached for my purse to silence it. I'd received three blocked calls at dinner. Including the one from yesterday, that made four in two days. Logan insisted on answering them himself, but whoever was on the other end hung up at the sound of his voice every time.

"Give it to me," Logan said through gritted teeth.

I shook my head. "Let's just ignore it."

Miles and Declan were having their own conversation and weren't aware of what was going on. "Maybe Elle can help," Declan said, drawing my attention back to the table.

Miles cocked his head as if he understood what the glances and glares were about and then slid a pad of paper my way. "Can you show me what the keypad looks like?"

I knew it was my decision whether or not I tried to get into Michael's panic room, but I still found myself glancing back to Logan. When I saw his face was twisted up in anguish, my heart banged in my chest. I hated what this was doing to him, but I knew it had to be done. We had to find out the truth. Both Logan's and Clementine's futures depended on it. With that in mind, I averted my gaze to the empty paper in front of me and proceeded to draw the rectangular box as I remembered it.

When I was done, my heartbeat had not yet slowed. If just the very idea of what I had agreed to do was making me nervous, how was I going to react when I was actually doing it? With a deep breath, I slid the paper back over to Miles. "The outside was stainless steel, the inside was black with blue number pads. Above the numbers were a red, a yellow, and a green light."

He looked at my drawing. "It appears to be a standard digital two-relay keypad with a magnetic lock."

"Which means?" Logan asked with a harshness in his tone that made me wince.

Miles ignored Logan's hostility. "It means once you enter the assigned code, the number sequence will deactivate the magnetic lock, and the door will open. If the keypad is programmed to toggle mode, then when you enter the same code it will either release the lock again or reactivate it."

"I don't understand. Why would Elle have to release the lock again?"

"These types of locks are complicated. Once the lock is deactivated, there are two possible outcomes. The door could automatically close itself after thirty seconds or it might remain in the open position."

"How will I know which one to expect?"

The sigh Miles gave told me the news wasn't good. "You won't. It's programmed during the initial installation and I have no way of knowing."

Logan cursed and scrubbed his jaw.

Stiffening my spine, I tried not to worry. Logan was doing enough of that for the two of us. "Okay, so worst outcome, it closes on its own. All I have to do is reenter the same code to get out. I got it," I said, my throat thick, my tone sounding choked.

I hated the weakness I was showing.

"There's one minor caveat."

Logan cursed again.

"If the alarm was not installed in toggle mode, and the door has closed, then there will very likely be a different release code. If you can't figure it out and you continually try, you could trigger the second relay. Most of the time, the relay is wired to the existing home burglar alarm and will set if off."

Then Michael would know what I was up to.

"Can't she just lodge the door open?" Declan asked.

"No, an alarm will sound if the door is programmed to close itself."

The fluorescent lights in the ceiling bounced off Logan's handsome face and I could see the torment in his expression. "So you're telling me if the release code isn't the same as the entry code, she'll be stuck in the panic room."

"Yes."

"And there's no way for you to determine this before she goes in there?"

"No. It all depends on how the door was initially set up, which unfortunately we don't have any way of knowing."

"Fuck that then. She's not going in there. We can't take that risk," Logan said. Then he added, "I'll do it."

"No," I gasped. "Michael would know."

"She's right, Logan," Miles said, then he looked toward me. "Do you think you know the code? It would be a series of four numbers."

My brain was thinking it through and I talked out loud. "His computer password was Clementine's birthday, which was six numbers. It would make sense that the code for the panic room would be similar. Maybe just the month and date or the month and year?"

The corners of Miles's mouth tipped up. "Sounds logical."

Miles was all muscle. Large, broad, and ripped, he was intimidating looking. He also had way more girth than Logan's lean body bore. But Logan didn't seem intimidated by this. He didn't seem to notice or care. My guess was that they were equally powerful.

"And if she's wrong?" Logan asked tersely.

Miles, on the other hand, seemed oddly nervous in the presence of Logan, especially tonight. Perhaps it was due to Logan's natural brooding demeanor or his obvious dislike for Miles's plan. I wasn't really sure, but as usual, he answered quickly. "If the house and panic room alarms are linked, a breach will trigger, and the entire house will be activated. If it is connected to the BPD, they'll be alerted to an intruder. If they aren't linked, then the lock will blink in a series of red flashes repeatedly until—"

"That's it!" I yelled, clasping my hands together and grabbing the attention of all three men in the room.

Logan's hand gripped my knee. "What's it, Elle?"

"That night I saw someone in Michael's study. I saw a red blinking glow. It had to be the keypad. And what if the person was my sister? She could have been trying to break into the panic room."

Logan nodded in agreement.

"But she must not have gotten in. That's why I saw the red blinking light. If Lizzy couldn't guess what the code was, then it can't be Clementine's birthday or her name or anything of significance to do with her daughter."

Everyone around the room looked grim.

Logan leaned forward and put his elbows on the table and his head down.

As it started to register, I realized that wasn't good news at all. "How many attempts can I make until the light is activated?" I asked Miles.

"Three; after that it will lock you out from even attempting a new code and continue to blink until a bypass code is entered."

"Shit!" Logan said, slamming his hands on the table. "She has to stop after two attempts. O'Shea isn't stupid. If he sees the red light blinking, he'll know someone was trying to break in and it won't be too hard to guess who."

Miles hunched over his laptop and hit a few keys. "You're right. I say we put that idea aside for now, but at least we know that the panic room isn't connected to the home alarm, which is good news because then O'Shea won't get an alert."

My phone beeped, this time with a text. I would have

turned it off, but I was worried Michael might be trying to reach me, and I needed to be accessible for Clementine. I pulled it out of my purse again. The text read, *Blessed are those who do not walk in step with the wicked or stand in the way that sinners take or sit in the company of mockers.*

Shivers went through me.

"Let me see."

I handed it to Logan.

He stared at it for the longest time. Perplexed, angered, and worried, he shoved my phone in his own pocket. "We'll talk about this later."

"Another message?" Declan asked.

Logan nodded. "A Bible verse. Doesn't make much sense."

"The Priest?"

"Would seem that way."

"Can I see?" Miles asked.

Logan handed him the phone and Miles stared at the screen for a bit, as if in contemplation.

With Logan's trust fund now accessible to him, he could afford to pay Miles and had asked him to work full time on this. Miles had agreed and taken a leave from his security job at the hotel. Sliding the phone back to Logan, he seemed to blink away his thoughts and went on. "Let's focus on something different, like trying to gain access to O'Shea's computer. Maybe we can learn something from what he has in his files that will help Elle come up with what the code could be."

Logan nodded in agreement.

"Okay, what do I need to do?" I asked.

"That's easy. Hang on," Miles said, and then started tapping his keyboard.

The muscle in Logan's jaw was tight with tension and his shoulders were rigid. I leaned over and placed my hand on his thigh and whispered, "Hey, it's going to be okay. I'll be careful."

He sucked in a deep breath and took my hand. "I don't

like this at all. If there was any other choice, you'd stay clear of O'Shea altogether."

I squeezed his hand. "You know I have to do this," I whispered.

He gave me a nod and stood up. I watched as he paced the room and then came back to his empty chair and gripped it with his hands. "What are you looking for, Miles?"

"O'Shea's IP address."

"You can find that?" I asked.

He gave me a grin. "I can do just about anything."

"How?"

Miles turned the computer toward me. "It's something I learned a long time ago working a short stint in white-collar crimes. Do you have an old email from him?"

I nodded and took control of the keyboard, logging into my Gmail account. "Here's one," I said.

Miles faced the computer again and started tapping some keys. "And . . . I got it."

"Won't he know?"

"Not at all," Miles reassured me as he turned the laptop around. "Here you go. Just enter his user ID and password and we're in."

My fingers were shaking and I think Logan knew how nervous I was, because he moved behind me and placed his warm hands on my shoulders. This helped calm my nerves, and I typed Michael's email address in the user name box. I had used that the other day and it worked. Then I typed Clementine's birthday in the password field. *Incorrect password* flashed across the screen.

"Try again." Miles pointed to the screen.

Slowly, I typed it for the second time, careful to hit every right key. *Incorrect password* flashed again. I glanced up, feeling defeated. "He must have changed it."

"Are you sure you have the right password?" Miles asked.

I nodded and swallowed, more nervous than ever.

Maybe Michael was more suspicious than I thought he was. Or maybe he had traced the site I had been on and knew I was lying to him. I hadn't divulged any of the lies I'd told to Michael yesterday to either Logan or Miles.

"Do you think he writes his passwords down anywhere?"

"I'm not sure, but I know he jots a number of things down. I'm going over there tomorrow to have breakfast with Clementine. I'll go in his office then and look around."

The noise that escaped Logan's throat sounded like a growl. "If he's on to you, he's not going to leave his password anywhere."

I tried to calm him by grasping his hands, which were still resting on my shoulders. "You're probably right."

Miles said, "Chances would be slim anyway, but the other thing you could do is install a program on his computer that will allow me to monitor his keystrokes so I can gain access that way." He started to tap the keyboard again and then pulled a small thumb drive from the side. "Insert this in one of his computer ports and when it loads, then hit install. It's untraceable and the next time he logs on, I'll be able to see every stroke."

"Elle, I don't want you doing this," Logan hissed as he took his seat beside me.

I needed to come clean. To tell him I doubted that Michael would ever hurt me. That he wanted me to be with him. But the fact that I had entertained those plans when I thought Logan had left me made me feel so guilty that I had a hard time getting the words out. Before I could push them up my throat, the door to the employee lounge flung open.

"Sorry about that, boys," Frank said, dragging his arm across his forehead. "Molly's going to burn the fucking place down with all these new electronics she's installing. Her latest gimmick is some fancy margarita machine that—" His eyes fell on me and for a moment they seemed haunted. I'd seen that look before on Sean McPherson the first time he saw me. *The ghost of Emily Flannigan,* I thought this time. It should have bothered me, but it didn't. Logan assured me I was nothing like her beyond a superficial similarity and that what he felt for me had nothing to do with her.

There was a chorus of *hey, how are you* from around the table.

"Oh, sorry, I didn't know we were in mixed company," Frank said, and he wiped his hands on his jeans before walking toward me and extending one. "Frank Reilly."

I smiled at him. "Elle Sterling."

I'd seen him once before, but he wasn't paying attention to me that night. He'd just wanted his daughter away from Logan. I wondered if with Patrick in jail and Tommy dead, he still felt that way.

"So what did you need?" He directed his question toward Logan, extending his hand and then pulling Logan toward him for a slight hug.

Frank was a big, billowy man. He'd been an informant for the BPD for years and had been the link between Agent Blanchet and Logan while Logan was being coerced to assist the DEA. As I watched the interaction between the two men, I couldn't help but observe the fondness Frank felt toward Logan. Odd; up until now I thought he didn't care for him.

But then again, he had allowed the break room at his pub to serve as the meeting place for this renegade task force, which, depending on what was really going on, could put him in harm's way.

"Got a minute to sit down?" Logan asked him.

"Yeah, sure," he said, and took a seat in one of the flimsy folding chairs that surrounded the small rectangular table.

The room was a hodgepodge of items that looked to be worn-out pieces from days better seen in the pub. Broken beer signs hung on the wall. The table was warped and the wood laminate was peeling off. Of the six chairs surrounding it, only two were sturdy enough to hold any real weight. I was worried the ones Miles and Frank were sitting in might just collapse.

"I want to pick your brain," Logan started.

Frank eyed him warily but gave him a slight nod.

"My grandfather told me a story once about Mickey O'Shea." He paused for a moment, and I knew the thought of Killian McPherson still made his heart heavy. I could see it on his face. With the slightest shake of his head he pushed the sorrow away. "He told me that when Mickey was a young man he went to prison, and that when he got out of prison he started up his own gang,"

"Yeah. They were small-time, though, a skeleton crew of twenty men at most. At the time, Paddy Flannigan was his number two. I don't know how much income they generated. I know they were extorting protection payments from the strip clubs, which is how Paddy got the idea to run his businesses through them, lots of cash I guess. But back then, they ran the cash through Mickey's mother's flower shop."

Logan nodded as if he already knew that.

Declan sat up straight.

And Miles eased his chair closer to the table.

"What do you know about Mickey?"

Frank looked uneasy.

"What?"

He shook his head. "I can't say."

"Is it about his gang?"

"His wife," Frank said flatly.

Everyone perked up. "What about her?" Logan asked.

Frank closed his eyes for a moment before speaking. "Have you seen a picture of his wife?"

I had, but everyone else around the room shook their head.

"Rose O'Shea was a knockout. Picture Maureen O'Hara mixed with Lana Turner and eyes the color of the clearest blue sky." He seemed to shake his head at the very thought of her but then cleared his throat, probably when he remembered I was in the room. "She was one of those women who turned every man's head no matter if he was in love, straight or gay, and she knew it. She loved the attention and often sought the company of other men. Word on the street was that she was a tease, which was ironic because she claimed to be such a good Catholic girl. Went to church twice a week."

Something like anticipation crested under my skin. The way he was talking drew all of us in, even the man I loved sitting beside me.

Logan crossed his arms over his chest and stretched those long legs. "Do you know how she died? I mean people say it was gang related, but that's all. Never any details."

Frank exhaled and looked away. "I do, but I swore on my life to keep it to myself."

Uneasiness moved through me. Whatever it was didn't sound good at all, and I wasn't sure any of us should know.

Logan eased forward. "Anything you can tell us about Mickey would be helpful."

Frank looked contemplative.

"Listen, Frank, this is going to sound crazy but I have reason to believe Patrick's former gang, the Dorchester Heights Gang, is reassembling. And that maybe Mickey is running it, going by the name 'the Priest' to keep his identity secret."

Doubt passed over Frank's face like a shadow.

"It sounds crazy, but it's not completely out of the question," Logan said.

Frank was shaking his head.

"Think about it—over the past few years the drug trafficking on the streets of Boston has been pegged to one supplier, but no one knows who he is. Cocaine use has more than doubled across all income levels, which means someone with a substantial network is supplying it. What if it's been Mickey this whole time using former Dorchester Heights members? The ones Patrick didn't welcome into

Blue Hill?"

My stomach twisted into a thousand knots. Clementine's grandfather running one of the biggest drug rings in the history of Boston meant that if word got out, she would be in constant danger. Kidnapping threats. Death threats. Mob danger. And to make things worse, I had no idea what Mickey felt for Clementine, if anything. At least I knew that Mickey wasn't involved in his granddaughter's care as far as I had observed. In fact, aside from my sister's funeral, I'd only seen him one other time, over at Erin's for her son Conner's birthday. I'm not even sure we ever spoke another word after we were introduced there. Still, the thought that he might be leading a secret life didn't make me feel good about Clementine's environment.

Frank stood up and walked over to the sink in the corner of the room. He opened the pine cabinet beneath it and rummaged around for a bit before he pulled out a bottle of Jack Daniel's. He raised the bottle. "Anyone else need a drink?"

Logan gave a shake of his head and leaned back on the wooden chair. I worried it might not withstand the pressure and tried not to wince.

"I'll take one," Declan said.

"Me too," I chimed in. I wasn't a drinker, but thinking about Clementine in possible perpetual danger drove me to want one.

With a quiet thump, Logan brought his chair upright and leaned forward. "You okay?" he whispered so only I could hear. It was as if he was thinking the exact same thing I was and also didn't like what that meant.

I nodded and put my hand on his knee. Just touching him made me feel so much better.

Frank continued to rummage around.

The room waited in quiet anticipation.

Logan placed his hand over mine, as if in reassurance that he'd make everything okay. The sentiment touched me. What we had together was so real, at times I had a hard time believing it. With Logan in my life, I knew what Charlie and I once shared wasn't real love at all because real love doesn't fall apart when someone is broken. Real love toughs it out . . . no matter what. Besides, according to Logan I wasn't the least bit broken, and I chose to believe him.

The liquid poured easily into the glasses Frank found above the sink and went down even easier. Logan's touch had already started to settle my nerves and this finished the deal.

Frank, on the other hand, downed one, then another glass. When he finished, he looked toward Logan, who seemed to have switched gears and suddenly gained patience. A slight trickle of perspiration broke on Frank's forehead. "It's not Mickey. I'm almost certain of that."

Logan looked perplexed. "What do you know, Frank? What makes you say that?"

He gulped another sip. "This is dangerous information. What I'm about to tell you has to remain in this room. Promise me it won't get out."

Logan raised his right hand. "I promise. I swear on my own life." He glanced around and Miles and Declan did the same, and then his eyes landed on mine. I didn't raise my hand. I didn't have to; he knew I'd never do anything that would hurt him.

Frank's words sputtered out. "He'd never run a gang once run by Paddy Flannigan. Never. Besides, he wouldn't have any trusted members. No one would work for him."

"What makes you think that?"

"Everyone knows his wife died because of him. He broke code and didn't protect his family. No one would work for a man like that."

"What really happened, Frank?"

"His wife took a bullet meant for Paddy."

Everyone's eyes widened to the size of saucers.

Logan twisted in his seat and his right foot was tapping furiously on the floor. "Are you certain about that?"

Frank nodded. "It happened right here, in my pub, in front of me."

"Who pulled the trigger?"

His response was an empty, "Mickey."

What?

I felt like the room was spinning. All the air was sucked from my lungs. I think I gasped. A chill went down my spine and I suddenly felt very cold. Mickey and Rose were Clementine's grandparents, and learning details of their tainted past made those knots in my stomach tighten even more.

Logan moved closer to me and the gesture warmed me instantly. I couldn't believe how much I needed him.

"What happened, Frank?" he asked, with a softness in his voice that surprised me.

Frank squeezed his eyes closed. "It was 1989, just after the New Year. The weather was miserable and the pub was empty, so I sent the bartender home. I'd thought about closing early, but my wife had just left me and the thought of going home to an empty bed wasn't appealing. In walked Paddy and he ordered his usual. He came in a lot back then. I used to joke with him that I was his therapist and was going to start charging. He and his wife were having trouble and I was no stranger to that."

Logan narrowed his eyes in concentration. "So you and Patrick Flannigan were friends?"

The hollow laugh that escaped Frank's throat sent chills through me. "Friends. That would be a stretch of the word. I did what I had to in order to stay on his good side. Molly's was between Blue Hill and Dorchester Heights turf but hadn't been claimed by either. That was enough to make me his best friend if he wanted me to be."

"You were afraid he was going to make you pay for protection?" Declan asked.

He nodded. "Fuck yeah, I was. Listen, things had changed by then. The Irish Mob was no longer about the cause; the IRA had long been forgotten. Like now, it was about profit, but it was also about pride. I was lucky I hadn't been forced to pay for protection like everyone else around me. I didn't care whose friend I had to be; I just wanted to keep it that way."

Declan raised a hand. "I'm not judging. My old man paid right up until the day Patrick Flannigan turned his back on everything Dorchester Heights for his shiny new Blue Hill Gang. That's the only reason we were able to save enough to expand our business."

Sympathetic looks passed between the men.

Logan squirmed a little, knowing he was the catalyst behind the merge, but in this case, it turned out to have had a positive impact on at least one family. "Go on, Frank. What happened next?"

"An hour or so had passed and he was pretty wasted. The door opened and Rose O'Shea came in, dressed to the nines. She was wearing a tight black dress, high heels, and a brand-new fur coat. I noticed it because I found it hard to believe Mickey could afford something like that. She strode right over to Paddy and sat down. Like it had been arranged. He ordered her a drink and they started talking. I didn't know if the two of them knew each other, but Rose had come in enough that I was aware nothing but trouble could come out of her flirting with him. Sure enough, it didn't take long for her to down a few martinis and for them to disappear into the bathroom."

My heart was in my throat. What if Michael was like his mother?

"What happened next happened so fast, it's all a blur. Mickey came in looking for Rose. The place was dark, but when she came out of the bathroom it was easy to see what she had been up to by how disheveled she was. Her hair was a mess and her red lipstick was smeared all around her mouth. Mickey lit up like I'd never seen him. The two were always physical, don't get me wrong—her slapping him, him pulling her out of the bar by her hair—but that night, the anger on his face seemed to transform to hatred."

My pulse started to race.

"'Your kid got arrested tonight,' he'd barked at her. She acted dumbfounded and he turned red as he eyed her.

"Rose started to throw a tantrum. She called him a liar. Blamed him for not loving the kid. Mickey's laugh was bitter when he told her that her kid was just as vile as her. She called him weak, pathetic, said he wasn't a real man. Out of nowhere, he charged at her, calling her a whore, a bitch, screaming at her, yelling. When he reached her he slapped her so hard she fell back, but before she hit the ground he grabbed her by the arm and the hair and started to drag her toward the door."

I dared a glance around the room, but everyone was focused on Frank.

Frank was in his own world. "That's when Paddy came out of the john and drew his gun. Told Mickey to let her go. Mickey shoved Rose away and went for his own gun, but Rose stumbled forward just as Mickey fired at Patrick and she took the bullet, right in the back of the head. Died instantly."

Everyone was in a state of shock.

My hand flew to my mouth and I gasped.

Mickey killed his own wife.

Michael and Erin must not have even been teenagers at the time. Michael never spoke of his mother, but her picture was everywhere in his house; he obviously loved her. Erin never spoke of her either, and as far as I knew she had only that one photo of a family of five in her house and none of only her mother. The older boy in the photo must have been the son Mickey was referring to who had been arrested.

The words *sins of the father* echoed through my head. And for the first time, Logan's theory that Michael had killed my sister didn't sound so insane. I couldn't dismiss the thought.

Logan pushed to his feet. "Kill a man's dog, he'll kill your best friend; kill a man's brother, he'll kill your mother; take a man's girl, and he'll kill you," he muttered.

"What?" I asked.

"Something my gramps told me once."

Frank nodded. "Old unwritten code of conduct, but in Mickey's case he killed his own girl."

"He must have blamed Patrick," Declan commented.

"I'm sure he did, but he was so much weaker than Paddy, there was nothing he could do about it. He didn't have any power. His own gang had already collapsed years before when he went after another gang's leader for flirting with Rose, and both gangs tore each other apart. He was just a florist by then. He really was powerless."

"I heard about that. Do you think Killian knew how Rose died?" Logan asked in a tone that was steely and sharp.

Frank slowly shook his head. "No one knew but the three of us. They both disappeared right after and I called the BPD. I claimed a guy wearing a ski mask came in, shot her, and then ran. They never questioned me. Gang violence was everywhere."

"You never told anyone else?" Miles asked.

"No! My life and my daughter's were on line. I knew to keep my mouth shut."

"You don't think Mickey could be pulling Patrick's strings somehow?"

"I don't see it," Frank said.

"So why would Patrick kill his own son?"

"I don't have a fucking clue," Frank answered.

"Like you said, a life for a life," Miles said to Logan.

Miles had grown up in Southie and still lived there. He was a beat cop before he went to work for the Gang Unit; he knew the way the streets worked here in Boston in a way I never would. But then again, so did Logan.

"That has to go much deeper than any of us could even have imagined," Logan said.

His words were spoken in an eerie context. One that made my pulse thunder through me and my heartbeat become so erratic, I thought my heart might pop out of my chest. I was clenching my palms so tightly that the indentations from my short nails were sure to draw blood.

My mind was spinning.

Would this information impact Clementine?

I started to feel like there was a black cloud over me that was never going to clear.

Uncertainty made me wary.

Worry controlled me.

Fear owned me.

If knowledge was dangerous, this was deadly information.

TWENTY-SEVEN

LOGAN

THE BACK DOOR TO Molly's had served well as my escape route over the past four months, but today I needed it more than ever.

My lungs felt like they were filled with rocks and I couldn't breathe. I pushed the door open with a force that made it bang against the brick wall.

Out in the cool night, air seeped into my lungs and I took two controlled breaths.

In.

Out.

I arranged my thoughts in my mind. A distant memory was nagging at me. One I'd been trying to place since Frank first mentioned Mickey O'Shea's wife.

Darkness was everywhere.

The night was so still, the water looked like a sheet of glass, the sky like a blank slate, and the wind was dialed down to a mere warm breeze.

The perfect summer night for chillin'.

I kicked my feet up and stretched my arms behind my head, letting my body rest comfortably on the canvas cushion beneath me. Relaxed in this way, I was in prime position for the swaying motion of the boat to lull me to sleep.

I was wiped out. My grandfather and I had spent the day

moving fast through the open water and finding the best spot to fish. Now, we were cruising on the sea of glass, doing nothing, and I could tell my grandfather wasn't ready to head back in yet. I didn't care; I had nothing better to do, and the truth was, I liked being out on the open water. It made me feel like my world wasn't crashing in all around me. Whether it was hormones kicking in or the simple fact that my parents didn't get along, and their constant arguing was making all of our lives miserable, I didn't know, and really, I didn't care. Life just sucked.

Sure, I loved hanging out with James, but being able to get away from the sailing lessons and polo matches of the Hamptons was like a breath of fresh air. I could breathe out here. I wasn't suffocating in fine linen or choking down a glass of Perrier.

My paternal grandfather, Killian McPherson, had come to my mother's family estate in Southampton to bring me back to Boston. Good thing, too, because even though I didn't have my license yet, I knew how to drive, and I was contemplating taking my grandfather Ryan's Bugatti out for a spin.

Killian McPherson and I had a tradition. September second marked the anniversary of his and my grandmother's wedding. Ever since my grandmother's death, my grandfather disconnected from the world on Labor Day weekend, and he just so happened to take me along with him every time.

The bitter argument my parents had over where I was going to start high school sent my mother fleeing from Boston in early July and she had taken me with her. But another one of my parents' longstanding disagreements wasn't going to keep my grandfather and me apart, even if Grandpa Ryan was around. The two older men hated each other. Then again, they were so completely different; there was no way they couldn't.

Whatever.

Exuding a confidence that always left me in awe, he scouted the area. Fully satisfied that we were nowhere, which was where he wanted to be, he twisted around. "Have your parents agreed where you'll start high school yet?"

I sat up straight, digging my sneakers into the floorboards for traction. "I told my mother I wanted to stay in Boston even if she chose to remain in New York, and like some sort of miracle she agreed to let me attend Boston's Blackstone Academy. For now, anyway. My father told me later she only agreed because I'd been wait-listed at NYC Prep and Collegiate, so we'll see what happens."

"NYC Prep, isn't that where James goes?"

I nodded. "If I have to leave Boston, I'll hold out until I get in there."

"Just stay on the straight and narrow, Logan. That boy seems to sniff out trouble."

I laughed and said nothing. James and I were way more alike than my grandfather wanted to know.

He maneuvered the boat around one last time and then shut the engine off. The way he drove this boat with such ease left me in awe every time I watched him. He was just a powerhouse. A very tall, well-built man with a strength that was greater than that of anyone I knew. It wasn't his size, though, that mattered. It was the power that oozed from him that allowed him to command the attention of anyone he came into contact with.

I'd never seen anything like it.

Turning all the way around, he ran a callused hand over the stubble of his white beard. "Well, since you're staying in town for a while anyway, I want you to come work at the News Parlor a couple of days a week. It will keep you out of trouble and I could use the help."

My brows popped. The News Parlor was my grandfather's store. He sold mainly lottery tickets, newspapers, and magazines, but there was a roped-off section that I was dying to get into. I'd been asking to work for him for the past year and he shot me down every time. "Really? You mean it?"

"Do I ever say anything I don't mean?"

I couldn't hold back my smile. "Will I be working on Dorchester Avenue or at the track?" I asked. Suffolk Downs was an awesome place and I loved when he took me there.

"Where do you think?"

"Dorchester," I responded with a sigh. It was worth a try.

He grinned. "I knew you were smart."

"Did you ever hire that girl who lives next door to you?"

Those dark eyes narrowed on me. "She's older than you and she's seeing that boy Tommy Flannigan. I don't want you getting involved with that shit. He's nothing but trouble."

"She says she's not seeing him, but I don't care either way."

It was his turn to raise a brow. "Then why do you want to know if I hired her?"

In my most I don't really care tone, I answered, "Just curious. She seems pretty smart. I might learn something from her." That was a lie. She had big tits and I wanted to feel them, along with the rest of her body.

"Well, as a matter of fact, I did. And everything else aside, inter-office romances, for lack of a better word, are never good business."

I kicked my feet up again against the chair in front of me and crossed my arms. "Who said anything about romance?"

He rose from the captain's chair he fit so well in and swatted me across the head. "Don't bullshit a bullshitter."

My grandfather might not have finished high school, but he was the smartest man I knew. With a shrug, I looked at him and answered truthfully. "I'm not. I'm dead serious." I didn't elaborate. I wasn't looking for a girlfriend, but I knew if I told him that I was just hoping to score, that wouldn't help me get the job.

The huff of laughter he gave me as he sat down beside me warned me another one of his stories was coming. "Well, there's something going on in that head of yours and I think its fair time I warned you . . . beware of the power of the dame."

With a glance in his direction, I rolled my eyes. "Gramps, please, anything but the birds and the bees."

I'd been jerking off for enough time now that I understood how everything worked. I didn't need him explaining it to me—again.

He shook his head and kicked his own feet up. "It happens before you know it. A woman can pull you in and get under your skin just like that. We all like to think we're immune, but before we know it we're under their spell. And then they own you in a way you never would have thought possible."

"That won't happen to me. I'm not interested in dealing with *chicks that way. Relationships are way too much work."*

The sky was the perfect shade of black and twinkling with stars as he stared up at it and closed his eyes. *"Yes, they are a lot of work, but learning to appreciate the beauty and the beast within women will take you far. It's something I can't drum into you enough."*

The laughter bubbled out of me. *"Did you just say* beast?*"*

Slowly, he opened his eyes and he looked my way. *"Let me tell you a little story."*

I settled in. This could take a while.

"All women are beasts. You just have to know how to tame them or when to let them go."

"Come on, Gramps, that sounds ridiculous."

"No, it's not. Let me tell you a little story about a woman who tore dozens of men apart. If that's not a beast, I don't know what is."

I nodded. *"Go on."*

"Many years ago there were these two gangs. Both were up-and-coming, both fighting for the biggest piece of the pie. Punch Leary was the head of the Charlestown Mob and he thought he could annihilate the Savin Hill Gang by distracting Mickey O'Shea."

"Distract him how?"

Gramps was shaking his head. *"By going after his wife."*

"What happened?"

"What happened, my boy, was a full-blown war. That wife of Mickey's was a dame, a tramp, but it didn't matter. Mickey O'Shea didn't react the way Punchy thought. He wasn't distracted; he was determined. And he went berserk. Kidnapped Leary and held him captive in some greenhouse miles from the city and slowly beat him to death. Kept him alive long enough to kill his entire crew. And he didn't just annihilate them; he stalked them. Made them aware of what was coming. One by one, he taunted them, black roses showing up everywhere, letting them know they should dread the upcoming day. It went on until every last one of that gang was killed and then finally Punchy."

Curiosity got me. *"How'd those guys let things get so far out* of hand?"

His dark eyes blazed with memory. "It was the beast. That woman. Savin Hill wasn't going to stand for another man trying to take one of their women. After that the Charlestown Mob vanished, but the war incapacitated Savin Hill so much they didn't survive too much longer, and it was all over some broad. Now, I'm not saying she wasn't gorgeous, because she was. Regardless, what I'm trying to tell you is that there have been wars waged over taking, or even attempting to take, another man's dame. Never get involved with a claimed woman, even if she's Helen of Troy. Come to think of it, especially if she's Helen of Troy."

Greek mythology had been the curriculum for my entire last half of eighth grade. For once, here was a topic I knew all too well and I couldn't keep my smart ass from rearing. "Moral of the story, then: beware of the Trojan, and not the one that comes in the small square foil."

My grandfather took my arms and pulled me closer to him. "No, Logan, this is no joke. Listen to me, and listen to me well — kill a man's dog, he'll kill your best friend; kill a man's brother, he'll kill your mother; take a man's girl, and he'll kill you."

He looked so serious I couldn't help but flinch. "Gramps, I'm not interested in Molly that way. It is really too much bullshit to deal with. Chicks just aren't worth it. You don't have to worry about me."

Silence filled the space between us as he let go of my arms. And then his hearty laughter echoed through the night sky. "Mark my words . . . someday you'll change your mind."

My phone buzzed and I carefully pulled it out of my pocket to sneak a peek. It was James and the text read, I finally scored.

"See, you know I'm right," my grandfather gloated.

The smile on my face wasn't meant for Gramps, but he didn't know that and I wasn't about to tell him what it was for.

The lecture that would ensue would be endless.

And I'd had enough of those for one night.

The wind picked up and snapped me back. My mind still a whirl, I tried to think this through. If Mickey had sought retribution for someone messing around with his wife, what would he have done if he killed his wife because of another guy—because of Patrick Flannigan?

Even if Frank didn't think so, Mickey O'Shea could very well be the kingpin to this entire operation. He had motive and reason to go after Flannigan. But why wait so long? It didn't make sense.

The Priest was someone, and if not Mickey, who? Michael? Payback for his mother's death? Or someone else entirely?

I didn't know the answers but was going to find them out. Frank gave Miles some names of former Dorchester Heights Gang members and he was going to ask around. We had to be close. There were too many coincidences. Too many connections. Too many deaths. And way too many threatening phone calls.

Shuddering, I moved faster through the alley. Elle's hand was safely in mine. I needed to get us away from here, from the chaos. I had to escape this madness if only for the night. Still, even as I thought it, I knew it wouldn't happen. Elle had to stay out of this. She shouldn't be taking risks. I had to convince her. Before we turned the corner onto Tremont Street, I stopped. "We need to talk."

Elle was shaking her head. "Logan, I know what you're going to say and you know I can't stay out of it. I have to protect that little girl, now more than ever. What if Lizzy married Michael because he was like our father? I don't remember what my father was like with us when we were little. Maybe he was just as loving as Michael is with Clementine now. And where will that leave her?"

Elle was practically hysterical and although I didn't want to understand her driving need, I did. In fact, I felt protective over Clementine myself.

"I have to be there for her, to make sure nothing bad happens to her."

I pinned Elle against the brick wall. I needed to calm her down. Standing in front of her, I looked down into her terrified stare. "I promise you I will help you to ensure she grows up happy, healthy, and normal."

Her eyes burned into mine. "You can't make me that promise, Logan. There is no way you can do that. This is all me. I have to do this myself."

The scent of her skin, the warmth in her tone, the pull of her body—they were all I needed to reassure myself that I could do this, that I could help her. I had to. I pressed my hands to the wall above her head. "Elle, I don't want you to do anything tomorrow when you go visit Clementine. It's too dangerous. Let Miles and me figure out a way to get the information we need and deliver it to Blanchet."

She shook her head violently, tears rolling down her cheeks. "I know I'm the reason you're in this situation with the DEA, why you're still involved, but you can't do anything with what you find out about Michael until I secure Clementine's future. I mean it, Logan. You can't."

I lifted her chin. "Hey, don't cry."

Her head dropped to my shoulder and she started babbling. "If something happens to Michael, I don't know what will happen to Clementine. I won't be able to live with myself knowing I might have been the one to wreck her entire life."

I pulled back. "Hey, that's not going to happen."

"It might. I don't think Michael has named anyone as her guardian yet. If he goes to prison, she could become a ward of the state until custody is determined."

"He hadn't filed—"

She cut me off. "Promise me, Logan. Promise me."

I clasped my hands to her face. I couldn't stand to see her so upset. "I promise, Elle. I promise."

Her eyes were wild now. "Even if Michael catches me, he won't hurt me. He has no idea about the two of us and besides . . ." Her voice dropped off.

"Besides what?" I asked.

She stared at me for the longest time and then dropped her gaze. "He wants me to move in with him. He thinks I can help him become DA and then judge. He said if I do that, I can be a bigger part of Clementine's life. That I could help raise her."

The words were unexpected. They were like a hard punch to the gut, and once again I couldn't breathe. "What the hell are you talking about?" I bit out.

She flinched at the harshness in my tone. "When I thought you left me, I spent the weekend at his house and he made me a proposition—if he could have me, I could have Clementine."

Everything around me seemed to be moving. The earth was no longer steady. There was a great divide between Elle and me. My world felt like it was falling apart. I fixed her with a turbulent look. "He . . . propositioned you? And what, you've been considering it while fucking me?"

"What?" she asked in shock.

I said it again. "Have you been considering his proposition while fucking me?"

"I can't believe you're asking me that."

My hands went back to their position above her head and I pounded my fists against the concrete. "You didn't answer me, Elle."

There was a hesitation in her movement when her palms lifted toward my chest. I wasn't certain if she was touching me. I couldn't feel anything. I was numb. She lifted her head to the sky. I did too. It was filled with a million twinkling lights and if I could reach up and grab some, I'd hand them all to her and assure her everything would be all right.

But I couldn't.

A horrible sense of foreboding washed over me. She was going to accept his proposal. My gaze swept her, lingered on her lips, and I could see that truth in the way her green eyes dulled, in the way her shoulders slumped, in the way she had yet to touch me.

Outrage burned in my blood. "Why won't you answer me," I demanded.

Her eyes flashed to mine but she just stood there, staring at me, saying nothing.

Something in the air shifted.

I was losing control again.

I couldn't stand the thought. I knew I was being too loud. I knew I shouldn't be so hostile. I knew what she was going to say. And that was just it: she was everything to me, and I was going to lose her.

With that thought in my mind, I turned and started for my vehicle. Oddly enough, I yearned for the day when I thought *I* was the threat to her safety. When her being with me was the problem, because at least then I had a solution.

She grabbed my upper arm. I thought she meant to slap me or push me—I wasn't sure. I froze. Her touch was doing something to me, snapping me out of the daze I was in. She placed her other hand on my other arm and stood in front of me, staring at me like I was the devil. I think she was talking, but the blood was swooshing so loud in my ears, I couldn't hear.

I was going to lose her.

I'd just found her and I was going to lose her.

She shook me. "Don't do this, Logan. Don't shut down on me," she pleaded.

I'd lost myself in my thoughts.

"I love you. Nothing has changed. I only told you that so you could understand that I'm not in danger around Michael. That I can use what he wants to get closer but I would never do anything to jeopardize what we have. Never. Do you understand me?"

I blinked. "You're not going to agree to his terms?"

Without hesitation she placed her palms on my chest. "No. I could never do that. I love you too much to lose you. But you have to trust me. You have to let me get closer to him. I'll stall him while I secure my place in Clementine's future."

I stroked my thumb over her bottom lip. "As long as he keeps his hands off you, I will try to come to terms with the plan Miles has laid out. But Elle, if he so much as touches a hair on your head . . . I might just kill him."

And this time, I meant it. I might not have had enough resolve to kill Tommy Flannigan with my bare hands, but if O'Shea violated Elle in any way, I couldn't be held responsible for my actions.

Her hands slid up my chest and dug into my shoulders. "He won't, Logan, I know he won't. He won't force me to do anything. He's not like that with me."

She was trying to convince me or maybe she was trying to convince herself, but either way, it wasn't as if I had a choice. "Okay, Elle, I'll go along with it as long as you promise to be careful."

She lifted on her toes and kissed me sweetly, softly. "I love you," she said again.

This time I said it back. "I love you, too."

I just hoped it was enough.

chapter
TWNETY-EIGHT

DAY 34

Elle

H IS BREATHING WAS STEADY and I timed mine to his.
In.

Out.

I'd been awake for hours, talking myself off the ledge I'd found myself balancing on.

I was worrying my lip.

I hadn't lied to Logan, but I also wasn't certain about what I'd told him.

I told him what I thought to be true. And the whispers in my head said everything was going to be all right. It was the logic in my brain that told a different story. I wasn't quite sure Michael wasn't going to pressure me the way I'd convinced Logan he wasn't. My hope was that I could continue to stall him while convincing him Clementine's future needed to be secured.

I had no idea if I could pull it off.

Lying on my side, watching him, I put my hand to Logan's chest and felt the beat of his heart. It was strong and unfaltering like him, and it helped to soothe my ravaged nerves.

His hand on my back started to stroke my skin, and that, too, soothed me.

He'd woken up. I knew I shouldn't have stirred him

before dawn, but he'd already told me he had to leave early and I needed him this morning.

As if he could sense this need, or maybe because he just needed me too, he kissed my head and then disentangled himself from my limbs so he could slide down to face me. On one elbow, he said, "Good morning. You're up early."

I kissed his lips. "I couldn't sleep."

I was done not being honest.

My signal must have been crystal clear because his mouth latched onto mine instantly.

He'd made love to me once last night and fucked me twice. Laying claim to me in a way he didn't have to. I was already his—heart, mind, body, and soul. There was no denying it.

His lips continued to move against mine, but the kiss was slow and sweet.

Wanting more, faster, I thrust my tongue inside his mouth and then took his hand and placed it on my breast.

"Elle." He whispered my name against my mouth.

"Logan," I breathed.

His thumb started rubbing my nipple to an aching tightness.

He shifted and I clawed at his arms. I wanted this. I wanted him to bury his cock as far inside me as he could. I didn't want slow and sweet, not this morning, I wanted hard and fast.

For a moment, he stopped and just gazed at me. He, himself, was a sight. His chest ripped, smooth, gloriously defined. Arms perfectly shaped. Legs strong.

My body pressed forward.

When I made contact with his, he flipped me onto my back and hovered over me, fingers almost magical as they reached between us and found my clit.

Caressing my pussy, his movements quickened, and then he started rolling my clit in little circles with his thumb while he tasted my mouth like he never had before. Desperate. Needy.

I felt the same.

A storm of desire hit me like a hurricane-force wind.

My hand reached down and found his beautiful length. I stroked it. Felt it. Circled it. As soon as I did, he groaned in such ecstasy I was beyond turned on.

"Logan," I moaned breathlessly, thrusting my hips up to meet his cock.

In an instant, he cupped me from behind and pulled me closer. I was all too happy to rub up against his hard, thick cock.

"Not yet," he whispered in my ear. He proceeded to tease me and kissed his way down my neck. When he reached my breasts he held them together to kiss the plumped flesh, both at the same time.

The sheets felt warm beneath me but he felt even hotter. It was a heat I yearned for and one I knew would never burn me.

His lips started to trail farther down my body and his throat made murmuring sounds of appreciation. No one had ever made me feel the way he did. Like I was special. Like I was the only thing that mattered. Like I was the one who kept his heart beating, his lungs breathing.

His hands moved in conjunction with his tongue, both at a busying pace, and I found the anticipation exhilarating. My body was at ease with his hands, lips, tongue, and teeth all over it.

Goose bumps rose on the bare skin of my hip bone when he passed over it and my body practically quaked when his finger started stroking my clit again. I bucked and wiggled beneath him when his warm breath teased me this time.

Lightly, ever so lightly, he stroked me again. It was tantalizing. It was teasing. It was delicious torture.

I found myself spreading my thighs as wide as I possibly could. I opened for him. Offered myself to him. And as soon as I did, he greedily took what was already his by sliding a finger inside of me and licking me with his tongue at the same time.

His groans of appreciation aroused me even more. The fact that I could elicit pleasure from him while he was giving it to me still messed with my head. I couldn't believe two people could be so in sync with one another.

My belly jumped when he put his mouth right on me and I rocked my hips when he added another finger.

"You like that?" he purred.

"Yes," I called out.

His hands were on me, his mouth was all over me, his tongue in me, and when I started to buck beneath him he held me down, never once stopping the exquisite pleasure he was administering.

If there was a heaven, I was in it. Every time with him brought new levels of pleasure and I was peaking once again. Up high above the clouds, stars burst behind my lids, pleasure shot through my veins. My legs tingled all the way to my toes, my arms all the way to my fingertips. He was my sun, my moon, and my rock-steady earth. I needed him in a way I knew I shouldn't. It made me weak, but I couldn't fight it. Instead I came beneath him and let the pleasure take me to that place I never wanted to leave.

I cried out. "Oh God, Logan. It feels so good. Don't stop."

I didn't want him to stop. I wanted this feeling to be enough to take me through whatever was going to happen with Michael because I knew, down deep in my soul, it wasn't going to be as easy as I wanted it to be. And I was going to take a piece of this with me to remind me not to trade my soul to the devil.

Logan nuzzled me for a moment before moving back up to bury his face in my neck. It was as if he was cementing that small gift in my soul he'd just given me when he placed his hand on my heart. I, in turn, put mine over his and held it for the longest time.

His erection was hot against my thigh and when I felt I could speak I told him, "Fuck me."

"Nothing I want to do more," he responded in that voice

that caused butterflies to take flight in my belly every time.

He pinned my hips down and pushed the first few inches of his cock inside me. Ecstasy filled the room in the form of moans. He held me in place. Watched me as he thrust inside me a few more inches. Pleasure swept through me. I wanted him so much that I had to rock my hips to get more of him inside me. "More," I breathed.

Repositioning himself, he drove his cock in deeper. My legs wrapped around him and my ankles locked together at his back. He was pulsing inside me and I loved it. My fingers went to his scalp and I pressed them against it.

The sounds of the sheets rustled beneath us. While he thrust all the way inside me, our movements were wild, wicked, out of control. Our stomachs slapping. Our eyes watching each other with such burning desire. In this moment, there was nothing else. Just him. And me. And the need to connect. To be one.

I could tell we were both close. When his breathing became ragged and he was about to come, I found myself on the brink again as well. I arched my back to meet his thrusts. He moved faster. And then he shuddered at the same time I climaxed. We were perfectly in sync and we came together in the most beautiful way. It almost made me cry.

The irony of it all was that we were made for each other, and who knew if we were going to be able to stay together. My conviction about my ability to fool Michael was waning and I knew if push came to shove, I'd do whatever I had to for Clementine.

All I could do was hope it didn't come to that.

LOGAN

MY FATHER WAS ON to me.

I didn't want to have to tell him what was going on, especially now that the stakes were higher and the DEA had threatened me. His life seemed less stressful and he was 120 days sober now. I worried that telling him I wasn't out of danger might push him to drink.

That was how I found myself speeding down the highway at seven in the morning. With Patrick put to rest since he was behind bars, I still had to investigate the Priest and Michael O'Shea, but I had to do so before and after office hours.

One of the conversations that purposely didn't make the table last night was that Miles had looked into www.evanmarks.com and it turned out it was a male escort service. Miles had found a charge on O'Shea's credit card from that very site. How he got the credit card number beat the shit out of me. His brilliance far exceeded my knowledge of the Internet in any capacity, but I'd take whatever he could come up with.

After verifying Michael's identity with the male escort indicated on the credit card receipt, Miles arranged to meet with him. In exchange for divulging what had happened when he met with O'Shea, the escort wanted a twenty-four-hour stay at the Onyx near TD Garden, complete with two escorts of his choice—before he'd meet with us.

I was happy to oblige.

I hadn't mentioned it to Elle yet because if it panned out like the last lead, it might give us nothing, and the last thing I wanted to do was burden her with more wasted shit about Michael, but I would tell her as soon as I left today. I had to. I had promised to keep her in the loop.

I pulled up to the swanky boutique hotel and tossed the valet my keys. "I shouldn't be more than thirty minutes."

"I'll keep it out front then, sir," he responded when I handed him a C-note.

That's what I was hoping for. Time was of the essence. I had to get into the office by nine.

I pushed through the revolving door and found Miles sitting in one of the plush red chairs. Red seemed to be a theme and I couldn't help but think I should bring Elle here. There was a red bike in the lobby, red chairs, and specks of red in the black swirled carpeting. On second thought, it looked like the devil's haven. "Hey, man, you ready?"

Miles stood and wiped his hands on his jeans. "He's in room 423. I called up and told him we were on our way."

We started for the elevator. "I'm sorry if I was a dick last night," I offered up.

Miles pushed the up arrow. "Don't worry about it. I know you're under a lot of stress."

The doors opened and we stepped in. "Why are you doing this?" I asked. "And don't say the money. I can see how invested you are."

He shoved his hands in his pockets. "I almost died when I was shot in the line of duty and it changed my perspective on life. I no longer wanted to fight crime on the street because I realized it wasn't only the bad guys who were getting hurt."

I nodded my head. He wasn't wrong about that.

"I look at it like this—some cards that are dealt are shit and if I can help someone who deserves it get a better hand, that's what I'm going to do."

I offered my hand to him. "Thanks, man."

When he shook it, I drew him close and pounded his back. I was never one for affection until I met Elle and I still wasn't a touchy-feely kind of guy, but this just felt right. The doors opened and we dropped the contact. That was enough of that.

I glanced up and saw a hooker and a tranny leaving a room. I glanced toward Miles. "I think that's our room."

"And there goes what you paid for," he huffed under his breath.

I raised a brow. "Hope he's happy enough to sing like a canary."

Miles laughed.

I laughed too.

Nothing was funny, but it felt good to find an ounce of humor in all this chaos.

Before the door fully closed, Miles shoved his foot in between the door and the jamb.

The dude opened the door and my eyes immediately went to the animal-print robe he was wearing.

"You Derrick?" Miles asked.

He pulled his robe closed to hide his junk. "That's me." He stepped to the side. "And you must be Miles."

He nodded. I preferred no introduction and Miles kept it that way.

I stepped in and knew I was never bringing Elle here. Everything was trimmed in red, but the pillow on the bed that read "Wicked Smaht" sealed the deal. The pillows were decorated with a Boston accent?

I walked over to the bathroom and glanced in. It was empty and I gave Miles a nod.

He opened the closet. "Clear," he said.

I nodded again.

"I'm alone," Derrick said and flopped on the bed. "So how can I help you?"

With my arms crossed, I leaned back against the red lacquered dresser.

Miles took a seat in the chair opposite the bed. "Tell me what you know about Michael O'Shea."

The dude twisted his lips. "The name doesn't ring a bell."

Miles looked annoyed as he pulled out his phone. "This guy." He flashed Derrick a picture of O'Shea's Facebook profile, and just the sight of his dark hair and icy blue eyes had me seeing double.

Derrick looked hesitant.

Frustrated, Miles went on. "It's the same picture I sent you when I contacted you."

With his blond, chin-length hair falling forward, he slicked it back with his palms. "Yeah, right, that dude. I remember him."

Miles's glare almost made me cringe. "You'd better. That's why you're here, to tell us what you know, not because we wanted to splurge on your sex life."

He straightened his spine and gave Miles a wry smile. "By the way, thank you for that."

If looks could kill, Derrick the dude would be dead. "Start talking," Miles demanded impatiently.

"What do you want to know?"

"When did you meet with him?"

He scratched his chin. "It was four, maybe six weeks ago."

"How did he contact you?"

"Through my email on Evan Marks."

"What was the purpose of the email?"

"He told me he was looking to watch his wife get off and that he wanted to tape it."

"He phrased it just like that?"

He laughed. "No, I doubt it. He was much more uptight."

"What exactly did he ask you, then?"

Derrick ran a hand through his hair. "I can't remember his exact words, man. Something like he wanted to schedule an appointment for him and his wife, and was it okay with me if he taped the encounter."

"Do you still have the email?"

"No. I can those daily."

Miles gave him a look.

He shrugged. "Can't take the chance of a scandal. You have to understand, I get contacted with messages like that all the time."

My stomach felt like iron bars and that someone had just clanged them.

Miles sat up a little straighter himself. "Okay, so you see a lot people, and yet you remember Michael O'Shea?"

The doubt was in his voice. I could tell he thought this guy was bullshitting us.

"His eyes, man. They were icy blue, almost haunted. Kind of gave me the creeps."

Miles seemed to believe him then. "Okay, so what happened?"

"I met them in a hotel room and he sat in a chair like you are in right now and never got up, and I mean never got up. His wife answered the door, his wife and I got it on, and she walked me to the door afterwards. He watched and didn't even jerk off."

Miles still had his phone in his hand. "Is this the woman that was with him?"

Derrick nodded in confirmation.

This meant it was Lizzy with O'Shea during the time she was supposedly missing.

Miles glanced at me, then back toward him. He'd drawn the same conclusion. "Did she seem like she was into it or more like she was being forced?"

He crossed his legs at his ankles. "To be honest, I'm not really certain. She seemed okay but not completely into it. I mean she consented, went along with it, got off, got me off, but said nothing."

"Did you think she was high or drunk?"

"She definitely wasn't drunk. High, I couldn't really say. She was just really sad."

Miles shifted a little in his seat and I was ready to jump out of my skin. "Do you remember anything else unusual?"

He gave another small laugh. "The dude started reciting some kind of prayer while we were going at it."

Miles's eyes shot to mine. "Do you know what prayer?"

"Something about repenting for her deeds."

"Anything else?"

"Look, threesomes are more my thing. That whole night was just freakin' bizarre. It was like they were putting on a show and neither one of them wanted to be there. Other than that, no, nothing unusual happened. Straight-up sex. Nothing kinky. He paid me, he never asked to see me again, and never contacted me again."

Miles stood.

I straightened.

"Thanks for the info." Miles handed him his card. "If you think of anything else, call me."

The dude didn't get up. "Yeah, no problem."

I started for the door and Miles followed.

"Hey," Derrick called. "I have the room for the morning, right?"

"Yeah, man. It's all yours," Miles answered.

There was nothing about what I'd just learned that made me feel any better. In fact, I felt myself twitching everywhere and I couldn't get out of there fast enough.

"Why would he do something like that?" Miles asked.

"I have no fucking idea."

My mind was warped. I couldn't think straight right now. My thoughts couldn't even be vocalized. O'Shea was with Lizzy when she was "missing." He'd never told Elle about it. He'd videotaped this fucked-up event for a reason.

I mean why?

What the fuck?

We walked toward the elevator and Miles managed to at least say what I couldn't. "What the fuck kind of guy does that with his wife?"

"The one who wants to lay claim to my girl," I muttered.

He pressed the button and turned his head toward me. "What did you say?"

"The same one who wants Elle," I said and closed my eyes.

The very thought was enough to drive me crazy.

chapter
THIRTY

Elle

IOPENED THE BACK door of my townhouse with my hands full.

I had my laptop on one shoulder, my purse on the other, and a giant plush elephant clutched in between. Logan had picked it up yesterday for Clementine. It was so big it had to be the size of her. I'd been unsuccessful in replacing Rosie and although Clementine had long forgotten her once precious rattle, he hoped this would fill any void the lost toy might have created.

It was really sweet.

Much to my chagrin, when I glanced toward the dark sky filled with gray clouds, I knew it was going to rain again. Boston in the spring was proving that my investment in a good raincoat was well worth it. I'd also picked up a red rain hat and red rain boots. Luckily, I had already shoved the hat on my head before stepping foot outdoors, but unfortunately my rain boots were at the boutique.

I took in the beautiful green colors that surrounded me— the trees, the grass, the stems of the flowers. Everything was starting to get so green and lush. I loved the Northeast and couldn't believe I'd spent so much time anywhere but here.

After a few moments of taking in the fresh air, I turned on my heels to lock the kitchen door. When I did, I felt something strange beneath my soles. The giant elephant was blocking my view but still, I managed to glance downward.

Black rose petals covered the stoop. Hundreds of them. The hairs on the back of my neck stood up and I felt a chill that was not from the cool temperature. I glanced around. Nothing. No one. Where did they come from?

That unease I'd felt earlier crept right back inside my soul.

Worrying my lip, I locked the door and hurried up the sidewalk to the street. The Porsche was parked behind the Mercedes, but there were no signs of anything or anyone unusual.

Today I was taking the Mercedes and as I rushed toward it, my mind was whirling. What I knew about black roses came from reading books and watching movies. Possibly total folklore, they meant to symbolize a warning for something like an impending death or a plot for revenge. Were these left for me or were they a prank by some neighborhood goth kid who dabbed black food coloring in his grandmother's rose garden? I tried calling Logan to tell him about it but the call went right to voicemail. I hung up. I was being silly. I'd tell him about it later.

I eased down the accelerator. Was it just my imagination, or could I smell the woodsy, pine-like smell of the outdoors in the car? I glanced around. Nothing. Odd. I was really losing it.

Driving fast, it still seemed to take me forever to get to Michael's. As I pulled onto his street, I looked in the rearview mirror and told myself I had to focus on what was important. I had to be brave. For Clementine.

I parked out front and double-checked that the thumb drive was still in the pocket of my black palazzo pants. I'd selected an outfit where the pants were loose and the top sheer so as to hide any evidence of what I was carrying on my body and draw attention up to the top. It wasn't the best plan, but I also hoped it wasn't one that was needed.

Hopefully, Michael would stay at work during my weekly breakfast date with Clementine—he always had. But then again, he hadn't propositioned me before now and wasn't awaiting an answer, either.

Knock. Knock.

I didn't want to scare Mrs. R and just go on in. This was her first week and she was still learning the ropes. In fact, I hoped Michael had reminded her to give Clementine only a small snack until I arrived.

There was no answer and I knocked again.

For some odd reason, I started to sweat even though it was cold outside.

The lock finally gave way and I felt a swoosh of relief. The door swung open and Mrs. R stood before me in her plain taupe pants, white blouse, and practical shoes. Her salt-and-pepper hair was pulled back in a tight bun. She was very proper. Like an English nanny. I both liked and disliked the idea of it. I wanted Clementine to have the freedom to express herself while understanding the rights and wrongs of the world. I wasn't certain Mrs. R would allow for the former, but at least I knew I would.

She moved aside. "Good morning, Miss Sterling. Clementine has been waiting for you."

I stepped inside. "How's everything going with her?"

"Very well. Thank you for asking."

I had the oddest feeling that I was like a stranger to her. Of course she didn't know me, but still, she knew I was a part of Clementine's life. When I'd first met her, I thought she would be ideal for Clementine, but maybe my state of mind wasn't exactly in top shape then because today she seemed cool, aloof. It was as if she didn't like me for some reason.

"Mommy!" Clementine called, barreling toward me at toddling speed with her juice cup in her hand.

"Don't run," Mrs. R warned, but her smile told me it was concern in her voice and not the need for obedience I'd heard in my father's voice every day of my young life.

I dumped everything in my hands and bent down with my arms extended. When Clementine reached me, I scooped her up and kissed her. "Good morning, silly girl. How are you today?"

Her hands clasped my cheeks and she opened her mouth for another kiss. Open-mouthed kisses were her thing. She breathed on me and she smelled of Cheerios and orange juice. A scent I had grown to cherish.

I held her tightly, the wave of love I felt for her as powerful as blood. She might not have been mine, but I felt like she was. "Look, I have a new friend to join your others." I set her down and handed her the stuffed elephant.

She giggled and threw her arms around the soft fur. "Rosie," she beamed.

My heart leapt at how much she loved her new Rosie.

"Mrs. Sterling, would you like me to prepare her breakfast now?" Mrs. R asked.

Still in the foyer, I glanced around at how tidy everything was. In the family room, all the toys were in the toy chest, the board books were placed neatly on the shelf, and Clementine's stuffed animals were nowhere in sight. "Oh, no, we do that together, but thank you. Did Traci come?"

She tidied her bun. "She came Monday and will come again tomorrow."

"Oh, it's just everything is so neat."

Mrs. R's eyes lit up. "Yes, Clementine and I did some straightening up of her things yesterday. They were in quite a disarray."

Panic set in and I didn't know how to stop it. "She has to be allowed to play," I found myself saying, knowing I was being ridiculous.

"Mommy," Clementine said again, but when my eyes darted down to hers she wasn't looking at me. She was looking at Mrs. R.

A twinge of jealousy struck and it was followed by unreasonable disappointment.

Mrs. R bent to Clementine's level. "Now sweetie, we

discussed this. I'm Nanny and," she pointed to me, "this is Aunt Elle."

Clementine was oblivious to the entire conversation as she pretended to give Rosie some juice, but I could see in that moment that Mrs. R truly cared for her and that my tension was tainting my view of the situation.

"How about I bring Rosie upstairs to your room to join your other friends in our tea party and you go make breakfast with your aunt."

She was correct. I was her aunt, not her mother.

I plastered a smile on my face and took Clementine's hand. "Come on, let's get those pancakes going."

Mrs. R gently took my arm. "I hope you don't mind that I'm trying to make the situation clear for her. We were in the park yesterday and she was calling every woman there 'Mommy.' I'm certain she misses her own mother and with no one constant woman in her life, she sees everyone as her mommy."

The sucker punch came out of nowhere, but I knew it wasn't intended to hurt me. Clementine did have a parade of women in her life. Nannies, housekeepers, Michael's sister, me, but none were here all the time. "No, not at all. You did the right thing."

Clementine and I went into the kitchen while Mrs. R left us alone and went upstairs. As always, I enjoyed my time with her. We made the batter, cooked the pancakes in the shape of princess tiaras, and then ate them with lots of syrup.

I shoved my own issues aside. Mrs. R was good for her. She was stable and reliable and could see what I had failed to see.

"How was it?" she asked Clementine as she entered the kitchen.

"De . . . lick . . . is," she said, rubbing her tummy.

My heart fluttered. She was cute beyond words.

"If you don't mind, Miss Sterling, I'm going to take her for a walk before the rain starts. It looks like it might just storm all day."

I was washing the frying pan. "Please, call me Elle, and that's a great idea. I'll just finish up here and be off. I have to get to work by ten."

"You can leave those. I'll clean them up later."

I pushed the hair from my face. "I'm almost done."

"Okay, then, we'll be off."

I wiped my hands on a towel. "Give me a kiss, silly girl."

In her shiny patent leather shoes she came over to me. "Bye, bye."

I gave her a big squeeze and kissed her. "I love you and I'll see you this weekend."

She gave me that open-mouthed kiss and then took Mrs. R's extended hand.

As soon as I heard the door close, I ran into Michael's office.

Sightless eyes were watching me, or that's how I felt as I plugged the thumb drive into Michael's computer and a series of letters and numbers flashed before me. The bar at the bottom moved at a snail's pace. I dug my fingernails into my palms as it inched ever farther toward one hundred.

Five.

Six.

Seven.

I glanced around and noticed the bouquet of roses on Michael's desk.

"That's it," I thought, and ran toward the tile that hid the keypad.

With shaky fingers I tried to move it. Nothing happened. I tried to turn it. Nothing happened. Had he relocated it?

Feeling defeated, I pushed in as I went to shove away and the tile popped open. I entered *7673*—the numbers that corresponded to *Rose*, Michael's mother's name. The dead woman whose pictures were everywhere. The mother he had obviously loved.

I couldn't believe it, but the bookcase to the left of the fireplace slowly started to open. My heart was racing and I bit my bottom lip in an attempt to steady my shaking body.

Anticipation clogged my throat. I wanted to run inside and see what all the fuss was about, but I was cautious and I waited for it to fully open. My eyes glanced back to the computer screen and the bar read 100 percent. Torn between the safe room and the computer program, I decided to eject the thumb drive first.

Once I did, I turned back and the door was still fully opened. I shoved the thumb drive in my pocket and wondered how long I should wait to see if it closed on its own. I should have asked Miles. I patted my pockets for my phone but it was in my purse, which was out in the foyer, and there was no way I could leave Michael's office with the door to the safe room, panic room, or whatever you want to call it the way it was.

It remained fully open. I stared at it. It hadn't closed by now and I knew it wasn't going to. I was certain of that. I saw a large five-prong handle on the inside and knew it was there for someone to pull it shut and lock the door quickly by turning it.

Bracing myself, I took a tentative step forward . . . nervous but filled with hope that going inside would lead me closer to the truth.

One step.

Two.

Three.

And I was inside.

It was smaller than I had imagined. Twelve by twelve at the most. The air smelled musty and dry like the basement. But it was neat and clean. The walls were a deep blue. There were three clocks across the one directly opposite me. Each was labeled—Tokyo, London, and Washington. Under them was a desk that stretched the entire length of the room. Two monitors were located on each end of the desk. To my right was a couch sandwiched between open shelves with bottles of water, cans of fruit, and first aid supplies. There was another couch sandwiched between cabinets.

Curious, I started with those.

The center of the room was clear and if Michael had money or drugs hidden inside the room, they'd have to be in there. My pulse was thundering in every pressure point in my body as I moved quickly. If Michael came home and found me in here, I'd have no excuse that would ring true. Clementine wasn't even in the house.

The bottom cabinet was a refrigerator that was empty. The top held a few guns, ammunition, and flashlights. The other cabinet was completely barren, but salt crystals were on the bottom of it. There was also a safe on the top that I wasn't even going to try to open.

The desk held the monitors and a keyboard. I clicked the enter button and was shocked to see rooms in the house pop up as well as the front and back doors. In plain sight were the kitchen, the family room, and Clementine's bedroom. Thank God, none of the other bedrooms were being monitored. Still, it made me a little jumpy to know Michael could watch me almost anywhere.

Oh, God, could he see me now?

I was just about to give up and run when a sheet a paper with what I knew to be my sister's writing caught my attention. Her letters always looked printed in all capital letters and they were easily identifiable. My heart stuttered a little as I reached for it. It read:

Gabby,
You must have known how much I need you right now. Things in my life are a mess. I need to get away. Please bring Clementine, a bag of her things, and as much money as you can. Meet me later tonight at 615 One Park Lane. Don't tell anyone, especially Michael, and please, be careful.

Love, Lizzy

Tears stung the back of my eyes and I sucked in a breath to hold them back. My sister had tried to contact me and somehow Michael intercepted the note. The wave of sadness I felt was excruciating.

"Miss Sterling, are you still here?"

My eyes darted toward the door and I spotted a sealed vanilla envelope on the desk labeled *Clementine's Paternity*. I had no time to look through it now, though; Mrs. R and Clementine were back and I had to get out of here. Frantic I was going to be caught, my hands were shaking hard and my mind was a scattered mess.

Clop, clop, clop, like a little racehorse I heard Clementine's small footfalls on the wooden floor in the foyer.

Snapping into action, I shot like a rocket out of the door. *The door.* How was I going to close it? I hoped it was programmed as Miles had described. Holding my breath, I re-entered the code and then closed the panel that covered it.

"Miss Sterling."

I felt a flicker of terror. Was I going to get caught?

The panic room door continued to close and I hoped it wasn't noticeable that I'd been inside. With no time to dwell over it, I tore toward the office doors, which, thank God, I'd shut before sitting at Michael's computer, and placed my hand on the knob. My heart was in my throat. A quick glance back told me I'd left the desk the way I'd found it and that the panic room door had completely closed. I heaved a sigh of relief and shut the door behind me. Then I crept out into the hallway and saw Mrs. R and Clementine in the hall powder room.

Mrs. R hadn't seen me, and I tiptoed toward the kitchen and then turned on my heels. I drew in the deepest of breaths that I could and said, "I'm still here."

She peeked out of the bathroom. She was soaked from head to toe and so was my little princess, who came surging for me when she saw me. "Mommy."

Mrs. R was still looking at me. I shrugged and gave Clementine a little huff of laughter. "What happened? Did you get rained on?"

"Wet," she giggled.

I laughed harder and held my hand out. "Come on, I'll take you upstairs and get you changed."

"Oh, I can do that, Miss Sterling."

"Please, call me Elle. And you get dried off while I take care of her and then I need to get going." Peyton opened on Wednesdays, so I could be a little late.

The rain had become a downpour by the time I pulled away from Michael's house. The minivans, swing sets, and porch swings along the road were a blur. Rain or shine, I didn't care. I was just relieved that I'd made it out of there without Michael coming home and without getting caught by Mrs. R.

That woodsy, pine-like smell was still potent in the car. I glanced in the backseat and saw nothing. When I got to the boutique, I'd have to check the trunk. Something had to be in there.

Taking the shortest way, I turned the corner and I swear I saw Michael's car heading in the opposite direction, toward his house. I hoped I was wrong.

When I felt like I could mask my overwhelming need to vomit, I fumbled for my phone and called Logan.

"Are you okay?" he answered, worried. "I saw you called and tried you back. Why didn't you answer?"

Even through everything, the sound of his voice made me smile. "I couldn't, but listen, I'm on my way to the boutique and everything went well. More than well, in fact."

"Did you install the program?" he asked, clearly concerned.

Suddenly, I felt a little proud of myself. I'd done it. "Yes, and I got into the safe room."

"What the fuck, Elle? I told you not to do that."

"I know, but the code hit me and I had to try."

His words were laced with anger. "I said it was dangerous. What don't you understand about that?"

I wanted to argue with him, but I knew he was right.

"It was a stupid thing to do," I agreed.

His sigh was heavy.

"Do you want to know what the code was?" I tried to extinguish his anger.

"Yeah." His tone was still off.

"It's *Rose*, Michael's mother's name."

"Son of a bitch."

There, he was fine. I laughed. "Can you believe it?"

"No. But you still shouldn't have gone in there. What if you had been caught?"

The car in front of me engaged its hazard lights. I pulled around it. "Since when do you talk in the hypothetical?"

"Since there was no plan A or plan B," he answered matter-of-factly.

The light turned yellow and I pressed the gas. "Okay, okay. Do you want to know what was in there or not?"

"Of course I do. Were the drugs still in there?"

"No, I looked everywhere. There were those crystals on the floor in one of the cabinets but nothing else. However, I found a note in there, and it was from my sister to me asking me to meet her. Michael must have gotten to it before me."

There was knock on his door. "Meet her where?"

"At some address at One Park Lane."

"Hang on," he told me.

The rain started to fall harder and I turned the windshield wipers up. "Okay," I said.

"Put him in the conference room and see if he wants some coffee, I'll be right there," Logan said to who I assumed was Sheila, his receptionist. "I'm back. Sorry about that."

The car in front of me came to an abrupt stop and I slammed on the brakes. The car behind me honked.

"Where are you, Elle? Are you okay?"

"Yes, it's just raining so hard I can't see two feet in front of me, but I'm almost to the boutique."

"Take it easy, okay? I don't want anything to happen to you."

"You're sweet, you know."

"Now, you're pushing it."

I laughed. "You are. Are you ready for the address?"

"Yes, shoot."

"It was Six-fifteen One Park Lane."

"That was one of the three buildings that cokehead pointed out to Miles."

All the spots were taken near the boutique and I found myself weaving up and down the side streets. "I want to go with you when you go," I said.

"No way."

I decided to give in and pay to park in a lot. I hated the high cost and very rarely did it, but the rain was cause enough to splurge. The lot I found was farther away from the boutique than I would have liked, considering I didn't have my rain boots. "Logan, please."

"No, Elle. Let Miles go with me and then I'll bring you there later if there's anything to see."

I switched the ignition off and fumbled for my debit card. "Do you promise?"

"Yes."

My bags were on the seat beside me and I pulled them onto my shoulder. "Oh, by the way, Clementine loved her new Rosie."

"Did she call her that?"

The lot was deserted. Everyone must have been waiting out the storm indoors. I opened the door. "She did."

"She's the sweet one," he joked. "Listen, I have to go. I'll call Miles after I meet with this client and let you know what we're doing. I have a few other things to fill you in about."

Water swooshed across my shoes with my first step onto the pavement and I swiped my card to pay the hefty twenty-dollar parking fee. I knew better than to complain to Logan about it because he'd offered more than once to pay the yearly astronomical fee for the parking lot just around the corner from the boutique.

I started to move faster. The quiet of the normally

bustling streets of Boston was eerie. "Logan, one more thing."

"Yeah, sure, what is it?"

"It's probably nothing, but when I opened the back door this morning to leave, it was covered with hundreds of black rose petals."

"Where are you?" he asked, panicked.

He took me by surprise and I stuttered. I wasn't exactly quite sure.

"Where are you?" he was yelling.

"I'm walking on a side street, heading toward the boutique."

It sounded like he was moving. "Listen to me and don't argue. Get back in the car, lock the doors, and come straight here. I'll meet you outside." The wobble in his voice told me to listen.

My legs buckled beneath me. "You're scaring me."

"I'm headed outside. I want you in your car and driving—now! Are you at the vehicle yet?"

The rain was coming down so hard it was whipping against me and it was hard to see. "No, I just turned back."

"Reschedule my clients for the day," I heard him say.

"I'll call you when I'm in the car," I said.

"No! Stay on the phone with me."

My heart was beating erratically. "It's just ahead."

"Okay, keep walking as fast as you can."

Panic like I've never felt gripped me. I hit the key fob and unlocked the door as fast as I could. "I'm getting inside. What's going on?"

"I'll tell you when you're safely inside and the door is locked."

"I'm in," I said, my voice nothing more than a whisper.

"Start driving. I'm outside waiting for you."

That woodsy, pine-like smell was still in my car. It was stronger than ever now and it no longer smelled like the outdoors, but more like the expensive aftershave I can remember my father wearing on special occasions. I wanted to gag. I couldn't stand it.

Just as my head turned to see what it could possibly be, an arm came around and covered my mouth. Terror plagued me. I tried to scream, but all that came out was a muffled sound. My eyes darted to the rearview mirror. There was a man wearing a black ski mask in my backseat. Icy blue eyes were all I could see.

Fear assaulted me.

My pulse started to thunder out of control.

All I wanted was for my defense mechanism to kick in.

My heart beat wildly as I figured out what I had to do.

The phone fell to the ground when I raised my arms to attack. But we weren't standing, and he had an advantage. As a result, my movements were jagged, not coordinated like they should have been. When I reached back to tear his eyes out, pull his hair, cause any bodily injury I could, he pressed something sharp against my face—a knife. "Don't move," he said through gritted teeth.

I knew better, but I tried to knock the knife from his hand by jabbing my elbow upward. His response was immediate and he pressed the blade harder. Along with pain, I felt warmth tricking down my face. He'd cut my cheek. How bad, I had no idea. Tears leaked from my eyes.

Then, in a rage, I went a little crazy. My hands going to my cheek, to the roof of the car, reaching behind me. My wild actions were enough to knock the knife from his grip, but in response he started to strangle me. I wasn't going to be able to get away from him. All my training, all the strength I thought I possessed, and I wasn't going to be able to fight him off.

"Elle?" I could hear Logan's frantic voice.

My attacker's hand was no longer on my mouth and I screamed, "Help! Help!"

In an instant he was covering my mouth again, this time with something thick and cottony. It smelled sweet and I immediately began to feel nauseous.

Moments later, his mouth was at my ear and I could

smell the foul scent of his breath permeating my membranes even through the chemical scent. "'They said to him, teacher this woman has been caught in adultery, in the very act. Now in the law Moses commanded us to stone such women; what then do you say?'"

My sounds, although muffled, had to convey my fear.

"You're much stronger than your sister. I thought you weaker. I thought I'd only have to hold on to you for a day or so. That all I had to do was convince you of the value of monogamy. I didn't realize you were snooping into affairs that have nothing to do with you."

I shook my head no.

He tsked. "Don't lie. He hath punishments for those who dare do so."

Again, I shook my head.

"I overheard your phone call. I know that you were looking around at things that are none of your business," he said in a whisper.

I tried to deny it, but nothing came out.

He removed the cloth from my mouth. "What do you know?"

"Nothing. I swear. The only thing I care about is Clementine."

The cotton was back in my mouth.

This time my gag reflex was triggered and I tried to push air from my mouth. I didn't like the sound of his voice at all. It was disguised in some way. It was familiar yet not. It was like he was deliberately trying to change it.

"You're the one who's been calling me," I tried to say.

Just then, everything around me became hazy. He let go of his hold on me. I wanted to open the door and run, but it was too dark. I couldn't see anything. The sound of the rain on the roof of the car seemed to be amplified and I felt like I was drowning, like I was lying on the sidewalk and the water was rushing over me.

I wasn't breathing. I gasped and sucked in a breath. Air. I needed air. The window. Could I open it? I tried to find the button on the door, but my fingers wouldn't move that far. The horn, what about the horn? I should pound my fists against the horn. But my body was sluggish and by the time I placed my hands on the center of the steering wheel and pressed, no sound came out. Wait, I wasn't pressing; I couldn't.

My limp body was like a puppet and he was tugging the strings. I could feel what he was doing, but I couldn't fight it. He pulled at my coat, took my arm out of it, and then he tore my top. I heard the sound of buttons popping and a cool draft hit my shoulder. I heard the familiar sound of a wrapper being torn, the *flick, flick* of nails against plastic, and then smelled the all-too-familiar scent of Band-Aids.

It was the nightmare of my mother's diabetes all over again, except I wasn't diabetic and he was going to give me insulin.

In a hopeless attempt, I tried to move away. I couldn't.

The needle plunged into my arm. It felt cool as the liquid swooshed through my veins, and then in the next moment I felt like I was falling. Falling into a deep, dark hole.

My father's face flashed before me. "You're so weak!" he yelled.

And this time I couldn't argue with him, because he was right.

chapter
THIRTY-ONE

LOGAN

A S THE CROW FLIES, Beacon Hill was only a hop, skip, and a jump from Dorchester Avenue.

At the most, it was ten miles.

Given Boston traffic, it was going to take me fucking forever to get to her, and in the pit of my stomach I knew I didn't even have five minutes.

Black rose petals.

They meant dread.

That was all I knew.

A chill ran down my spine, my stomach lurched, and my pulse skyrocketed. I hoped I could reach her in time. But as soon as I stepped out the door, I knew I was fucked.

The sky was dark, black clouds circling overhead, and the rain was pouring down like sheets of ice. It was fucking hailing out and the temperature was dropping by the minute.

Her sharp, agonizing scream echoed in my head and I ran as fast as I could to my vehicle. Just as I started it, the passenger door whipped open.

Fuck!

My gun wasn't on me. It was locked in my desk drawer back in the office and my other one was in the glove box right in front of where . . . my father was now sitting.

"Pop." I blinked in surprise.

He pounded the dashboard. "Go, go, go!" he yelled.

My hands gripped the steering wheel. My heart thundered and I pressed on the gas full power. "Call the cops," I ordered.

"No, we can't do that, son."

Of course, he was right. Who knew which cops would be dispersed and whose payroll they were on?

I wove in and out of the traffic, the cars moving at a snail's pace with their hazard lights on.

"Watch it!" my father yelled.

Suddenly, I skidded to a stop at the traffic light and the burning red circle seared into my brain like a hot poker. I was being way too emotional to think this through tactically. The jerk and skid checked my emotions, though, and focused me on the task at hand—getting to Elle.

In one piece.

"Where are you headed?" my father asked.

"The boutique," I managed.

The urgency in his voice told me he must have heard me on the phone with Elle. "Take the back way to Ashmont Street and then cut through the small alley to get to Neponset Avenue."

I nodded. "Call Declan—tell him someone grabbed Elle in her car. She's in the Mercedes and it was parked . . . *fuck*," my throat was tightening, "I don't fucking know where she was parked."

My father pulled out his cell.

"And tell him to get a hold of Miles," I managed to say even though my throat was almost fully constricted now.

"Declan, are you at the coffee shop?" he said. "Okay, we have a problem . . ."

Elle's cries echoed in my head and I found myself driving blindly through the haze.

"Logan, turn here!" my father yelled.

Fuck. Pay attention, asshole, I told myself. I took a right and then an immediate left and got my head back in the game.

"He's out looking for her now and Miles is on his way. They'll both probably beat us there."

I laid on the horn at the slow traffic in front of me. "Move, move, move."

"Go up on the sidewalk, get around the cars, and take the next right. That will get us to 93 faster in this traffic."

My tires climbed the curb and I moved around the cars on the pavement until I got to the turn he'd told me to take. "What are you doing here?" I finally asked as I swerved around the bend in the road and went over the railroad tracks somewhere in Boston I'd never ventured.

He spoke calmly and rationally. Nothing like me. "Logan, I don't know what you've been up to but I know whatever it is, it's dangerous. I heard the terror in your voice from my office and followed you. Now tell me what's going on."

I chanced a single glance toward him. "That's just it, Pop, I don't have a fucking clue what just happened. She told me she'd found black rose petals on her back step this morning and a sinking sensation hit me like a ton of bricks. A story Gramps told me."

"Yeah, they were the calling card of the Savin Hill Gang back in Mickey's short heyday. Left as a warning."

Ring. Ring.

It was my cell, and the name *Miles* flashed across my dash. I pressed the accept button on my steering wheel. "Tell me you're there. That you've found her."

"No, I'm in Beacon Hill though. Her vehicle isn't anywhere outside the boutique. Declan's on foot combing the side streets, I'm almost to the end of Charles, and then I'll start looking in the parking lots. Listen, Peyton saw Declan and wanted to get him out of the rain. He had to tell her Elle was missing and now she's near hysteria. What do you want me to tell her?"

"Fuck!" I slammed the steering wheel.

My father's voice filled the car. "Miles, let's not say anything right now until we figure everything out, but she shouldn't be anywhere alone."

"Yeah, I agree. I'll tell her to lock up the boutique and go to Mulligan's Cup. The streets are a ghost town, but Declan said the café was packed. She should be safe there."

It was odd listening to the conversation, because the one thing about the Irish Mob that had really changed over the years was that they never made a move in public. The days of shootouts in public places were over. Not enough police protection. Not enough men in their pockets. Therefore, Miles's plan for Peyton was a good one.

"Keep in touch," my father told him, "And we'll call when we're closer."

"Roger that," Miles said and hung up.

The familiar blue and red sign for Interstate 93 was just ahead. That meant less than eight miles to get to her, but it could have been the entire two-hundred-mile distance of 93, which ended in St. Johnsbury, Vermont, that I had to travel because the traffic on the highway was at a complete and total standstill.

"Fuck!" I cried out.

The sigh from my father told me he felt the same. "Turn around and go back to Dorchester Avenue."

"It was worse there."

"We'll double back to Washington Street and then over to Blue Hill Avenue."

"That's at least ten miles out of the way."

"Logan, trust me, son, it will get us there faster."

I threw the car in reverse and looked backwards as I zoomed the wrong way off the on-ramp. I felt raw and nervous inside in a way I never had. Back on the road, I hit the gas, spraying water, speeding to the corner, and turning left so fast that I almost fishtailed up Washington Avenue.

My father gripped the handle above the door but said nothing else.

I kept control of the Rover and when the light ahead turned red, I hit the gas and powered through the intersection.

Nothing was going to stop me from finding Elle.

Not now, not ever.

Elle

T HE SUN WAS SHINING.
    Clementine was chasing me through a field of dandelions as fast as she could.

"Mommy," she called. "Please slow down, I can't keep up."

I was in front of her, trying to get away. I couldn't slow down. I wanted to be with her but I knew I shouldn't.

"Please, please, Mommy, don't leave me."

My heart stung and I turned around. I couldn't stand it and I had to comfort her. To explain to her it was safer for her not to be with me. I bent down and picked a dandelion and handed it to her. "Blow, just blow," I said. "And everything will be okay."

She took it and blew on it, but still she wouldn't stop crying. Although I knew better, I reached my hand out for her to take, but instead of feeling her smooth, baby-soft skin, I touched something damp, gritty. Dirt. The ground. Sand. I couldn't tell. All I knew was that I wasn't in a field and a hammer was pounding against my brain.

I tried to move but couldn't. It was as if my arms and legs weren't attached to my body. Chemical fumes stung my nose. I was aware I was somewhere, I just didn't know where. I couldn't see anything but that retched blackness.

With all my might, I concentrated harder. Slowly, my consciousness was coming back.

Something was around my eyes, but it wasn't thick

enough to prevent me from making out shapes. Trees. Flowers, maybe.

The smell of chemicals was everywhere in the air.

I could hear noises. Water running, maybe.

A figure stepped toward me.

I didn't dare even try to move now.

"I think she's waking up, Father. What do you want me to do with her?" an unfamiliar voice said.

"I'm not ready for her to begin her repentance yet. Keep her quiet so I can concentrate."

That was the voice I'd heard in the car. I'd heard it before. I still couldn't place it.

"Why don't you use the same sermons you prepared for her sister?"

"She's not a drug addict. We don't have to take her through withdrawal to repent for the unholy sins she committed on her body."

"What about her adultery? Perhaps you could use the lessons you already designed to atone for the sin of adultery."

"Enough! She's not an adulteress—yet. My goal is to prevent her from becoming one. I need some time to think. Her repentance must be unique to her."

Was I in church? What was going on? I started to squirm. Tried to scream.

"Give her another injection so she doesn't get away from you like her sister."

My sister. He had taken my sister?

Frantic and scared, I scraped at the ground beneath me. My hands were tied together, but still I tried to heave myself up. I wasn't weak. I did know how to defend myself. I could take him . . . if I could just figure out which way was up and which was down.

Before I could distinguish direction, that horrible Band-Aid smell was back in the air and I heard a *flick, flick*.

"No, please no," I pleaded.

With a yank of my hair, whoever was beside me sat me

up. "Shut the fuck up or you won't like what I do to you."

"Leave her alone. I told you I don't want you to touch her. You'd be mindful yourself to recite your own lessons and repent for your own weaknesses."

"Yes, Father." His tone had completely changed to subordination.

"Let me hear it," that familiar voice ordered.

"Now?"

"Yes, now." I heard a slam and flinched.

Fingers crept to the back of my neck and I was left hanging there by my hair. "'To preserve you from the evil woman, from the smooth tongue of the adulteress. Do not desire her beauty in your heart, and do not let her capture you with her eyelashes; for the price of a prostitute is only a loaf of bread, but a married woman hunts down a precious life. Can a man carry fire next to his chest and his clothes not be burned? Or can one walk on hot coals and his feet not be scorched?'"

"Very good, now remember that."

My body slammed against the ground as the one holding me dropped me like I was nothing more than a child's stuffed animal. "Now, be a good girl and stop moving around," he hissed low in my ear.

Good girl.

My mother used to say those words to me when my father was on a rampage. It was her coping mechanism. I didn't understand it then, but in later years I did. It was the only way she knew how to deal with my domineering father. She couldn't fight him; all she could do was try to make me understand that if I followed the rules I would be better off. *"Now, Gabrielle, be a good girl and finish your peas and you won't have to sit here all night. Now, Gabrielle, be a good girl and be brave; it will be over before you know it. Now, Gabrielle, be a good girl and don't cry. You know he wants you to be tough."*

I wanted to scream. I hated those two words. I didn't listen then and I wasn't going to listen now.

I squirmed and flailed my body. He yanked my shirt up, exposing my bra to the cool air. Vomit got stuck in my throat. His fingers were on my stomach and he was pinching the skin. I didn't whimper. Instead I tried to fight him off, but I knew it was hopeless.

The more I fought, the more his hands wandered, so I stopped. The feel of his hand drifting down ever so slightly to the waistband of my pants frightened me more than anything else. *Please, please, please God, don't let him rape me.* I knew of all the things that had happened in my life, that would be the one thing to send me over the edge.

I hadn't prayed in years, but I was praying now.

If I was in a church, maybe God would hear me.

As if my prayers were answered, I felt the sharp prick of a needle and liquid started to spread through my body like fire.

"Good job, son. Now, allow me to concentrate. We have to save her because she's going to be our savior." The voice was clearer now, not so disguised.

If only I could remember it.

If only the ground wasn't so cold.

If only the blackness wasn't sucking me in.

chapter
THIRTY-THREE

LOGAN

"**T**HIS IS A BAD idea," Miles warned.

I shot him a look.

"Let me go in there alone."

"No fucking way."

Elle had been missing for almost eight hours. I'd gone ahead and notified the authorities, but they hadn't had any luck either. With nothing to go on, there wasn't much they could do. There was no evidence of a struggle. Nothing to go on. Nowhere for them to look. Miles's influence got a bulletin out quickly, but even so, there was no sign of her or the Mercedes—anywhere. The fucking rain hadn't let up and that wasn't helping. I was desperate, and if confronting O'Shea led me to her, I didn't really give a fuck what it cost me.

I'd sell my soul to the fucking devil if it meant saving her.

Taking the doorknob in my hand, I wanted to rip it from its socket. The adrenaline rush from my pent-up rage was what was keeping me going. I flung the door open, and Miles put his hand out to stop it from slamming against the wall.

"Hi, can I help you?" A tall blonde with big tits stood from behind her desk.

I breezed by her. "I need to talk to O'Shea."

"Do you have an appointment with Mr. O'Shea?"

The door to his office was closed and I burst in. "Where is she?"

The prick was sitting there, all pompous with his reading glasses on like he didn't have a care in the world. At my appearance, he removed his glasses and his brow creased. "Who?"

My body was all taut energy and I was ready to snap. "You know who. Now cut the bullshit and tell me what you want."

He stood up in his finely tailored suit looking all polished and put together. "It's Logan McPherson, right?"

"You know who I am. Now tell me where she is," I barked.

He cocked his head to the side as if confused. "I have no idea who you're talking about."

My nerves were shot. I was running on pure adrenaline. And I had no reason to care about anything but where the fuck Elle was. I stepped toward him. Anger flowed through my veins. "Elle, asshole, now where is she?"

He looked at his watch. "As far as I know, she'd still be at work."

"Well, she's not. She's missing."

"She was at my house visiting my daughter this morning."

I stepped even closer, and Miles put a heavy hand on my shoulder. "And shortly after she left, someone attacked her and took her."

His skin seemed to pale. He was a good actor, I'd give him that. He grabbed his office phone and hit a series of numbers that I could only assume had to be her cell phone. After about a minute, he pressed the receiver and hit some more numbers. "I'm calling the boutique now."

Silence.

His empty hand clasped the desk.

A moment later he hung up. He tried another number. What maybe her home phone?

"She's not going to answer. She's gone. Now stop fucking around. Where is she?" I said through gritted teeth.

Something darkened in his eyes as he listened to a ring that wasn't going to be answered. "I don't know. Did she go home sick?"

"She's not fucking sick, someone took her. Tell me who." I lunged toward the desk, but Miles grabbed me.

"Calm down, buddy. Getting physical isn't going to help."

I tried to shove him off me. O'Shea was my ticket. He was the one who was going to take me to her. He had to fucking know where she was.

O'Shea ran a hand through his hair. "How do you know Elle?"

I stopped trying to lunge for him. "It doesn't matter."

He seemed a little disoriented. "Why do you think she's missing?"

That's when I snapped. I flew across the room and pinned him to the bookcase behind his desk. "Because she is. Because I was talking on the phone with her when someone took her. I heard her crying for help and now I can't find her."

"I don't know where she is, I swear." He was gasping for breath and his words were barely a whisper.

"Fuck," I cursed and let go of him. I wanted to collapse where I stood because I had no other direction.

O'Shea straightened his tie. "I care about her. I wouldn't hurt her."

My chest tightened so much it ached. I wanted to pummel him just for saying that, but I had to think about Clementine, and Elle's relationship with her. I might have already damaged it and I knew I shouldn't cause any further destruction.

I turned toward Miles, who was shaking his head at me.

"We're wasting time here—let's go."

Miles gave me a nod and stepped toward O'Shea, who was looking like he was in a fog. He ripped a piece of paper off the legal pad on his desk and wrote something on it. "Here's my number. I used to be in law enforcement and I'm trying to find Elle. If you think of anything that will help or if you hear from her or anyone concerning her, give me a call."

With clenched fists, I shook my head and sprinted out of that office.

Maddening futility enveloped me.

I felt crazed.

Wild.

Insane.

Out of control.

My pulse was pounding louder than the rain, drowning out everything but the memory of her scream.

As soon as I hit the sidewalk, I felt it. My world was tilted. I took off with my fists flying and my feet stomping on the bricks of the sidewalk. Faster and faster I went. My legs cramped and my stomach knotted, but I didn't stop. I didn't falter. Until I realized I had no destination.

"Logan! Where are you going?" Miles called after me, gaining strides on me with my new slower pace.

The rain was coming harder, making it impossible to see more than a few feet ahead.

His hand grabbed my shoulder and jerked me back.

I stared at him, having forgotten the purpose of that visit to begin with until I saw his face. "Did you plant the bug?"

Lightning flashed like a warning to get off the street. "Yeah, I did. Now come on, man, let's go to your old man's and see if he makes any calls."

We were both freezing, shivering even, as we turned around and headed for the car. "Sorry for losing it back there," I said. "I knew he wouldn't tell us anything, but I didn't think he'd be so fucking convincing."

"I don't think he was lying."

Thunder rumbled through the sky. "Are you shitting me?"

He shook his head. "Up until my recent retirement from

the force, I'd been grilling suspects for years, and they have a tell about them when they're lying. O'Shea didn't have one. In fact, he looked more terrified than he let on. I could see it in his eyes. I honestly don't think he's involved, but I'm not so sure he doesn't know who is."

I had to give credit where credit was due; Miles was always one to keep a level head. "Okay, so what if you're right? What's next?"

"We wait and see what he does. If he knows anything he'll make a move soon."

Rain slid down my face and into my mouth. "Yeah, it's not like we have a choice."

"What about the sister's place? Do you want me to go alone?" he asked.

"No, I want to go. Maybe we can find something that will help us."

"Yeah, okay. Let's make a quick stop there. I can monitor O'Shea with my phone for now."

I shook my head to get some of the water off it.

We got to the Rover and Miles took the keys from me. "I'll drive."

I handed them over without complaint.

Once we were inside, we sat there, in silence, listening for something, anything, to come from O'Shea's office.

As he started driving, he turned to me. "We're going to find her."

"I know," I said.

There were no other words I could say, because the thought of never seeing her again was too much to even think about.

When we first met, I thought we were better off apart.

But it didn't take long for me to realize we were so much stronger together.

Now, alone just wasn't even an option.

chapter

THIRTY-FOUR

Elle

*L*ONG AND LEAN. DAUNTLESS. *Fearless. He was right in front of me. I lunged for him, twining my arms around his neck, feathering kisses across his face, his cheek, his chin, his nose, his scar, his lips—warm, lush, soft, blissful.*

Logan. Logan. Logan. I said his name a million times.

My body felt cold, though; even in his arms I couldn't get warm.

I held him tighter, but the chill was still inside me.

I was so cold.

Awareness started to sink in. He wasn't with me. I was alone.

My eyes heavy, I wanted to open them.

Curled on my side, a sharp pain radiated though me.

I felt beneath me.

There was a rock there.

I tried to move it.

I tried to move myself.

I could do neither.

My throat was scratchy. My mouth was dry. My skin itched. My body ached all over. The chill I had been feeling had settled in my bones.

I was cold, so cold.

Muted voices were incomprehensible.

My head jerked toward them.

They were too far away for me to see any more than two figures. One dark and looming, the other tall but much thinner, wirier.

It was then I noticed that I was no longer bound or blindfolded.

Okay, where was I?

I glanced around. There were windows everywhere. Plants. Dirt. Sprinklers.

I was in a greenhouse.

Shadows approached me. It was dark and hard to see.

Suddenly, hands gripped me. I wanted to fight them off.

I wanted to be strong.

I just couldn't.

That smell was back in my nose—the expensive aftershave and foul breath.

My stomach retched.

One of the men pulled me upright and sat me in a chair. His face was covered again with that ski mask. "Good, you're awake. I'm almost ready for you."

I opened my mouth and found I could speak. "Ready for what? Why am I here?"

"You're here so you won't make the same mistakes your sister made. You need to understand the value of remaining faithful to the one who loves you."

His voice. It was the same voice from the phone calls. "What are you talking about?"

"Not what, who. Michael," he snapped. "If you can see the path set forth for you, you won't have to worry about the wee little one and her future. Walk down that path, and walk toward Michael."

"Clementine," I whispered.

He ignored me and went on. "You're also here to learn you must stop meddling. If you can learn the value of these things through God's word, then you will live through this,"

My whole body quaked.

My brain was fuzzy.

This man had taken my sister.

"Let me go!" I screamed.

He laughed.

Make him feel something, Logan had told me when he took me to the boxing gym just last week and I showed him my moves.

With all my might, I lifted my leg and kicked my foot right into his groin.

He yelped and leapt back, grabbing himself.

Another set of hands were on me. The wiry one's, the younger one's. He got right in my face. I knew him. He was the young man who'd delivered flowers to me last night. Without hesitation, he pulled me up by my blouse and slapped me. "You bitch."

I thrashed back. Kicking, screaming, hitting.

It did nothing.

"Sit her down, I'll get the rope," the man in charge barked.

The younger one manhandled me, groping and touching me in places he didn't have to before he had me in the chair.

The man in charge wrapped a blindfold around me and then tied my wrists behind my back. "Here, silence her. We'll try again in the morning."

Moments later there was that horrible Band-Aid smell back in the air and I heard another *flick, flick.*

"No," I pleaded. "I'll be good. I'll be good. I'll be good. I promise."

My blouse was lifted. Fingers smoothed across my skin. Feeling me. Making me want to scream.

"Watch yourself, son." The voice came from a distance.

The fingers ceased. He was pinching the skin on my stomach. Then I felt the sharp prick of a needle and liquid started to spread through my body like fire again.

"Not the entire vial, you fucking idiot. We can't afford to lose her. We need her alive."

This time I didn't whimper.
I didn't cry.
I didn't try to get away.
I wanted to.
But I was too tired.
I was weak.
I'm sorry.

chapter
THIRTY-FIVE

Day 35

LOGAN

TALKING WAS OVERRATED.

For hours I'd paced like a caged tiger and listened to Miles and my father try to talk me down from the ledge I was dangling from.

"We'll find her. She's going to be okay."

Arteries pumping with adrenaline, muscles bunched, ready to spring into classic fight style, I had no direction and that was enough to drive any man crazy, let alone a man whose girl had been taken.

We'd moved from my pop's to Miles's place. Miles was sifting through all the shit on O'Shea's computer. He'd logged on about an hour ago and Miles had gained access. It was late and I was going fucking nuts. I'd looked at every file and seen enough of O'Shea's videos that I knew he was arranging these escorts for a reason and not for his sick pleasure.

As soon as my old man left, I found myself doing something I rarely did—taking refuge in a bottle of scotch.

I had to do something.

I was going crazy.

Time was passing and nothing, still nothing.

I had no leads.

My mind was so fucked that I had to escape the madness,

even if for a little while. I wasn't a drinker, so when I say a bottle, I don't mean it all went in my mouth. Some landed on me, some on the floor, some on the couch.

But come on, I'd watched sex tape after sex tape of Lizzy, and other men, all the while O'Shea sitting by watching. Whatever the reason, there couldn't be one strong enough to justify this shit. It was then that I realized just how fucked up O'Shea really was. And Elle had slept in the same house with him. The very thought sent me right over the edge.

Eight more hours and I could call Blanchet. When I'd called her earlier, she hadn't turned me down like I thought she would. Hadn't told me it wasn't within her duties to find missing persons. All she told me was to pursue normal police channels and if Elle was still missing after twenty-four hours, to call her back. Obviously, the police couldn't find Elle and I couldn't find her on my own either. No matter what the consequences of getting the DEA involved, if they were able to find her, I'd deal with the fall-out when it came.

I threw myself down and closed my eyes.

Where the fuck was she?

Someone was shaking me. "Come on, Logan, get up."

My eyes came unglued in the blind-darkened room. I quickly looked around. I was in Miles's townhouse. I must have passed out. My pulse was pounding. My hair was damp. My white T-shirt was glued to my sweat-plastered skin. "It's like a fucking sauna in here."

Miles opened the blinds. "You're sweating all the alcohol out of your system."

"Is that what it is?" I squeezed my eyes shut. Pressed the heels of my hands into my eye sockets as hard as I could, hoping that would help.

Miles nudged me and shoved a cup of coffee in my face. "O'Shea just arrived back at his office. Go take a shower. Your father stopped by earlier and left you some clothes. They're on the counter. He said he had a couple of early clients and he'd be back."

Even the cup was warm when I took it. "Anything?"
He shook his head.

There was a knock on the door, and I practically bolted out of my seat and swiped the bottle from the floor to shove it under the couch. Last thing I needed was for my father to see me like this.

Miles eyed me as he swung the door open. It was Declan and Peyton, not my old man.

"You look like shit," Declan commented.

I gave him a slow nod and then glanced at the clock. It was just after eight. Two more hours and I would be sitting in Blanchet's office.

"Good morning," Peyton said. Declan had told her most of everything last night.

"Morning." I looked toward Declan. "Don't you have to be at work?"

He strode to the kitchen. "Charlene opened up and agreed to work the day. I'll drop Peyton at the boutique and meet your old man."

"Want a coffee, Peyton?" Miles asked.

"No, thank you," she answered, and then looked at me with eyes like saucers. "Still nothing?"

I gave her a slight shake of my head. "Nothing. I'm going to take a shower. I'll be back."

"Anything on the computer?" I heard Declan ask Miles.

Jogging up the stairs, I felt my stomach turn and took the steps two at a time. The bathroom door was close enough that I was able to get to it to block out his answer. Yeah, there was shit on that computer. Nothing that could help me find Elle, but enough for me to know she needed to stay as far away from that freak as she could.

The bathroom was tiny and I pulled the shower curtain open to turn on the water. After I pissed about a gallon of what had to be the booze, I hopped in. Yesterday was a complete waste of a day, and today didn't look promising.

Every lead led us nowhere.

I held onto everything I could. The feel of her lips on

mine, the kisses she blew to Clementine when she spoke with her on the phone, the sound of her voice.

And yet I worried those very vibrant things would be crushed by the fact that she was missing and I couldn't find her.

My old man and Declan were going to watch Mickey's floral shop for unusual activity. I'd talked over with my old man the possibility of Mickey resurrecting the Dorchester Heights Gang. Just like Frank, he highly doubted it. Said Mickey had lost his drive when his gang folded. What he was going to do, though, was visit Patrick. It was doubtful he'd tell my old man anything but on the off chance he would, it was worth the visit.

Then there was O'Shea. He'd cut loose yesterday after we left. Turns out he went home. The monitoring device that Miles had left in his office didn't give us shit. He didn't so much as sneeze before he left.

The videos from his computer, though—fuck, I couldn't block them out no matter how hard I tried.

In them, it was O'Shea and Lizzy and a second man, but that man was never the same. One video was with Derrick, and what he'd told us about his encounter was true. The hotel rooms were always different but Michael was always sitting in a chair, watching, and then praying. Some verse about bearing with one another and, if one has a complaint against another, forgiving each other. Miles looked it up. It was Colossians 3:13, a scripture on forgiveness.

Perhaps forgiving adultery?

I had no idea.

The videos had all been taped within a one-week time span.

Regardless of the date, they all played out the same. O'Shea sat in his suit. Lizzy turned the camera on and opened the door, where a man would be standing. He'd go in and they'd get right to it. The fucking was different, but her face the same—saddened. When it was over, the hired escort would leave, O'Shea would take Lizzy's hand, and they would pray. Then the camera would turn off.

It was like some kind of test.

Only once did the camera remain on after the little prayer session, and it appeared as if it was left on by accident.

Lizzy stood beside Michael and reached to turn the camera off, but it didn't turn off.

He took her in his arms.

"No more," she cried.

He kissed her head. "This was the last time. I promise."

"I can see Clementine now?"

He shook his head.

"Michael, please, you promised."

"It's not my choice. He doesn't think you're ready."

"But I did what you asked."

"That's just it. You didn't pass."

"What do you mean?"

"Don't you see? You aren't strong enough to fight off the evil. You shouldn't have fucked those men."

"But you told me to!"

His eyes glassed over. "Turn it back on—he'll know we talked."

"What's this about?"

"Turn it on."

She reached again but the camera didn't turn off. She had to be doing it on purpose—like she planned to use it for it something. Then she went back to stand beside him.

Once again, he took her into his arms, but this time he asked, "Do you feel repentant?"

She raised her chin, but not in defiance, more in resoluteness. "Yes."

"Do you still want to fuck other men while married to me?" he asked.

"No, Michael, I don't want to. I love you."

"Then why do you?"

She stared at him.

"Tell me!"

"You told me to," she cried.

"But I didn't tell you to fuck Tommy while you were married to me and you did."

"I said I was sorry. I've said it so many times. I don't love him. I love you."

"Are you sure?"

Just then there was a knock on the door.

Neither moved to answer it.

"Open the door, Michael, it's time for me to take her back."

"No," Lizzy cried.

And Michael seemed to be crying too.

It was then that he shut the camera off.

Everything about it disturbed me. Him, Elle's sister, the random johns, the praying, the demands, and the guy behind the door. After seeing the videos, I couldn't even discuss them. My stomach had lost its contents more than once last night and my nerves were on the brink of being fried.

He was one fucked-up person.

And Elle was tied to him in a way I couldn't sever.

Knock. Knock.

I turned the water off. "Yeah."

"O'Shea just got a call from the Sudbury Police Department. The Mercedes turned up abandoned near the old Fort Devens Annex early this morning."

"The wildlife refuge?"

"Yeah, that's the place."

"I'll be right there," I yelled.

"I'll be in the car," Miles said.

Like lightning, I bolted out of the shower. I didn't bother to dry off before I put my clothes on.

My heart thundered in my chest. I hadn't asked him if . . . I let the thought hang there where it was.

Outside, Miles was in his car. An old Mach One Mustang. I wasn't sure what year it was, but I knew it was older than my old man's Porsche.

I hopped in without hesitation. "Any sign of Elle?" I

asked, worry clear in my voice.

He gunned it and the engine roared. "No. I called an old buddy on the force in Sudbury; no signs of anyone, anywhere."

I took a deep breath.

"I also called Blanchet."

My head whipped in his direction.

"It was close enough to the twenty-four hours."

"And?"

"Turns out Michael reported her missing early this morning."

My head snapped in Miles's direction. "O'Shea reported her missing?"

That wasn't good news at all. That meant he really didn't know where she was.

"We're monitoring his office calls, so if anyone contacts him there we'll know."

Unable to take anymore, I shook my head. "And what about calls to his cell and house?"

"I'm working on that."

"When will it be done?"

"I had to ask for help. I got four guys on it. Hopefully within the hour."

I pointed ahead to the road, where I eyed the cars stacked up, their red taillights a glowing line, their exhaust trailing white flares of smoke. The day was overcast and cold again. The traffic looked bad for miles, and it was at least an hour drive to Devens without it. I linked my hands behind my head. All I wanted to do was plow through the cars.

Like magic, Miles reached under his dash and pulled out a siren.

"No fucking way."

The grin on his face was one I'd hardly ever seen. And he opened his window and jammed that thing onto his roof.

With a small glimmer of hope that had no right being anywhere in my chest, I looked over at him. "I fucking love you, man."

"You better. I'm breaking so many laws right now." He punched the gas and off we flew through the traffic, weaving in and out and around the line of cars.

We hadn't even known each other a month, and he was putting himself out there to help me, which only proved it wasn't how long you knew someone that mattered but the relationship you forged.

And the one I'd forged with Elle was unbreakable.

I was going to find her.

We were going to spend the rest of our lives together.

Interstate 90 was a breeze to get to on the Miles Express. My gaze was out the window, my mind a scattered mess of thoughts. Elle had to be okay. Why hadn't anyone heard anything from her kidnapper, though? That's what bothered me the most. If she wasn't kidnapped for a ransom of some kind, why was she taken?

There was a green and white sign on the side of the road that read boston university school of theology. "Holy fuck!" I pounded the window with my fist.

Miles jerked his head my way but kept up his speed. "What is it, man?"

My head snapped back as if Miles could read the sign even after we passed it. "When I went to see Tommy in prison and he told me he suspected O'Shea had killed his wife, he said something I totally disregarded as babble."

"You know the police have no evidence that leads to O'Shea. He has a tight alibi, so chances are it *was* babble."

"Yeah, yeah, I know, but that's not what I'm saying. Tommy told me the Priest had taken Lizzy."

Route 2 was ahead and Miles eased off the gas. "I'm not following."

"What if all this time we thought Lizzy abandoned O'Shea, she hadn't really left him but she'd been held captive?"

Miles's head nodded slowly. "I'm following you now, but what about the videos? They were filmed last month."

I sighed. "I know, but if those men were tests of some kind?"

"And she failed."

"She'd have still been held. It's the only thing that makes sense."

"What about when we saw her on the hotel footage with Tommy?"

"Maybe she'd gotten free and that's why she was sneaking around. Why she was trying to contact Elle, but not Michael. Why she didn't see her kid."

Miles nodded. "It makes sense. It also makes sense that *the Priest* was the man behind the door in the videos."

"And the one calling Elle."

Miles nodded again.

"We have to find *the Priest*."

"Another visit to Michael?"

I nodded. "Once we get back. What other choice do we have?"

"Not many. I've exhausted my resources. They've all heard of him but no one has seen him, nor do they know where to find him. I can bring in some guys from the Gang Unit, but it's going to cost you."

"However much, I don't care." I checked my watch, the one my grandfather Ryan had given me, and for once was thankful for the trust fund he'd set up for me, for the fact that money would never be an obstacle in getting Elle back.

"And Patrick?" he asked.

"My old man is set to meet with him this afternoon."

The rain had stopped about thirty minutes ago. Finally. And was replaced by blasting sunshine. With the change in weather, we arrived at the wildlife refuge in record time considering we were coming all the way from the East End.

A blue-shirted county sheriff's deputy was blocking the way down the road, the road the Mercedes was found abandoned on.

Miles rolled down his window. "Hey, man. Can you let me pass?"

Rolled-up sleeves, buzz cut, and iron face, the guy appeared at the open window. He took a swig of water from a plastic bottle he was holding and then shaded his eyes and peered in. "Miles, my man, I thought the car looked familiar."

Miles held his hand out and the two shook.

"I'd love to help you, but I need to know why."

Miles nodded in understanding. "The woman who was driving that car is a personal friend and I'm trying to help find her, private work."

The deputy pounded the hood. "I don't have to tell you not to touch anything."

Miles gave another nod.

"Carry on then, and if I can be of any help, let me know."

It was crazy how police connections worked.

Two uniforms comparing paperwork on the dirt road gave the tow truck driver a thumbs-up. Since Elle was reported missing, and the car she last drove was found abandoned, crime scene investigation was on site. Just as we pulled up, their vehicles started rolling away, as did the other sheriff cars. "Keep your mouth shut and let me do the talking," Miles warned.

I paused and then said, "Yeah, sure."

He opened his door and cruised over to them.

I followed.

The remaining guys were both young, had to be fresh out of the academy when Miles retired. "Hey, Miles Murphy. Not sure if you remember me—"

The uniform with a build like a boulder stuck his hand out. "Miles Murphy, of course I remember you, you're a legend. Took a round in a gang turf war in the West End and lived to tell the story." He turned to the other officer, who was even broader shouldered and more barrel chested. "You remember the story, don't you?"

"Yeah, of course I do. How can we help you?"

Miles lowered his chin and nodded toward the clipboard in the linebacker's hand. "I'm working the case of a missing woman and she was last seen driving the Mercedes you just towed off. Find anything that might help me find her?"

There was no hesitation in his response. "Nothing really. Small amounts of blood were found and we're sending them off to the lab, but CSI initial analysis showed two different blood types. Purse, laptop, and wallet for a," he glanced down, "Gabrielle Sterling were found, which rules out a simple mugging. There are signs of a struggle but really, not much more."

Suddenly, the sun seemed blazing hot even though it was only April. I couldn't speak if I wanted to. I couldn't move if I were asked to. What if someone just took her and we never hear a word about her again? What if she just vanished? Who would care—other than me? O'Shea would move on like he had since his wife went missing. Elle had no family to speak of—except for that little girl she loves. The one she adamantly wanted to keep safe. Who would make sure Clementine was safe?

Somehow, some way, I knew I would.

Miles's expression was blank. "Anything else I should know about that might lead me to where the perp came from?"

The other cop scratched his head. "No, that's about it. But leave me your number. If something comes up, I'll give you a call."

"Hey, thanks, man, I really appreciate the help."

The two officers nodded and the linebacker said, "And if you come across anything, you'll let us handle it, right?"

"Yeah, of course."

The other one indicated me with his finger. "Who's this, by the way?"

The Sheriff's car that was blocking the road started down the path.

Miles blew off the question. "We'd better let you get to it. Thanks again."

Back in the car, it took all I had not to lose it.

My head felt heavy.

My vision slightly blurry.

My heart strained.

Memories of Elle burned in my eyes. The way she'd wiggle out of my hold. Blow me a kiss as she went off to work. Laugh on the phone.

She was so full of life.

The landscape blurred as we headed back to Boston. We were about halfway when Miles broke the silence. "Let's head over to the address Elle gave you yesterday."

"There's no point to that," I muttered, staring straight ahead.

"Well, we're going anyway."

I shrugged.

He kept on. "Do you think it takes a special dye to make roses black?"

I shrugged again, gaze on the landscape now. "I'm not . . . I don't . . ." I had to clear my throat, try again. "I'm not sure."

"We need to get a sample of the rose petals, have the dye run, and then query that to see what stores sell it."

I didn't look at him and muttered, "There could be hundreds."

"It doesn't matter. At least it's a starting point. Also, the Mercedes was found out in nowhere land. Why?"

"Who knows? The perp could be west, north, south, or back in Boston and trying to throw us off for all we know."

"Yeah, but like I said, it's a starting point."

I looked at my watch. She'd been missing twenty-four hours. Things weren't looking good. "A starting point." My laugh was harsh.

The car swerved to the side of the road.

"What the fuck?"

Miles got out, came around to my side, opened the door, and yanked me from my seat.

"What the fuck are you doing?"

He shoved me.

I shoved him back.

With his hands, he took ahold of me. "You are Killian McPherson's grandson—act like it, for fuck's sake. The Killer would be rolling in his grave if he saw the shape you were in over a chick."

"Fuck you." I shoved him harder.

He moved toward me and put me in a headlock. "She's just a chick. Either decide you want to find her or give up, but don't fucking waste my time."

"She's not just a chick!" I shouted.

His hold got tighter as I struggled to free myself. "Then what is she?"

"The woman I love!" I managed to scream.

He released his hold of me and started back for the car. "Then start acting like it."

With my hands behind my head, I paced the side of the road, and then with new resolve got back in the car. "Let's do this. Let's find her."

His cell rang. "Murphy here," he answered.

Silence.

"Organic soil amendments?" he questioned.

"Yeah, okay, thanks for letting me know."

"What's going on? I asked.

"Initial lab results have identified either compost or manure in the carpet fibers of the trunk, the backseat, and the driver's floor mats."

I looked at him questioningly.

"Fertilizer, like the kind used to grow plants and flowers."

My mind snapped back to the memory I had the other day of the story my gramps had told me.

"Holy fuck, that's it."

"What's it?"

"How fast can you get us back to Boston?"

I knew where she was. All we had to do was figure out where the fucking greenhouse was that Mickey O'Shea had held Punchy Leary captive. Elle had to be there.

Morning faded into afternoon.

Hours passed.

I paced, feeling like a storm growing stronger and ready to lash out.

Miles worked tirelessly on searching county records for greenhouses. There were way more than we had suspected, and none were deeded to Mickey O'Shea.

He was going through the list again, in more detail.

"Fucking A," he bit out.

I was behind him in an instant. "What?"

"There's a greenhouse about fifty miles east of Sudbury owned by a Rose Corporation. Do you think it could have any connection to Rose O'Shea?"

"Yes, it has to. Let's go."

"It's a good two hours away, Logan. Let me call the Sudbury Sheriff's Department and see if they can send someone closer."

"No, I want to find her."

He stood and gripped my shoulder. "You did, but you have to let someone else get her. Someone closer. Someone with authority."

Gearing up, I stared at him, daring him to stop me.

He stepped closer. "Logan, listen to me. I know you're going crazy right now, but her life could depend on this. We don't have any backup. We don't know what we'd be walking into. Let the authorities take care of this."

"Make the call." I conceded.

Although I hated to admit it, he was right.

chapter
THIRTY-SIX

Elle

*M*Y FINGERNAILS BIT INTO *my own skin.*
Digging, gouging, tearing, trying to free myself.
I was an animal being held captive.
No, I was a girl, a good girl.
Wait, I was a woman.

As I rose to consciousness, I wasn't sure how long I'd been here. I wasn't sure about anything. The only thing I was certain of was that more than likely I was going to die, and it was going to be sooner rather than later.

Muted voices were incomprehensible, but I didn't care anymore. I was shrouded in darkness and I couldn't fight it anymore. It wasn't my choice. My body was making the decision for me. I hadn't eaten. I'd been injected with insulin at least three times that I knew of. My confusion was evidence that hypoglycemia was setting in. It was a symptom I knew well. One I'd helped my mother overcome many times. Except, I knew the outcome when untreated. And it wouldn't be long before my brain shut down.

Far in the distance, I thought I heard sirens. No, I wanted to hear sirens. I wished I heard sirens.

Suddenly, the voices became clearer. "Get the fuck out of here, now."

"What about the girl?"

"Leave her."

Oh, God.

"Don't leave me," I tried to scream.

But the sound of a car's screeching tires and the silence in the room told me they were gone. And that I was all alone.

Logan's face flashed before me. I spoke to him. *I love you. I'm sorry. I'm sorry I'm just not strong enough.*

The whistle of sirens seemed to be closer.

Hope rose in my heart.

There was the sound of a door.

More voices.

Talk louder. I can't hear you.

Then my body slammed against something hard and I heard a thud. I think it was me. I wanted to open my eyes. To see where I was, but I just couldn't.

I was weak.

More hands were touching me. I wanted to scream. I did scream, but I don't think anything came out.

Words were echoing all around me.

The moon was strangling the sun—no, the sun was strangling the moon.

Tires were spinning.

I was in a car.

No, I was on a train.

Another thud.

I could see.

Lights were bright above me.

I was moving again. Fast. Really fast. I was back on the train.

Or had I been in a car?

This time I focused on only one of my senses—hearing, for now. I concentrated hard and when I did, I could make out what was being said.

"She's in and out of consciousness."

"Drug overdose?"

No, I don't do drugs. I was trying to talk. Could they hear me?

"I don't think so."

No, they couldn't. "Call Logan. I need Logan," I said.

"How'd she get here?"

"Sudbury Sheriff's Department brought her in."

They weren't listening to me.

"Symptoms?"

"Sweating, tremors, palpitations."

"Pupils?"

"Dilated."

"Sounds like insulin shock. I need a CBC, stat."

A pinch.

"Her pulse is steady."

Was I in a hospital?

Yes, yes I was. But was it too late?

I couldn't think anymore.

And then everything went black again.

Time passed. I had no idea how much or how little.

There was an incessant swooshing noise that woke me up.

My eyes flew open.

I felt a bit drunk.

Yet still, I could see things. There wasn't a mask of darkness around my head anymore—the blindfold was gone.

I could hear things more clearly—they were no longer muffled.

The sounds were coming from machines.

One in particular making that beeping noise that made me want to scream. I'd heard it only once before—when I was in the hospital having my kidney removed and ended up barren.

It was tall and obnoxious and it stood beside me, blinking red numbers, and it was then that I noticed the long plastic tube that ran up from the back of my hand to the pole.

Panic gripped me.

Where was I?

I was on my back, propped up. The material beneath me was utterly foreign. It was white and stiff, and smelled faintly of bleach—I wasn't on a hard, damp ground anymore.

I wasn't in heaven.

I wasn't in the fiery pits of hell.

I was in the hospital.

How?

My head pounded as I tried to remember what had happened. I struggled to sit all the way up. I needed a phone. I had to call Logan.

Everything was a scattered mess in my head; even his number was a jumble. I was dizzy, light headed, and still I reached for the phone that should have been beside my bed but there wasn't one there.

I glanced around.

The small amount of rectangular blue sky I could see through the slats of the blinds to my right told me it was daytime. I had no idea what day it was, though, or how long I'd been here.

Clementine. Would she have been waiting for me?

Anxious, I folded the covers back as gently as I could and sat on the edge of the bed. I had to find a phone. I glanced down. My fingernails still had some dirt under them; my legs were clean but bruised, my arms the same. I touched my face. It stung—my lips, my cheek, my nose.

The pole worked well as a crutch for support and I wheeled it into the bathroom before I would make my way into the hall. I looked in the mirror to find a bandage across my cheek; my lips were cut and bruised, and my nose looked slightly burned.

A murmur of voices from outside my door put me on alert. I hurried back to my bed, my pulse skipping.

Who was coming?

When the door handle turned, I held my breath, hoping it was Logan.

But how would he know where I was?

Familiar eyes greeted me. As if I'd been struck by

lightning, my body jerked. His eyes. They were the same icy blue eyes as the man who had taken me.

I felt the blood drain from my face.

The room began to spin.

My fingers gripped the sheets.

The noise coming from the machine now sounded as loud as a hammer and I wanted to smash it.

My breathing felt irregular and I took a huge breath. Blinking a few times, I talked myself off of the ledge. Of course, I knew it wasn't Michael who had abducted me. It couldn't have been. I'd have known if it was.

Still, fear crept around the periphery of my mind.

"Elle, you're awake." He rushed over to me, his cell ringing as he crossed the room.

"Where am I?" I asked. Everything seemed to be happening in slow motion and I wasn't sure my words would make sense.

His arms were around me and he was hugging me.

I felt nausea rise in my throat, but swallowed it down.

His cell rang again. The ringing of the cell phone was agitating. Still ignoring it, he pulled back and grabbed my hand as if relieved to see me. "You're in a hospital in Springfield."

An anxiety I couldn't name formed in my chest. I tried not to flinch but I did, and I ended up pulling my hand back. I closed my eyes and attempted to reject the feeling that he had anything to do with my or my sister's abduction, but in this moment, he was a stranger. Nothing made sense.

His phone was driving me crazy. "Answer it," I said rather harshly.

With a heavy sigh, he pulled it from his pocket and glanced at it. His features darkened in the strangest way, but he still didn't answer it. Instead he switched the ring to vibrate and focused on me again. "Are you in pain?" he asked. This time there was a new tone in his voice. One I'd never heard.

Hushed.

I didn't like it.

As if my lack of response was a yes, he started for the door. "I'll get the nurse."

"No, not yet."

I could see his phone vibrate in his hand. I wanted to ask him if I could use it. I wanted to call Logan, but I knew I wouldn't be able to explain myself. Still, I stared at it the entire time he poured me a glass of water. "How's Clementine?" I asked, more concerned about her than ever.

With the glass in one hand and his phone in the other, he handed me the water. "She's fine. Here, drink this."

Once I'd taken a sip, I looked up at him. "How did you know I was here?"

His sigh gave away his concern and he sat in the chair next to the bed. "I was at the Sudbury Sheriff's Department when units were dispatched to the scene." His last words trailed off.

I looked at him strangely. Town names didn't matter to me. I could have been on Mars, that's how far away I'd felt.

"I was worried about you. You were missing and I'd filed a missing persons report. I was notified when the Mercedes was found and I wanted to talk to the men who impounded the vehicle, directly."

With a shudder, I forced myself to talk even though I didn't want to. "I wasn't missing. A man took me, Michael, a man who told me I had to walk down God's path, a path that leads to you."

Silence stretched between us. "Shhh . . . you don't have to talk right now. I've told the police we'd go down to the station tomorrow in order to give you some time to think, to get everything straight in your head," he finally said.

Straight? How did he know it wasn't straight? It wasn't, but I hadn't told him that. Did he know who had taken me, who had taken my sister? Any calmness I might have had in me, any patience or tolerance, had been left on that dirt floor wherever I had been. I felt raw inside and I wanted answers. "Michael, the man who took me said he had taken Lizzy, too."

His phone was buzzing again and when he glanced down at it, all the color drained from his face. And then just like that, like what I'd said wasn't news to him, he jumped to his feet. "Listen, I need to go," he said, and headed for the door.

"Michael!" I called.

He turned back. "The doctor said you should be released tomorrow. I have something I need to take care of, but I'll be back later to check on you."

"Michael!" I called again, but the door closed.

What just happened?

chapter THIRTY-SEVEN

LOGAN

I WAS A FORCE to be reckoned with.

As I strode down the hospital corridor, nothing or no one was going to stop me from seeing Elle.

As soon as Miles had gotten the call that Elle had been found, he slapped the siren on his car again and we took off. Unfortunately, no one would violate HIPAA policies, so I had no idea how she was. All I knew were three things. She was alive. She had been admitted and was on the fifteenth floor. And I was going mad.

My legs couldn't move any faster. I wanted to run, but didn't want to draw attention to myself. I hadn't stopped at the desk, hadn't checked in. I snuck by with my hat on and sunglasses on my face. Somehow, I managed to slide right past the reception area without so much as a whisper. I wasn't going to take a chance at being denied access.

The hospital was huge and it took fucking forever to navigate. When I got in the elevator, there was no button for the fifteenth floor. I turned around to find a nurse with a cup of coffee in her hand. "Excuse me, how do I get to room fifteen ten?"

She gave me a smile. "Take the red elevator to the third floor, follow the sign for the green elevator, then take that one to the fifteenth floor."

Something tight in my chest exploded like a grenade.

I thought it was my heart, blown into a million pieces.

This journey was taking way too long.

What if she needed me right now?

"Thank you," I said, and this time I ran.

At the door to the room, I came to a stop and braced myself for the fact that O'Shea might be there already. When Miles made the call, he had learned that O'Shea was at the Sudbury Sheriff's Department. He was more than an hour closer than us.

Resolve, resignation, hatred, and rage were just a few of the emotions that passed through me. Tempering all of them, I took a deep breath. I wasn't going to stay in the shadows anymore. I couldn't. Elle was mine, and I was going to claim her for all the world to see.

Elle and I would deal with the fallout of O'Shea finding out about us, together.

A small huff of laughter escaped my lips. I talked the talk, but in the end I knew I'd do what I had to in order to make sure Clementine remained in Elle's life—even if that meant stepping away.

Pushing all the shit aside for now, slowly, I pulled the door open.

My heart was a drum banging in my chest as I eased it open. The room was dark, and emotion flooded me when I saw her lying so still in the bed. So much so, I almost dropped to my knees and prayed. Something I hadn't done since my grandmother was alive.

It really was Elle.

She was alive.

Somewhere deep in the fiery pit of my soul, I doubted it was really her. I feared that because I was a sinner, my punishment was going to be losing her.

Absolution.

Redemption.

I vowed to seek both.

Her profile was beautiful and I stopped where I was to just stare at her. The woman in front of me was more than an alignment of features. She had become the one thing that kept my heart beating and my mind sane.

I needed her.

Before I moved any farther into the room, I looked around over the rim of my sunglasses.

No O'Shea.

When I was certain I was the only person in the room, I took my sunglasses off.

As if she could sense me, her head snapped in my direction. "Logan!" she cried.

I rushed toward her and my stomach fell when I saw the bruises on her face. Not because of how she looked, but rather because of the pain she must have endured. My fists balled at my sides and anger welled beneath the surface of my very being. "Elle," I said, my own voice broken, gruff. When I reached the bed, I fell beside her and took her hand. "Elle, I can't believe it's really you."

She struggled to sit up.

"No, don't move," I insisted.

She ignored me and reached her arms out, her hands reeling me in. "Logan," she cried again.

There was no hesitation as I moved to embrace her. Gently, so gently, I lifted her chin before I pressed her body to mine. "Are you okay? Tell me you're okay." That voice wasn't even mine.

She nodded through the sobs and slammed her head to my chest. "I am, now that you're here."

Suddenly, I was a live wire. My world, the one that had seemed tilted, cracked in her absence, was righted with her in my arms, and despite knowing this was nowhere near over, I couldn't help but feel happy.

I wasn't a poet, nor was I a romantic, but at that moment everything seemed just a little brighter.

I climbed onto the bed. I had to be beside her. Her tears were bordering on hysteria and I needed to help calm her down. I lifted her head, careful not to look too closely at her wounds right now or the thought of them having been inflicted on her might just cripple me. And I couldn't afford that handicap, not here, not now.

"Oh, Logan." She said my name again as if I were her savior.

I wished I had been.

I wished I'd found her yesterday.

No, I wished I'd gotten to her before anyone took her.

I wanted so badly to rewind time and be the one to take her place.

"It's me. I'm here. I'm here."

"How . . . how . . . did you find me?" she cried.

I reached to stroke her hair. It was matted, and a mess, caked with dirt.

Oh, fuck. What had happened to her?

Again, I forced myself to focus. She needed me and she needed the calm me, the one that had never existed until she entered my life. "Later. I'll tell you everything later."

Her body was trembling despite the warmth in the room. "He had eyes like Michael's, the man who took me, he had eyes like Michael's. He told me he had taken my sister to set her on the right path, to repent for her sins, and that he had taken me so I could avoid the path she had taken."

My mind flipped back to being at her sister's apartment yesterday, which, according to the leasing office, she'd had for almost three years. There were some men's things in it—enough to indicate Tommy had been living there. Yes, she must have committed adultery. But who would hold her captive because of that?

The lease was in her maiden name, and was signed when she first moved to Boston. Employment records from Lucy's corresponded to that date. Facts indicated that she blew into town, got a job at Lucy's, and formed some kind of bond with Tommy. Where O'Shea fit in, who the hell knew?

It seemed that even after she married him, she spent a great deal of time at her apartment. The rent had been paid in cash every month through January. February, March, and

April hadn't been paid, and an eviction notice was getting ready to be processed.

I slipped the agent five hundred to lose the eviction paperwork for a few days. I didn't want the place cleaned out just yet. In there we'd found the missing garage door opener to Michael's place and signs of a struggle. The place smelled like bleach and antiseptic, as if someone had cleaned it thoroughly, and not that long ago. But what struck us as odd was the Bible on her counter. It seemed out of place based on what I'd seen and what I'd known about Elizabeth O'Shea. As soon as we'd left, I'd called Blanchet to let her know about the apartment.

"*The Priest*," I said without even realizing I'd said it.

Her eyes widened as she looked up at me. "He's the one who took me."

She already knew this.

I nodded. I knew it too. "Who he is, is the missing piece to all of this."

"But why take Lizzy and me . . . I don't understand why."

I squeezed her tightly. "Neither do I . . . but I will."

"Logan, I was terrified. After all my self-defense classes I still couldn't protect myself. I never even had a real chance. They kept injecting me with insulin to keep me quiet."

"They?"

Still trembling, she nodded. "There were two of them. One was the boy who delivered the flowers to me. The other one wore a mask."

Blood pulsed in my ears and my calm façade began to crack.

As if she had to get it out, she went on. "I knew what too much insulin would lead to. I'd lectured my mother about it all the time when she became reckless with her injections. And that sound, the sound of nail against plastic, I knew what it meant each and every time. I begged them to stop. I promised to be a good girl. I promised, but they still kept doing it."

I had to man up. I was having a hard time breathing, but what kind of sick fuck does that to someone? "Elle, baby, I'm so sorry. I'm so sorry."

Tears streamed down her face. "They used to do that to psychotic patients in the twenties to experiment on them."

I swallowed—hard. The lump in my throat was making it difficult to breathe.

Before I could say anything, the door started to swing open. The nurse's back was to me and I bolted off the bed, my hand behind my back ready to take action if I had to— hospital or not. I relaxed when I saw a tray of food in her hand.

"Miss Sterling, you're awake." The nurse smiled crossing the room to open the blinds. Once they were open, she turned around and then glared at me. "I don't believe visitors have been authorized."

"What happened to her? What state did she arrive in? What did the doctors say?" All my questions, the ones I didn't want to ask Elle, came streaming out.

Her glare reached around me to Elle. "Is this man bothering you?"

Elle's laugh was a surprise, but the sobs that followed were not. "No, he's the only thing in my life that seems sane right now."

At that she relaxed. "I'm glad to see you're feeling better,"

"We've talked?"

"Yes, I brought you up here. You were quite out of it, though, so it's not a surprise that you don't remember. You kept asking me to call Logan, but I couldn't make out his last name or the number you were giving me."

"This is Logan, Logan McPherson." She pointed to me with a smile on her face that eased all the pain I was feeling in my heart.

The nurse's smile only grew, and she set the tray on the table beside the bed and then went over and took Elle's pulse. "You need to eat. Perhaps this handsome man could make sure you do. I'll go notify the doctor that you've woken so he can come by and check on you."

Elle pushed the tray away. "I can't eat. My stomach is really upset."

The nurse pointed to a needle on the tray beside the food. "The doctor ordered Zofran. It will help, I promise."

Elle went to stand. "I need to use the bathroom first."

The nurse nodded and assisted her.

Closing the door, the nurse stepped back into the room. "Now, I'm going to bend patient confidentiality and answer your questions. Just know I don't do this on a regular basis, but Miss Sterling was asking for you. First, I want to ease your mind. She was not sexually assaulted."

Relief flooded me. I'd been a coward and unable to ask Elle myself.

"Upon arrival, she was very close to slipping into an insulin coma, but thankfully she was brought into the ER just in time. There doesn't appear to be any sustaining injuries. The cut on her cheek looks like a knife wound but should heal with very little scarring."

I flinched as visions of Tommy in my grandfather's kitchen came to mind.

"The doctor will suggest having a plastic surgeon take a look at it. I'm not so sure that's needed, but it's up to her."

The door opened and my Elle stood there, looking so frail and thin. Her cheeks looked hollow, her skin pale, and her eyes dulled.

"She was slightly dehydrated, but the IV has helped with that. She still needs to take in a good amount of fluids in the next few days. I hope I can count on you to make sure she gets what she needs."

I nodded.

The nurse insisted on helping Elle to the bed, but I stayed close to her side. As soon as Elle was back on the bed, the nurse inserted the needle into the IV. "Now, this will make you drowsy, so I'll make sure the doctor waits a good two hours before coming by to check on you."

"Thank you," I said. "For everything."

She gave Elle's arm a pat and mine a squeeze. "Listen, I don't get involved in my patients' business, but whatever happened, I hope you tell the police. It's noted in your chart that your statement was vague upon arrival and that you postponed questioning until tomorrow. Please go down there and do it. I'd hate for this to happen to anyone else."

I looked at the nurse. "You don't have to worry about that. I'll be escorting her personally."

She glanced back down. "Oh, okay. It states here a Mr. O'Shea would be doing so."

"His mistake," I noted, and I couldn't help but wonder what his involvement was.

The nurse left and when I swung my eyes back to Elle, that's when I noticed the bruises on her legs and couldn't hold back my loud gasp.

"Logan," Elle whispered.

I looked at her face.

"I'm okay, really I am."

"I love you," I said, and had to fend off the tears that I felt welling in my eyes. I'd never cried in my life, but looking at her bruised and battered was going to break me.

She reached for me. "I love you, too," she whispered, and then pressed her lips to mine.

It was something I had wanted to do but wasn't sure I should. Her lips looked so battered and bruised. The thought of why they might be turned my stomach and I couldn't ask, not yet.

She flinched at the contact and I kissed my own fingers and gently placed them on her lips. "This is me, kissing you."

Tears welled in her eyes again, and she kissed her own fingers and placed them on my lips. After a few moments, she took my face in her hands. "You don't look so great."

I had to laugh at that. "Yeah, I've had a rough night."

Moving faster than she should, she wrapped her arms around me, and I let her hold me for a long, long time. I held her too and in her arms I gained strength. She brought it to me. I knew then we had a lot to discuss. When I finally let go of her, I cleared my throat and pulled a chair up so I could swing the food tray around to feed her.

She put her hand out. "I can do it."

I smiled at her. "I want to. And while I feed you, I want you to talk to me. Tell me everything and anything you can remember. Then I'm going to help you take a shower. And after that I want you to get some rest. Once you're discharged we are going to go down and talk to Blanchet. This is much bigger than me and Miles, and I think it's time we let the authorities handle it."

"Are you sure?"

"I am."

The sun slammed through the window and she squinted. "Here, I'll shut the blinds."

She shook her head and reached for the sunglasses that were hanging from my long-sleeved T-shirt. "I want to feel the sun on me. It feels so good. I was cold for so long."

That fucking lump was back in my throat and my hands were shaking as I tried to feed her the chicken broth.

She opened her mouth and accepted the spoonful. She swallowed slowly.

As I went to give her another, I said, "Listen, before you start, I need to tell you something."

Fear riveted her and her entire body went rigid. She stopped me from giving her another spoonful by taking hold of my hand. "What is it? It's not Clementine, is it?"

"No," I said immediately.

She relaxed.

"I went to see Michael. He didn't believe me that you were missing, so I told him I was talking to you on the phone when you were abducted. I didn't tell him anything else about us, but I'm sure he can figure it out."

She took her hand away and indicated I could continue.

That was a good sign.

I scooped another spoonful.

After she swallowed it, she said, "I think you are right. It's time to come clean about everything. Michael loves Clementine and I know even if he's angry with me, he'll do what's best for her. In the end, he will."

I wasn't sure if she was trying to convince me or herself, but I agreed with her.

She ate everything on her plate and told me what she remembered, which wasn't much. I helped her shower and then put her back into bed. She didn't have any clean clothes, so a clean hospital gown had to do for now. Once she fell asleep, I'd slip out and head to the lobby. Miles was downstairs and I needed to fill him in. And I was also certain he wouldn't mind heading back to Boston to grab a few things—including one very important thing.

"Lay with me," she whispered.

"I'd do anything for you," I said as I took my place next to her.

"Even jump through fire?" she asked sleepily as her head found my chest.

"Jump through fire, leap from the tallest bridge, scale buildings, anything."

"My hero."

I wasn't her hero.

Or her white knight.

But I knew what I could be and as corny as the thought was in my mind, I was going to be . . . her Prince Charming.

chapter THIRTY-EIGHT

Elle

ATINY DETAIL SAT on the outskirts of my consciousness.

It was right there but I couldn't place it. I was in the bathroom when it hit. I'd just woken up and Logan wasn't back yet. Feeling clearer-headed than I had earlier, I replayed the events of the past few days in my head. It wasn't long before my mind felt overworked trying to pull everything together and I wished Logan were here to bounce my thoughts off of.

Unfortunately, that tiny piece of the huge puzzle was lost before I could figure out what it meant. Frustrated, I stared into the white porcelain sink, trying over and over to bring it back.

I didn't know how long I'd been standing in front of the mirror. Just looking. Thinking. Concentrating. Until eventually, I gave up and let my mind wander. I wondered if I'd have a scar. When I could kiss Logan without my lips scorching in pain. If the day would come when he could look at me without feeling racked with guilt. This wasn't his fault. Whatever this was.

"Elle?"

The hairs on the back of my neck stood up.

The voice caught me off guard. I gripped the sink, feeling panicked. Shifting my eyes around the small space, I knew I had no choice but to answer. There was no escape.

Still, I didn't move.

Michael tapped on the bathroom door. "Elle?"

"Yes, I'll be right out," I called in a shaky voice.

Why was I frightened? I had no reason to be. He said he'd be back. Why hadn't I thought to call and tell him not to come?

Stupid.

Stupid.

Stupid.

Logan had left me his phone in case I needed anything while he went down to talk to Miles, but that left him without one. My instructions were to call Miles if I needed anything, but the phone was on the table beside my bed.

Standing straight, I opened the door. It was when I looked at Michael that the small fragment I'd been trying to recall from somewhere in the back of my mind came to me in a flash. The memory was of me getting out of Michael's car after Lizzy's funeral. I was trying to avoid a conversation I didn't want to have with him and was rushing for the door when a man called out to Michael. I twisted my head and the man calling to him had icy blue eyes, the same eyes as Michael. The same eyes as the ones I had seen in the rearview mirror. And his son was with him, the same boy who had groped me and injected me with insulin. Seamus. The man's name was Seamus. Michael called him that.

I felt myself pale and squeezed my palms shut.

"What is it?" Michael asked.

Pensive, I stepped out into the room very aware that I was naked beneath my gown and hating it. It made me feel vulnerable. I shook it off and decided it was time I came clean and that Michael did as well. "Who was the man who came to the house after Lizzy's funeral with all the flowers?" I asked sharply.

Michael's entire demeanor instantly turned aloof. "How would I know? There were a lot of people there that day."

I knew he was lying.

"Why do you ask?"

My mind was wandering again, back to the picture in Erin's house, the one with the family of five—Michael, his sister, his mother, his father, and the fifth unknown. I changed tack. "Do you have an older brother?"

Michael took a step toward me. "What are all these questions about?"

I stepped back. "Do you?"

For a moment, neither of us moved or talked. "Have you thought about my proposition?"

Stunned, I couldn't even comprehend why he'd bring that up now. "No, Michael, I haven't. I'm sorry, but someone just kept me captive and injected me with insulin until he could figure out how to put me on the right path."

Blatantly ignoring me, he matter-of-factly stated, "You have something I need and I have something you want. It seems like such a simple choice, but still, I need to hear your answer."

"I don't understand why you're changing the topic," I said, exasperated.

He took a deep breath. "There are so many things you don't understand."

I sighed. "Then help me—tell me what I need to know."

"Elle, before I leave here, I need to know your answer. That's all you need to know."

I threw my hands up. "Why? Why before you leave here do you have to know?"

"Clementine's safety depends on you saying yes," he said in a broken voice.

Panic tore through me. "That's not true. You're using her to get what you want."

He frowned. "I wish I was."

No more. I couldn't take any more of this tiptoeing. He had to stop his lies now. "I'm in love with Logan McPherson and I want to be with him, not you."

Physically shaking, he ran his fingers through his dark hair. "I figured as much when he barged into my office looking for you."

I shook my head. "Then why did you still ask me about us?"

"Because I need an answer."

My knees felt like rubber. "It's no, Michael, it's no."

That fear seemed to grow on his face. "I'm sorry to hear that."

I needed to sit down, so I made my way to the bed. Once there, I turned to him and softened my gaze. "Please, don't take Clementine away from me. Don't punish her for my choices. She needs me in her life."

He seemed so distant, even though he was just across the room. "If you're not standing by my side before the District Attorney nominations, her life will be in danger and there is nothing I can do about it."

I got to my feet and ran over to him. "What are you talking about? Tell me what you mean."

Five seconds had passed before he spoke. "I can't."

My fists were pounding against his chest and tears were leaking from my eyes before I knew what I was doing. "Stop saying that. Just tell me. Tell me now."

As if defeated, he closed his eyes. "I don't even know where to start."

"The beginning, Michael. Start there."

He nodded, and after a few seconds he began to speak. "Your sister and I didn't fall in love. She was a prostitute I used for sex on a few occasions and although I fell in love with her, she never really loved me. She couldn't, because she was in love with someone else."

"Tommy Flannigan?" I asked, already having determined Lizzy had some kind of connection with him from what Logan had uncovered.

Another nod. "He wasn't right for her. He couldn't help her turn her life around, and that was what she needed."

I had nothing to say. I was certain she did need that, but experience had told me no one could do that for her; she had to want to change.

"And yet she loved him anyway. He was her pimp, for fuck's sake. He used her to make money. I hated that. Couldn't stand it. He didn't want her to clean herself up, didn't want her to get off the drugs; all he wanted was for her to keep her mouth on other guys' dicks."

I'd never heard him talk like that. "What changed, Michael? If she didn't love you, why did the two of you get married?"

"I'm getting to that. Like I said, we knew each other."

My temper flared. "Yes, you were one of those dicks she kept her mouth on."

"Don't judge me, Elle. At least I wanted to help her. And I tried many times to get her to walk away from that life, but she wouldn't. When I was done trying, I gave her my card and told her if she ever needed anything, to call me. For the longest time, she didn't. But then about two years ago she got picked up on a possession and prostitution charge. That's when she contacted me. I took her case free of charge, vouched for her, and bailed her out of jail—the court contingency was that she come work for me, my contingency was that she stay away from Tommy. She didn't really have much of a choice. It was me or jail time. So she agreed to my terms. And as the days went on, she was doing so much better. Every day I could see the light shining brighter in her eyes."

An overwhelming sadness stabbed at my chest for what she had become.

"At that time in my life I was just starting to think about running for District Attorney and I thought having a woman beside me would be beneficial, so I asked her to marry me."

I'd surmised that Michael and Lizzy, although married, weren't truly in love, so this wasn't a surprise. "Why her? You could have had anyone, I'm sure."

"There was something about her that I couldn't let go of. Not only was she beautiful, but also I really, truly believed that I could fix her. Change her life. And I thought maybe she could change mine. You know, the whole 'two lost souls' thing. I had a lot of hope back then, hope that she'd learn to love me."

I hated hearing this. Lizzy and I had both been so broken.

He went on. "The offer I made her was more than fair. All she had to do was marry me, play the dutiful wife, help me get the nomination, and stay clean. In return, I'd give her forty thousand dollars for each year she stayed with me. It really would have been a picture-perfect campaign—selfless attorney helps struggling woman and they fall in love."

I narrowed my eyes at him. "Manufactured love for the polls?"

He went on. "It didn't start out that way. I told you, I really did love her."

My eyes widened. "So my sister married you for money?"

He nodded. "Sadly, yes."

I didn't know what to say.

"It wasn't long after I'd made my offer that we went down to the courthouse and got married. About a month later she discovered she was pregnant. I didn't question who the father was. A baby was going to change every-thing. At first I thought the pregnancy would bring us clos-er together, but it didn't. I found her withdrawing more and more. I tried to help her, but she wouldn't talk to me. She stopped coming to work, said she was too tired. Then she started to disappear for days at a time, only to turn up hungry and exhausted. I never asked where she'd been. I knew where—to see him. I think that's when I gave up on her. Turned my mind off to love and focused on my career. With a family, I would more than likely be able to climb the political ladder so much quicker."

My jaw dropped and my body shook. "You took your tragic situation and made it about politics?"

"No, Elle. I took control of my life and tried to make

something out of it."

"Spin it however you want."

"You weren't here. You didn't see the way she treated me, the way she'd talk to me. She had absolutely no respect for me or for what I'd done for her."

"Why'd you let her stay, then?"

"She was pregnant. I couldn't kick her out. I knew if I did, she wouldn't take care of herself. So day after day, I endured all the crap she threw my way. After she had Clementine, things only got worse. By then, I'd stopped trying to make her happy. One day, out of the blue she threatened to leave me, take the baby, and run away with Tommy."

"But Clementine was legally your daughter. Lizzy couldn't just take off with her. You had rights too."

He laughed. "Your sister didn't care about the law. I knew there was a very real possibility that I could come home one day and find her and Clementine gone and that I'd never see them again. I couldn't have that. Clementine meant everything to me. That's when I went to someone for help who didn't care about the law either."

"What kind of help, Michael?"

"Someone who could offer Tommy the job of a lifetime."

"I don't understand."

"Your sister used to tell me the oddest things, either during one of her rages or later, once she had calmed down. One time she had told me that Tommy wanted to be successful on his own and break free of his father's hold. He really felt that his ticket out of the Flannigan shadow was the drug market. I knew this, and I used this information. Within hours of your sister telling me her plan, Tommy was offered one of the very coveted positions as wholesaler for Boston's biggest drug supplier. There was no way he was going to leave town and give that up. And with him staying, I wouldn't have to worry about Elizabeth leaving. This would give me a chance to get her help and for us to cement as a family. Or so I thought."

Shock wasn't even what I was feeling. "You're an attorney, Michael. You uphold the law. Why would you even know a person who runs a drug empire?"

His eyes, so icy blue, had tears in them. "Elle, if I would have known that it was going to cost me your sister anyway, I would never have let Seamus back into my life."

My heart was in my throat. "Who is Seamus to you, Michael?"

"You already know, Elle. He's my older brother."

My own shock finally seemed to register as I put it all together in my mind. Seamus ran Boston's drug empire. Seamus was the Priest. Seamus was the one who'd kidnapped me. Seamus was Clementine's uncle. The delivery boy was his son. Clementine's cousin.

Oh God.

Tears were leaking from Michael's eyes and he grasped his hands with his hair. "I can't take it anymore. I just can't."

"Take what?" I screamed.

He flinched and words stumbled out of his mouth. "Ever hear of selling your soul to the devil?"

I didn't know what to say to that.

"That's what I did when I asked Seamus to give Tommy a job. I had no idea my political aspirations were so significant to my brother. It turns out, they were even more important to him than they were to me."

I was losing him. He wasn't making sense. I needed to pull him back. In a softer voice I said, "Michael, finish your story, please. What happened after you got Seamus to give Tommy a job?"

His facial features tightened. "Things got worse instead of better. I asked Elizabeth to stop seeing Tommy and she ignored me. She was around less and less, and I couldn't get her to stay at home. She wasn't even spending time with Clementine. Then one day I got a call from the nanny that Elizabeth had come home and made her leave. That wasn't like Elizabeth. She didn't like to be alone with Clementine. I frantically called Seamus to find out if Tommy was still working for him. Once he reassured me that he was, I rushed home and found her packing. When she saw me, all she did was ask for the money I owed her."

"The forty thousand?" I asked, trying to understand what my sister could possibly be thinking. Why she'd want to uproot her child for a life on the road. She should have known better.

Michael scrubbed his face. "Yeah, and I went crazy. Called her some names and told her to go to hell. That's when she told me to go fuck myself. That she didn't need my money. That soon she and Tommy would have enough to never have to worry about money again. I laughed at her. That's when she told me she had five million dollars' worth of drugs in her car. While she packed, I took the drugs and put them in the panic room where she wouldn't be able to get to them. I had to. There was no way I was letting her leave the house with Clementine. When she started loading the car, and figured out what I'd done, she freaked out on me, went nuts, and then drove off alone. She had done it all the time; I thought she'd be back in a few hours once she cooled down."

I stood there, wordless. She was so much like my father. I hated that.

"But she didn't return and I started to get worried. I thought she took off for good, and that's when I called you."

I felt sick. "That's when Seamus had taken her?"

He nodded. "I didn't know it at the time, but yes. It turned out Seamus had picked up Elizabeth right after she left the house that day. My call had alerted him. It was my fault."

I had no sympathy for him, although he looked truly regretful. "So when you called me, you didn't know where she was?"

He shook his head.

"When did Seamus tell you he'd taken her?"

He ran a hand through his hair. "About a month ago."

"You knew where she was a month ago and yet you kept letting me think she was out there alone? Why would you do that?"

"How could I tell you any of this? Tell you what I'd done. I begged Seamus to let her go. He said he would when she was ready. He wanted her to repent for her sins and prove she would no longer be an adulteress."

My mind was a whirl. "What about Patrick's threats? You had the drugs; why didn't you just give them back when he made the demand?"

"I couldn't. By then Seamus had already sent a team in to package the drugs and have them delivered to his warehouse. When I received the threat from Patrick, Seamus told me he'd get me what I needed by the deadline."

"But he only sent half the drugs to the boutique?"

"I know. He said he was worried that the DEA was watching and he wanted to make certain the delivery arrived safe. We know how that ended up."

I shuddered. Thankful he didn't really know.

"Things went from bad to worse after that."

"What do you mean?"

"Elizabeth somehow escaped from Seamus and she started calling me. Threatening me. She wanted the drugs back. She even broke into the house, trying to get into the panic room."

"The note," I said. It slipped from my mouth, giving away the fact that I'd broken into the panic room.

He nodded, seemingly surprised. "Yes, she left you a note in the Mercedes, but I found it first. And then you found it—in my panic room."

"Is that why your brother kidnapped me? Because I broke into your room?"

A shake of the head.

"Then why?"

Michael averted his eyes.

"Why?"

He sighed, resigned. "After his son delivered flowers to

you, and saw you with Logan, Seamus was worried you were going to walk away from me. Believe me, I had no idea he'd taken you. I even went to the police."

My breath, coming faster, blew the first word away. "But who I choose to love isn't Seamus's concern and I wasn't doing anything wrong."

"I know that," Michael whispered. "But now he's resorted to threats against Clementine to keep us together."

"We were never together."

"In his mind, we should be."

"Tell him to find you someone else."

"I've tried. Presented my secretary, the nanny, a few others, too. He had me run them through a few of his loyalty and faithfulness tests; none of them could pass. Since they wouldn't say yes to my first order, the second test could never even be administered."

The website. It made sense. *Pick one. Show loyalty and obedience.* I felt a little sick. "I must have failed too, then."

He nodded. "He wasn't testing you; to him you were the perfect match for me. He just needed to instill his family values in you."

I threw my hands up. "Fuck him. Why does he care so much about who you end up with?"

Resolve seemed to overtake him and he spoke like he wasn't talking to anyone. "I already told you, Seamus's political aspirations for me were bigger than even my own. Mayor. Senator. White House. He saw his ability to rule more than Boston through me. To show my father he could be so much more than my father had thought he could be. However, if I was going to climb the political machine, he knew I needed a woman by my side and he thought, no he *thinks*, you are the perfect woman to fill that role. I've already told you this. You're the key. Say yes and Clementine will remain safe."

I stood open mouthed. Was Michael playing me? "I'm not going to say yes, Michael. But you have to be able to stop him from doing anything to Clementine. She isn't a part of this. You have to talk him out of it."

He was shaking his head.

"Talk to him!" I screamed.

"I have."

"Then go to the police."

"I can't."

"Why can't you?"

He shook his head violently as if he wasn't going to tell me.

"Michael!" I was hysterical now. "Why can't you? She's your daughter, it's your job to protect her!" I screamed even louder.

As he spoke, his shoulders began to shake. "I know. I know. But my choices have been stripped away from me, Elle. You don't understand."

Everything I saw was red. "No, Michael, your choice is to keep her safe, no matter what you have to do. Go to the police. Tell them everything."

Kill him, I thought.

"I can't."

"Then I will."

He shook his head. "You can't."

"Why not?"

"He'll know I told you and then he will go after Clementine."

"He almost killed me."

"Elle, he's obsessed with having connections. He thinks that's how he is going to grow his empire. Nothing is going to stop him."

"You have to turn him in," I begged.

His laugh was dry. "Like I said, you don't understand."

My fists balled at my sides. "Then tell me."

His eyes closed again and minutes passed before he spoke. "That Saturday morning that your car was at the mechanic's and I went there, that was when I found the note Elizabeth had left for you folded on the visor in the Mercedes. That night I didn't go out of town like I told you, but I went to the address on the slip of paper."

My stare was one of complete anger.

"I didn't mean for it to happen. She was threatening me. Blackmailing me—the drugs for Clementine. Was she kidding me? She couldn't take care of Clementine. She had no idea what that even meant. But yet, she kept taunting me, threatening to steal her away, and I lost control. All I was doing was trying to shake some sense into her. To calm her down. She wasn't thinking clearly. Clementine needed stability and she couldn't provide that. She insisted she could. She kept threatening me. She was hysterical."

My stomach lurched.

"She didn't like what I was saying about her relationship with Clementine and she started clawing at my coat. Clementine's rattle fell out of my pocket and she picked it up like it meant something to her. Like she really was her mother. Biologically she might have been, but that's as far as it went. I tried to make her see that, but then she went wild, denying what I'd said like it wasn't fact, she started hitting me, punching me, screaming at me. I had to defend myself so I shoved her back. That's when she fell and hit her head. She was dead instantly and there wasn't anything I could do. If I called the police, I'd go to jail, I knew that, so I called Seamus to help me get rid of her body, and now he owns me. You see, there's nothing I can do. He owns me."

My entire being was shaking. Inside and out. Tremors rocked me. Anger tore through me. I shoved him. "Killer."

He looked at me then with resolve and regret in his eyes. "I know. But listen to me, Elle, I can make this right."

I slapped him. "You killed my sister."

Tears streamed down his face. "I never wanted any of this to happen. Just know that you're the right person to take care of Clementine, to be her mother. I've spent the day arranging it all. Promise me you'll take her and leave Boston. It's the safest thing for her, and when you do, and she grows up happy, never tell her about her mother or me. Tell her she had parents who died loving her but nothing else."

"What are you talking about?" I screamed.

He grabbed my arms. "Promise me," he cried.

I stared at him blankly.

"Promise me you'll take care of her," he cried again.

I shrugged out of his hold. "I promise. I love her. You know I'd do anything for her."

My assumption was that he was going to turn himself in.

Just then, I heard the door open and Logan yelled, "Elle!"

That's when Michael pulled a gun from his suit jacket.

Terror shot through me.

I didn't know what to do.

Michael pointed the gun.

"No!" I screamed.

"Elle," Logan called for me again frantically.

I turned my head for only a fraction of a second. "No, Logan, go. Get out of here."

Ignoring me, the look on his face was determined. He looked fearless, dauntless, as his long, lean body rushed toward me.

I screamed again, "Logan, leave the room!"

He wasn't doing it.

"Stay clear of the gun!" I cried.

My head was bouncing.

From Logan.

Toward Michael.

And back.

I didn't see the gun go off, but I heard it.

An icy chill slivered down my spine.

The gunshot shattered the atmosphere.

The sound was deafening.

My ears were ringing.

I'd never realized just how loud a gunshot could be.

Blood splattered all over me. Warm, yet so chilling. It covered me from head to toe.

I was screaming, but nothing was coming out.

Pure terror was all I felt.

My entire body shook and I couldn't move.

Whose blood was covering me?

Mine?

Logan's?

Michael's?

I turned back and that was when I saw Michael on the ground. He'd killed himself. Strong arms wrapped around me, pulling me backwards, trying to turn me around. There were voices, screams, sounds, but I couldn't make out the words. All I knew was that I was pressed against a hard body.

Logan's body.

Everything was white noise. The walls, the blinds, and the window were splattered in red and the floor looked like it was bleeding.

My stomach revolted.

My feet were off the ground.

What happened next . . . I don't remember.

Slowly, so slowly, the walls closed in around me and then finally, I was lost between them.

LOGAN

PRINCE CHARMING I WASN'T.

He was supposed to walk into the room where his sleeping beauty lay and kiss her. Or at least that was how Declan thought the story went. My plan was to do that and then slip my grandmother's ring on her finger.

That's not what happened.

Rather, the ring sat in the silver box waiting for the right time and instead of being with Elle, who needed me right now, I was sitting in a room with Blanchet, Miles, and a team of DEA agents who love drawing on a fucking white-board all day.

There had been some wrong assumptions made, Mickey O'Shea being the Priest one of the biggest. But I was confident now that we had all the dots. It was connecting them to compose the right picture that was slow in coming together.

My old man had gone to see Patrick and surprisingly, Patrick told him everything. That Seamus wanted vengeance on Patrick. For his mother's death. For being sent away to Ireland. For his whole fucked-up life. That Seamus had kept his identity a secret so that when he was ready, he would come out guns blazing and annihilate the Blue Hill Gang. Tommy's fuck-up with the drug fiasco had only served to accelerate his plan and only made it sweeter.

A voice pulled me out of my thoughts. "This is the only photo we have of Seamus O'Shea, otherwise known as the Priest," Blanchet said, pointing to a copy of the picture from Erin's house that Elle told her about when Blanchet went to see her in the hospital this morning. "Immigration is sending us over a more recent one but it hasn't arrived. Details surrounding this man are sketchy at best, but it seems he was a miracle child, born seventeen months after Mickey O'Shea," she pointed to a picture of an old man taken walking into his flower shop, "went to prison."

O'Reilly, the poor sucker who was appointed her subordinate, coughed out, "It's called conjugals."

She narrowed her stare at him. "Prison records show Rose visited her husband every Sunday for the three years he did time but during family visitation hours only."

He cleared his throat. "Sorry, go on."

Another guy raised his hand and then glanced down at the report in front of him. "It says here Mickey was sentenced to five years."

She shook her head and flipped the page of the report she held. "Early parole for good behavior."

The red marker scratched against the smooth surface. "Juvie records show the young Seamus caused a lot of trouble. Didn't go to school. Break-ins. Fights. Public disturbances. Then Rose O'Shea is gunned down in a bar and subsequently the bad seed is shipped off to Ireland to some seminary school, supposedly never to be heard from again."

"So what happened?" an agent called out.

The she-devil herself was in full form and ready with every answer. "Immigration records show him reentering the United States about three years ago, with a wife and kid in tow."

"Should we assume he didn't go to seminary school if he was married?" O'Reilly asked.

"You don't assume anything because if you do, you'll be

wrong. He went to seminary school in Dublin and just before he was to be ordained, he disappeared. No one knows what he did between the year of his disappearance and his reappearance in the U.S., but sources say he has strong ties to the Continuity Irish Republic Army, which is more than likely his pipeline for the drugs."

"And you said he's known on the street as the Priest?"

She nodded in confirmation but her eyes said, "No shit." I almost laughed out loud.

"How could the DEA have been unaware until recently?" one of the agents shouted out.

"You tell me," she sneered.

"And we've never had eyes on him?" another guy asked.

She shook her head. "As far as I can tell by flipping through old reports, he was a myth. No one ever laid eyes on the Priest, so the DEA assumed he wasn't real. Something conjured up to take our attention off what it should be on. Happens all the time. We have so many leads that go nowhere and so many hyped-up heads of drug rings that never existed. According to these reports, any investigation into the Priest led to a dead end."

"Makes no sense," someone mumbled.

Irritated, Blanchet slammed her fist down. "All I can say is either he was really good at staying underground or all of you are really stupid."

O'Reilly stood. He had some balls. He strode over to the whiteboard and started writing. "Seamus O'Shea is still at large. We believe him to be traveling with his wife and son. No known direction."

"We have this composite of his kid," Blanchet added, pointing to a taped-up photo Elle helped a sketch artist render.

"Looks like another sick fuck," one of the guys muttered.

That earned him a look from Blanchet. "Let's stick to the facts. Text messages and voicemails from Seamus O'Shea on the day of Michael O'Shea's suicide clearly show threats made toward his sister-in-law, Elle Sterling, and his daughter." She pointed to screen shots taken from his phone.

The hairs on the back of my neck stood up.

"Are they still in danger?" someone interrupted.

"Not that we have reason to believe. As far as we can ascertain, the reasons for the threats had to do with Michael O'Shea's political career and well, since there won't be one, I would surmise they should be out of danger."

Miles was leaning against a window with his arms crossed. "What do you say we concentrate on finding Seamus O'Shea?"

Blanchet's head snapped in his direction.

The room quieted.

And then she gave him the slightest smile of agreement.

Another agent raised his hand like we were in class.

Blanchet nodded.

He pointed to the board. "What does Seamus O'Shea have to do with Tommy Flannigan's murder?"

"A life for a life," I muttered.

Blanchet looked at me.

"It's an old mob saying."

"Whose life?" he asked.

The last thing I was going to do was get Frank involved, so I shrugged and said, "I have no idea." I did, of course. Mickey must have told Seamus what happened years ago, how when he went to shoot at Patrick, Rose got in the way, and then once Seamus was holding the cards, he ordered Patrick to have his own son killed to avenge his mother.

A life for a life.

I'm sure Patrick had a choice, just as my father had years ago. His life or his son's life.

There's always a choice.

Blanchet started writing on the board again.

Hands went up.

Miles took the lead and answered most of the questions. In time, he would share Mickey and Rose O'Shea's tragic story with the DEA. Just not yet. We needed some time to let things settle for all of us first. For Clementine's sake, Elle wanted the O'Shea name out of the press as much as possible. I understood that.

I watched Miles in action.

Where Blanchet was good, Miles was better. But since she officially worked for the DEA and he didn't, he had to follow her command. I had a feeling that it was just a matter of time and soon he'd be on her team or possibly managing her. Either way, combined, they both had enough of the facts, and I was certain together they would bring Seamus O'Shea to justice.

With Seamus O'Shea on the lam, and no political hopeful in his pocket anymore, we all really did believe Elle and Clementine were no longer in danger. I had to give it to Michael O'Shea: in the end, he took care of his family the only way he could.

He had made the right choice.

Completely over all of this, I rose to my feet. "If you'll excuse me, I don't think I can be of any more help."

She nodded. "Thanks, McPherson. You're free to go."

The way she said it, I knew what she meant.

My father was free. I was free. Elle was free.

Finally, Elle and I could be together without outside forces pulling us apart.

And if that didn't sound like a happily ever after, I didn't know what did.

chapter
FORTY

DAY 85

Elle

I HAD NEVER BEEN much of a romantic.

I'd never even thought about it. My time was spent searching the world for treasures. It was odd, but it wasn't until Logan entered my life that I thought about the person I was before him as being a nomad. A gypsy. Traveling around in search of nothing yet never stopping.

Sure, there were times I'd watch romantic comedies and get that little high that comes with happy endings, read chick lit for the sheer pleasure of smiling, and once I think I might have thought the idea of ice-skating in Central Park while holding someone's hand could be fun, but in all honesty that was as far as my romantic thoughts had ever gone.

Until now.

While I lived with Clementine at Michael's house, Logan stayed at my place. We had both agreed that easing Logan into Clementine's daily routine was the best way to move forward. Also, with Michael's absence, I didn't want to compound her confusion by moving her out of her home right away.

Small, baby steps, we both agreed.

A saying that never could be applied to our relationship. We'd started full blast, but over the past several weeks we'd learned how to temper the inferno that lived within us both. It was fun. We actually went on the most incredible dates. Real dates. He picked me up and we went out to dinner, sometimes to the movies, and other times we went sightseeing. We double-dated with Peyton and Declan, something I had never done nor had Logan, and sometimes we brought Clementine on our dates.

We also indulged in classic movies from the eighties that for most kids were a rite of passage. Neither of us had a normal childhood, so this was all new to us. Logan bought a Best of the Eighties DVD complete set and it included *The Breakfast Club, Pretty in Pink, Back to the Future, Sixteen Candles,* and so many more favorites of that decade. At the end of each date, he would drop me off and kiss me good night. The kisses were never soft and sweet, though; they were much more reminiscent of the very first night we met.

Hot and heavy.

Breathtaking.

Unforgettable.

Mrs. R had stayed on, which allowed me to go to the boutique and work on transitioning it over to Peyton. The plan was that I'd remain the owner, but she'd be my managing partner, and once she was ready to be independent, I'd sell her the boutique. And since I was easing out of my duties, I had the luxury of sneaking off during my lunch break and meeting Logan at my place, but today we had a completely different agenda.

Today was the start of our new life.

Logan and I would be saying our goodbyes to everyone.

And leaving Boston.

It was early, around eight, and he was waiting for me on the stoop to my townhouse. With a kiss, he took my hand. "Morning."

Butterflies bounced within my belly. "Good morning."

"Come on, we have a lot to do today, so let's get started."

I followed him, and as I watched him open the door, I thought, *I'd follow him anywhere.*

He turned back before entering. "Are you sure you want

to do this?" he asked tenderly.

I nodded and let my gaze devour him. The soft tone of his voice was such a sharp contrast to the strong man standing before me. Logan was wearing a black T-shirt that hugged his torso and faded jeans that hung low on his hips. His arms were chiseled in such a way that didn't make him appear bulky in the least. He was all long and lean and hard. Powerful. Strong. Competent. There was no one else in the world I trusted more than he to help me raise Clementine.

"It doesn't matter to me. You know that, right? I will love her no matter who her biological father is," Logan said.

I nodded again. My heart in my throat, because I knew he meant that with all his heart and soul.

The envelope marked *Clementine's Paternity* that had been in the panic room was in my hand, and Logan and I were standing in front of the fireplace in a home that was soon to be owned by someone else. I'd be turning over the key today at noon to the real estate agent. The townhouse was completely bare, except for him and me, and a fire in June.

With trembling fingers, I tossed it into the flames. That envelope contained DNA results that Michael had run. Logan and I both knew there was a very likely chance Tommy Flannigan was Clementine's father, but it was equally as likely to have been Michael, or someone else entirely.

We both watched as it went up in flames.

Blood isn't thicker than water. It took me seeing the way Logan interacted with Clementine and seeing the sacrifice Michael made for his daughter to really believe it. After all, I'd grown up in such a completely different environment. A place where carrying on the bloodline was all that mattered—no matter what the risk.

Logan pulled me close. "Are you sure you're ready to leave Boston?"

I smiled at him gleefully. There was no hesitation in my

voice at all. "Yes. Yes. Yes."

His laughter was such a beautiful sound. "Say that again," he whispered.

"Yes. Yes. Yes," I said with even more excitement in my voice.

It was he, and I, and Clementine, and we would be starting fresh in a new city.

His fingers were stroking my thighs. It was finally summer, and I'd worn a pair of lightweight khaki shorts and a silky white top. Easy, breezy fashion is what Peyton called my wardrobe. I'd never thought of it like that before, but she was right.

Those competent hands moved up my body, over my hips, my belly, my breasts, up to the buttons of my blouse. Goose bumps covered my body.

"Are you cold?" he asked coyly, his warm breath scathing my neck.

I laughed. "No, it's summer."

His grin was wider than mine. He knew what he did to me.

My laughter came to a halt when his mouth fastened itself to my neck. I tipped my head back to allow him full access. Just the way he knew I liked, his tongue trailed down to the buttons he had undone and his teeth skimmed my skin along the way. When my blouse was completely opened, he dragged his tongue all the way back up to my mouth.

"Are you sure you're not cold?"

"No," I said, a little breathless.

"You're practically shivering," he said around his kisses.

"It's the way you're touching me."

I could feel his mouth turn up with satisfaction. "Come with me," he said.

I looked at him questioningly.

"We have some time." His voice had that husky edge to it.

I loved that sound.

With my hand in his, he led me up the stairs to my now empty bedroom. He seemed a little nervous when he opened the door. With a step back he shoved his hands in his pockets, and curiosity had me looking inside. My hand flew to my mouth and I gasped when I did.

Last night it had been completely empty. Today it wasn't. There was a blanket in the middle of the floor, with small red tea lights surrounding it and twinkle lights hanging from the ceiling. My heart felt so full it was banging around my rib cage.

He reached for my hand and led me inside.

I licked my lips. "And you say you don't have a romantic bone in your body."

He shook his head. I think he was blushing, and if that wasn't the most adorable thing.

It didn't last long because his mouth was back at my neck and his hands were taking my shirt off, then my bra, then my shorts and panties. "God, I need you," he breathed.

And God, I loved to hear it.

In a blink I was completely naked and he was fully dressed. I couldn't have that, so with much haste, I stripped his clothes off.

Gently, he picked me up and carried me to the center of the room, laying me down on the blanket and hovering over me.

I looked at those hazel pools, so much greener today. We'd been through so much, and every night when Clementine and I said our prayers, I thanked God for him, for the day he came into my life.

His hand went between my legs. His fingers slid against my slick flesh, then inside me, and I moaned. "I love when you touch me like that."

He moved in and out in a rhythmic pattern that could easily bring me to orgasm in a matter of minutes.

And he knew it.

My own hands sought his beautiful cock, fully erect and ready for me.

"Not yet," he said. "I want to hear the noises you make when you get turned on, when you come, and I can't concentrate when you're touching me."

I laughed. I knew exactly what he meant.

Logan teased me, moving slowly, feathering soft strokes over me with his fingers and circling his thumb with just the right amount of pressure.

I trembled on the edge and I knew he'd take me over when he felt the time was right. I let him know how much he turned me on, with my sounds, my nails, my arched back, and then finally, I exploded and my orgasm rocketed through me. "Logan!" I cried and took a breath before calling out his name again.

When we were together, everything went away but the two of us. The intimacy we shared was erotic and beautiful and joyful, and made to last a lifetime.

My body was still tingling when he thrust inside me.

I loved the feel of when he first filled me. The way his body shook from head to toe, the sounds he made, the way he made certain not to crush me.

He moved slowly.

Up.

Down.

In.

Out.

I met him thrust for thrust, and I knew how much he was enjoying it by his groans of pleasure. Loving how I could turn him on, rev him up, make him lose control, I started to move a little wildly beneath him, and he did the same above me.

We were two pieces of a puzzle that fit together perfectly.

Our union felt so incredible.

Raw and real and sensual.

If oblivion was a place we could go, he took me there.

It wasn't long before his breath got hoarse in my ear and he slid his hand between us to caress my clit.

My fingers practically clawed his back it felt so incredibly good.

We moved harder, faster. Skin slapped and mouths sucked.

I moaned in delight.

He cried out, "Elle! Oh fuck, Elle."

"Logan," I called.

"Come with me."

I already was. "I am. I am. I am."

I closed my eyes and behind my lids the universe opened up. Stars, moons, planets, and comets surrounded us in my empty bedroom.

Logan thrust inside me once more with a shout, and then stopped with a shudder. He moved a second later, once, twice, then stopped again. When he dropped his head to the crook of my neck, he said, "I love you."

My own planetarium show came to an end and as I tried to catch my breath, I held on to him as tightly as I could. "I love you, too," I said in a whisper.

"You okay?" he asked.

Funny, I'd forgotten all about the floor until that moment.

"More than okay," I said and kissed him.

Beep. Beep.

Beep. Beep.

Beep. Beep.

"Fuck. Shit. Fuck. Shit," Logan cursed as he jumped to his feet, not exactly startled by the car horn but rather flustered.

Blinking, I sat up and watched as he shoved his feet into his jeans and then scurried to the closet and opened it.

"What's going on?"

"Get dressed, fast."

He was in such a state of distress, I did what he said without question. My nerves got a little frazzled, but it didn't seem like he was worried. It seemed like he was nervous. I buttoned my blouse and said, "What's going on?"

He blew out the candles and looked at that expensive

watch that he seemed to have become fonder of. "They're early."

"Who is early?" I questioned, combing my fingers through my hair.

Logan had a bag in his hand, and he pulled out the red blindfold we'd taken from the boutique months ago but had not used.

I raised a very curious brow.

He shrugged and the corners of his mouth tipped up. "I thought we'd have time for this, but now I have to ask you to put it on."

I narrowed my eyes.

"Please," he begged and stepped toward me.

I held a finger up. "Hang on. You were going to let me blindfold you?"

He nodded. "That was the plan, but then I got lost in you."

I bit my lip. "I didn't mind, really."

His grin was devilish as he strode toward me. "Turn around."

With a shake of my head, I waved my finger back and forth. "No, no, no, *you* turn around."

Beep. Beep. Beep. Beep.

"Please, I promise you can use the blindfold and the handcuffs on me later if you just turn around and let me put this on you now."

He was vowing to give up control one night in the future. I didn't have to think twice. I stuck my hand out in shaking position.

He raised a brow.

"Deal," I said.

He shook his head and then my hand. "Deal."

With the blindfold over my eyes I was surprised it didn't freak me out, but it didn't. I always felt safe with Logan.

Step by step he guided me down each stair, and when we were at my front door he opened it.

Music started to blare and I heard the sound of Peyton's

laugher. "Declan, turn that off," she chided.

"Dumb ass," Logan muttered.

I heard other voices too. "What's going on?" I asked Logan.

He tugged my blindfold and it fell to the ground. "Well, this is not how this was supposed to happen, but I'll just have to roll with it."

Everyone we knew—Frank, Molly, Sean, Declan and Peyton holding hands, Rachel and her boyfriend, Miles, Erin and her husband and kids, and even Mrs. R and Clementine—were standing in the street with red balloons in their hands. "I thought we were supposed to go see each of them."

Logan shrugged. "I thought it would be better this way."

I nodded. I had to agree it was. I'd come to love each and every one of these people and I was going to miss them, but I'd made a promise to Michael and I intended to live up to it.

Logan gave a slight nod toward the crowd and then they all backed away to reveal a shiny red Prius. "Bon voyage!" they yelled.

Tears stung the back of my eyelids and I brought my hands to my mouth. "How did you even remember I'd wanted one in the midst of everything going on?"

His grin was cocky. "A very wise man once told me that it's the little things that make the biggest difference."

I threw myself at him. "He wasn't wrong."

Logan twirled me around on the stairs and then tossed me over his shoulder and started to carry me to the car.

"Hey, this isn't very romantic."

He laughed. "I told you I wasn't good at romance."

I think I might have been giggling and crying at the same time because he couldn't have been more wrong.

When he opened the driver's door, he set me down and smiled at me with that smile that from the very first time I saw it made my stomach flip.

"Mommy," I heard Clementine say.

"I got her." Logan closed my door and extended his hands to Mrs. R, who brought her to him. He strode around the car whispering something to her and then the two of them got in on the passenger side.

I smiled at her. "Hi, silly girl."

"Shiny," she kept saying.

I was laughing. "It is very shiny."

"She's not talking about the car," Logan said, holding her on his lap.

I glanced into the backseat and all I saw was a car seat.

When I turned back around, Logan had his hand around Clementine's. "Open it," he whispered.

She did.

I gasped.

"Elle Sterling, will you marry me and let me be a part of your and Clementine's life?"

My jaw dropped. My body shook. Never in a million years was I expecting this. Happiness surged through me and I was fighting to hold back the tears. I couldn't remember a time in my life ever feeling like this.

"Say yes, say no, say anything," he said, sounding mildly distressed.

"Yes," Clementine answered.

My laughter and joy turned into big, sobbing tears as I struggled to talk. "Yes. Yes. Yes."

The ring was the absolute most beautiful thing I had ever seen. "Logan, it's exquisite," I said through my tears.

He slid it on my finger and it fit perfectly. "It was my grandmother's and before my grandfather died, he gave it to me and told me he wanted you to wear it. Somehow, some way, he knew you were made for me."

I threw my arms around him and Clementine and found his lips. "That's because he knew we were made for each other."

When Clementine would have no more of being constrained, Logan opened the door and handed her to his father. Then he turned back and honked the horn. As if it was a signal, everyone let go of their red balloons.

Clementine was clapping her little hands together like it was a show.

I watched as the sky filled with my favorite color. The color I always saw as hope.

"You ready to say goodbye?" he asked.

I nodded. I knew we wouldn't be saying goodbye forever. There would be visits. But it was time to go.

The three of us were starting a new life together away from the madness of Boston. I never in my life would have thought I'd have a family of my own. I never in my life would have thought I could be so happy. But here I sat in my new car, with my new fiancé, and my newly court-appointed daughter, and life couldn't be any sweeter.

The sorrow that brought us here would always remain in my heart, but I wouldn't wear it on my sleeve.

I was stronger than that.

We held hands and watched through the windshield until we couldn't see any more balloons, and then we turned toward each other.

Logan ran his finger over the slight scar on my cheek.

I ran mine down the one under his eye.

War wounds.

Tragic memories from our past that we would never forget but together would be able to put behind us.

Together.

Not apart.

Not alone.

Together.

chapter
FORTY-ONE

Day 275

LOGAN

BROOKLYN IS THE PLACE we call home.

Here, I found myself no longer divided between worlds.

My grandfather Ryan owned an authentic brownstone built around the turn of the century by his father's father and when he heard how much Elle loved the architecture of Beacon Hill, he gave it to Elle and me as a wedding gift.

It's odd because before I met Elle, I never wanted to get married, but with her, I couldn't even tell you anymore why.

We married in the Botanical Gardens with fewer than thirty guests. We both decided on something small and meaningful. The vows we recited included Clementine, and she even stood up at the altar with us.

My father had moved to Brooklyn as well, and together we opened McPherson and Son Family Law.

Elle chose to run her online boutique from home to be closer to Clementine and I try to stay home one, sometimes two days a week to pull my share and give her time. She loves her life and her circle of friends. She's even recruited them to help her. Phoebe, Lindsay, and Lily go with her as she combs through antique stores looking for the best of the best.

I'd been thinking about my grandfather Killian a lot lately. He was a man of great wisdom and guidance. Sure, I knew he was an outlaw, but that was a part of his life I never saw. To me he was one of a kind. A man who loved his grandson. And there's not a day that goes by that I don't miss him. I'm thankful, though, for the time he spent with me because those memories are what will keep him alive in my mind forever.

There's this pizza place in Brooklyn called Paulie Gee's. Elle and I took Clementine there last week.

It was then that I saw it on the menu, and for the first time since my grandfather's death, I laughed at the thought of him. "Forget the pepperoni, kid," he used to say, "Corned beef is the way to go."

I would never try it and always made a face in disgust.

Today, I came here alone. "I'll have the pizza with corned beef," I said to the waitress.

She was older and smiled. "You must be Irish."

I nodded, proud of my roots.

As I waited for my pizza, I pulled the note from my pocket that was in the safety deposit box along with the ring. *Do not open this until you smile when you think of me* was written across it.

I set it on the table. He had given his life for what I'd done and that was one guilt I'd never shed.

The television was on over the bar and a news alert flashed across the screen: *Record-breaking drug bust in Boston shuts down the biggest cocaine ring to hit the streets since the seventies: DEA officials to comment soon.*

I smiled. They got Seamus, that son of a bitch. He'd been MIA for months. Video footage showed Blanchet and Miles with DEA-issued jackets leaving a church.

I sat back in the booth and crossed my feet at the ankles. Chapter closed on that son of a bitch. Miles always said he wasn't stopping until he could put him away for life. Now it looked like he got what he needed and finally nailed the bastard.

When my pizza arrived, I stared at it for a bit and remembered that little boy who sat across from the old man and never took a bite. I folded a slice in half the way he did and brought it to my mouth. I smelled the corned beef. *Not so bad smelling,* I thought, and then took a bite. "Not so bad, old man," I said aloud with a smile.

I wiped my hands and opened the envelope, sliding the piece of paper out. With a deep breath, I read it.

Logan,

Choices are made and consequences paid. It's the smaller man who dwells and the bigger man who moves forward. I've spent my life making one bad choice after the other, and the only choice I can say that I never regretted was marrying my Millie.

I've tried to teach you the things I faltered in, so that hopefully you wouldn't take the same wrong steps I had. It wasn't until after you left today that I realized I don't have to worry about you. You are your own man. Strong. Confident. Competent. And I hope I had just a little to do with it.

But it's time for me to join my love.

Don't let my choice crush you.

Don't be sad that I'm gone.

Don't dwell.

Know I'm where I'm supposed to be.

I love you.

I swallowed down the emotion I felt and read the note again. After I finished reading it for a third time, I couldn't help but think my grandfather was a man of infinite wisdom.

The road I had taken in life wasn't always easy. In fact, sometimes it was extremely difficult. Still, in the end he was right . . . I truly believed we all ended up where we were supposed to be.

EPILOGUE

Day 1,220

Elle

"COVER YOUR EYES."

"They are covered, Mommy," Clementine insisted.

"You have to squeeze your fingers together."

"They are."

I put my hand sideways over my eyes with my fingers touching each other, not splayed apart as hers were. "Like this, silly girl."

With her fingers wide she looked at Sean. "Grandpa, tell her I can't see this way."

He raised his brows, fighting back his grin. "Elle, she can't see like that."

I rolled my eyes as I walked toward the front door and muttered, "She's got you wrapped around her little finger."

Logan was waiting on the other side of the door and I hurried to swing it open wide. Carrying the small blue bundle in his arms, my husband stepped inside. My heart skipped a beat when I looked at him. Passion. Love. Lust. Desire. And family. It was all standing right in front of me—long, lean, and incredibly sexy. His grin was absolutely adorable, as was he, and what he was holding.

I looked down. "Clementine, are you ready to meet your new baby brother?"

The pitter-patter of little feet had long since morphed into the thump-thump of what she liked to call big-girl feet. In her miniature classic Converse sneakers that she had to have because they matched her daddy's perfectly, she ran toward Logan and her new baby brother. "He came, he came!" she yelled in excitement.

Logan crouched down as she approached him. "Clementine, meet Killian."

I lowered myself beside Logan and adoringly gazed at our new son and my incredibly sexy husband. The adoption had been arranged, but we weren't expecting Killian to be born until next month. When we got the news, we didn't tell Clementine about his early delivery because we wanted to surprise her.

Her eyes were wide as she looked at him.

"What do you think?" I asked.

She twisted her lip.

"Clementine?" Logan prompted with unwarranted concern in his tone.

She put her little hands on her hips. "Daddy, I told you I wanted the one with the curly hair."

All of us burst into laughter.

Infectious as it was, she didn't laugh. Instead, she eyed Killian and then pursed her lips. "Where's the button to push? I want to see what he says."

As if on cue, Killian Sean McPherson began to cry.

Clementine covered her ears. "Turn it down."

I took her hand and lowered myself to her level. "We talked about this, silly girl. He's not a Build-A-Bear."

She seemed to contemplate this for a long while.

"What do you think, Mommy?" Logan asked, placing a soft kiss on my lips.

"I think we all have some things to learn, Daddy," I said, kissing him back.

This had Clementine now covering her eyes. "Not again," she whined.

We both shook our head.

She was just too funny.

Logan stood and held his free hand to her. "Come with me, Clementine. You and I are both new at this baby thing and we need to figure out how to feed him."

Her grin grew incredibly wide. "Oh, Daddy, I already know how to do that."

Looking absolutely adorable himself, Logan said, "Well, maybe you could show me."

Clementine looked over at me. "Mommy, could you please get us a bottle? I have to teach Daddy how to feed my new baby brother."

Tears stung the corners of my eyes. "I have one right here," I said as I reached in the diaper bag I had set next to the door when I came in before Logan to prepare Clementine.

I watched as Clementine and Logan, with baby Killian in his arms, made their way to the couch, matching sneakers and a matching bounce of optimism in their steps. And when they sat down and Logan helped Clementine onto his lap so she could show him how to hold the bottle, my tears could no longer be contained.

"We're very lucky," Sean said, placing his hand on my shoulder.

"Yes, we are," I managed to say and squeezed his hand.

The days had turned into years, and everything bad that had happened around Logan and me when we first met now seemed like a lifetime ago.

Just then the cuckoo clock on the wall chirped and my eyes went to his hazel pools. Every time it went off, Logan rolled his eyes, and it made me laugh. This time was no different.

As I stepped toward my family, the one thing that ran through my mind was that all those years ago I had been wrong about love.

It really does conquer all.

AUTHOR NOTE

ALTHOUGH I TRIED TO stay true to Boston, I did take some liberties with locations, dates, and timing.

If you enjoyed this book, there are a number of ways that you can support it.

First, please call or email friends and tell them about it. If you really want them to read it, gift it to them. If you prefer digital friends, please use the 'Recommend' feature of Goodreads to spread the word, or make a post about it on Facebook.

Second, please consider leaving a review for this book.

If you'd like to read more of my books, on the next page is a list of other titles.

OTHER BOOKS
BY KIM KARR

BLOW

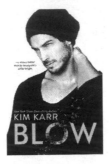

2 fatal sides.

1 epic love.

7 days to survive.

They met in the face of danger. They weren't looking for love. They both knew better. But they couldn't stay away, and they fell hard.

He is heart-stoppingly handsome, fearless—and haunted by deadly ties.

She is breathtakingly beautiful, determined—and in harm's way.

They should have parted. They didn't. They never should have fucked. They did. And now time is running out. One hundred sixty-eight hours. That's all that remains. While Logan McPherson fights to save them, Elle Sterling is forced to make a choice that could change everything.

When torn between right and wrong, tainted love doesn't have a chance . . . or does it?

TOXIC

Meet Jeremy McQueen, a sexy, intense, brooding entrepreneur who goes after what he wants, and Phoebe St. Claire, a socialite-turned-CEO who's been drifting through life searching for something she thought she'd never find again—the right man to share her future.

Phoebe St. Claire has devoted herself to saving her family's hotel empire—but her best efforts have not been good enough. With her whole world in turmoil, the tenacious go-getter turns to the once love of her life. Far from innocent, Jeremy McQueen was a guy from the wrong side of the tracks, and her parents would never have approved. Their years apart have only made the sexy bad boy more irresistible than ever—and their reunion is explosive.

When she asks Jeremy to help her salvage her family business, he agrees immediately, with only one condition—he wants her in his bed.

But soon surprising circumstances leave Phoebe reeling. Was this fairy-tale romance just too good to be true? Will Jeremy's secrets pull them apart all over again?

NO CLIFFHANGER. STANDALONE ROMANCE.

THE 27 CLUB

Janis Joplin. Kurt Cobain. Amy Winehouse. Zachary Flowers. I always knew my brilliant brother would one day be listed among the great artistic minds of our time. I just didn't know he would join the list of exceptional talents who left us too young, too soon.

I was always the calm one, the perfect foil to his free-wheeling wild spirit. But since his death shortly after his 27th birthday, I'd found myself adrift and directionless.

I knew it was time to face my destiny, and I was ready to yield. But then I met Nate, Zachary's best friend. Only he could help me put the pieces together, fill in the blanks that Zachary left behind. I needed him to answer my questions—and I wanted him for more. He awakened in me a sensuality that had never been explored, never satisfied. Nate's presence controlled me, his touch seared me, and it was up to me to convince him that he was brought into my life for a reason. . . .

NO CLIFFHANGER ENDING.

THIS IS A STANDALONE ROMANCE.

THE CONNECTIONS SERIES

Connected
Torn
Dazed
Mended
Blurred
Frayed

KIM KARR IS A *New York Times* and *USA Today* bestselling author.

She grew up in Rochester, New York, and now lives in Florida with her husband and four kids. She's always had a love for reading books and writing. Being an English major in college, she wanted to teach at the college level, but that was not to be. She went on to receive an MBA and became a project manager until quitting to raise her family. Kim currently works part-time with her husband and recently decided to embrace one of her biggest passions—writing.

Kim wears a lot of hats: writer, book-lover, wife, soccer mom, taxi driver, and the all-around go-to person of her family. However, she always finds time to read. Kim likes to believe in soul mates, kindred spirits, true friends, and happily-ever-afters. She loves to drink champagne and listen to music, and hopes to always stay young at heart.

CONNECT WITH KIM
Twitter @AuthorKimKarr
Facebook *www.facebook.com/AuthorKimKarr*
Website *www.authorkimkarr.com*
Instagram https://instagram.com/authorkimkarr/

And don't miss Toxic, where, as a reader you'll first meet Logan. It is an unforgettable stand-alone romance! Available now. Continue reading for a preview.

TOXIC

FAMILIAR FACES

MY MOTHER TAUGHT ME many things . . .
To stand up straight.
To be thankful for what I had.
To never talk to strangers.
And to always answer when spoken to.
I didn't always listen.
"I miss you." The text had arrived early this morning and I hadn't been able to reply. I didn't know what to say but I knew why Dawson had sent it.
It was October fifteenth.
Our wedding day.
Or it was supposed to have been anyway.
The rain was steadily falling as Lily and I left the movie theater and quickly made our way to the waiting car.
As soon as I got in, I collapsed in the smooth leather seat and looked next to me. "Thank you."
"For what?"
"For always being there for me."
"That's what best friends are for," she smiled.
And that's what she was. Lily Monroe had been my best friend for as long as I could remember. And like me, she was in a strange place.
"Has he called yet?" I asked, uncertain if I should bring it up.
Lily shook her head.
"You should just call him."
She shot me an *if looks could kill* glare. "No, I will not.

And we're not talking about him. As far as I'm concerned, Preston Tyler is dead."

Okay then.

I knew when to shut up.

Lily and Preston were always breaking up and getting back together but this was the longest they had been apart in the three years they had been a couple. The breakup was going on nearly four weeks.

Lily opened her purse. "Here," she said as she unscrewed a small bottle of wine. It was the kind you get when you're flying. A glass for one.

I took it and gave her a smile and when she pulled out a second, I had to laugh. "Always prepared."

"You know it," she said raising her hand. "To rainy days."

"And rainy nights." I clinked her bottle.

"To new beginnings."

"And old endings," I said, and then I drank the wine.

All of it.

I needed it.

After a final gulp, I let my forehead fall to the window. The sound of faint raindrops that drizzled down it as I stared out into the night triggered something inside me—that lonely ache that I couldn't seem to ever shake. And for the first time since I had woken up that morning, I allowed a melancholy wave of sorrow to wash over me.

I'd second-guessed my decision to end things with Dawson every day. So when I woke up this morning, I thought I'd be sadder than I had been.

But I wasn't sad at all.

I was relieved.

I was ready for the shadow that had been looming over me since I broke off the engagement to be gone. Even after the wedding was canceled, the countdown to the big day was still there. Just because two people ceased to exist as a unit, it didn't mean you no longer felt the other person's presence in your life.

And Dawson Vanderbilt, even with his gallant stand-up and let's be friends attitude, had felt like a constant mark of failure in my life.

The seemingly perfect man, a wedding planned with all the trimmings, and I still couldn't go through with it. I knew the chemistry wasn't there to sustain a life of happiness together.

I loved him, yet the spark I wanted to feel each time I saw him and the leg I wanted to kick back with a pointed toe when he kissed me—neither ever came.

My phone rang and glancing at the screen, I rolled my eyes.

"Your mother again?" Lily asked.

I nodded. "She's called me every hour since I left her at lunch. She says she's checking on me but I can't help but feel like it's more. Like she's punishing me for not going through with the wedding by reminding me of all the things we would have been doing today."

"She means well, you know she does."

"I suppose," I said as I glanced again at the ringing phone.

"Give it to me."

I looked at Lily questioningly.

"Give me your phone."

She powered it off. "Everyone you need to talk to will be right inside there." She pointed to the large brick building we were coming up on in the Meatpacking District.

I gave her a weak smile and slipped my phone in my purse.

When the car slowed, Lily put her hand on my leg. "You sure you're up to this? We could just go back to my place and watch another movie."

I flashed her a huge grin, letting my pearly whites show as the black Escalade pulled up to the curb. "Are you kidding?" I chuckled. "And miss the funeral tonight?"

She giggled. "Speaking of, did you see Danny's tweet?"

I shook my head.

She pulled out her phone, tapped a few buttons, and showed me. "May our ideals RIP. #Bestfuckingfriends #Somethingsshouldneverdie."

"I really have missed him," I sighed.

"Me too but at least his social media obsession keeps us up to date with his daily life," Lily replied with a wink.

"That's true."

"Last chance," she said.

For one moment, I thought about backing out but I plastered a smile on my face instead. "I'm fine. Now let's go have some fun."

The door opened and a big black umbrella was held above it. I placed my hand on Hugh's shoulder. "I'll take a cab home, so don't wait up for my call."

Hugh had been our family's driver since I was eight years old.

"Miss Phoebe," he said in his heavy English accent. "You know your father insists I see to it that you make it home safely."

With one foot out the door, I tried not to laugh at the irony that even from his jail cell, my father still felt the need to watch over me. "I promise I will."

He shook his head with a heavy sigh, conceding quickly before an argument arose that he knew he'd never win.

I gave him a little squeeze before dropping my other foot to the ground. "Have a good night."

As of that morning, Hugh's duties had been transferred from our family's personal driver, to a driver for the Saint Hotel. He'd still drive my mother as well, of course. Poppy had all but refused to cut back and I knew losing her driver wouldn't sit well. Soon enough she would be feeling the repercussions of not doing as I had suggested. The Hamptons house went on the market last year and sold right away so that kept her bank account full over the past year. But with no money coming in from The Saint Corporation, I estimated within a year she'd have nothing left.

The trust fund I had access to was also almost empty.

My grandfather had divided the money in half—I got the first half when I turned twenty-one and the second when I turn thirty-one, which was still five years away. Most of what I had was used for my father's legal defense when all of his and my mother's assets were frozen. I was surprised that my father dragged the proceedings out as long as he did. I knew he was guilty. Everyone knew he was guilty. He'd been charged once before though, when I was little, and had gotten off. I think that's why he refused to plead guilty. But this time it cost him—no us—a fortune. And he wasn't acquitted as he was over twenty years ago. I had never thought of my father as selfish, but I did now. After everything, in the end, to receive a lighter sentence, he finally did plead guilty.

By then the St. Claire fortune had been nearly depleted. My parents had been living beyond their means for years anyway, so it didn't take much to empty them once their accounts had been released.

I had to turn the company around. If not we were not only going to be penniless, we would be homeless. My apartment was a rental, with a steep rent. My lease would be up next month and I planned to move out of the Park Avenue apartment my mother had insisted on when I went to grad school. But my mother would never leave her home on East Seventy-Sixth Street until she was forced to. And a small part of me didn't want her to. It was my childhood home after all. But the reasonable side of me knew that even after the second mortgage was paid off, the five-story home would sell for enough that she'd never have to worry about money.

And then I wouldn't have to worry about her.

The open velvet rope was only a few feet away but it seemed so much farther. I grabbed on to Lily's arm to steady myself. I was feeling slightly tipsy from the wine and my mind was running in a million different directions.

My mother.

My father.

My job.

I took a deep breath.

The cool air felt good in my lungs. It helped to shift my mind away from my problems. I looked at Lily; she was worried about me, I could tell. But I knew I'd be fine. Today I was allowed to be down but tomorrow I would pick myself back up. Still, I wanted to ease her mind. With thoughts of the flick we had just watched, more specifically of the very hot, very sexy Captain America, slamming into my head, I decided to do something to convince Lily I was okay.

So I held my phone to my ear in mock conversation and spoke loud enough for her to hear. "Hello, Marvel Studios, I really want to play the Black Widow in the next *Captain America* movie."

She looped her arm through mine and her dirty-sounding chuckle was loud. "Gorgeous, all legs, and sexy vixen with a husky voice—yeah I'd say that part works for you."

Flashing a smile at the bouncer, I stopped. "We're Danny Capshaw's guests, Phoebe St. Claire and Lily Monroe."

He glanced down at his clipboard and nodded for us to pass.

Danny belonged to some entertainment circuit that had come to the city last year, called Jet Set. It was the hottest new thing—membership not only allowed exclusive weekend access into some of the city's hottest clubs, it was the only way to gain VIP status. It was brilliant. Nothing the rich and famous valued more than exclusivity. And they were more than willing to pay—a lot. Membership fees were ridiculously high.

The soles of my high heels clicked on the red and white checked floor, and as soon as we entered the club, my vision blurred as the pink walls coated everything in my sight with a slight blush. I looked over to Lily. "By the way, I was thinking more like a pistol-toting badass, but I'll take sexpot."

Right in front of a fifteen-foot Rorschach print by Andy

Warhol, Lily snorted, "You'd have to remove the cobwebs from your vagina to even remotely gain that title."

"It hasn't been that long."

She rolled her eyes.

"What? It hasn't. Just because when you and Preston are on, you do it morning, noon, and night doesn't mean the rest of us do."

She shrugged. "I can't help it if I have an overactive libido."

I had to laugh.

"And besides, most younger couples do it more than once a week."

"Dawson and I did it more than that but even if we didn't, I'm sure we'd be considered way more normal than you and Preston."

With a tug of my hand, Lily led me toward our table. "Let's see what everyone else has to say about it."

"Oh God, let's not."

Everyone else was our four best friends. We had pledged growing up we wouldn't turn into our parents but as of that very morning the last of us entered the ranks. Now, each and every one of us had joined our prospective family businesses. Making it official, we've broken the vow. And now we're doing the only thing we can—gathering together to bury it.

Morbid yet true.

Making our way through the crowd, I noticed the way the glass shelves that towered over the bar seemed to shimmer with the aged scotches and exotic liquors. It was a Saturday night, and like most Saturday nights in every nightclub all around the world, the patrons were out to celebrate. But unlike everyone else, we were coming together to mourn the death of our young ideals.

Coincidence the burial was taking place on the same day as my canceled wedding?

I hardly thought so.

It had to have been a sign that it was time to put them

both to rest.

The Rose Bar was the newest addition to Jet Set. Danny met the owner of Jet Set last year while he was partying in a club in Miami. Under its new management, the Rose Bar had been touted as one of America's swankiest clubs. It even had a fleet of white cars, including Hummers, Lamborghinis, Ferraris, and Porches, used to pick up and drop off Jet Set members.

The club was packed and brimming with wealthy men and women, some of whom I was sure would turn up on Page Six. Because the men and women inside weren't just anyones, we were all someones—the great-granddaughter of Eisenhower, the great nephew of Ford, a great cousin of Kennedy. No one needed to know how many greats were before our name—it was irrelevant. The bloodlines were all that ever mattered.

I rolled my eyes at the thought and draped my leather jacket over my arm. My little black dress fell a few inches above my knees and the vertical lines of crystals gave it some shape. I preferred comfort to style in a way that seemed to separate me from my peers whose motto was all fashion.

Lily and I passed a brilliant red billiards table and a loud cackle of laughter caused me to look up. At the center booth, in the middle of the VIP section sat a bunch of guys. Even as Lily continued to pull me along, my eyes stayed locked where they were, as if some kind of magnetic force wouldn't allow my gaze to shift.

The guys in the booth toasted one another and then slammed back their drinks, laughing boisterously. However, when a group of scantily clad women walked by their table, they all stopped talking. The women eyed the guys as languorously as they possibly could, hoping for an invitation to join them, I was sure. The guys stared back with equal vigor.

I knew those guys.

I dropped Lily's hand and walked closer. Standing at the

edge of the stairs, I recognized a few of the girls' faces from grad school at Stern. My eyes redirected to the horseshoe of men in the booth, also from Stern. Lars Jefferson was the bookend to the group. In grad school he was always the loudest, most obnoxious, and most arrogant guy on campus. He held his elite social status as a pass—a pass to do and say anything he wanted. Unfortunately, he was also Dawson's best friend.

I never could stand him.

He leaned forward and that's when I saw the blond hair I'd have known anywhere.

Dawson.

I froze, glued to the spot I was standing in.

It had been three months since I'd broken up with Dawson. Six weeks after we set the date. The day I was supposed to move in with him. Now I couldn't help but stare. Of all the places to run into him, I never thought I'd see him here.

Lars stared at the women. He took his time choosing the girl he wanted and then beckoned her with his smile. I watched as it went down, needing to see if my ex-fiancé did the same. Lars tipped his chin and sure enough the woman beamed with glee. Dawson just sat there while a few of the other guys followed Lars' lead.

The girl Lars showed interest in brushed her jet-black bangs away from her face, patted her hips with her hands, and walked slowly to the table. I was certain she must have known who he was and probably also knew he was involved with someone, but from the white-toothed smile Lars gave her as she walked over, she must have been confident that didn't matter.

"Hi," she said to him.

I was good at lipreading. I'd spent a great deal of time watching people. No, I'd studied couple's interactions. It was an unhealthy habit I had picked up when I was lost. But it was Dawson who had helped me stop. It was Dawson who helped me live again. It was Dawson with that group of men looking to fuck any girl they could. And it was Dawson who I had let go.

Ice formed in my belly.

Lars ran his eyes up and down the girl's body, as if he was trying to assess her dress size. Then he gave Dawson a sideways look. Dawson shrugged. If it was because he wasn't interested or didn't care, I couldn't tell. But then Dawson shifted his eyes toward a pretty blonde who walked by and Lars did the same. I had to assume Lars maybe just wanted what Dawson was interested in.

Prick.

Hand on hip, the woman did a runway turn, like a schoolgirl in front of her bedroom mirror and started to walk toward them again. When she passed, Dawson nudged Lars. Comically, Lars got up and chased her.

My eyes settled on Dawson. There were so many guys in the club and they were just as handsome as the ones at that center table, but none of them were as eligible as those bachelors sitting together. None of them had ever been married, each was under thirty years old, and surprisingly, each was very gainfully employed. They were New York City's biggest catches and every Eloise could only hope to land one of them.

Why had I been the exception?

"Stop shooting daggers his way. He's not doing anything wrong," Lily barked at me.

I blinked a few times, suddenly realizing I was doing just what she said I was. The shock I felt that Dawson would join that crowd looking for a meaningless hookup was quickly replaced by hurt.

Over the thumping bass of the music, Lily said, "Come on. You're staring."

I gaped at her. "I'm not staring," I snapped.

She took my hand. "Hey, are you okay?"

I nodded.

"Do you remember why you broke up with him?" she asked.

I nodded again.

"Then let's go."

I didn't move. "I just feel a little confused right now."

Her grip around my fingers tightened. "I know. And you know I love you and I'm only looking out for you when I remind you again that you broke up with him for a reason, and a good one. So quit looking like you wish you were still together."

My eyes focused on my best friend. "I don't regret the breakup."

She dropped her hold on my hand and moved to stand in front of me, blatantly blocking my view. "I know you don't and you shouldn't. He wasn't right for you."

I pursed my lips. "I wasn't right for him."

Her face filled with concern. "You weren't right for each other. So why the sad face?"

I bit my lip in contemplation. "This is the first time I've seen him since he brought over my stuff. He looks happy."

She grabbed my hand and squeezed it. "Good. Now you can stop feeling guilty."

I nodded.

I wished it was that easy.

She turned on her heels. "Come on, tonight's the last night we'll all be together for a long time."

With a genuine smile forming on my lips, I shifted my eyes to find our friends. Jamie was lounging in a booth on the other side of the VIP section. The neon lights from the disco ball above the dance floor flickered all around him as he took a large gulp of his scotch, maybe trying to wash down the bad taste of the last foreclosure he had to make that put someone on the street.

Emmy was filming him with a video camera, probably wishing she could film the two of them together. When we were younger, she had aspirations of going to Hollywood and being an actress. She settled on home movie production for the time being and brought her video camera everywhere. Her parents held her trust fund over her head to keep her in New York. Soon though, when she turned thirty, she would have complete ownership and then, we were sure, she'd be gone.

Logan was in a deep discussion over in the corner of the bar, about what was anyone's guess—he never discussed his job or his life. Although a good friend, I knew very little about him. He was the quiet, secretive one.

A lot like me.

But his reasons for remaining quiet were different from mine—mine were internal, the way I felt about myself and this world of ours. His were more external. He'd grown up in two very different worlds and I think he struggled with which one he belonged in.

Danny made me laugh. He was dancing with some guy I'd never seen before. Throwing his hands around like a rapper, more than likely mourning the loss of his free-dom. Always the happy-go-lucky one in the group, he'd recently joined the ranks of the employed, sitting beside his father and learning the ropes of the gaming industry that had made his great-great-grandfather billions. Of all of us he had held out the longest. Went on sabbatical af-ter grad school to find himself but when he came back he found himself all right, right beside his tycoon father being groomed to run the family-owned business.

These people gathered here tonight were like my family. We grew up together, went to the same parties, to the same schools, and once upon a time we all hated the life that hav-ing money brought. Those days were long over. We'd tried our best to hold on to them, but life took over and crushed those ideals. We had all decided further education was the quickest and easiest way to avoid the family binds that awaited us. Me, it wasn't the business I was avoiding. I just didn't care what path I took and where it led. But none of it had mattered because when we graduated, whether it was with an MBA, law degree, or other certification, the family calling was inevitable.

Lily Monroe, textile heiress, was learning the apparel

business that had been started by her great-grandfather. She loved to shop, knew clothing well, what fashions worked and what didn't. She would make a great figurehead for the House of Monroe someday, but running the company didn't interest her. Her goals were all short-term. She had become the true socialite of the group and hated working more than any of us. Her passion was ballet and what she wanted more than anything was to be a ballerina. But a knee injury in her freshman year at Julliard changed all that, and as time passed, Lily's dream had too. I prayed Lily would never have to take over the family business like I had, and so did she.

Logan McPherson was the grandson of a hedge fund manager and philanthropist worth an estimated twenty billion dollars. His grandfather was one of the wealthiest men in the city, but Logan never seemed to care and he never discussed money. He was an attorney who spent most of his time in Boston. I knew he was licensed in both states but wasn't sure if he was practicing in either. No one knew much about his work.

Emmy Lane, publishing heiress, refused to learn what it would take to run a long list of publications owned by her family and because of her resistance, her parents were not on board with her plan to relocate to LA. She hadn't gotten the big break she was waiting for but she still continued to audition for parts here in the city. Swan Publishing might have been her family legacy but her passion was acting and she still hoped someday she would be a star.

James Ashton, Harvard graduate and real estate heir, acquired his real estate license shortly after grad school and learned quickly how to wheel and deal with the bigwigs.

And Danny, poor Danny just recently settled into his destiny, marking day one of the rest of his life. Danny had choices though. His father was a gaming heir from very old money and his mother was of the European "fast set." Her family had founded Fiat and led a glamorous life that included elaborate parties, streamlined yachts, fast cars, and luxurious villas. Although Fiat was no longer family owned, he could have joined the board. In the end, he opted for the gaming industry. Churchill Downs was where his training would begin and he'd be based in Kentucky for the next year. He had mixed emotions about leaving the city but since he'd been back and forth for the last two years, what was one more? Well, that's what he said anyway.

And then there was me. Phoebe St. Claire—heiress to a hotel empire that was crumbling before my eyes.

My great-grandfather bought his first hotel at the height of the oil boom. His father disapproved of the investment but the hotel broke all records and soon my great-grandfather expanded throughout the country, adding hotel after hotel. Just before his death The Saint Corporation, known as TSC, expanded internationally to be the first international hotel chain promulgating a certain worldwide standard for hotel accommodations everywhere. Through the years, the international division was sold off, and under my father's reign, all that remained were the US operations. As my father's only child, I always knew I was next in line to run what was left of the hotel empire. It simply happened sooner than I thought. The circumstances only compounded the financial distress of the already vulnerable company.

With a whistle, Jamie held up a bottle of Piper-Heidsieck champagne. Danny and Logan headed toward him and Emmy without any further prompting. Together, Lily and I climbed the steps up to the booth.

Jamie stood and pulled me close to him. "You doing okay today?"

I put my finger to his lips. "We'll talk later."

"Dawson's here."

"I know," I said, and glanced over my shoulder toward his table.

If Lily had always been my very best girlfriend, Jamie held the spot as my very best boyfriend. In fact, I think I was always more open with him than I was with Lily. We just had an ease between us.

"My man," Jamie said turning to Danny. "How was your first day on the job?"

"Fucking sucked. But I expected worse."

I turned around and hugged him. "Something tells me you loved it."

Shoulders lifting he said, "I'll let you know after a month in Kentucky when I'm not under my father's watchful eye."

"Phoebe, you made it," Emmy greeted me with a hug and Logan joined in.

I purposefully moved myself to the other side of the booth so my back was to the center of the room. Nothing good would come of me staring at Dawson all night.

Once we all sat down, James passed glasses to each of us, and then raised his. "Today, we have gathered to mourn the loss of our youth. We were once young, wild, and free but all that remains now is for us to get even wilder. So let's get fucking drunk."

"Cheers," we all said in unison as we clinked our glasses.

An hour later, and after too many bottles of champagne and wine, for what had to have been the twentieth time of the night, we brought our hands to the center of the table. The six of us shared a bond that could not be broken by anyone, and we all knew it. And this time, as our flutes clinked, we said together at the top of our lungs, "Friends forever," and pressed our glasses to our forehead.

It was a private signal between us. We'd seen each other through so much; no words could describe what we felt for one another. And no one knew any of us like we knew one another. Through thick and thin, united we stood.

Dramatic—yes.

Real—absolutely.

After we finished our toast, I stood on wobbly legs. "Excuse me, I have to use the restroom."

"Do you want me to come with you?" Emmy asked.

She was nestled close to James and seemed pretty happy right where she was. Some things never changed. "No, you stay put."

I looked down at my watch. It was only twelve ten, or maybe it was two. Funny, I couldn't tell which was the big hand and which was the little one.

The stairs nearest to our booth offered me the chance to glance toward Dawson but I had a strange feeling someone was watching me. A silver button on a distressed leather jacket caught the reflection of one of the beams of light flaring down from the twirling disco ball. The leather stood out in a sea of fine fabric suits and sequin dresses but then faded into the crowd. For a moment, a sense of familiarity stirred in my belly. But I pushed the feeling aside and just thought—too much alcohol.

The restrooms were near the back—I'd been here before it changed owners and I remembered. Or I thought I did. I tried to peer through the crowd to locate the bathrooms but the place was way too big to see around the bar or the dance floor.

"Hello gorgeous. Long time no see. I was just coming to say hi," Lars leaned down and kissed me right on the mouth.

I quickly stepped back, surprised by his close proximity and repelled by the feel of his lips on mine.

He shoved a glass of wine into my hand. "I bought you a drink. Thought we could celebrate . . . you know, moving on."

I stepped back again.

And when I did, Lars' eyes widened and his grin was wicked. "Whoa, you look sexy as hell. Did you start celebrating without me?"

I stood as straight as I could, trying to shake off the feeling of bugs crawling all over my body from the prickle of his stare. "No! I'm here to celebrate Danny's new job." That wasn't really the truth, but I wasn't about to explain to Lars.

"Well, fuck me upside down, but Phoebe it looks like you want to do more than celebrate."

I considered his comment. My dress was shorter than I'd normally have worn, and the neckline much lower than I'd ever worn. But Lily had bought it specifically for me, for my unwedding day as she called it, and dropped it off that morning. How could I have refused her?

He lifted my chin. "You changed your hair too."

"I cut it."

After I broke up with Dawson I needed a change, so I cut my long tresses to just above my shoulders and darkened them a bit at the same time. My once long, wavy, golden blond hair was shorter, darker, and straighter.

My mother hated it. She said it looked like a bob and she detested bobs. I happened to love it. The whole change made me feel lighter, freer.

Lars tugged on the ends of my hair. "You changed the color too. It looks sultry." He licked his lips. "You look sexy as fuck."

I jerked my head back and just stared at him. Unsure where he was going with this and not really caring, I just wanted to escape his scrutiny.

"You've put some weight on too. Not so skinny anymore."

I shrugged. I couldn't control my weight. If I lost my appetite for even day, I looked unhealthily skinny. Everyone thought it was great to have such a high metabolism. But it wasn't. I had to work at maintaining a healthy weight or my frame looked boylike.

"Has Dawson seen you yet?"

Disbelief clouded my narrowing eyes at the nerve of him. Like my ex-fiancé seeing me looking differently would change anything about our relationship?

My vision began to blur at that point and I knew I had had way too much to drink.

Lars' mouth was at my ear before I could move away. "Your outfit makes it look like you have curves in all the right places though, don't worry."

I thought I might vomit.

Was he for real?

Words flew out of my mouth at lightning speed. "You're

such a dick. Go find some other woman to harass who's into your kind of foreplay."

An evil grin formed on his lips. "A dirty mouth too, just the way I like them."

"You like them anyway you can get them," I spat back.

Bile rose in my throat and I wasn't sure if it was his attention or the alcohol causing the sick feeling.

"Feisty," he grinned. "What was Dawson thinking letting you go? I bet you're an animal in the sack."

"Get lost," I told him and turned to walk away.

He grabbed my wrist. "Now that you're all worked up, what do you say we get out of here? I won't tell Dawson."

I tried to free myself of his grip but he wouldn't let go.

Someone stepped between us. The distressed leather was the first thing my eyes were focused on when my skin started to tingle with a sense of familiarity. The tingling quickly turned into trembling as my gaze lifted and I saw the bluest of blue eyes.

They were soft, concerned, knowing.

They were the eyes of my past.

It was *him*.

I was surprised.

I was shocked.

I was mesmerized.

My body started to tremble even more and I downed the glass of wine I had been holding to help calm my nerves.

Still, I couldn't stop staring. He looked the same. No, he looked better, if that was possible. His hair was shorter but his devastating good looks were even more striking.

This time I knew he was real—he wasn't a figment of my imagination. Just that one look into his eyes and all the hurt was forgotten. It was as if the last five years had never happened. And we'd just met.

I lost myself in his eyes and I couldn't stop myself from going back to when we'd first met.

It was the day I came alive.

As an extra, included is a preview of Kim's very first novel. If you haven't read Connected, you haven't met River Wilde. Buckle up and get ready for the ride. It's one you won't want to miss!

CONNECTED

NEXT LIFETIME

WE WALKED THROUGH THE open door to the University of Southern California Campus Bar and Aerie pulled her tail up. "At least they aren't playing that Halloween crap in here," she yelled a little too loudly. As my ears adjusted, I heard a velvety soft voice singing an unfamiliar yet captivating song.

Aerie stopped to put her devil horns on, and I glanced around the large room recognizing a lot of students, while trying to get a look at the band. I shouted directly into her ear, "They sound really good. Have you heard them before?"

She was on her toes trying to see over the crowd. I laughed at how short she was until her pointy devil horn hit me in the eye. "No, but I love their sound," she responded, still trying to see the stage and almost falling over.

I had been coming here for the last three years and couldn't ever remember it being so crowded. I could barely see the long wooden bar to my right, and with the mass of bodies bumping and grinding on the dance floor, I couldn't even catch a glimpse of the stage.

"Do you know their name?" I asked Aerie.

"I think they're called the Wilde Ones," she hiccuped and laughed. She winked at me as she started to dance her way toward some friends on the dance floor and yelled over her shoulder, "By the way, I love them! Great name and an even greater sound."

"I'll get drinks and meet you out there in a bit," I said

to no one since she was already gone. When the bartender acknowledged me, I ordered two beers, one with ice and one without, and tacked on two shots to help Aerie drown her misery.

The live music stopped and typical Halloween songs were blasted through the speakers. I turned my back to the bar and scanned the crowd for Aerie. You would think she would be easy to spot in her red sequin devil costume. She said she was out for vengeance and if her outfit was any indication, she would be vindicated.

I didn't see her anywhere but I did spot an attractive guy. He was still too far away for me to zero in on any specific feature, but something—no, everything—about him drew my attention.

I watched how he moved; his confidence captivated me. He seemed relaxed, like he knew exactly where he was going. And as he headed in my direction, I became mesmerized. Biting my bottom lip, I was unable to focus on anything but him. My head was still a little foggy from the three beers I'd consumed earlier and I was clearly not thinking straight when I made eye contact with him, and then slowly studied his body from head to toe.

As the distance between us narrowed, I could see that he was alarmingly attractive: long, lean, and muscular but not bulky. He wore a black beanie hat with his light brown hair sticking out. When I looked into his eyes, they undid me. Although I couldn't see their color, I could feel their intensity. I almost feared that if I looked into them for too long I might never walk away. His eyes aside, the words *handsome* and *gorgeous* weren't strong enough adjectives to describe this man.

My mind wandered to where it shouldn't. Knowing better than to compare this guy to my boyfriend, I did it anyway. I felt incredibly guilty, but I couldn't help myself. Ben was all surfer. He was attractive, hot, and sexy with an ego to match. This guy was equally as attractive, hot, and sexy, but there was something else—something more. I couldn't quite put my finger on it.

Easing his way through the crowd, he removed his beanie and ran his hands through his hair. When our eyes connected it felt like minutes, but only seconds passed. Suddenly I felt an electric pull forcing me to keep looking at him. Everything I felt indicated he was dangerous. I knew I should look away, walk away, but I didn't. I couldn't. He was just too alluring.

He was finally close enough that I could tell his gleaming eyes were green. I was instantly drawn to his smile. It wasn't a full smile, more like a half grin emphasizing his dimples. His skin was smooth with no facial hair and that made me weak in the knees. His full lips were begging for a kiss. I'd never looked at a guy like this before, not even Ben. So why was I eyeing him this way, and why was I unable to avert my gaze?

Aside from his overall sex appeal, his clothing made him even more irresistible. He wore faded jeans, a black Foreigner concert T-shirt, and black work boots. I had to laugh a little when I saw the concert T-shirt because I was wearing one, too—my dad's U2 T-shirt, knotted on the side, hanging off my shoulder.

Having made his way through the crowd much better than I had, he was now standing in front of me. His face was breathtaking; he had a strong chin, a small straight nose, perfectly shaped eyebrows, and long eyelashes. He was a vision of utter perfection and I couldn't help but smile.

The bar was crowded and there was no room on either side of me. Putting both hands in his pockets, he smiled back at me. Then, running his tongue over his bottom lip, he asked in a low, sexy voice, "Were you staring at me?"

I pouted my lips and rolled my eyes. I took a deep breath as I straightened my shoulders and placed my hands on my hips, "No, I was just looking for my friend while I waited on my drinks. You just happened to be in my line of vision."

He chuckled a little then said, "That look was hot."

I huffed out a breath and tried not to laugh. *Did he really just say that?*

When the bartender brought my order and set it in front of me, my phone started ringing in my pocket, but I ignored it as I continued to stare at him. "Why would you think I was looking at you, anyway?"

As the person beside me settled her tab and walked away, he moved to fill the empty space and tossed his beanie next to my drink. His proximity caused my pulse to race and my heart to pound faster. Leaning sideways, he rested his hip against the bar. With his eyes still locked on mine he answered, "Because I was staring at you, hoping you were staring back."

I looked directly into those powerful green eyes, so full of intensity, and I instantly lost my train of thought. With the electric pull only growing stronger between us, I feared I wasn't going to be able to get out of this encounter unscathed.

He dragged his teeth across his bottom lip and his eyes scanned my body. The expression on his face told me he wanted to do more than just talk. I wanted to do more as well.

A moment of comfortable silence passed before he cocked his head to the side in the most adorable way and grinned. "With all this talk about who was staring at whom I think we forgot the basics. I'm River," he said as he extended his hand with the most devilish grin on his face.

Feeling bewitched by him, I put my hand out to shake his but quickly pulled it away. Unfortunately, I also bumped into the person standing next to me and accidentally spilled his beer.

He gave me a dirty look and swore under his breath. River's grin quickly turned into a frown, and he gently moved me away. In a clipped tone he apologized, "Sorry, man, just an accident, but let me buy you another."

The now drinkless man with a wet shirt looked at him and nodded. River pulled out his wallet and handed him a ten. "Buy two." The man took the money and walked away, muttering something under his breath. River immediately returned his attention to me, and I bit the corner of my lower lip and smiled at him.

There we were, standing face-to-face, with only a few drinks separating us. Sliding one of the beers toward him, I took a sip of my own even though the ice had melted. "Thank you, that guy sure as shit wasn't happy with me. In fact, he kind of acted like an asshole."

Taking a sip of his drink, he started to laugh, almost spitting it out. Skimming his finger over my bare shoulder, his eyes locked on mine. "You're more than welcome."

Quivering from his touch and intense gaze, I took a step back, fearful of where this might lead.

Moving forward, he traced my last step. He was not going to let the distance widen between us. He stared intently into my eyes. "Now, where were we? Do we need to start over?" He waited for my response as he watched me swallow my drink.

I pulled my lower lip to the side with my teeth and smiled playfully. "We were introducing ourselves."

"Okay, so let's try again. I'm River and you are? . . ."

"I'm not sure you need to know that information right now. I'm kind of thinking you might be a stalker."

His eyes widened as he laughed. "You're not serious—are you, beautiful girl?"

Unable to control my own laughter, I simply said, "Maybe I am," but my laughter subsided when I registered the sweet name he'd called me.

Leaning toward me, he was close enough that I could inhale his fresh scent. It was a soapy, just-out-of-the-shower smell.

"What? If you're not going to tell me your name then I get to call you whatever I want."

Averting my eyes from his gaze, I looked down.

After taking another sip of his beer, he set the mug down. He hooked my chin with his finger and tilted my head up toward him. His touch seared my skin and left it tingling. He stared at me with his intense green eyes and chuckled. "Can we talk about you thinking I'm a Jack the Ripper type? I just want you to know, I'm definitely not. In fact, I think it's safe to say you were staring at me first, but in no way do I think you're a stalker."

My mouth dropped open. I was unsure of what to say. I knew he was right. I had stared first.

"So we can get past this; let's just say I was staring first. Not that it really matters."

We were looking into each other's eyes as the bartender passed me my bill. When I turned to pay for my drinks, our connection was broken. Handing my money to the bartender, I thanked him and told him to keep the change. This distraction gave me some time to think about how to handle this potentially dangerous situation.

I watched River as he ordered two more beers, and realized I had to work out my conflicted feelings. I pushed my guilt aside and handed him one of the shots.

"Cheers."

"It's a beautiful day," he replied before shooting back the shot.

I tried not to show how turned on I was that he had just quoted lyrics from one of my favorite songs.

Setting his shot glass down, he put his hand in his pocket. "So, does this mean you forgive me?"

His voice was strong, but soft, and made him even more tempting. I found myself thinking that he was not only adorable, but unlike anyone I had ever encountered before. I knew I shouldn't be doing this. I had a boyfriend that I loved waiting for me.

I raised an eyebrow and asked, "Forgive you? Forgive you for what?" I was having a hard time concentrating on the conversation and honestly had no idea what the apology was for.

He shifted on his feet. "You know what. Never mind," he muttered in my ear. His warm breath brushed my neck and I wanted to feel it everywhere.

Looking me up and down, he changed the subject. "What, no costume?"

Continuing our dangerous flirtation, I glanced down, motioning with my hands from head to toe. "How do you know this isn't my costume?"

While tugging on my T-shirt and pulling me a little closer, he seductively whispered, "If that's your costume you're definitely taking first place in the contest because it's the sexiest one I've ever seen."

We were silent for a minute; not even our heavy breathing could be heard. The noise from the bar and the crowd around us had quieted, but his words, his touch, they inflamed me, excited me, and sent fire through my veins.

"Where'd you get this, anyway?" he asked, tugging at the knot on my shirt, pulling me closer.

It felt like the room was spinning and I wasn't sure if it was him, the alcohol, or the fact that he had just asked me a question I didn't want to answer. "My dad managed the Greek and was a collector of concert T-shirts," I said, trying to push back the emotions welling up inside me.

He seemed to understand my hesitation before nodding, clearing his throat, and once again changed the subject. "So, have you ever seen Foreigner play?" he asked, now pointing to his own shirt and grinning.

As I looked at the bold white letters across his chest, I pushed aside my sadness and refocused on our conversation. We were just two people who had a lot in common— or at least that was what I wanted to think. When our drinks were gone, he ordered another round. As I finished the shot, I accidentally slammed the glass on the bar, and the bartender glowered at me. "Sorry," I mouthed.

River reached out and grabbed a strand of hair that had come loose from my ponytail. He very slowly tucked it behind my ear, sending shivers down my spine. Circling his index finger around my ear, he lightly tugged on my lobe. He sparked a fire in me that never before existed.

Gulping the drink I didn't need to be drinking, I hoped to extinguish the flame. I hoped no one had seen him touch me that way. Ben would be fucking furious. He was ridiculously jealous. We had many arguments about other men, all unjustified. At least until now.

As the strobe lights started to flicker and I leaned my hip against the bar for support, he put his hand on my waist and turned me so my back was against the bar. I wondered if he noticed me almost lose my balance from the flashing lights and drunkenness. Moving to stand directly in front of me, he put his hands on either side of me and pressed his palms into the bar. He was enveloping me, but I didn't feel trapped. I didn't know what I felt, but I knew my heart was pounding out of my chest; my stomach was doing flips, and I became light-headed as goose bumps emerged on my skin.

I thought he was going to kiss me as he stared intently into my eyes. I closed my eyes preparing for it but I felt him abruptly pull away. Immediately, I heard a high-pitched voice squeal, "River, don't forget we're leaving right after the show," and before I could catch a glimpse of the girl, she bounced away.

Smirking at me he said, "My little sister has the worst timing."

I was going to respond when I heard a drumroll echo through the bar. Glancing around, I tried to figure out what it was for. Amused, he rolled his eyes before looking at the stage and then back to me. "That would be for me," he laughed, leaning in so we were face-to-face. "They want me back onstage. I've gotta go unless you'd rather I stay and we finish what we started? Because that certainly would be way more fun."

I really hadn't heard anything he said, but everything seemed to finally make sense. He was the voice I heard when I came into the bar. He was so charming, so captivating, and so aware of me. I was pretty sure I was drunk because I was feeling things I should not have been feeling.

As I stared into his powerful green eyes, I knew I should've been trying to escape them.

Before I could say anything in response, he moved his head slightly back, lifted my hand, and slowly kissed it. Then he leaned into me and whispered in my ear, "Guess not. Not yet, anyway." My hand was on fire, my ear scorched.

That same drumroll rumbled through the sound system again and he quickly turned his head back to look at me. "I gotta jet."

He was still holding my hand, as he looked straight into my eyes. "You'll wait for me until after the show."

It wasn't a question. It was a statement. And then motioning between us, he added, "Because this isn't finished."

At that moment I realized that what had started as harmless flirting had turned into a situation that had gotten way too dangerous.

He placed his hands back on the bar and waited for a response. Since he hadn't asked a question that I wanted to answer, I just smiled and said, "If you're in the band you'd better go, you shouldn't leave your fans waiting."

He gave me one last heart-stopping grin and then leaned in and kissed me. My body reacted strangely; a rush of something I couldn't identify surged through me. At first he only lightly touched my lips with his then for a few short seconds he pressed a little harder before pulling away. I didn't kiss him back, but felt light-headed.

"I hope you've become a fan," he said, winking at me before grabbing his hat. Then he turned and walked away.

I brought my fingers up to my lips and watched as his silhouette disappeared through the crowd. I became vaguely aware that *"Superstition"* was playing, but my mind was focused on him.

I shook my head, trying to rid myself of the thoughts that shouldn't be there. I knew I had to leave, or I would end up doing something I would regret. I loved Ben, and Ben would fucking kill River just for looking at me the way he did. And then there was the kiss; yes, Ben would certainly kill him.

Knowing these things, I wondered why I hadn't walked away in the first place. For a moment there, I felt as though I believed in love at first sight, which I didn't. And how could love at first sight even exist when you were already in love with someone else? I didn't want to keep thinking about what happened because I was confused as hell, and I knew the meaning of it all wasn't what I wanted it to be.

I smiled about our encounter. He definitely was not a stalker. He was adorably charming and utterly charismatic, a guy who had a simple ease about him that I really liked, and a guy I didn't ever need to see again. This I knew for certain.

With thoughts of River swirling through my head, I made my way through the crowd to the dance floor where I found Aerie with some kind of pink drink in her hand. "We have to leave. Now!" I shouted at her while pulling her off the dance floor.

"What? Why? Are you sick?" she asked, struggling for words.

Then she turned and pointed to the stage. "Because if you're not, I want to see that hot guy sing first."

I turned to see where she was pointing and sure enough it was him, River. I then realized I'd never even told him my name.

Pulling Aerie through the crowd under protest, I heard the audience chanting, "River Wilde, River Wilde." I glanced up to the stage just in time to see him grab the microphone. Before the live music started we exited through the door, and Aerie started yelling obscenities at me. As we walked away I found myself thinking I had just had the most magical encounter and might never be the same because of it.